"Wher 　　　　　　　　　　　**ove gone?**

"A moder 　　　　　　　　　　　and happiness. I cou 　　　　　　　　　　　—*ening News*

"Brilliantl 　　　　　　　　　　　"
　　　　　　　　　　　　　　　—*Daily Mirror*

"Page-turn 　　　　　　　　　　　*an & Home*

"A British 　　　　　　　　　　　—*Dorset Echo*

"If you are a fan of well-written chick lit, you will love this book. . . .
The plot keeps the reader guessing right to the very last page."
　　　　　　　　　　　　　　　　　—*Refresh*

"A touching story with a modern heroine

A Hopeless Romantic

"A delicious romcom, surprisingly believable."

—Marie Claire

"Touching, engrossing, and convincing . . . a rollicking ride of joy, disappointment, and self-discovery, which you'll want to devour in one sitting."

—Daily Telegraph

"Hard to resist."

—Elle

"Harriet Evans has scored another winner . . . will warm you up like brandy on a winter's night. . . . Witty, entertaining, self-reflective, and full of characters you'll grow to love."

—Heat

"An entertaining page-turner."

—Closer

"Superior romcom with heart and soul."

—Bella

Going Home

Also by Harriet Evans

A Hopeless Romantic
Going Home

Harriet Evans

The Love of Her Life

Downtown Press

New York   London   Toronto   Sydney

Downtown Press
A Division of Simon & Schuster, Inc.
1230 Avenue of the Americas
New York, NY 10020

First Downtown Press trade paperback edition June 2009

DOWNTOWN PRESS and colophon are trademarks of
Simon & Schuster, Inc.

For information about special discounts for bulk purchases,
please contact Simon & Schuster Special Sales at 1-866-506-1949
or business@simonandschuster.com.

The Simon & Schuster Speakers Bureau can bring authors to your
live event. For more information or to book an event contact the
Simon & Schuster Speakers Bureau at 1-866-248-3049 or visit our
website at www.simonspeakers.com.

Manufactured in the United States of America

10 9 8 7 6 5 4 3 2 1

ISBN: 978-1-4391-1315-8

It's not love. It's just where I live.
—Nora Ephron, "Moving On," *I Feel Bad About My Neck*

Set me as a seal upon thine heart, as a seal upon thine arm;
for love is strong as death.
—Song of Solomon 8:6

Darling Kate,

I'm sorry.

Perhaps one day, when you're grown-up,
you'll understand why I've done it. Relationships are complicated,
that's the truth. Darling, I love you, and your father loves you.
You mustn't blame yourself. You are our little girl,
and we're both very proud of you.
You must come and see me soon.
Lots and lots of love,

Mummy

xxx

P.S. Happy belated fourteenth birthday, darling.
I do hope you like the telescope. Is it the one you wanted?
Zoe helped me choose it, so I do hope so.
Lots of love xxxxx

Part One

One

*H*er father wasn't well. They kept saying she shouldn't worry too much, but she should still come back to London. He had had an operation—emergency kidney transplant; he'd been bumped right up the list. He was lucky to get one, considering his lifestyle, his age, everything. They kept saying that, too. Kate had even been tested, to see if she could be a donor. She couldn't, which made her feel like a bad daughter.

It all happened so suddenly. It was Monday afternoon when she got the call telling her it had happened, the previous day, after a kidney miraculously became available. He'd been unwell for a few years now, the diabetes and the drinking—and the stress of his new life, he was busier than ever—but how had it got to this, got so far? Apparently he had collapsed; the next day he'd been put at the top of the transplant list. That afternoon, Kate's stepmother, Lisa, had rung to let her know.

"I think he'd very much like to see you." Lisa's rather nasal voice was not improved by the tinny phone line.

"Of—of course," Kate said. She cast around for something to say. "Oh God. How . . . how is he now?"

"He's alive, Kate. It was very sudden. But he's got much, much worse these last few months. So he's not that well. And he'd like to see you. Like I say. He misses you."

"Yes," said Kate. Her throat was dry, her heart was pounding. "Yes. Yes, of course."

"He's going to be in intensive care for a few days, you know. Can you come next week? You can get the time off at the office, I presume." Lisa made no other comment, but a variety of the comments she could make hung in the air, and rushing in next to them came millions of other guilty thoughts, all jostling for attention in front of Kate till she couldn't see anything. She rubbed her eyes with one hand as she cradled the phone on her shoulder. Her darling dad, and she hadn't seen him for eighteen months, hadn't been back to London for a real visit in nearly three years. How the hell . . .? Was this emergency, his rapid decline, was it her fault? No, of course it wasn't, but still, Kate couldn't escape the thought that she had made him ill herself, as certainly as if she had stuck a knife into him.

Out of the window, Manhattan looked calm and still, the gray monolithic buildings giving no clue to the arctic weather, the noise, the hustle, the sweet crazy smell of toasted sugar and tar that hit you every time you went outside, the city she had grown used to, fallen in love with, the city that had long ago replaced London in her affections. Kate looked around the office of the literary agency where she worked. It was a small place, only four full-time members of staff. Bruce Perry, the boss, was in his office, talking on the phone. Kate could see his head bobbing up and down as he violently agreed with someone and what they were saying. Doris, the malevolent old bookkeeper from Queens who openly hated Kate, was pretending to type but in reality was listening to Kate's conversation, trying to work out what was going on. Megan, the junior agent, was in the far corner, tapping a pencil against her keyboard.

"Kate?" said Lisa, breaking into Kate's thoughts. "Look, I can't force you to come back, but . . ." She cleared her throat, and Kate could hear the sound echo in the cavernous basement kitchen of her father and Lisa's flashy new home in Notting Hill.

"Of course I'll come," Kate heard herself say, and she crouched into herself, flushed with shame, hoping Doris hadn't heard her.

"You will?" Lisa said, and Kate could hear incredulity and something else—yes, pleading—in her voice, and she was horrified at herself, at how cold she was capable of being to Lisa. Her father was ill, for God's sake. Dad.

It was time to get a grip and go back home. And so Kate put the phone down, booked a flight for Saturday evening, getting into London on Sunday morning. Then she went into Bruce Perry's office to ask for two weeks off. No more. She wasn't staying there any longer than she had to.

Bruce had grimaced a bit, but he'd been fine about giving her the time off. Perry and Co. was not exactly the fast-paced business unit it might have been, which is why Kate had got her job as assistant there in the first place. In fact, to the outside eye, but for one author, Anne Graves, it would seem to be a mystery that they managed to stay in business, employing as they did five people, and with no books sold to any major publisher, no scripts sold to any studio, for years and years, so it would seem.

"Where will you stay?" Bruce asked. "Will you go to your dad's?"

"No," said Kate firmly. "I've . . . I've actually got a place there." Bruce raised his eyebrows, and Kate could see Doris put down her ledger and look up, intrigued.

"Your own place?"

"It's . . . kind of," Kate told him. She cleared her throat. "I part own it. I was renting it out, but they've just left. Last month."

"Good timing," said Bruce, pleased. "That's great!"

"Yes," said Kate. She wasn't sure that it was good timing, the ending of Gemma's rental lease coinciding with her father's emergency kidney transplant, but still, look for the silver lining, as her mother was always telling her. She shook her head, still trying to come to terms with it. "Wow," she said out loud. "I'm going back to London. Wow." She bit her thumb. "I'd better see if I can get hold of Dad. Lisa said he'd be awake in a little while. . . ."

"Well, what will we do without you," Bruce said, more for effect than sounding like he meant it. He stood up languidly. "Hurry back, now!"

"I will," said Kate, although she was kind of sure she could simply not ever appear again and all they'd need to do after a few weeks would be to hire a temp to filter through the fan letters to Anne Graves. "I'm sorry to leave you in the lurch like this—"

"Oh, honey," Doris said, standing up and coming over. She patted Kate's arm. Kate reared back in horror, since usually Doris wore a murderous expression when she came near her. "Don't you worry about that. My niece, Lorraine, she can cover for you. She'll do a real good job, too, you know it, Bruce."

"Great idea!" Bruce said happily.

He went back into his office, whistling, as Kate swung back around toward her computer. She bit her lip, not sure whether she wanted to laugh or cry.

Kate walked home that night, the twenty-odd blocks that took her back to her mother and Oscar's apartment, a slight feeling of unease hanging over her about the task that lay ahead of her, and the conversation she would have to have with her mother and stepfather. It was a milder March night than it had been thus far that year, and though it was dark and the clocks wouldn't go forward till Sunday, there was still a sense that spring was in the air. She walked up Broadway, following its slicing path through her beloved Manhattan. She didn't try to think about anything, just walked her usual walk, drinking it all in. This was her home. Here she could walk the streets and be part of the glorious, jostling mass of humanity, anonymous even if she wore a pink wig and rode a giraffe. No one here cared, no one here recognized her, knew her. Here she bumped into no old school friends, work colleagues; here she saw no ghosts getting in her way. Just the wide stretch of the road, leaving midtown behind her, as she headed up past Lincoln Center, watching the lights get dimmer, a little cozier, seeing people out running, walking their dogs, living their lives in the thick of the metropolis—that was what she loved best about New York.

She knew she was nearly home when she got to Zabar's. The huge, cheery famous deli was as busy as ever. Families doing late-night shopping, solitary coffee drinkers hunched over a paper in the cafe. Warmth, light, color bursting out of every pore. Kate stared in through the window. They were advertising gefilte fish for Passover, only a few weeks away in mid-April. I'll be back by then, she thought. Only a couple of weeks. Really, that's all it is.

Dad's going to be fine, she told herself as the traffic purred beside her and she looked wildly around, wondering where she was for a moment. She thought about him for a minute, considering with terrified fascination what it would be like to see him again. Her father, so tall, so commanding, so handsome and charismatic, always the center of the room—what would he be like now, what would his life be like after this operation? What if the kidney didn't work? How had it come to this, that she could push down the love she had for him, push it down so far inside her she had been able to pretend, for a while, that it was all OK?

But she knew the answer. She'd become an expert at the answer, since she'd left London.

Deep inside her came a stabbing pain at the top of her breastbone. Kate gently rubbed her collarbone, as her eyes filled with painful tears. But she could not cry, not here, not now. If she started, she might never stop.

I'll go back, see Dad, make sure he's OK, check on the flat, try and find a new tenant.

And I'll see Zoe.

At the thought of seeing her best friend after all this time, Kate felt the hairs on her neck stand up, and though the memory of what had happened still sliced at her, she smiled, a small smile, until she realized she was grinning through the window at a rather bewildered old man with thick white hair, who was trying to read his paper in peace. Kate blushed, and hurried on.

It was Oscar's sixtieth birthday in a few weeks, and Venetia, Kate's mother, had given him his present—a brand-new baby grand piano—early, back in January. As Kate arrived at the apartment building, on Riverside Drive, the window of Venetia and Oscar's apartment was open, and Kate could hear the sound of the piano floating down to her on the sidewalk.

"Hello there, Kate!" Maurice, the doorman, called happily, opening the door for her into the small marbled foyer. He pushed the button for the elevator. Kate smiled at him, a little wearily.

"How are you, Maurice?" she said.

"I'm just fine," said Maurice. "I'm pretty good. That spray you told me to get, for my back—well, I bought it yesterday, I meant to say. And it's done a lot of good."

"Really?" said Kate, pleased. "That's great, Maurice. I'm so glad."

"I owe you, Kate, that's for sure. It just went away after I used that spray."

Kate got into the lift. "Good-o. That's brilliant."

"Hold the elevator!" came a querulous voice, and Mrs. Cohen, still elegant, tall, refined in a powder blue suit, shuffled into the lobby. "Kate, dear, hold the elevator! Hello, Maurice. Would you be a dear, and—"

"I'll get the bags from the cab," said Maurice, nodding. "You wait here."

There were times when the geriatric street theater of the apartment building made Kate's day; there were other times when she would have given fifty dollars to see someone her own age in the lift. Just once. When they were installed in the lift, bags and all, and when Kate had helped Mrs. Cohen to her door and put her bags in her hallway, she climbed the last flight up to her mother's apartment, hearing the sound of the piano again as she reached the sixth floor.

Venetia was born to be a New Yorker; it was hard to believe she'd ever lived anywhere else, really. Of course, Kate could remember her in London, but it seemed rather unreal now. The mother she'd had until the age of fourteen, when, the day after Kate's birthday, Venetia had left her and her dad, was like a character Kate remembered watching in a film, not her actual, own mother. She had to remind herself that it was Venetia who'd picked her up from school every day, Venetia who'd smoothed her hair back when she'd been sick after eating some scrambled eggs when she was eight, Venetia who'd collected her from the Brownie camp in the New Forest a day early after Kate had cried all night for her. The idea that she and Kate's father had lived together—that Venetia had taken Kate to watch Daniel play at the Royal Albert Hall, that she had entertained myriad numbers of Daniel's friends in their cluttered basement in the tall house in Kentish Town, had wiped tables down, collected wine bottles up, fielded calls from agents and journalists and critics and young, lithe music students—had long disappeared. She was a New Yorker now, and more important, Kate thought, she was the star of her *own* show.

Venetia and Oscar's apartment was straight out of *Annie Hall*—from the framed Saul Steinberg prints and posters of the *Guys and Dolls* revival that Oscar had done a couple of years ago to the copies of *The New Yorker* on the coffee table; the view out over Riverside Drive in the long, low room that served as a sitting room, dining room, den and Oscar's office (he worked at home mostly; he was an arranger, a composer and a conductor); the pictures of Kate in silver frames that she always found hugely embarrassing: her as a baby, sucking her toes, sitting on a lawn somewhere (Kate never knew where; there was no lawn in the Kentish Town house); her smiling rather rigidly outside her college after getting her degree; with her mother, the first time she came to New York to visit, when Kate was fifteen, just after Venetia had married Oscar. And there was one she always wanted to take down, just because: Kate, beaming, holding the first issue of *Venus,* the magazine she'd worked on in London. There had been other photos, other remnants of Kate's life. They had been taken down—no one wanted to see them, now.

As Kate opened the door to the apartment, the smell of onions, something cooking, hit her. Her mother was in the tiny galley kitchen singing; Oscar was playing "Some Enchanted Evening" on the piano in the long room.

"Hi!" she called, injecting a note of jollity into her voice. "Something smells nice."

"Hello, darling!" Venetia appeared in the corridor, wiping her hands on her apron. "I'm making risotto, it's going to be lovely." She kissed her daughter. "Thanks for calling. It'll be ready in about fifteen minutes. How was your day? Did you get hold of Betty? She rang earlier. She was wondering if you wanted to meet for a drink on Friday."

Kate disentangled herself from her scarf, and from her mother, backing away toward the door to hang her things up. She pulled her long dark blond hair out from her coat and turned to her mother, chewing a lock of hair as she did.

"I'm starving," she said indistinctly. "I'll give her a call in a minute. Mum—"

Oscar called from the long room. "Hello, Katy! Come and say hi!"

Kate poked her head around the door. "Hi, Oscar," she said. "How was your day?"

"Honey, I'm home!" Oscar said joyously, launching into a ragtime version of "Luck Be a Lady." "I've been home all day!"

Oscar made this joke roughly three times a week. Kate smiled affectionately at him.

"What a lovely evening," she said, staring out over the Hudson at the purple-gray sunset. "I had such a nice walk back."

Oscar was only half listening. "That's good, dear," he said. "Would you like a drink? Venetia, can I get you another drink, darling?"

Venetia appeared, carrying her gin and tonic. "I'm fine with this one, thanks, darling," she said, carelessly caressing the back of her husband's neck as she passed by. "I'd better lay the table—darling, did I mention that I saw Kathy today? And she and Don can't make it to your party?"

"Dad's ill," Kate said. Her voice was louder than she'd meant. The room was suddenly deadly silent.

"What?" Venetia turned to look at her daughter. "What did you say?"

Kate gripped the side of the sofa. "Dad's really ill. He's had a kidney transplant. He's in intensive care."

"Oh my God," Oscar said, looking toward his wife. "That's—well, that's awful."

"I'm going home," said Kate. "On Saturday. To see him."

"Back to London?" her mother said. Her face was white.

"Yes," said Kate, shaking her head very slightly, willing her mother to do the right thing.

"My God," said Oscar. He chewed at a cuticle nervously. "Will he be . . . OK?"

"Yes, yes," said Kate, wanting to reassure them. "I mean—it's dangerous, but he's very lucky. I hope so—" She swallowed, as black dots danced in front of her eyes, and a wave of panic swept over her at the thought of it, her poor darling dad. "Yes, Lisa thinks he will be. . . ."

Lisa's name dropped like a stone between them. It was Venetia who broke the silence. "You're going back Saturday? What time's your flight?"

"Nine. In the evening."

"Right." Venetia put her drink down; she patted her collarbone, her slim white fingers stroking her skin. "We'll drive you. Oh, darling. How long are you going for?"

"Two weeks, probably," said Kate, coming toward her. She wanted her reassurance, for her mother to tell her it was going to be OK, not just for her dad, but everything to do with it. "I'll be back for Oscar's party, of course I will—I'm just going to make sure he's OK."

"Course you do!" said Venetia. She put her arm around her daughter, squeezed her shoulders. "Darling, it's just—well. It'll be hard for you. That's all."

There was silence again in the room as Oscar looked from his wife to his stepdaughter. Kate gazed out of the window. The sunset was almost over; it was nearly dark.

"Yep," Kate said. "It will be hard." It felt strange; it felt alien here suddenly. She hated that feeling. "I had to go back sometime," she added, and Oscar nodded and sat back down at the piano. "Just wish it wasn't for this, that's all."

Two

Kate had lived with Oscar and Venetia since she came to New York. She was always just about to start looking for an apartment of her own—or a studio, more likely, for even though she had the rental money from her flat in London, renting in New York was still staggeringly expensive. Still, it was ridiculous, being thirty, living with your mother and stepfather, and when she'd moved to New York she'd thought it would only be a temporary measure, that she'd be moving out soon. But the right time never seemed to happen. She and Betty often talked about getting a place together, but Betty's love life was erratic to say the least. Whenever Kate was at her most desperate to move out, move on, move away from her domestic situation, it coincided exactly with Betty and her latest five-star full-on love affair being at its height, whereupon Betty would say, "I think we're getting married. . . . Or at least moving in together . . . in a couple of months, I'd say, so no Kate, sorry . . . I can't!"

Then they would break up, awfully, and Betty would be too heartbroken to contemplate anything, and Kate would have to soothe her back to sanity with a variety of cocktails all over the SoHo area, and Betty would gradually perk up and say, "We should really look for a place soon!" and Kate would say, "Yes!" and then, without fail, the next day, Betty would go to a gallery opening, and there she would meet Brian (public schoolboy with nappy fetish) or Johan (Norwegian bike courier) or Elrond (poet with long hair), and the whole apartment thing would go quiet for a while—and Kate would tell herself to wait a little longer. So the weeks turned into months, and the months turned into years. To her surprise. And still she didn't move, still she stayed on Riverside Drive.

On Friday evening, Venetia and Oscar gave Kate a farewell supper. It was early because Kate was going out to meet Betty, and Venetia and Oscar were off to a drinks party held by Alvin and Carol Da Costa, on the third floor. Venetia made quiche, Oscar made a beautiful mesclun and pomegranate-seed salad. They drank a toast to Daniel, said bon voyage to Kate.

The last few days seemed to have flown by; how could it be Friday already? Kate wondered. Escaping their ministrations— "Remember to take an *adaptor*." "Did you collect your dry cleaning?"—she excused herself and shut the door of her bedroom slowly and sank down on the bed, wondering when she should pack.

Now that she was alone, she wished, as she had done these past few days, she was going tonight, that she was already there, even though Lisa had told her there was no point in coming over till Daniel was out of intensive care; still, Kate wished she was there even if he wouldn't have realized it. "It'll give you time to sort your stuff out before you come," Lisa had said. She supposed she meant it kindly.

The truth was, really, that she didn't have that much stuff anyway. Clothes, yes, but all her books, her old things from her old life—they were all in storage in the basement of her flat in London, like her old self, trapped in aspic, while the new self gazed longingly into the window of Pottery Barn or Bed Bath & Beyond, picking out covers for imaginary cushions, towels to hang on illusory rails. She'd bought a new duvet and pillow set for her room in the sales this year and she was *still* excited about it.

Kate shook her head, smiling. She realized now, with a start, that this had been going on for three years—three years that she'd been with her mother and Oscar, too. The truth was she enjoyed it. Not just because they were fun—Oscar *wanted* people to be happy in his presence, and he wanted Venetia to be happy more than anyone else and, therefore, her daughter, by extension. It was fun living with them, especially for a girl like Kate, who was, as Zoe had once pointed out, old before her time anyway and more likely to prefer an evening around the piano singing show tunes than queuing for ages to get into a loud, sweaty, pricey club (as she saw it).

But it was also nice because Kate had got to know her mother again, after years of never really seeing her, years of her name being persona non grata with almost all her father's friends and family in London. Even Venetia's sister, Jane, who was much more stiff-lipped than she and lived a life of rigid, middle-England organization in Marlow, could barely tolerate any mention of her. It was fun living with her mother again. Especially this happy version of her mother. She didn't put any pressure on Kate to do anything she didn't want to—she was just happy to have her living there.

Still, perhaps that's why it's a good thing I'm going back, Kate told herself as she climbed up on a stool to take her big suitcase down from the top of her wardrobe. It was dusty with lack of use—when was the last time she'd used it? She couldn't remember. Cars honked faintly outside: Kate looked at her watch. It was time to go. She pulled some slouchy boots on over her skinny jeans and ran out into the hall.

"You look lovely, dear," Oscar called, spying her through the open doorway.

"Thanks, dear," said Kate. "I won't be too late."

"Stay out! Enjoy yourself!" called her mother. "Where are you going?"

"Downtown, to the Village," said Kate. She sighed. She wanted to see Betty, of course, but Betty was on a matchmaking drive and tonight, Kate feared, was to be the culmination of this. The last time Betty had set her up with someone, he'd turned out to be gay and only going along with Betty because he wanted her gallery to show his work, so Kate didn't hold out much hope.

"So, will you stay in London?" Betty wiped her fingers on the napkin and stared at Kate, who paused with a bowl of miso soup halfway to her lips. "I bet you will."

"Stay there?" she said, in astonished tones. "Good God no, Bets. Are you mad? I'm going back to see Dad after the op, then I'll wait till he's through it OK, I'll see Zoe and the kids, and I'll be back on the first plane that'll take me. It's Oscar's sixtieth in a couple of weeks anyway. I can't miss that. Can you imagine?" Betty said nothing. "Come on."

"Hm," said Betty. "Well, I'm just saying, that's all. It's going to be weird. Three years!" She turned to Andrew, who was next to her, and gestured at him. "What do you reckon?"

Kate and Betty had been friends since university, so Kate should have been used to her ways. She reminded herself now, as she stole a glance at Andrew from under her lashes, that Betty—and Francesca, for that matter, so thank God she wasn't here, too—always said what they thought, always had done. It was funny, really. Most of the time. She blushed as Andrew suddenly met her gaze.

"I hope she comes back," Andrew said. He coughed, awkwardly, and was silent again. Betty rolled her eyes significantly at Kate and made nudging motions at her. Kate ignored her. She was too astonished, and pleased, at what Andrew had said, for usually he said nothing, let alone anything conclusive.

Kate had known Andrew now for a couple of months purely because, since he'd moved into Betty's building in January, Betty had wasted no time in throwing him into Kate's path. This was made easier by Andrew's eagerness to meet Kate when he heard she worked for a literary agency. For Andrew was that not-so-rare creature: the boy with a book inside him. Kate had met enough of them both in London, when she worked on various magazines, and in New York, since working at Perry and Co., to recognize Andrew as conforming fairly typically to type: he was angry about a lot of things, not least the parlous state of the Great American Novel; he had thick hair he brushed back from his face a lot, mostly in anger; and his novel was extremely difficult, both thematically and practically. He hadn't written more than a word since Kate had first started talking to him about it. He was "circling round the themes," he had told her when she'd asked.

"Right," Kate had said politely.

"Honestly, that's not exactly true," Andrew had added with a rueful smile. He scratched his cheek. "Could also be that I'd rather be out having a few beers after work than writing." He smiled at her, and Kate had instantly liked him again.

She found that, over the following weeks, she alternated between not being sure whether she liked him or not. Sometimes he was really very funny, coruscatingly rude or charming about something. Sometimes—too often—he was moody, virtually silent, as if oppressed by the weight of matters on his mind. Betty was running out of excuses, of social events to ask him to. Sooner or later Kate was just going to have to make a move, she told her. Ask him out for coffee.

As Andrew got up to use the bathroom, Betty said this to Kate, in no uncertain terms.

Kate was horrified.

"Ask him out? No, no way, Bets. I couldn't. Get him to."

"He's not going to," said Betty decisively. She looked around her to make sure Andrew wasn't on his way back and hissed across the table, "It has to be you. Come on. You've got to seize the moment. Otherwise it'll be over, and—and then what? You could have missed the chance to get married. For*ever*. How would you feel then?"

"Oh," said Kate. "Relieved?"

Betty shook her head. "You are weird, did you know that?"

"No I'm not," said Kate.

"You're like a metaphor for . . . argh. Intransigence."

Betty worked in an art gallery in SoHo and was prone to remarks like this. Kate suppressed a smile.

"Oh dear," she said. "Damn."

"Don't you want to get married?" said Betty. She stabbed at a dumpling with a chopstick.

Kate stared at her in astonishment. "No, I don't want to get married."

"Why? Why don't you?" Betty said, but as she was saying it recognition flooded her face. "Oh my God. Kate, I'm sorry—"

Kate held up her hand and smiled, "It's OK! It's fine. Now—" she said as Andrew came back to the table, "I kind of need to get an early night, I'm afraid, and I have to pack. Can I get out before you sit back down again?" She shot up and scooted along the plastic bench.

"Kate—" Betty said.

Kate looked up at her.

"Sure." Betty nodded. "Sure."

"Bye, Andrew," Kate said, turning to him. They stood to one side against the table as a Japanese waitress bustled past them, bearing a huge tray of sushi, and Kate felt the pressure of his arm against hers.

"Sorry," he said.

"It's fine," Kate put her bag on her shoulder. "So I'll see you when I get back. . . ."

"Let me walk you outside," Andrew said, in a loud, rather unnatural voice. He cleared his throat.

Outside on the crowded sidewalk, in the heart of the tiny Japanese restaurant district on East 12th Street, Kate cast around to see if there was a cab.

"I've got something to ask you," Andrew said, staring intently at her in the evening gloom.

"So, thanks," she said. "I'll see you when I'm back—"

"Kate, Kate," Andrew said rapidly. "I gotta say this now."

"Oh," said Kate, with a dreadful sense of foreboding. "No, I should walk to the—"

He gripped her arms. "Kate, let me finish."

"No, really," Kate said desperately, stupidly hoping that if she warded him off then what was about to happen might not happen.

Andrew stepped back. "Look," he said, crestfallen at her apparent horror. "I just wanted to ask you out when you get back. Maybe see if you wanted to go for a coffee, see a movie sometime. But I guess—I guess that's not such a great idea at the moment. With your dad and all. I'm sorry."

"Ah," said Kate, feeling rotten that she was hiding behind her dad's kidney transplant to get out of a date she didn't want to go on. "You're right. It's—not a good time for me right now."

God, I sound American, she thought. I really must go home.

"Of course it's not." Andrew nodded. "Hey. When you get back, if it is a good time—call me. OK?"

"Sure," said Kate. "Sure."

"I promise not to talk about the novel," said Andrew. "Much."

She looked at him, into his big brown eyes, as he smiled at her in the street, the lanterns from the bar next door swaying in the breeze behind him.

"I just kind of like you, Kate," he said. "There's . . . there's something about you. You're cool. I . . . I guess."

He scuffed the sidewalk with his toe and she watched him, her heart pounding. It had been so long since someone had said anything like that to her, and to be honest, she had never thought they would again.

"Oh," she said, and a lock of her dark blond hair fell into her face. He looked at her and pushed it off her cheek, his fingers stroking her skin. Kate met his gaze, shaking her head. Something was wrong.

"Andrew," she said. "I—"

He bent his head and kissed her. His touch, his warm lips on hers, his hands on her ribs. Perhaps—

But she couldn't. And the force of her response surprised her, for Kate pushed him away and said, breathlessly, "No. I'm sorry, no."

She gave a huge, shuddering sigh.

Andrew stepped back, blinking uncertainly. He looked bewildered.

"I'm—my God, I'm sorry."

"No," Kate said. She was almost backing away from him, she realized, trying to escape, like a cornered animal. "It's not you. It's me."

He wiped his mouth with his hand, almost in disgust. She smiled. "No, really. I mean that. It's the oldest cliché in the book, but in my case it's totally true—it really *is* me."

"Right," Andrew said formally. He brushed something off his shirt. "Betty said something."

"What?" said Kate.

Andrew nodded, and looked at his feet. "Hey, it's no big deal. She said some guy screwed you over. Something bad happened to you in London."

She loved the way certain Americans always said the word

London, investing it with a certain amount of reverence. "You could say that," she said. She winced and looked up at him, not sure how he was taking all of this. "Hey—" she began.

"It's no big deal," he said. "Truthfully, it isn't." He ran his hands through his hair. "You wanna cab?"

"Sure," said Kate. "That'd be—"

Andrew whistled, and almost immediately, as if he were calling up the Batmobile, a cab zoomed around the corner. "So," he said. He held the door open. "See you around, I guess."

"Sure," said Kate. "Yeah. Upper West Side, Eightieth and Broadway. Thanks."

The cab pulled off; through its greasy window she watched as Andrew turned and walked off. Kate touched her fingers to her lips as the car sped through midtown. She was shaking, and she didn't know why.

The traffic was light, miraculously. Please go through Times Square, she willed the cabdriver. Please, go on. She stared out of the window as the lights of Broadway grew closer and they headed past Macy's, and a sense of disgust came over her. Why had she let that happen with Andrew? Why couldn't she just have kissed him and jumped into a cab? Maybe arranged to see him when she got back? Why did she have to behave like that? What was she going to say to him, to Betty?

"I'm too good at running away," she said softly under her breath. She put her head against the glass, watching the reflection of her skin as the streets rushed by and they came to Times Square. Kate loved Times Square, much to Oscar and her mother's horror. She couldn't tell them why she loved it, quite, it never seemed to make sense. She loved the anonymity of it, the adrenaline that came with it. You could be wholly yourself, a unit of one, walking through the concrete, neon-lit stage there. You could stand in the center of the traffic all day and twirl around— and no one would look at you. She loved the contradiction of it—when she first came to see her mother and went looking for Times Square, she had spent ages trying to find an actual square. Now, she didn't know what she'd been picturing in her head: a stately, square of London houses, with a garden in the center, railings around the edge, perhaps? And when she'd realized this was it, this gray meeting of roads stretched out over three or so blocks, she had laughed. It was unlike anything she'd ever seen before; it was utterly unlike London.

Twenty-four hours' time, and she'd be on the plane. Twenty-four hours' time, and her dad's operation would nearly be over. Forty-eight hours till she saw him again. Till she was back there again. . . . The lights of Manhattan flickered and flashed into Kate's cab, the theater signs, the road signs, the bars and restaurants and clubs, flickering on her face, keeping her awake, though then, suddenly, she was very tired.

Three

There was a backlog at Heathrow, and Kate's plane circled over London, coming in from the east, flying straight across the center of the city. It was the perfect bird's-eye view. Kate shifted in her seat, her hands resting lightly on the stack of magazines she'd been reading, and stared down, out of the window, craning her neck in excitement. The huge jet followed the path of the Thames, its tiny black shadow flickering through the streets and places below. The river was bluer than she remembered. She'd forgotten how green it all was, how many open spaces there were. They flew over the Houses of Parliament, glowing gold in the early morning light, as the center of the city stretched away in front of them. Kate twisted in her seat, looking down, following the path of Regent's Street all the way up to Regent's Park, the Telecom Tower, King's Cross away to the side, as they headed west.

It looked like a toy town, Legoland, and she couldn't reconcile it with what had gone on before. In those tiny streets below her, in that park there, in that tall building just beyond the river—yes, it was all still there.

Kate never understood people who said airports were full of romance or love. Not only had no one ever met her at an airport (except her mother, and that hardly counted), she wouldn't want them to meet her. Be reunited with the love of your life surrounded by polystyrene ceiling tiles, strip lighting and gray upholstery? No thanks. She struggled with her luggage trolley, flaring out her elbows to maneuver it around corners, trying not to let hopelessness and the strangeness of the situation overwhelm her. Taxi. She needed a taxi—a good old black London cab—and she pushed on through to the arrivals hall, vaguely registering the expectant faces of people waiting as she went. Kate had learned, now. She didn't even bother to look around. She had long given up playing that game in her head.

It was a sunny day. Warm and fresh, with a cool little breeze whipping about. It smelled of spring, of something in the air, even there at the airport. Spring had come in London, and she felt it as she crossed the tarmac to the cab line, as a man in a blue sou'ester waved her into a cab. Although she kept expecting something dramatic to happen—for someone to leap at her and stop her, or yell at her—nothing did, and so the taxi moved off, gliding along smoothly heading into London.

On a gray motorway—how prosaic, but there it was—and so that was how Kate came back to London. As the redbrick streets flew past and the old familiar signs appeared, she stopped trying to think and simply sat there, drinking it all in, wondering how she'd got there, and most of all, how her father was and what would happen now.

And then suddenly they were there, turning off Maida Vale into the long tree-lined boulevard, where the buds on the elms were just visible, and they were grinding to a halt outside the redbrick building, and the bin with the face painted onto the lid was still outside.

Kate didn't get out of the car. She looked around only as the cabdriver pulled her bags out onto the sidewalk, puffing, and said, "All right, love?"

He opened the door, regarding her curiously. She knew he was probably thinking, Uh-oh. Is she actually a bit . . . mad? Kate blinked at him suddenly, as if he were speaking Martian.

"Oh," she said. "Yes."

"Is this where you want?"

"Yes," said Kate, stepping out onto the sidewalk, though actually what she really wanted to say was, I've changed my mind, can we go back to the airport? "Yes, it is."

She gave him money and thanked him; he drove away, with a hand wave out of the window. She felt like an alien; she couldn't remember how to behave. She looked down at the paving slabs on the sidewalk. Rectangular, scratchy dark gray, slightly cracked. It was silly. She'd forgotten what they were like here.

Shoulders squared, Kate picked up the bags and stood at the foot of the stairs that led up to the hallway of the flats. A bird called in a nearby tree, a large black car hummed next to her, its engine running, but otherwise it was silent.

It's strange, the things that are stored in your brain but that you haven't thought about for years. The black front door of her old building was really heavy, on a spring. You had to wedge your body really firmly against the door to stop it clapping shut in your face; she forgot. It banged shut behind Kate, practically trapping her with its force as she lugged her bags into the hallway and looked rather blankly around her at the large, beige, sunny hall, quiet and dusty in the cool sunshine.

She was just wondering how she was going to get her huge suitcase upstairs; she'd brought back such a lot of stuff, and the thought of lugging it to the first floor, her body bone-tired, made her feel rather blue. Impossible not to think about the first time she'd come here, with him, impossible not to think about how it had been the day they'd moved in, three years ago in spring. Then the mailboxes had been over there; they'd been moved around now. Kate peered inside the box marked FLAT 4: two catalogs, five pizza delivery leaflets, four minicab cards, three Chinese takeaway menus, a plethora of random letters addressed to assorted names she didn't know, and some bills, addressed to her, greeted her. FLAT 4 had obviously become the storage depot for everyone's unwanted post; and Gemma, the tenant, had only moved out last week. Lovely.

Kate looked briefly at the pile in her mailbox then down at her bags, and decided she'd deal with the post later. She pulled her suitcases across the hall, overcome with fatigue. She was not usually given to moments of girlish weakness, but she was suddenly very tired. Up till now coming back to London had been anonymous, impersonal. The taxi driver, the man at customs, the lady at the passport desk—they didn't know her. Now she was here and she was in the flat where people knew who she was. This was when it started to get . . . messy. Somewhere above her a door opened; she heard voices. Kate shrank back against the wall, like a prisoner on the run. Perhaps this was a mistake, a big mistake, perhaps she should just turn around and . . .

Suddenly there was a loud noise, a thudding sound, and then boots on feet thumping across the landing, coming downstairs, several pairs of feet, she thought. Kate pushed her bag up into the nook by the banisters and peered up. There was muffled cursing; they were obviously carrying something heavy, and she heard an old, familiar voice say, "Thank you. Thank you very much. I'll see you later, then."

Swiveling her neck, Kate turned and peered up through the banisters. There was a coffin coming down the stairs. A coffin. She blinked, and to her alarm a hysterical, horrifying urge to laugh bubbled up inside her, before she swallowed it down, frantically scrabbling to push her suitcase out of the way.

"Can you open the door, Fred?"

"No, mate," Fred answered. "You've got the front, you take it."

"It's heavy, remember?"

They were turning the last corner, outside her own flat, just appearing at the top of the stairs, and Kate called up, "I'm down here. I'll hold the door open."

"She's down there," said the other man. "There's someone down there."

"Thanks, love," Fred said. "We've got a coffin here, you know."

"Yes, a coffin," the other man added.

"Yes," said Kate gravely, wondering if she were being filmed as an extra in a hidden-camera Pinter play. "Don't worry. I'll stay here."

She leaned against the door, holding it flat open.

It was, indeed, a coffin: sleek and brown, borne gently by its bearers to the bottom of the steps, held only slightly at a diagonal angle. She stared at it as they reached the bottom step and gingerly readjusted their load.

"Been on holiday?" Fred said politely. He nodded at her suitcase as they walked toward the front door.

"I've been away," said Kate vaguely. "Just got back, yes. This is . . . er . . . sad." She gestured pathetically at the coffin. "Who . . . who is it?"

"Old lady who lived upstairs. Had a husband. Nice fellow." Fred jerked his head up, indicating where in the labyrinthine view they might live. Kate followed his gaze. They passed through the front door and left her standing there on the threshold.

"Second floor?" said Kate, her voice faint.

"Yep," said Fred, nodding kindly at her.

"Mrs.—not Mrs. Allan?"

"Yes, love," he answered her. "Sorry. Not the best welcome back for you, is it now?"

Kate loved him then for apologizing, as if he were personally responsible for Mrs. Allan's death. She smiled at him and shook her head as if to say, Please, don't worry. She followed them onto the sidewalk as they slid the coffin gently into the hearse.

"There he is," one of them said under his breath to the other. "Ah." And they looked up. There in the window, one floor above

Kate's, an old face looked out through the glass. She recognized him then, of course she did—it was Mr. Allan. Mr. Allan pressed a hand to the glass, looking down at the street, his face impassive. He was much older than she remembered.

The car drove off. Kate raised a hand in greeting to Mr. Allan, not sure whether to smile or not. Once again, she wasn't sure what to do, how to behave.

She hadn't spoken to the Allans since she'd left. They'd written to her in New York—Mrs. Allan had sent her newspaper clippings, articles she thought she might like—but Kate hadn't written back, and the communication had dried up. Mr. Allan's face now looked down at her, gray and yellow through the sun on the glass, and she waved again, uncertainty flowering within her, and looked around to realize she was standing on the sidewalk alone. She pointed in, toward the flats, as if to say, I'm back, and looked up—but he had gone.

"I'll—" she started to say out loud. *I'll see you later.* Climbing up the stairs, she shut the front door behind her, picked up her heavy bag and dragged it upstairs.

Four

*T*he lock that clicked in the door, the floorboard in the hall with the big hole in it, where you could see the Victorian pipes underneath, the sunny little sitting room down the corridor with the bay windows, the radiator in a fretwork-covered box. The bookshelves, still filled with her books, gaps where he had taken his books away—all these things, stored somewhere in her memory, forgotten till now. She didn't remember leaving her flat for the last time. She remembered scenes within it, though. She remembered coming here for the first time with Sean, the first Christmas here . . . waking up on a Sunday morning, in bed together, the papers, friends for lunch . . . As Kate stood in the living room, keys in her hand, and looked around, she smiled grimly. Every bloody couple cliché under the sun, like an ad for a Sofa Workshop or a kitchen sale.

The previous tenant, Gemma, was about her age, and though she'd left everything pretty much as it should have been, for a furnished flat, she'd moved the armchairs around. Frowning, Kate pushed them back to where she'd had them before, one next to the sofa, the other in front of the window. She leaned against the windowsill and breathed in, memory flooding over her with the smell of wood, of lavender, of something indefinable, dusty, earthy, cozy—the smell of her flat.

Funny that it should be so comforting to be back here. Funny. She put the keys quietly down on the table, almost as if she were afraid of disturbing someone, and took off her coat, putting it gingerly on an armchair. She went into the kitchen, noting with pleasure that the pots and pans hanging on the hooks she'd so lovingly put up a couple of months before she'd gone were still there. On the tiny little balcony that led off the kitchen door—no more than a doormat size, really—she could see the thyme and rosemary were still going strong. She opened the door, pulling it slightly, remembering how it always used to stick.

There were people walking on the street outside—families pushing strollers, people chatting outside the little row of shops down the road. Kate craned her neck to watch them, to look down over the wide boulevard of redbrick apartments, lined with trees that were sprinkled with fat, green little buds. Over past the shops was Lord's cricket ground, a ten-minute walk, then Regent's Park, the zoo, the canal . . . down Maida Vale, which she could just see, was Edgware Road, leading into the park, to Mayfair, into town. All just outside. She could go out now, could be in any of those places, which she'd dreamt of over the past three years with increasing frequency. She could do that, she was back.

A loud noise from the bedroom made her jump. Kate turned and ran, relishing the size of the space that was her own now, and she saw that her suitcase, which she'd leaned against the wall, had fallen over, bringing down with it her telescope. She smiled at the sight of it, memory leading her back down a path. Her telescope! She hurried over to the corner of the room, straightening it out, setting it right again. How she had loved that bloody thing when she was a teenager—it made her smile to think of it, that while Zoe and most of her other friends had been standing outside tube stations of an evening with their waistbands rolled up and over, to shorten their skirts, ponytails high on their heads, usually to one side, smoking Silk Cut Menthols and chipping their nail polish,

Kate had been—where? Yes, at home, looking through her telescope, high up in her attic bedroom, or curled up on her ancient patchwork bedspread, reading *Gone with the Wind*, or *Forever Amber*, or some yellowing Victoria Holt novel.

"Hello, old thing," she said to the telescope, stroking it gently, brushing the light film of dust from its casing. It had been so long since she'd looked through it. She caught herself, and the memory of her teenage self, and smiled, grinning widely at how touchingly and unintentionally hilarious she had probably been. Poor Dad, she thought, gazing away into nothing. What he had had to put up with, on his own, looking after this strange, solitary teenager who didn't understand why her mother had gone, who blamed herself for it more than anyone. Still partly did, though it was more than half her lifetime ago. Kate's hand flew to her collarbone.

The reverberations from the crash had toppled some photos on her bedroom shelves. Her parents on their wedding day, in black and white, her mother in a dark velvet minidress, almost painfully young and thin, her beautiful red hair swinging about her shoulders, her father, so pleased with himself—and with his wife. They were clutching hands, so tightly that even through the years and the monochrome, you could see the whiteness of her mother's knuckles.

It was stuff like that that got in the way, Kate thought, carefully putting the picture back on the shelf. Nice of Gemma to leave it out for her, but it was best put away, along with the marriage itself, and the photos next to it—her twenty-first birthday, taken by Zoe, her and Steve and Sean, hilariously awkward in suits, for some reason, and, a sop to her new family, her stepmother and Dani, at Dani's christening, nearly five years ago, her half sister resplendent in a little gown and white hat embroidered with flowers.

Kate turned away from the photos, frowning. She felt out of kilter once again, remembering why she was here, and she went into the sitting room and picked up the phone, calling Lisa again.

"Yes?" Lisa answered immediately. "Hi, Kate." She added, more warmly, "How are you? Good flight? Everything . . . OK?"

"It's fine. How's Dad?" Kate said, running her fingers along the bookcase in the corner of the room, staring out of the window.

"He's OK. He's having a nap," said Lisa. "He can't wait to see you."

"Oh—" Kate pursed her lips, shaking her head and looking down at the floor. "Oh. I can't wait to see him. Lisa, can you give him my love? Is it OK if I come over now?"

"Give it an hour or so, if that's all right," said Lisa. "He's still quite weak, Kate."

Kate turned and looked back at the picture of her parents on the shelf behind her, perfectly still. She had spent the last three years with her mother, making up for lost time; she had always known, though, that once she came back here, everything that she had neglected would hit her, hard. It struck her now that she had almost become too good at what she did: shutting out a whole area of her life. She had crossed the ocean and simply closed the door behind her on her life in London. As if, for the most part, it didn't exist. As if she could.

She needed to keep moving, keep busy here. She'd go and get Mr. Allan some flowers. Yes. She turned away from the telescope and the photos and went into the sitting room again. She grabbed her bag and left the flat, running down to the shops on the corner of the road, marveling at the price of a pint of Rachel's Dairy milk. She got some flowers, daffodils, bought the papers and some Marmite and hummus and crisps. The old corner shop now sold posh Président butter and had its own orange-juicing machine.

As she unlocked the front door to the building, she realized how quiet it was. She climbed the stairs slowly, listening for sounds. There was nothing from upstairs, and she didn't know whether to go up now or wait till later. When had Mrs. Allan died? Was it too soon?

The phone was ringing as she unlocked the door to her flat again; she ran for it but missed the call, and she couldn't work out who it was. But it reminded her who else she was here to see, as if she could have forgotten. Kate picked up her mobile, fingers toying over the keypad, and after a minute she shook her head. No, it would be too weird to speak to Zoe right now, after so long, to hear her voice—she could still hear her voice—when she was going to see her later. She texted instead:

> Hi. I'm back. Can't wait to see you. Shall I come
> round about seven? K x

Almost immediately, so that it felt she had barely finished writing the message, her phone beeped back at her with the reply.

> Seven is perfect. Can't believe you're back! Can't
> wait! Lots of love, Z xxx

She unpacked, hung out her washing, pottered around in the kitchen and then in the bedroom, listening to the radio in an effort to cheer herself up. As Kate reached for a hair tie on her dressing table, she looked up at herself in the mirror. She hadn't seen herself in this mirror for years, and the effect was rather like coming back from holiday and seeing in the mirror you look into every day how tanned you'd got after two weeks away. She looked . . . different. Older, probably. Thinner, but not in a good way. Mostly she looked tired. Her dark brown eyes were smudged underneath with circles, her dark blond hair was longer. Had she always looked that serious? The hairbrush she'd been holding gently slid out of her hand and Kate stared at herself, silence echoing around her.

She shut her front door behind her, and as she did she remembered Mr. Allan. She looked at her watch. She didn't have time to go and see him tonight, she would go tomorrow. The thought crossed her mind as she slung her bag over her shoulder and tripped downstairs: What else would she do tomorrow, other than seeing her father again and seeing Mr. Allan? But over the past couple of years, Kate had got very good at filling in hours of time, doing not very much, lying low, staying in the shadows. She just hadn't done it in London before.

It was getting late, and she glanced into her mailbox again, remembering too that she had meant to go through her post. The pile of letters was still there, undisturbed, but as she peered closer something in the compartment caught her eye, and it was then that she saw the letter.

A new letter, at the top of the pile.

In handwriting she would never forget as long as she lived.

Kate Miller
Flat 4
Howard Mansions
London W9

Kate's hand froze in the air, the letter clutched in her fingers. Air trapped in her throat; she felt hot, boiling hot. How did Charly know she was back? And more important, why the hell was she writing to her?

Five

*D*aniel Miller had not been an ideal father to a teenage girl, in many ways. After Venetia left, his professional decline had been rapid: in 1990 the *Times* had said that his interpretation of Beethoven's violin concerto was probably the best ever—yes, ever—yet by the time Kate was taking her A levels, four years later, he hadn't had a proper solo recital for months. The gigs were starting to dry up, as Daniel was late for rehearsals, argued with conductors, cried in his dressing room, got drunk at lunchtime, and sometimes didn't turn up at all. When he'd had a reputation as being one of the best, if not the best, he had been—for a musician, admittedly—modest about it. Now that it was on the slide, he had turned into a prima donna, sulking in the house in Kentish Town, skulking angrily, smoking furiously, talking, always talking to friends, on the phone, around the kitchen table.

It wasn't as if Venetia had been the world's most regimented mother, either; but when she'd been around there had at least been some semblance of order, some idea that there might be food in the fridge or water in the boiler; now Kate and Daniel simply got used to muddling through. Dinnertimes were sporadic, usually set by Kate, school parents' evenings went unattended. Daniel never knew where he was going to be on any given day, or indeed where his daughter was: it was luck on his part that his only child was a shy girl, more likely to be in her room reading Jean Plaidy than out in London somewhere raising Cain. Daniel remembered Kate's birthdays, but only after he'd been reminded by others. But he forgot to ask about most other things: when her university interviews were, when she started her exams, how she might be feeling about everything.

In other ways though, for Kate, her father was the perfect father. Kate was tall and ungainly from her teens onward, with long, spindly legs that rarely did what she told them. She was thin, flat-chested—like a stick drawing. Later, of course, she would come to see that being tall and sticky wasn't so bad; in fact, lots of other girls wished they were like that. But being tall and sticky, with bangs that were always too long, short nails, bitten and with chewed cuticles, and with no social skills whatsoever, it was a long time before she could see it. She was not particularly sure of herself, much as she longed to be, much as she desperately wished she was like her charismatic father or her mesmerizing, much-missed mother, or the confident, smiling girls at school who hung around at the tube station. She would gaze at them shyly from under her bangs as she passed them, going down the stairs to the platform, going back to her dad, to an evening of homework, of music, of conversation around the kitchen table with Russian composers, Italian singers, obtuse German conductors . . . and Daniel, directing the evening, shoving his floppy blond hair back with his hand when he got excited, as young Kate collected the plates, dumped them in the sink, drinking the dregs of the wine quietly behind their backs, alternately fascinated and bored by their conversation as only the wistful outsider can be.

She wished she could be one of them. Not necessarily the band gathered around her father, but the band of girls outside the tube station, gossiping about *Eastenders*, about who Jon Walker liked best, about whether Angie really got fingered by Paul at Christa's party on Saturday and did her dad know because he was really strict? Whether Doc Martens were just totally over. But she knew she never would be.

Kate thought about this, how much things had changed, as she came out of the tube station and walked toward her father's new house. New—well, not anymore, she supposed. It was a long time since the days of the house in Kentish Town. And it was years now since Daniel Miller had not only found himself a new wife, but a new career, as a recording artist who released albums that were either ABBA tracks or modern classical music like Barber's Adagio for Strings, posing for the covers artfully with a loaned Strad in black and white, standing on a clifftop. He'd even been nominated for the Classic FM Awards (and whether he had been outraged not to win or secretly relieved, Kate couldn't be sure). Just before his health had declined a few months ago he had emailed Kate to announce that his next project was an album of Barry Manilow's greatest hits.

She was proud of him—she was his daughter, how could she not be, having seen him at his lowest, and how he'd built himself up again? But Daniel Miller's change of career had been greeted with absolute outrage in the more traditional musical world— open letters to him, pleading with him to pull his album of ABBA songs, signed by the six biggest music critics in the *Telegraph,* offers of "proper" work, third desk in the Bournemouth Symphony Orchestra publicized far and wide, making Daniel a scapegoat, almost, for what the more puritannical elements of the classical music world saw as the selling out of genuine talent for big bucks. Daniel had stuck to his guns, though, and his bank manager thanked him for it, and the *Hello!* interviews started, as did the chats on the GMTV sofa orchestrated by Lisa, who was herself an ex-PR person. For Lisa was behind it all; it was Lisa who Kate had to—reluctantly—credit with turning her father's life around, even if Kate didn't love her the way she felt she should.

Now Daniel and his new wife and daughter lived in Notting Hill, in a cream town house off Ladbroke Grove, with a huge, clean, neutrally colored basement kitchen, not a chaotic, eclectic basement kitchen, leading through to a perfectly manicured garden, artfully designed, with an enormous communal garden out the back. A distressed chandelier hung in the hallway; aluminium window boxes with ferns adorned the windowsills; the 4x4 stood outside. Yes, times had changed for Daniel Miller: until now, for the better, as he had frequently told his eldest daughter, almost daring her to challenge him on it.

As Kate rang the door of her father's house, just after five o'clock that Sunday evening, she was shaking somewhat, though she tried to hide it. In her hands were some more of the daffodils—she wasn't sure what to bring her father, not knowing what he would and wouldn't be able to eat.

The door was suddenly flung open. There, like an action heroine and her matching miniature doll, were Lisa and Dani, as if they'd been standing there, simply waiting for her to come along.

Lisa was standing with her hands on her hips, her tiny frame encased in an expensive brown velour tracksuit, chocolate UGGs on her feet, and Kate goggled at her rather stupidly, not knowing what to say. She stared at Lisa's beautiful, unlined face, her skin moist and tanned, perfectly buffed and cleansed and possibly peeled by a team of high-tech beauticians, and just said, blankly, "Lisa!"

"Kate, hi," said Lisa. Her expression was neutral. She pushed Danielle forward. "Dani, it's your sister. Kate. Say hi."

"Hi-yerr," Dani said loudly.

"Hi, Dani," Kate said, and bending down, kissed her.

"Hey there! Hi!" Dani said, showing her tiny teeth.

"Why's she got an American accent?" Kate said, peering at her half sister as if she were an alien. Dani stared back at her impassively, her curly blond pigtails bobbing slightly as she sucked her thumb.

"Kate, she hasn't got an American accent," said Lisa. She cracked her face into a smile. "Dani, we're going to get you ready for bed in a minute, OK? Then you can come back and talk to Kate." She turned back to her stepdaughter. "Look, it's lovely to see you."

"Oh, and you," said Kate. She held out the daffodils, and Lisa reached out for them. "Um, these are for Dad," Kate went on, and Lisa dropped her hands like stones. "I mean, you know. Shall I show them to him?"

Lisa stared at her with something close to exasperation. "Whatever you want," she said. "He's through there."

She guided Kate with her hand on her elbow, pushing her down the cream-carpeted hallway to the sitting room, where she said, "Dan, darling? Kate's here, and I'll be back soon."

Kate stood in the center of the huge space and stared at the figure at the other end of the room.

"Kate?" came a low, raspy voice from the sofa underneath the window, and Kate walked down toward her father.

"Hello, darling girl," he said, reaching up and putting his hand around Kate's neck, pulling her down to him as he lay on the sofa. "How's my Katya? Look at your old dad, eh? Bit of a shambles, I'm afraid."

Kate hugged her dad, kissed him awkwardly. She stuck her lower lip out, unintentionally mimicking her thoughts. She was totally, utterly knocked sideways by what she saw. His face was yellow, his hair colorless, the creases in his cheeks looked like folds, and his lifeless hands were crossed pathetically on his stomach, like an old lady waiting for a bus. Those hands, which once coaxed sounds of pure heaven from a three-hundred-year-old wooden box, the hands that were insured for a million dollars when Kate was ten—they looked flat, deflated, like the rest of him. Where once his hair was dark browny blond like his daughter's, slippery and uncontrollable, his gray eyes snapping fire as he waved a fork at a friend, violently disagreeing about something, or turning a page with a noise like a whip, where once his tanned, healthy face smiled excitedly down at an adoring crowd, now did he smile gently at his daughter and pat the sofa.

"Come and sit here, old lady, come and tell me how you are."

"God, Dad," said Kate. "I'm so sorry . . ." She trailed off and bit her lip. A tear rolled down her cheek. Daniel looked at her.

"Oh, darling," he said, "come on," and he pulled her arm so she sat down next to him. "It's a bit of a shock, isn't it? But I'm having a bad day today, leaving the hospital and all. You haven't seen me for a while, Kate, that's all. Normally it's much better than this. Never mind, it's over now, isn't it? I just have to concentrate on getting better."

"I didn't realize," said Kate. She felt almost dizzy with sensation overpowering her. How could this have happened, how could she have *known* this was happening to her dad and not come sooner? Forget her mercurial, vague mother; he was, without a doubt, the person she loved most in the world. How could she have shut herself off so completely? She stared at him frantically, and he looked at her.

"My goodness, you look quite mad," he said. "Are you OK?"

Kate looked around the immaculate sitting room, at the white sofas, dim lighting, the lilies on the pale wooden table, trying to hold on to something she knew. She found nothing, and the incongruity of her and her dad in this room struck her, as it had before she left for New York, so many times. She was overwhelmed with memories of how she used to feel and think about all of this.

As if reading her thoughts, her father said, "Lisa's been amazing, you know. I don't know what I'd have done if she hadn't—"

"I know, Dad," said Kate. "I'm so sorry I wasn't here sooner."

"She has been brilliant," her father persisted. He lay back on the sofa again. "And Dani—gosh, she's quite different from you at that age. Very noisy!"

"I bet," said Kate, smiling at him, holding his hands.

"But it's nice to have a young person around the house again. A little Katya." He blinked. "Ah, here she is!"

Danielle rushed into the room in her pajamas. "Daddeeee!" she cried. "I'm here!"

Her pajamas were pink; she had a glossy, huge teddy under her arm and slippers in the shape of bunny rabbits, and she looked very small and totally innocent, her chubby legs thumping across the carpet.

Kate bit her finger sharply, the pain flooding through her, calming her down, and she looked away from her father to her half sister.

"I like your pajamas, Dani," she said. "Pink pajamas, like the song."

"What song?" said Dani, in an American accent.

" 'She'll Be Coming 'Round the Mountain,' " said Kate. "Do you know it?"

"No," said Dani. "You're lying, man."

"I'm not lying," said Kate. She sang.

> *"She'll be wearing pink pajamas when she comes,*
> *She'll be wearing pink pajamas when she comes,*
> *She'll be wearing pink pajamas,*
> *She'll be wearing pink pajamas,*
> *She'll be wearing pink pajamas when she comes."*

" 'Singing aye-aye ippy-ippy aye,' " Daniel boomed loudly, suddenly, from the sofa, and Kate jumped and Dani laughed.

" 'Singing aye-aye ippy-ippy aye,' " they sang together.

> *"Singing aye-aye ippy*
> *Singing aye-aye ippy,*
> *Singing aye-aye ippy-ippy aye."*

Dani laughed again. "I like it," she said, jumping onto the sofa. She wiggled in between Kate and her father, her warm little body writhing with excitement. Kate put her arm around her and hugged her, inhaling the scent of her damp hair. She looked over at her dad, watched him smiling down at his small daughter, then up at her, and she squeezed Dani a little tighter.

"Sing it again," Dani said.

"I'm tired now, darling," said Daniel. "Tomorrow."

"No!" said Dani, jumping up. She stamped her bunny-clad foot and said in her best American accent, "I wannanother song! Why?"

"No, Dani," said their father.

"Dani, leave it," said Kate. "Dad's tired. You can have a song tomorrow."

"Oh my God!" Dani screeched. "I wanna song, man!"

"Jeez Louise," Kate said, under her breath.

"Jeez Louise!" Dani repeated in piercing tones after her, rolling these exotic words around on her tongue. "Jeez Louise!"

"I know," her father said softly, to her embarrassment. He spread his hands out helplessly; he didn't look at his youngest daughter, but raised his eyebrows. "She's always like this."

"Daniel," came a clear voice from the door. "Is Dani giving you trouble? Is she being a bad girl?"

"I'm not, Mom!" Dani screeched in a slow, high voice. "Kate wouldn't sing me another song and she promised!"

"I'm sure she didn't mean to," said Lisa.

"I didn't," said Kate, sounding totally unconvincing. Lisa walked into the center of the room, and Dani ran toward her and clutched her leg with the desperation of a man finding the last life vest on the *Titanic*. Lisa looked down at her daughter.

"Ah, mum's darling girl," she said. "Is she tired tonight?"

"Yes," said Dani, sucking her thumb loudly. "Rilly, rilly tired. Night, Dad."

"Say good night to Kate, darling," Daniel said, shifting on the sofa. "She's come to see you too, you know."

"She should have come earlier," Dani said. "Mum told me."

Silence like a blanket flung itself over the room, broken only by the noise of Dani sucking her thumb again.

"Nonsense!" exclaimed Lisa, looking flustered for the first time in her life. She ran a hand over her forehead, the other resting on her daughter's head. Kate thought how tired she looked, for a second. "Sshh, darling," said Lisa, looking at Daniel, who ignored his younger daughter.

"Lisa." Her husband's voice was quiet but firm. "Why don't you put Dani to bed, and Kate and I can catch up."

"See you in a minute, Kate," said Lisa, ushering Dani out of the room.

"Bysie bye, pink pajamas," cried Dani as she skipped out of the room, utterly unconcerned with the familial havoc she, the only person in the room related to everyone present, had wrought.

"She didn't mean it," Kate's father said. "She's got a lot on her plate at the moment."

"Dani?" Kate said, smiling gently.

"Hah," said Daniel. "Lisa. I'm not easy at the moment. She's very . . . organized." The thought that this was the best thing you could find to say about your wife, for whom you had almost had to throw your daughter out, for whom you had worked yourself into the ground, moved houses, made new friends, gone on flashy, expensive holidays to "network" with flashy, expensive people that you didn't really like that much, for whom you had essentially reinvented yourself, struck Kate as singularly depressing. But she said, "I know. Yeah. She must be great to have around at a time like this."

"Oh, sure," said her dad, and they both fell silent, the two of them sitting awkwardly in the pristine sitting room like refugees from another world. Kate shifted on the sofa.

The letter from Charly was in her bag. She could feel it in there, humming with intent. She hadn't opened it; she didn't want to open it, knew she couldn't. She didn't know why she hadn't thrown it away. But she hadn't. Now, silent next to her father, she slid her hand into her bag again, to touch it for the umpteenth time since she had left the house.

"What's that?" said her father curiously, his voice resonant in the stillness of the vast room.

"Nothing." Kate pushed the envelope hurriedly into the darkest recesses of her bag. "Just something that was waiting for me. Post."

"You must have a lot to deal with," her father said. He shunted himself up slightly on the sofa, grimacing as he did so. "Sorting out the flat and everything."

"Yes," said Kate.

Daniel looked up at the ceiling, then at the floor. "Um—while I think of it," he said casually, "are you going to get a new tenant while you're here? Approve them yourself?"

Before she left for New York, her father had bought half the flat, so Kate owned it jointly with him, and he was entitled to half the rent. Kate skimmed her foot along the carpet. "Not sure yet," she said. "I might wait till I go back and get the letting agents to do it again. I need to think about it. I mean, Gemma leaving and me coming back—it was all quite sudden."

"Right," said Daniel. "Still." He coughed—Kate thought rather awkwardly. "We don't want to lose rent on it, do we? You don't, I mean." He cleared his throat extensively.

"Two weeks I'll be here, Dad," Kate said gently. "You won't lose that much rent, I promise. I'm sorry—" She didn't know what to say. "I'll get onto it," she said. "I'm sorry," she said again, wondering what else to say. A germ of an idea formed in her head; she rejected it. Surely not. "Anyway, Dad, you mustn't worry about that at the moment. It's not important."

"Easy for you to say," her father said quickly. He breathed out, heavily, a sort of groan.

"Dad, you OK?"

"Yes, yes," Daniel said, almost impatiently. He shifted slightly.

"How long till they—till they know?" Kate said. "Whether it's taken, I mean?"

"What's taken?" He shook his head, not understanding.

"The kidney." It felt like a dirty word.

"Oh, I see. I don't know. If it hates me, it'll tell me pretty soon; I'll go into arrest and probably die," he said, smiling mordantly. "They've got me on enough different pills, though; good grief, I could practically set up a bloody pharmacy."

"Dad." Kate put her hand on his, which was lying on his chest. Her hand was shaking.

"Oh, Kate," he said. "God, it's lovely to see you, darling. I miss you."

She looked down at him; his eyes locked with hers, blue, fierce, with a flicker of their old fire.

"I'm sorry," said Kate, and she meant it. "I am so sorry."

"No need," said Daniel mildly. "I could have come to see you more, you know. But you should have come back. Dani hardly knows who you are. And she's your sister. You've only seen her once in the last three years."

Kate had a childish, stupid impulse suddenly to scream like Dani, to stamp her feet and say, *I don't care about Dani, I hate her, it's you I want to see,* but she merely tightened her grip on her father's hand.

"You know why I had to get out of here," she said instead.

"You did the right thing," Daniel said. "It was right you left, you know. I just think you've left it too long. That girl," he added casually. "Charly. It was Charly, wasn't it, the one you met in your first job?"

"Yes," said Kate.

"Well, I never liked her, I have to say."

Since this was patently untrue, and Daniel had always had a crush on the long-legged, tousle-haired, foul-mouthed Charly, Kate said nothing, but she smiled at him, and he twinkled back at her. "Well," he said after a while. "Maybe just a bit." He was silent for a moment. "How's your mother, then?"

"She's well. She sends her—well, she sends her love," Kate said, cursing herself for phrasing this so badly. What Venetia had actually said at the airport, hands clasped to chest, while Oscar struggled with the bags, was, "Oh my God. My darling Daniel. Tell him . . . God, what? You know, he's an ogre, but I still can't help loving him."

"How's that gay husband of hers?"

"He's fine. He's not gay," Kate said automatically.

"Hmm," said Daniel, flicking back his hair in an unconscious gesture. "Do you or do you not remember your engagement party? When he told me he'd had a manicure specially for the party? My God." He shook his head.

"Some men like manicures," Kate said defensively.

"Not any men I know," said Daniel.

"Dad!" Kate said, hitting him gently on the arm. "You used to wear gloves in the summer to protect your hands!"

"That's completely different," Daniel said crossly. "I was a musician, they were my tools."

"Well, so's Oscar. He's a musician."

"No, he's a tool," Daniel said, chuckling to himself, coughing a little bit. He recovered. "And he's not a musician. Arranging camp songs about farmers and cowmen is not being a musician."

"He doesn't—" Kate wasn't going to get into the merits and

demerits of *Oklahoma!* with Daniel, nor point out to him that actually it was probably the greatest musical ever written. She and her father had fallen out about this many times before. So she frowned at him, smiling, too, but her frown quickly turned to alarm.

"Dad, are you all right?"

"I'm fine. Well, I'm not fine. Aarrpff."

She looked at her father, panic rushing over her; perspiration covered his forehead, and he was terribly pale all of a sudden.

"Lisa," she called, getting up. "Dad, I'm going to get Lisa," she told him, shaking free of her father's frenzied grip.

"No, don't," he said, flashing a ghastly rictus grin at her. "I'll be fine. When do you have to go, darling?"

Kate looked at her watch. She didn't want to look at him. "I'm going to see Zoe, but it really doesn't matter if I'm late."

Lisa appeared in the doorway. "Dan? You OK?" she said, bustling forward. "What's wrong with him?"

"He went a bit . . . funny," said Kate. She looked down at her father as Lisa put her hand on his forehead and checked his pulse.

"Went a bit funny," Daniel repeated. "That's the medical term for it, I'm sure." He closed his eyes. "God, I'm tired. It really knocks you for six, this business. And I'm so bored. So bloody bored."

He was a man of action, used to doing, speaking, thinking, striding around and yelling. Kate could see how much he hated this confinement. He needed constant distraction, attention to keep him stable, otherwise—she remembered this much from her childhood—the consequences were awful.

"I'm sure you are," said Kate, still standing and watching him. Her eyes met Lisa's. "Look, Dad," she said, bending down, "I'm going to take off and let you get some rest, OK? But I'll be back tomorrow."

"How great!" said Lisa, smiling thinly. "That'll be great for you, won't it, Dan?"

"I look forward to it," Daniel said, slightly inclining his head, mock formally. He took his daughter's hand and kissed it. "Until tomorrow, my darling, so wonderful to have you back."

"Yes," said Kate, stroking his hair. "Bye, Dad. I love you."

Her eyes filled with tears as she followed Lisa out into the hall, her fingers in her shoulder bag again, absentmindedly touching Charly's letter. Lisa handed her her jacket with an air of polite efficiency.

"Kate, can I ask you something?" she said as Kate put her jacket on.

"Sure," said Kate.

"Did your father mention about the flat, about whether you're finding another tenant again or not?"

Kate wanted to laugh suddenly, the urge bubbling up within her, overwhelming her. She felt hysterical. "Yes," she said. "He did."

"Oh," said Lisa. "Right." She looked expectantly at her step-daughter, waiting for more information. "So—are you getting a job while you're over here?" Lisa said suddenly. "How did you leave it with them?"

"In New York? I said I wasn't sure when I'd be back. They've got someone to cover for me, don't worry. She's really good."

"It's not that hard to learn the skills, though, is it?"

Uh-oh, Kate thought. She steeled herself for another blow. "What do you mean?" she asked, trying to sound polite and friendly.

"You're the office assistant." Lisa sounded exasperated. "Aren't you?"

"Er . . . I . . . ." Kate didn't know what to say.

"I'm just surprised, that's all," said Lisa. She drummed her fingers on the stone-colored wall. "I never thought that's what you'd end up doing."

"Right," said Kate briskly. "OK, well, thanks, then I'll—"

"It was such a shame, what happened, wasn't it," Lisa said conversationally. "Because, you know. You were doing so well on *Venus*. Your dad thought you'd be editor of the magazine in a few years. Or writing a novel or something. He always said that. He's a bit surprised, I think—"

"Right," said Kate again, nodding furiously. "Lisa, look, now's not the time for—"

Lisa held up her hand briefly. "I must say this—" she began. Kate's heart sank. "That's all very well. But I don't think you quite understand how much your dad worries about you now, Kate."

"I know he does."

"He feels very let down." Lisa looked at the floor.

Kate was angry suddenly. Angry at herself for mismanaging this situation, angry with Lisa for her insinuations, her nasty barbed comments.

"Look, I'm very tired, and so are you, much more so than me. I haven't seen you for eighteen months, or Dad or Dani. Please, Lisa," she said, surprised at how scary she sounded, "let's not get into this." Being angry made her stronger, she realized. She wasn't scared of Lisa anymore. "I'll see you tomorrow, is that OK?"

Lisa stared at her. "Yes. Yes of course. Look—"

But Kate made her escape, hurrying down the path into the crisp March night.

Six

Kate took out her phone and called Zoe. "I'm on my way."

"Oh my God."

"I know. Zoe, I need a drink. Put some wine in the freezer."

"Already in the fridge, love. Got some Twiglets here, too."

"Twiglets! Oh my God, when was the last time I had—"

"I know, I know. Now stop wittering and get on the tube. I'll see you when I see you."

Kate picked up her pace. She was going to see Zoe! Actually see her, look at her face, be in her presence. Sit at her kitchen table, see Henry, meet Flora for the first time! She was terrified, but she couldn't wait. After seeing her father, nothing else seemed as bad as that, and it was with a curious lightness of heart that she stepped off the curb, looking around her in the evening gloom.

Zoe, Henry, who was invariably called Harry, and Flora lived in Kilburn. When Zoe and Steve were first engaged, they had bought a garden flat in a terrace house, moving from a spacious, airy flat in Muswell Hill because, as Zoe kept saying, Kilburn was the Next Place. The Next Place that was going to go stratospheric, the new Notting Hill/Clapham/Shoreditch. By the end of the year, where there were roadworks and rubbish and drug dealers there would now be potted plants, widened sidewalks, and tapas restaurants. Zoe and Steve would be able to stroll out in the evening to sample the delightful new Italian restaurant and friends would say admiringly, "You live in *Kilburn*?" much as one might say, "You live in *Mayfair*?"

Three years on, and everything else had changed. They'd bought the flat upstairs when Harry was born. But Steve was gone now, Harry and Flora were here, yet Kilburn was still more commonly bracketed with Soweto and South-central L.A. than Fulham or Battersea. But by then, other things were simply much more important.

Kate realized, as she stumbled along in the dark, that she knew the route to Zoe's house from the tube so well she could have almost done it blindfolded. There were the broken cracks in the paving stones; there was the parking ticket machine; there was the gate that half hung off its hinges. It was so unlike Daniel and Lisa's house; it was more like Kentish Town, where she'd grown up. She ignored the lounging youth who sat on a wall two houses along from Zoe's, staring balefully at her; she even smiled quite sweetly back at him and hammered on the door impatiently, all thought of fatigue gone.

And then darling Zoe opened the door. They didn't say anything. Zoe just smiled at Kate and held out her arms, and Kate remembered what she'd forgotten, that Zoe and Steve's house was more of a home to her than she'd ever known, that she loved Zoe more than most people in the world, probably. Zoe looked exactly the same, like a little brunette imp, and as she stepped forward and hugged her best friend, Kate felt her heart hurting, physically hurting.

"Missed you." Zoe's silky thin brown hair muffled Kate's voice; after about a minute they laughed and stepped back, Zoe still gripping Kate's elbows.

"Look at you, lovely girl. You're so grown-up. What's happened to my Kate?"

"Hardly," Kate laughed, and shook herself free. She crossed her arms. "Where are the children?"

"In bed," said Zoe. "Sorry," she added. "I knew if I let them stay up to see you we'd never get rid of them. I told them if you came around at all it'd be very, very late. And I told them you wouldn't have had time to buy any presents yet, because there aren't any in America."

"Ah." Kate followed her in and shut the door behind her, looking around in pleasure at the long corridor littered with small Wellington boots, a bike with training wheels, and coats hung on various things. A birdcage hung off the umbrella stand.

It was like being home again. She hadn't realized how much she'd missed this house. Zoe gazed around rather helplessly, then clapped her hands and said, "Right, let's get some wine. Put your coat . . . er, there. That's right."

"Thanks." Kate followed her through into the sitting room, piled high with brightly colored videos, books, toys, cushions and more cushions. Kate had forgotten this, that Zoe was incapable of entering one of those Cath Kidston–style lifestyle shops so beloved by her, the kind that stocked chipped enamel jugs and beautiful cups and saucers for the modern vintage home, without walking out with a cushion under her arm. She must have had about twenty. It made sitting on sofas in Zoe's house extremely hard.

"So how was—"

"So how are—"

There was a constraint in the air all of a sudden; they broke off and laughed. "You go first," Kate said.

"How's your dad?"

"Fine. Weak, a bit shaky, but basically fine, for the moment. They won't know if it's been a success for a while."

"Must have been great to see him."

"Yeah." Kate couldn't articulate it all. She scrunched up her nose and nodded, and Zoe nodded back. She understood.

"How was the flight?" said Zoe, brushing the worn edge of the large blue sofa.

"Good, good, thanks," said Kate.

"How's New York! I want to hear everything. How's it going?"

"How's it going?" is one of the world's most annoying questions. It is not a request for specific information, but more a general "Fill me in" command. Kate didn't know where to start. Trying not to sound churlish, she said, "What do you want to know about?"

"You know!" Zoe's enthusiasm was loud, too loud. "How's everything going, what's it like in NYC, are you liking living there? What's new?"

"Um. Well, I saw Betty on Friday—"

"Yeah? How's she?"

"She said she'd just spoken to you." Betty was an old friend of both of theirs.

"Yeah, she rang last week, actually." Zoe cleared her throat. "Who's Andrew?"

"Andrew?" Kate was blank for a moment, then she remembered. It seemed years ago. The drinks, the kiss, her running away . . . Andrew. She tried to picture his face, mortified, in the darkness. She felt her cheeks flame red; she raised her hand to her face. It was another life.

"He's—no one, really," she said. "Someone Betty's always trying to set me up with."

"Oh!" Zoe said, too loudly again, like this was a jolly, great conversation between two normal friends. "Oh you!"

"No," said Kate flatly. "I kissed him and then I felt sick and had to get into a cab and run away. If you want the truth."

Zoe's brow furrowed. "Right."

"Nothing really to talk about," Kate said. "Honestly."

Zoe took the hint. "So, then. That's—great. So, how's the flat? Did the tenant leave it in a state?"

"No, it's fine, actually," said Kate. "I've unpacked; it's nice to be back there."

"Yes, it must be." Zoe ran into the kitchen, collecting the wine out of the fridge. "Is it . . . er, is there a lot of stuff in it still? From . . . before?"

"Yep." Kate took the glass she handed her. "Most of it's in the storage area in the basement. But quite a lot's still in the cupboards in the hall. Just . . . you know. Books. Photos. Clothes I should have thrown away years ago. Joint stuff we had together."

"I'm the same," Zoe said. She waved her hands around. "Too much stuff of Steve's around still. It's been a while now. Why can't the bastard come and pick it all up, eh?" She smiled, her eyes filling with tears.

"I know," Kate said, feeling inadequate. She could feel her heart hammering away in her throat, it seemed. This was it, now. "Look, Zo—"

"Can I say something?" Zoe interrupted her, her voice high, nervous. "Darling. Can we just—catch up, you know? Not have some long, awful, depressing conversation that leaves us both in tears and makes us feel hugely guilty?"

"But—" Kate had come expecting that; she deserved it, she *was* guilty. But Zoe put her hand on hers.

"Look, Kate. Darling Kate." Her eyes were bright with tears. "Do you know how much I miss you?"

"Zoe—" Kate said, easy tears coming to her eyes. "I—"

Zoe interrupted her again. "This is what I mean. I miss you so much. There's so much to say, and so much I want to know about. I don't want to sit here having a maudlin conversation about all the crap that's happened. It happened. You ran away."

"I did."

"But I'm the one who kicked you out."

"No you weren't."

They were facing each other.

After a few moments, Zoe sighed, deflated. "It doesn't matter. Oh, Kate. I was furious with you, but now you're back so, oh, please let's not waste time being apologetic and wringing our hands about it all. I want to know how you *are*."

She sat back on the sofa and nodded her head solemnly.

"But—" There was so much Kate could say to this, and she fumbled for words.

"I mean it," Zoe said, almost fiercely, and Kate saw that she was struggling with emotion, emotion that threatened to overwhelm her. Kate nodded back.

"Right. Of course," she said.

"Yep," said Zoe, recovering herself quickly. "Cheers, darling Kate. Cheers. Welcome back." She stood up, and Kate followed suit. "God, it's good to see you again."

Their glasses, clinking heavily together in the quiet room, made a harsh clanging sound. After they'd each taken a large sip, they both sank into the sofa and looked at each other.

"So really, how's your dad?" Zoe said first. "Were you at his house?"

"Yes," said Kate. "He came out of hospital this morning. Um, he's OK. Not great, actually."

"How was Loosa?"

This was the childish name Zoe and Kate had given Lisa after her appearance on the scene, six years ago. "Loosa" made them cackle for hours in the pub, at Kate's flat, and so on. Even Charly tried to claim she'd thought of it. It was less of a joke when, after about nine months together, Loosa and her dad announced they were expecting a baby and were engaged. She was Lisa after that.

"She was . . . er, fine," Kate said. "You know what she can be like."

"Was she mean?"

"Noooo . . ." Kate grimaced, remembering the conversation. Then she smiled, it had been so stupid. "Umm, she told me I've wasted my life and I'm a disappointment to Dad." She nodded at Zoe's outraged expression. "Oh, and then she had a go at me about the rent, wanted to know when I was getting someone else into the flat and I needed to sort it out ASAP."

"What a cow." Zoe's dark eyes snapped fire. "Don't worry about her. She's always been a cow, Kate. She's a cliché—I thought they didn't make them like her anymore. Evil stepmothers, I mean."

"Still . . ." Kate was trying to be fair. She knew Lisa had it pretty tough. And as she thought about the huge, spotless house, perfect without and within, she felt weirdly sorry for Lisa, and Dani, just a little, and desperately sorry for her dad.

There was silence—another awkward silence. Zoe cradled her glass of wine in her hand; there was a noise from upstairs, a creak, but then silence, and they looked back at each other and smiled.

"Oh, by the way. I should have mentioned," Zoe said after a moment, "Mac's back."

Kate looked up sharply. "I thought he was living in Edinburgh again?" she said, rolling the words around on her tongue, almost dizzy with the luxury of talking about him.

"No, he came back. He's looking for somewhere to live. He wants to move up here, find a flat closer to us, actually." She looked curiously at Kate. "Hey! Maybe he should rent your flat when you go back!"

"That's a good idea." Kate rummaged for some imaginary item in her bag so Zoe couldn't see her face.

"He'd love to live in your flat, I bet. I always thought he had a bit of a crush on you."

"Did you!" Kate waved her head around, as if this were hilarious.

Zoe nodded, her brown bangs bobbing up and down her forehead. "Yes, seriously, me and Steve used to talk about it." She looked at her friend curiously. "But . . . well, it didn't work out, did it."

"I suppose not." Kate nodded, seemingly interested. "So, how's his job?"

"Good, good," Zoe said. "He's a resident now in a hospital down here, actually doing pretty well, I think. It's just—since everything happened, it's good to have him around," she said, looking glum. "It's nice for Harry and Flora to see their uncle. He's so good with them." Zoe smiled. "Oh, he's lovely. He's just a gentle giant, you know."

"Yes," said Kate, smiling gently at her. "He is lovely. I can imagine he would be."

"Anyway." Zoe shook her head, recovering herself. "When he heard you were back and you were coming over, he said he'd pop around tomorrow instead. He said he didn't want to intrude, you know. On us catching up and everything."

"Of course," said Kate. "That's really nice of him. Still, it'd be great to see him."

So Mac *could* be on his way over as she sat here on the sofa. But he wouldn't come over, Kate knew it. Once he knew she was back, he'd no more pop around to Zoe's to say hi than he would eat a glass vase. And she couldn't blame him.

"So how's work?" Kate said a bit later as they ate dinner, two more glasses down.

"OK." Zoe swallowed. "OK. Good, actually. They've really been great about the kids and everything. And it's a nice place to work. I like going there."

Zoe worked as a garden designer for a picture-perfect little garden nursery near Primrose Hill. Having been a lawyer at one of the top London firms, averaging eighty-hour weeks and earning double that, suddenly three years into her job she chucked it all in. Memorably—or this was how Steve told it—she'd told a partner at the firm that she didn't want to end up like him.

She'd trained as a garden designer because they could afford to; Steve was a management consultant, still working long hours and bringing home the bacon, and when they had the children her job was flexible. It was perfect—until Steve left them, and now she was struggling to make ends meet. But as she said, she'd rather struggle, working in the open air with the flowers and seeds and picking her children up from school, than work all the hours of the day and be able to afford five-star holidays to Dubai.

"You should come and have lunch with me one day, when I'm at the nursery," Zoe said, patting the table flatly with the palm of her hand. "What are you going to do for the next week or so?"

"Not sure, really," said Kate. "I need to sort stuff out in the flat. See Dad. Spend some time with Dani, too, I suppose. And catch up with people, Francesca and all that lot."

"How's your work going?" Zoe emptied the rest of the bottle into her glass.

"OK," said Kate. "Someone's covering for me while I'm away."

"Are you—what's happening with the agenting? Are you handling any stuff of your own yet?"

She took another swig of wine as Zoe watched her, waiting for her answer.

"Not really, no," she said honestly. "And I like it that way, Zo. I know it's terrible, but I love it. I like not having to be me anymore."

Zoe nodded. "I thought you'd be editor of some huge magazine some day," she said. "*The Devil Wears Prada,* that sort of thing. Or writing a bestselling novel." She shook her head. "That's all."

"You sound like Lisa," Kate pointed out. "I thought you'd be well on your way to being a judge by now."

"You thought lots of things would happen," Zoe said. "So did I. Look at us."

The cluttered kitchen was silent; the house was quiet. Kate tried to imagine what it must be like for Zoe, alone every evening while the children slept upstairs. Tears pricked her eyes; a painful lump rose in her throat.

"Hey," she said, trying to change the mood. "Do you remember your housewarming party here, all those years ago?"

"My God," said Zoe. "I always forget about then. We only had the ground-floor flat, before we bought the upstairs one. Isn't it weird, how different it was then?"

"Sure was." Kate nodded. "That was a great party, though."

"You wore your blue and gold dress."

"You stood on a chair and sang 'Cabaret.' "

"Oh dear," said Zoe ruefully. "Didn't Betty snog that Finnish gate-crasher from the flat upstairs?"

"Yes, she did," Kate hit the table, memory flooding back.

"And—oh my God. Wasn't that the night you got together with Sean?"

She cleared her throat as Kate was silent, memories flooding back over her.

"No, it was a few weeks later."

"But you were flatmates, weren't you?"

"Yes, we were. . . ." Kate squashed a piece of bread into her fingers. "Yep. That was a weird night. I'd forgotten." And she had, strangely. It had been one of those event evenings that mark the beginning of a new time in one's life and thus the end of another, she realized now. "Nine years ago," she went on. "I can't believe it. It seems . . . well, it's weird."

"So near yet so far," said Zoe, and Kate nodded.

Kate unwrapped an after-dinner mint and carefully smoothed the foil out onto the table. "When did you buy the flat upstairs?" she asked. "I can't remember. Was it after you got married?"

"After," said Zoe flatly. "Steve flirted totally disgustingly with the estate agent and I didn't speak to him for two days. But he got the price down by five grand, so I couldn't hate him anymore."

Kate remembered Steve's flirting well. There was nothing she could say to this.

"Typical of him," Zoe went on. "Bloody typical." She blinked rapidly. "Anyway, what was I saying? Yes, Mac. Mac!" Kate nodded. "You see, I always thought he had a bit of a thing for you. That night at our housewarming party, you know. He was mad about you for a while, you know that, don't you?"

Kate was silent, and then she said, "Well, it's a long time ago, isn't it."

"Yep," said Zoe. "It's just a shame. We should get you two together before you have to go back, you know." She looked Kate over appraisingly, like she was a prize heifer. "You haven't seen him since—how long?"

"I don't know," said Kate. Keep your voice light, she told herself. "Is he—" She opened her eyes wide. "Is he well, though?"

"Yeah." Zoe nodded. "He's OK. Got a bit of gray hair. Works too hard. Doesn't talk about stuff much. But he's OK. I know he'd love to see you."

Kate looked around the bright, cozy room, feeling cold suddenly, and very tired.

"It's weird talking about this," Zoe said, sighing. "I never talk about it, about all of us, anymore. I'll have to make the most of you while you're here. It'll be a while, won't it? Perhaps you'll love it back here so much you won't go back. Yay!"

"I am going back," said Kate. "Seriously. I love it there. I've got a new life, you know."

"I know you have," said Zoe. She crinkled her nose. "You needed it. I like thinking of you leading this superglam New York life, meeting up with Betty for cocktails, running around like Sarah Jessica Parker. Sort of means I cannot hate you for not being here, Katy."

Since her last birthday party had consisted of her mother, stepfather, and the Cohens (from down the corridor), and Maurice, the doorman, having a slice of cake out on the sidewalk, Kate didn't know what to say to this. She smiled and nodded, sagely, as if hinting that a life full of incident and drama lay waiting for her across the ocean.

At eleven o'clock, Kate left, by then a little worse for the wine. As she was putting her coat on, Zoe opened the door and said, "Bye, darl," Zoe said. "I love you. It's so good to have you back."

"It's good to be back," Kate said, and then, that moment, as she hugged Zoe, it was.

• • •

When Kate got back home, the letter from Charly was still in her bag. She waited till she was in bed, face washed, warm chunky bed socks from Bloomingdale's, which her mother had given her last Christmas, enclosing her feet. Her old bedroom smelled faintly of familiar things, COCO perfume and peonies. Outside, someone somewhere was yelling at someone else, or perhaps at no one, and way beyond her the city flickered, lights gradually going off one by one, still at its heart never asleep. Kate smoothed her hands over the duvet and blinked, the fatigue of the day finally catching up with her as her fingers fluttered on the glue of the envelope.

She drew out a letter. A letter and a photo. It was of Charly and Kate, dressed up at the office Christmas party, their first year at the magazine. Kate winced at her ill-advised Spice Girls–era black clompy platform boots, black miniskirt, waistcoat, and hair in a high ponytail, and then, almost greedily, her eyes drank in Charly, glorious as always, her long, tousled hair tumbling around her tanned shoulders, the little black dress with spaghetti straps, the gorgeous, still-covetable knee-high black suede boots. It had been so long since she'd seen her; she'd forgotten how beautiful she was, how hilariously different the two of them were.

Hilarious, yes. That they'd been friends, so close you couldn't slide a finger between them, so obsessed with each other it was almost like a relationship, so heart-stoppingly sad that she hadn't seen Charly for years, that Kate rocked back against the bookshelf, as if a ray of something had just shot out and hit her in the chest. That was the effect Charly still had on her, nearly eight years on, all those years since they'd first met.

Dear Kate—
　　It's been a while, hasn't it. How are you?
　　I'm fine, I suppose, working hard, not.
　　I found this photo of you and me at the Christmas party,

the year you started at Your World!, thought you'd like to see it? What did we look like back then??!!

Kate, I'm writing to say hello. Also to remind you I'm still alive. I wonder if you still care about that.

This is hard for me to write, you know I never was one for letters. I wanted to apologize. For everything, I suppose. Well, I thought I might as well try. Also, I'm writing because I wanted to let you know I'm having a baby. We don't know what it is yet—

Kate didn't read any more. She screwed the whole lot up, jumped up out of bed, and the cold hit her. She ran into the kitchen, opened the little thin French doors, and threw the letter, the photo, the envelope, over the balcony railing. She wondered, as if watching herself from above, why she hadn't just opened her bedroom window, or thrown it in the bin. But it wouldn't have been far enough away.

It was only when she felt something drop onto her chest that Kate realized tears were running down her face. In the dark corridor there was no sound. She crawled wearily back to bed, turned the light off, praying for a deadening sleep.

But the thoughts crowding into her brain danced there all night. She should have realized that those scenes would go through her head again, that she would dream about it all again. Back when she was starting her life as a grown-up, they all were. Look how it had turned out. She'd told Zoe she never thought about it, she'd practically forgotten everything.

But that was a lie. Although she didn't want it to be, it was imprinted on her brain, for always. How could it not be? And the dreams always ended the same way, with Kate realizing what, deep down, she carried around with her every single day in New York. That she shouldn't be here. She didn't deserve to be here. That was why she didn't let herself remember.

Seven

"*H*ey. New girl. I'm going to Anita's for lunch. Do you want to come?"

Kate blinked up at the vision before her and pushed her tortoise-shell glasses slightly farther up her nose.

"Er, yes, please," she said, shocked. "Thanks."

"I'm going *now*," the vision said. "I'm bloody bored, and Catherine and Sue are going to be gone for fucking *ages* on that conference meeting thing. Let's get out of here."

Two weeks into her exciting new job at *Your World!* and Kate had yet to have lunch with anyone; she was too terrified. She sat on a bench by Lincoln's Inn each day at lunchtime, eating her sandwich and hiding behind a book if she saw anyone from the magazine. The offices were near Holborn, a big glass building housing all the magazines in the stable of Broadgate UK, and every morning the revolving doors sucked in these gorgeous, coltish girls who strode past Kate, hair flowing in the breeze, expressionless and cool, and every evening it spewed them out again, as she flattened herself against the wall, trying not to get in their way. She spoke to her boss, Sue, to Gary, the postroom boy, with whom she was insanely jolly and chatty, the way new people always are with the photocopying man, the postroom boy, the security guards. They're men, they're not bitchy, they don't ignore new people as a point of principle.

To everyone else, however, she felt miserably, she might as well be invisible. If by chance one of the tall goddesses who hustled and bustled around Catherine Baldwin, the fearsome editor, should be forced to address her with some features-related query that only she could answer, Kate heard herself replying to their careless questions in a voice rusty with lack of use, and a tone hopelessly fulsome and inane.

"Hi!" she'd squeak. "Hi there! No, Sue's not here! She's still out at lunch! Sorry, sorry," she would say, practically bowing, as Georgina or Jo or Sophie looked bored and, not a little, contemptuously down at her.

Because it was now October, the whole new job thing had a curious resemblance to going back to school, or university. The days were still dry and relatively warm, the leaves dusty and crunchy on the trees, the streets of town suddenly busy again after the dog days of August and September. They were still playing "Everybody's Free (To Wear Sunscreen)" and "Livin' La Vida Loca" on the radio, but they sounded flimsy, summery, silly, out of kilter. The Argos Christmas adverts had started appearing on TV, even. As Kate and her new flatmate, Sean, walked to Rotherhithe station in the mornings, the still-rising sun would hit them in the eyes, and in the evenings, though they tried to deny it, it was too cold to sit outside at the pub.

Kate and Sean had been friends at university, but they were more friends-in-a-group than friends who went out for drinks on their own together. Tall, laconic, with a Texas drawl, Sean was Steve's best friend. Steve was a good friend of Kate's, too. In the Easter term of their first year at university, Kate had introduced Steve to her best friend, Zoe, and Steve and Zoe had been going out ever since. So Kate and Sean had spent a lot of time together in the past few years.

Still, though, Kate was fairly surprised to find herself sharing a flat with Sean, but then lots about her life now surprised her—the fact that she was south of the river, for starters, was a shocker, as was the fact that she didn't like cheap cider anymore—she preferred a glass of Chardonnay. She'd been to TopShop and bought a black and gray checked miniskirt, which she mistakenly wore with a black polo-neck and black tights, in the warm, dry weather of September, but it made her feel supermature. She did her own shopping at the supermarket, picking out Things to Cook from her new Jamie Oliver cookbook. She bought the *Evening Standard* on her way home each night and felt super-grown-up, reading it with a concentrated expression on her face on the tube.

Three weeks into her new living arrangement and all was going swimmingly—too swimmingly, in fact, because Kate had started to dread saying good-bye to Sean each morning. He sometimes perplexed her with his constantly flirty ways and optimistic, can-do attitude, as well as intimidated her since he was, without doubt, usually the best-looking man in the room. Now he was the friendliest face Kate saw most days, and she would cling to him at the ticket barriers.

"I don't want to go to work today," she'd say, clutching his arm.

"Hey now. Don't be silly," Sean would say, gently prising her off him with a giant pawlike hand. "It's only been ten days. You'll soon make friends, Katy. You're shy, that's all."

"They're horrible," Kate would mutter, biting her lip. "Don't like it. Don't want to go to work and be grown up."

It was true, in its way. Part of her wished this wasn't happening, that she was back at home with her father, cheerfully cooking stew, throwing insults around at each other, listening to music. Warm, safe—but a little boring. Wouldn't it be easier if she just moved back in with her dad again and never left the house or faced the real world, with all its terrifying complications that she wasn't at all good at? Yesterday she had spilled coffee over one of the girls at work—Georgina. Georgina had given her what Kate could only identify now as a death stare and said, "That top was *new*," even though it was only a teardrop-sized spot of coffee. Kate was thinking of having plastic surgery to change her appearance.

"Look," Sean would say, punching her playfully on the arm. "You're Kate Miller, aren't you? All you ever wanted to do since I've known you is work in magazines. Haven't you?"

"I'm not right for them. I don't fit in."

"You got a First in English from Oxford, Kate," Sean would say. "You're right for anyone. You gotta see that. You're young, you're cool! Man. They're lucky to have you, OK?"

Kate would rather die than use her university education to impress people, and she refrained from pointing out that at college she'd done nothing *but* work while everyone else was off having fun, drinking, putting on plays, drinking, sleeping with each other, going to balls, going to silly parties, drinking and sleeping with each other. She wasn't cool, she was the opposite of cool, she was . . . lukewarm. She was destined for the shadows, watching from the sidelines, not center stage. Ugh. But Sean, whose nature was as sunny as his hair color, couldn't see that about her, and it annoyed her.

"You'll find some friends," he said one Thursday, nearly three weeks after she'd started there. He patted her on the shoulder, moving her away from the ticket barriers. "You'll love it there soon. This is your time! You're in the big wide world now, and you're gonna find your niche. I promise."

Sean was untroubled by self-doubt. "It's easy for you," Kate said childishly. She looked down at the floor, knowing she was being stupid, feeling eleven again, like she was back at school trying to persuade her mother to let her stay at home. Sean put his finger under her chin, and she turned her face up toward him.

"Hey," he said gently, looking into her eyes. He smiled, his tanned, kind face crinkling into lines. "It'll be easy for *you*, Katy. You're wonderful. We all know it, *you* just need to know it."

She clutched at his wrist, taken aback. "Oh, Sean." She was

embarrassed, she didn't know why, and she smiled back at him shyly. "You're just saying that."

You're just saying that. She sounded about five; Kate cringed inside, then asked herself why it mattered, as awkwardness fell upon them. She tightened her hold on his wrist, reached up and kissed him on the cheek.

"Thanks," she said, and she smiled at him, feeling happy all of a sudden. "You're right, Sean. Thanks a lot."

"I know I am," he said, and he was still watching her. "Now, you're gonna be late. Have a great day. I'll be there when you come back, after a long day slaving over some JavaScript. OK?"

"OK. Bye. Thanks."

His mouth curled a little. "No, thank *you*."

He was a flirt, such a flirt, she told herself as Sean walked away. Kate watched him, shaking his head at her over the ticket barrier as the sea of commuters bustled past them, off with lives of their own, full of promise and exertion and interaction and . . . Oh, all the bloody things she was no good at. It was so sweet of him to try, she told herself. She stared after him. He would be there tonight when she got home, watching TV, and they'd sit on the sofa together and chat about their day, and yet another day would have passed with her being shunned, like the Amish. So she'd cook him something and he'd teach her how to mend her bike or how to rewire a plug or something, and they'd spend the evening together, like they always did. She'd be fine, if she could come home to that life. It was a nice life. Who said you had to love your job?

But Sean was right. Because that very day, Charly decided to notice Kate.

They went to a traditional Italian place, around the corner from the office. It was free of Broadgate employees, by dint of the fact it served food—in particular, food that wasn't just leaves. Charly seemed to know them all; the waiters practically clapped as she slunk in, her long legs sliding into a table by the window.

"God, Sue's a real cow, man," she said as they were seated. She pushed her small frameless sunglasses up on her head and nodded at a waiter. Her honey-colored hair tumbled around her, she smiled at Kate, the freckles on the end of her nose wrinkling. "Yeah, we're ready," she said to the waiter hovering nearby, a look of adoration on his face. "What're you having? Salade niçoise for me. No dressing. With extra olives. And a Coke. Thanks." She flung the menu back at him without acknowledging his presence.

Kate said, "Er . . . me too."

"The same?" the waiter said, raising his eyebrows.

"Yes," said Kate, not wanting to be conspicuous. She handed him back the menu.

"You don't want dressing either? The same?"

"Yes!" said Kate, trying to affect an incredulous laugh.

"You want extra olives, too?"

"Oh, go away," Charly said, batting the waiter away. "Just bring her a normal one. Leave us alone. So. D'you like Catherine? What do you think of Sue?" she demanded, leaning in, her long, slender fingers plucking a stale roll from the basket in front of them.

Kate was taken aback by the directness of the question and a little terrified. She hadn't imagined she'd have to speak, more that she could just sit there and listen to Charly, whom she'd noticed striding around the office, effortlessly glamorous. She never seemed to hang around with the Georginas and the Jos, the Pippas and the Sophies—she was her own separate entity. More beautiful than them, cooler than them (she had been wearing cropped trousers and heels for ages—long before Madonna in the "Beautiful Stranger" video, as she informed anyone who wanted to listen)—less posh than them, less fake than them. She knew it, and she didn't seem to care.

"Come on," said Charly impatiently, and Kate was shaken

from her reverie. "Is Sue a good boss? She really annoyed me today, you know, telling me to recheck that piece on gloves for autumn."

"Er . . . aah," Kate said, hating the impaired speech she seemed to have developed since her arrival at *Your World!*. What would Sean say if he could see her? She thought about it and smiled. "I like her. She's nice. Bit uncommunicative—I mean, I wish she'd tell me what's going on a bit more."

"Yeah," said Charly, nodding. "She seems to think you'll just guess. She's OK, but I know what you mean. I used to work for her."

"Did you?" said Kate. "How long—how long have you been here?"

"Not long," said Charly. "Too long, you might say. A year. I was her assistant, now I work with Catherine and Georgina"— Kate nodded, she knew this—"and I sometimes write the editor's letter when no one else can be bothered to do it, and I do a couple of featurettes."

"You do the Letters Page, don't you?"

A frown passed over Charly's beautiful face. "Yeah, and I hate it. Load of weirdos writing in to tell you how to make stuffed animals out of the lint from the washing machine, or wanting you to print a picture of their grandson just 'cause he's done a poo that's shaped like Alma Cogan."

"Really?" Kate was fascinated.

"Not the last one, no." Charly shook her head. "Barbara Windsor, actually."

Luckily the salads arrived, saving Kate from further comment. Charly ate like a demon, shoveling food in her mouth, throwing out odd comments, inviting responses from Kate, making jokes about the office, filling her in on what she hadn't known— Barbara in Sales had slept with Fry Donovan, the new Broadgate publisher, a couple of years ago, and he'd given her a job to keep her quiet, so the rumors went, which is why Barbara giggled helplessly whenever Fry walked into the room. Claire Cobain on the subs desk threw up into Phil's yucca plant the day after the Christmas party. She'd forgotten and he hadn't realized for three days, except they all kept gagging on the smell. And Jo and Sophie weren't speaking to each other after Sophie heard Jo saying to Georgina in the loos that she looked rank in her new black patent platform boots.

All Kate had to do was throw in the occasional question, raise her eyebrows at the required moment, but Charly was a great companion, and soon Kate found herself opening up, telling her about her flatmate, Sean, about her best friend, Zoe, about how she'd started to dread coming into work, how she'd eaten her lunch on a park bench for the past two weeks.

"By yourself?" Charly demanded. "Sitting in Lincoln's Inn eating a sandwich from Pret A Manger by yourself? God, that's sad. What did you do if someone you recognized came past?"

"I'd look down at my book, or else I'd turn my head so they couldn't see me," said Kate, and as she said it, she realized how silly it sounded. Charly laughed, her eyes wide open with surprise, and Kate joined her.

"That's the saddest thing I've heard for a long time," Charly said.

"I know," Kate agreed. She looked at her watch. "We should get back, you know."

"Yeah, in a bit." Charly looked carelessly at her watch, then pouted. "Let's have a coffee first. So—where were you before here?"

"Here?" Kate gestured to the building behind them. "Nowhere. This is my first job."

"Your first—jeez," said Charly. "How old are you?"

"Twenty-two. I left university this summer."

"Oh my God," Charly said, peering at her as if she were an

exotic specimen. "And you started work right away? Didn't take any time off?"

Kate shook her head uneasily. She didn't want to disabuse Charly of the notion that she'd gone straight from university to a job, when, in fact, she'd had a solitary, dusty summer at home in Kentish Town, slowly driving herself mad with the future. Her mostly absent mother and stepfather were in the Hamptons for the summer and incommunicado; Daniel had a new girlfriend and was rarely at home; Zoe had skipped off into a job at one of the top law firms as had Steve; Francesca and Betty, two of her closest friends, had gone traveling together for six months, not back till after Christmas. A few weeks prior, Kate had nearly put the phone down on Zoe when she'd told her that Mac, Steve's older brother, had just been put on some special fast-track system for the best surgeons in the country. People she hadn't even *met* were falling over one another to outdo each other while she had whittled away the dog days of summer, saving up for a trip to the newsagents each day. But that was over now, she hoped. OK, it was *Your World!*, it wasn't *Vogue*, but it was a start.

"What's your ambition, then?" Charly asked. It was a strangely childish phrase, that; it touched Kate, though she wasn't sure of the answer. She wrinkled her nose. Charly persisted. "What do you want to do, what's your dream job, I mean?"

It was what Sue Jordan, her new boss, had asked her a month ago at her job interview, and Kate gave the same answer then as now. She looked over and above Charly to the shelves behind the counter in the little restaurant. They were lined with spreads, old jars, tins. "I want to work in magazines, that's all," she said. "I love them."

"Really?" Charly sounded dubious, but Kate had heard it before.

"Yeah," she said, smiling and shaking her head. "I was a geek all through school, and the one thing I loved that wasn't geeky was

Vogue. Don't know why, just did." She did know why, though; it was an entrée into a world she wasn't part of, a world she could only aspire to: glamour, style, elegance, beautiful clothes. It wasn't the posh people she was interested in; it was something more fleeting than that—she supposed it was that idea of a blueprint for how to live your life. With style, flair, purpose, and organization. The cold, beautiful women in those magazines, they weren't ignored by boys or by their coworkers, they didn't have mothers who left them, fathers who were messy and annoying. They—all of them, whether they were the writers, the models, the society people— they had black shift dresses, scented candles, fresh linen. Boughs of apple blossoms in big glass vases, thick black velvet evening cloaks—that sort of thing. She loved magazines, that was all; the smell of the new pages, the sheen of the pictures, the slice of life, the answers to her curious questions about things, how other people behaved, reacted, everything. She was happy simply to observe— she knew that, too.

"Well, good for you," Charly said, sounding uncertain. "So, you'll be wanting Sue's job in a year, then? Better tell her to watch out."

"Oh no," said Kate, looking horrified. "It's not—"

"Calm down," said Charly. "Don't get so worked up about it. It's a job, OK? When you've been here longer you'll realize it's not worth having kittens about. Me, I'm happy if it pays me enough to buy a couple of glasses of wine and some new boots every few months."

"Really? What do you want to do, then?" Kate said curiously.

"I don't know," said Charly. "I want to marry someone rich and go and live in Spain. Have a house here, too, in the Bishops Avenue. With a heated indoor swimming pool and lots of Sophie's friends." They both laughed; Sue had just signed off on a feature that morning about the millionaires' row of houses in north London, and Sophie had spent a lot of time saying in a Very Loud

Voice that she knew someone who lived there. "I think she's reading the map wrong. It's probably Bishops Avenue in Acton, more like," Charly had said loudly that morning, and Kate had smiled as Sophie turned on her heel and flounced back to her desk.

"Hey," Charly added as they laid their money on the table. "You been to the Atlas pub? Around the corner from the office?"

"No," said Kate.

"It's nice. Fancy a quick drink there tonight?"

"Really?" Kate said, then corrected herself. "That'd be great." She looked at her companion. "Thanks, Charly."

"What for?" Charly slung her bag over her shoulder and pulled out the hair that was trapped underneath it. She shook her head, and the waiters in the cafe watched in adoration. Like a Timotei ad, Kate thought with amusement.

"Just—thanks for asking me out to lunch and stuff," she said as they stepped out onto the street. "It's weird when you start a new job. Not knowing anyone, you know."

"Course I know," said Charly. She didn't look at Kate. "When I joined last year no one spoke to me for three weeks. Hey." She pushed her hair out of her face. "I reckon we could be a bit of a team, don't you think? Show Sophie and Jo and Georgina, show them we've got our own thing going on. OK?"

"I'm not bothered about them," Kate said, surprising herself.

"Sure, whatever," said Charly darkly, and Kate wondered which one of them had incurred her wrath. "No worries. But still, we're going to stick together. I've decided. You up for a drink, then?"

"Definitely."

"I'll see who else is around, too. Introduce you to some other people. We're going to have a great time."

The sun was warm on Kate's hair; she felt relaxed, herself, for the first time since she'd started there. "Great," she said as they turned the corner and walked up toward their building.

"Look at that loser over there, with the Beckham haircut,"

said Charly, flinging her arm out so that she nearly knocked over a teenage boy who was staring at her. "What a jackfruit."

The loser with the Beckham haircut was coming out through the revolving doors. He raised his sunglasses and smiled at them. He was extremely good-looking.

"Hey," he said.

"Hey," Kate said, then wished she hadn't.

"You never called me back, Charly," he said, looking hopefully at her. "When are we going out again?"

"Shove off, Ian," said Charly. "It's not happening. Kate, I've got to get some gear from the postroom. See you later, OK? Atlas, straight after work? I'll come and pick you up."

"Great," said Kate, and Ian stared at her, annoyance crossing his otherwise perfect face.

That night, when Kate rolled back to Rotherhithe at 12 a.m., swaying and singing softly to herself like a sailor on shore leave, Sean was still up watching American football on Channel Five. As she staggered into the sitting room, Kate waved at him nonchalantly, trying to prove she was sober, and her hand flew back and hit the door frame with a loud *thwack*.

Sean smiled to himself but only said, "Good night, then?"

Kate's mind was whirring, through the white wine that was pooling in her stomach, in her throat, in her head. Good night? The best night, that's what. She and Charly, Claire, and Phil had gone to the Atlas, sunk a few drinks, then some more, then Sophie had joined them, and the five of them had played the pub quiz machine, screaming with joy when they got one of the questions right. It was Kate who knew that Chairman Mao died in 1976. She didn't know how she knew, she'd just known, and as she'd leaned forward, punching the big plastic square on the machine, shouting, "Yesss!" she felt, slightly hysterically, as if all those years of being the class swot, the one who got their homework in, the one who really never did anything bad, they were paying off. Charly had screamed, jumped up and down, and high-fived Kate, and then "Spice Up Your Life" had come on the jukebox, and they'd both jumped off their stools and danced like crazy.

"I hate the Spice Girls!" Charly had shouted. "They're bloody awful!"

"I love them!" Kate said. "Sort of . . ." she continued as Charly looked on at her in horror, and both of them laughed again.

Gorgeous Ian had turned up. Charly ignored him all evening, drinking beer from her bottle, cheering Kate on in the quiz and then, as they all stood around outside the pub after they were kicked out, suddenly walking off down the street with him, her hand carelessly clutching the back of his neck. Kate had been almost shocked, impressed by her total insouciance, the very *Charly*-ness of it, and then it had made her smile.

As she sat on the night bus home, trying not to acknowledge that she did feel a bit sick, she thought how great life was, how all the usual things that worried her—her dad, her mum, her sad little life, her fear that since she split up with Tony, her university boyfriend, nearly two years ago, she would never find love again, her fear of her job, that she was just a big fat failure—all these things seemed to vanish, with the optimism of youth, and what she remembered instead was Charly's face as she bought them all another round of drinks with the winnings from the machine. Charly's amused expression as she said, "You're hilarious, Kate, you know that?"

"Thanks, Charly," Kate had said. "This is great." She patted her arm.

Charly had shrugged. "My pleasure." She'd looked strangely pleased.

Kate fell onto the sofa next to Sean, put her head under his armpit, and smiled, ridiculously.

"Found some friends, then?" Sean said. "Or have you been drinking alone again?"

"Shurrup," Kate said, her voice muffled by Sean's sleeve. "Friends from work, nice."

It was so cozy on the sofa, next to him; she loved Sean. "So, where did you go?" he said, muting the sound on the TV. He turned in toward her and stretched his arms, yawning, and pulled Kate toward him. She wriggled into him, happily.

"Just pubs near work, near the work building," she said. They were silent together, for a moment, and she could hear his breathing, feel the rise and fall of his chest, her head against him.

"Oh, Kate," he said softly.

Kate sat up slowly, suddenly not feeling so drunk, knowing he was looking at her, and their eyes met.

Sean was a closed book to her in so many ways; she had known him for years, though they had never been best friends or gone out with each other. He was a genial, all-American kind of guy—on first appearance, and then you realized that, in his quiet, understated way, he was more British than that. His clean-cut, sporty appearance belied his more studious, careful character; though she knew him well, Kate never quite knew what he was thinking. Through the waves of cheap white wine, spirits, and exhaustion, she looked at him, blinking, wishing he would speak first, not knowing what was suddenly now between them. Someone more worldly-wise would have known what to do, on the sofa, having a moment with their flatmate. They either would have leaned over and kissed him or got up and made some coffee.

Watching him, watching his softly twitching lips, Kate suddenly wanted to kiss him, wanted it fiercely. But she couldn't. It was strange, new, scary. It was *Sean,* after all. Her flatmate. And she was drunk. No.

"Pfff," she said, rather helplessly, smoothing her skirt with her hands.

It broke the tension, and Sean smiled at her. "Oh, babe," he said kindly, and he patted her arm. "You're hilarious."

"That's what Charly said!" Kate said, remembering the evening again, happily.

"So the mean girls aren't being mean to you anymore?" Sean said lightly, sitting back and taking another sip from his bottle of beer.

Kate sank against the sofa. "Oh," she said, her eyes closing, glad the moment was over and it was normal again. "No, hope not."

Sean nodded, and looked back at the screen. After about a minute, he realized that the head next to his arm was lolling and that his flatmate was fast asleep.

The last thing Kate remembered that night was Sean's gentle shove as he pushed her onto her bed, where she pitched headfirst onto the duvet. She woke up early the next morning as the October rays were creeping into her room, the curtains wide open, having not been drawn the night before. She lay there, reconstructing the evening slowly, from its unexpected start to its slightly strange finish. Had any of it really happened? Had she imagined the lunch with Charly, the drinks, the general knowledge? The night bus—and that moment with Sean last night, had she made it up? She patted the bedside table next to her, feebly, feeling for her water glass, and then sat up slowly. Her mouth was dry, her head was ringing, she felt as if she wanted to die, but for the first time in what seemed like a really long time, Kate realized she was looking forward to the day ahead.

Eight

*M*ore than a year after she'd started at *Your World!*, the pie chart of Kate's friendships was clear. Charly was her best friend. Zoe was her newly engaged, other best friend. Betty and Francesca were happily ensconced in their chaotic flat in Clapham, Betty worked in a gallery and tied her short dyed hair into pigtails, while Francesca, who was a banker and the person Kate had been closest to at university, was now extremely grown-up, wore gray suits and worked in Canary Wharf, which was suddenly where everyone was working.

Charly and Kate were still editorial assistants, and they sat across from each other and helped each other, went to the same Italian deli around the corner for lunch (where Kate happily stuffed her face with carbs and fats and Charly gingerly picked out the tomatoes in her sandwich and ate them), and occasionally got the tube to TopShop on Oxford Circus, where Kate would try on clothes that didn't suit her and buy them and Charly would try on clothes that made her long, leggy form look even more stunning and complain that nothing fit her, and leave buying nothing. In the evenings they went to the pub, where they gossiped and bitched about the day at work, their sometimes eccentric colleagues, and their endless fascination with the microcosm of the office.

Kate was changing; she only realized it when other people remarked on it. "Nice work, Kate," Sue had said briskly to her a couple of months ago, after she had written a little piece on Alma from *Coronation Street*. "You're really coming out of your shell, aren't you?"

The truth was, she loved it—she loved her life now. She took to it like an ugly duckling to water, having feared the life outside her experience before. Now Kate strode to the tube station in the mornings, her long legs flying out in front of her, her long hair catching in the breeze. She laughed with the postroom boys, she said hello to Catherine, the editor, with a bright smile on her face, not a mumbled, half-horrified grunt, in fear lest she try to engage her in conversation. She loved answering the phone to random readers, calling to ask whether *The Darling Buds of May* was ever coming back on TV again or where they could get the recipe for hot pot that had been in last week's issue. And she looked forward to relaxing, drinking, chatting, laughing in the evenings as she had never done before.

One Friday afternoon in March, Kate sat at her desk, trying to concentrate on the letter she was writing while resisting the temptation to play with her new mobile phone, her first, which she had picked up that very lunchtime. She hadn't actually called anyone on it yet, but she had taken down the numbers of everyone in the office, entering each one in the address book, slowly and painfully. It was four o'clock, and the office felt dead. Kate felt dead, too—it had been Sophie's birthday drinks the night before, a long, messy night, culminating in Kate not getting home till two because of the vagaries of the night bus. Charly had disappeared at midnight, with a random ad exec she'd picked up hanging on to her arm. Charly had been in a strange, cool mood, and Kate could tell a storm was brewing.

Kate chewed on her biro and looked up from her desk, where she had been idly pressing buttons on her mobile. "So—did you go back to his place?" she asked.

Charly was flicking through a magazine, exaggeratedly pouting. She was supposed to be checking the text for the recipe card layout.

"God, I love Britney Spears," she said. "There's no way she's a virgin. No way. Look."

She waved the magazine in front of Kate.

"Fake boobs," said Kate, glancing at the magazine.

"No," said Charly. "They're real."

"They're fake!" said Kate. "Come on! Where did they come from! She used to have no boobs at all."

"From growing up, she's only nineteen," said Charly, as Kate's boss, Sue, zoomed into view, her heels clicking madly on the thin lino. Charly carried on flicking through the magazine as Kate turned back to her computer screen.

"Are you in next week?" Sue said, not slowing down or making eye contact with Kate.

"Yes," said Kate, who was used to her boss. "Why, what do you need?"

"I'm on holiday next week. Bloody half term. Malcolm's booked that stupid riyadh. Can you do the Editor's Letter for me? I thought you might like to do it."

"Sure," said Kate, half standing up, like a captain in the mess when the general pays a visit. "Of course, Sue. Wow, how great! Thanks—thanks a lot."

Sue stood still, several steps ahead of Kate, on her way out to the lifts. "Great. Good one. Get it to Catherine for her to look over by Tuesday morning. OK?"

" 'Thanks—thanks a lot,' " Charly mimicked, half smiling, as Sue walked away. "You big suck!"

"I know," said Kate, embarrassed. Charly rolled her eyes.

"Well done," she said, after a pause. "Good one. I'm going to be really kind and take you out for a drink to celebrate tonight. And there's a new club in Soho just opened. Virus, it's called. We could go there afterward."

Kate bit her lip. "I can't, sorry. Steve and Zoe are having a housewarming party. Sort of an engagement party thing, too. It's fancy dress. And especially not after last night."

"Ooh-la-la," Charly said. "Sorry I asked. How about just one after work instead?"

"OK," said Kate. "Great." She swiveled happily around on her chair. "The Editor's Letter! Hurrah!"

"Good for you, that's great," said Charly, and she reached opposite, to Kate's desk. Her hand couldn't pat Kate's hand, it was too far away, and she ineffectually patted the dictionary there instead. "Back to work, then, Kate Miller," she said, her hand slapping against the pages of the magazine as she carried on flicking through it. Kate turned back to her desk, and they sat in silence for another hour—well, near silence, as Charly sighed loudly, like she always did, and in the background was the muted clicking of keyboards and faint office sounds of whirring machines. It was Friday, it was nearly the weekend.

"Where shall we go?" said Kate as they left the office an hour later, striding out together in the dusk of the March evening. "The Crown?"

"No," said Charly firmly. "Anywhere but The Crown."

"Oh God," said Kate. "Who did you do there?"

"Shut up!" said Charly, glaring at her, but smiling. "I didn't 'do' anyone there, thank you very much. It's just Phil and Claire . . ." She trailed off, chewing a strand of hair.

"What?"

"They're there tonight, heard them say it as they left."

"So?" Kate liked The Crown. It had nice bar snacks, like mixed nuts, and though it didn't have a quiz machine, it had a jukebox, a rarity in a central London pub. And it was by the Inns of Court, tucked away on a little side street—she thought it was rather nice, like something out of a Dickens novel. There were barristers in there, sometimes in gowns. "Go on. I love it in there."

"No, come on, we're going to The Globe."

"*Again,*" Kate moaned, like an unwilling child being forced to the shops on a Saturday. "What's wrong with Phil and Claire?"

"There's nothing wrong with Claire," Charly said grimly, jabbing the button for the traffic light. "Claire is great. I don't have a problem with *Claire.*"

"You—and Phil?" Kate was aghast, not because she was surprised Charly had slept with someone, but because she hadn't noticed. "When?"

The lights changed. Charly marched across the road, impossibly fast. Kate ran behind her. "Hey, slow down. When? Didn't you know he and Claire—"

Of course she knew he and Claire were an item, it was the worst-kept secret in the office, two best friends at work also having an affair. It wouldn't have mattered, either, except it was blindingly obvious Claire was mad about Phil and Kate could see he wasn't that into her. He was a bit of a player; nice enough, but he was twenty-seven, he didn't want to settle down yet.

But Charly didn't answer, and they arrived at the pub. The welcoming smoky fug of The Globe drew them in, and after they had settled down with their drinks (double gin and tonic for Charly, white wine spritzer for Kate), Kate said, tentatively, "Look, Charly, sorry. I didn't know. What's going on?"

"Nothing's going on," Charly said, and there was a tone to her voice Kate hadn't heard before, dark and bitter. She smiled, a small, sad smile. "Just me. Screwing things up as usual, OK?"

"So you—?" Kate made a gesture with her beer mat, waving it around, hoping it would convey the question "You've been shagging Phil?"

Charly tutted, impatiently. "Yes."

"How many times?"

"Jeez, Kate, do you want a tally?"

"Oh." Kate nodded. "So more than once, then."

"Yep," said Charly, and she gave a ragged sigh. "It started a few weeks ago—well, it started at the Christmas party. I went back to his flat, and we saw each other over Christmas—you know I'll do anything to get out of Leigh." Kate nodded. "So I'd come down to London and stay the night with him, we'd wander around town, no one around, all that shit. It was—lovely." Her voice cracked.

"Oh my God." Charly never talked like this. Like a person with emotions. Kate watched her friend, she patted her arm. "You've fallen for him, haven't you?"

"No," said Charly furiously. "He's an idiot, OK? We were supposed to be meeting up last week and he called and said Claire was getting suspicious! He said it had been fun but we should call it a day, he couldn't have two secret office affairs going on! What a—"

Her hand clenched into a fist and her lovely face crumpled. "Oh, Charly," said Kate unhappily. She didn't know what to say. She liked Phil, but she couldn't understand why he was so secretive about his relationship with Claire, either. Was it that big a deal? Was it naive of her not to understand why he was so weird about it? She put her arm around Charly's bony shoulders, clad in slithery oyster silk. Charly sniffed loudly and caught Kate's hand.

"That's why I don't want to go to The Crown tonight. OK?"

"Yes, that's OK," said Kate, kissing her hair. "It's always OK. Now, we need to plan our next move. Tell him he can't get away with it."

Charly looked at her in surprise. "Are you serious?"

"Yes," said Kate, feeling incredibly protective of Charly, who was so screwed up in her own weird way. "It's Claire I worry about now, don't you? He's just going to mess her around like he has you." She got out her new mobile phone, her pride and joy.

"What are you doing?" said Charly.

"I," Kate said proudly, "am now going to send my first text message." She typed, laboriously, for a minute. "God, this is annoying, scrolling through. There!" she said eventually. Charly peered over her shoulder.

I know what you did to Charlx. If you mess Claire arovnd we will tell her. Have a god eveming. K x

"Hm," said Charly. "The typing's a bit crap."

"So?" said Kate, pressing SEND.

"Well, Kate Miller," said Charly admiringly. She cleared her throat and sat up straight. "You are turning into a bad girl, you know that?"

"Hardly," said Kate.

"Slept with your hottie flatmate yet?"

Everyone always thought she was having a torrid affair with Sean. "No!" Kate said, and she blushed. "It's not—there's nothing going on. Shut up!"

"Yeah, right," said Charly, draining the last of her drink. "In your head there is. I don't blame you, he's gorgeous. Dull as hell, though."

"No he's not," said Kate defensively, though Sean had, in fact, this morning in the kitchen, droned on about the new Microsoft enabling functions for five minutes while Kate held her hungover head in her hands and prayed for death. "He's just passionate about his job, that's all."

"Bor-*ing*."

Kate thought back to the weekend before, how Sean had showed her how to use his new laptop, set her up with her own Hotmail account and everything. They had sat side by side at the computer for hours, she listening, he explaining, their legs touching, neither of them acknowledging it. "No," she said quietly. "Not all the time."

"He's so not the one for you," said Charly. "Don't shag the flatmate just because he's there and you're busy playing husband and wife. *Textbook*. I mean it."

Kate was silent, uneasy, all of a sudden. She looked at her watch. "Let's get another drink, and then I'd better be off," she said.

Charly sprang up, suddenly alive again. "These are on me, doll," she said. "Thanks. Thanks a lot." She sashayed to the bar, and every man in the vicinity glanced in her direction.

Nine

*I*t was after eight when Kate got back, and she was two-white-wine-spritzers drunk, which is to say not sober but not disastrous. Sean was watching TV as she barreled into the sitting room.

"I'm late!" she cried loudly, hoping that by making a drama of it she'd get the guilt over quickly. Sean hated being late, it was the one area of flatmate life where they diverged wildly. If Kate said Sunday lunch at 1 p.m., she expected people to pitch up by two and to serve food by three. Sean meant lunch on the table at 1 p.m.

Sean didn't look up from the TV. For some inexplicable reason (Kate said it was because she was being all grown-up), Zoe had decreed that tonight was to be evening dress, and Sean was immaculately dressed in black tie. He was that kind of boy, the sort who always had nicely shined shoes and owned his own dinner jacket.

"Are you furious?" Kate said, unwrapping her scarf and throwing her coat on the floor. "Sean, it'll take me two minutes to change, I'm sorry—"

He looked up and she saw his face.

"What's wrong?" she said.

His big blue eyes were curiously expressionless; but Kate knew him by now, knew him well enough to know something was up. "Jenna's engaged," he said.

"Oh." Kate sat down next to him and took the remote out of his great big hand. She turned the TV off. "Oh, Sean, that's— that's crap."

Jenna had been Sean's girlfriend all through high school in Texas, and most of university, till they'd broken up before he came back to England for his third and final year. She was, as far as Kate knew, the only woman he'd ever loved, and the circumstances of their breakup were mysterious. Sean had been really unhappy. Kate had met her only once, in their second year, when she'd come to visit. She reminded her of a girl from a seventies perfume ad: long, wavy brown hair, flicking out at the sides, endless long legs, the shortest skirts, the widest smile. And she was nice, which was the killer. Kate and Francesca had hated her.

She patted her unresponsive flatmate's leg, feeling the hard muscle beneath the black cloth. "How did you hear?"

Sean cleared his throat, and flicked his eyes wide open, then shut them rapidly. He did this several times. "She called me. I was just leaving work, and she called me."

"Are you really upset?" Kate said gingerly.

"No," Sean said, sitting up and shaking his head. "Hell no!"

Rubbish, Kate thought. He reminded her, fleetingly, of Charly and her earlier bravado.

"It's just—hey, Jenna was my first proper girlfriend, and I was really into her, you know. She's marrying some farmer guy called Todd. Ugh." He shook his head again. "He grows maize, has, like, thousands of acres. It's such a *cliché*, man!"

Kate looked around their warm, small flat, crammed full of mementos of their happy flatmate life together. Sean followed her gaze and she nudged him, desperately wanting him to feel better, be happy. She hated seeing him like this, it hurt her, too, and it was then she realized how close they'd become. "I know," she said, almost desperately. "Oh, love." She clutched his hand a little tighter and he turned to look at her with something like surprise on his face.

"Kate—"

"Who wants to be a bloody maize farmer, eh? Aren't you glad that's not you? Aren't you glad you're here instead?"

There was silence as they looked around the flat again together: on the floor was a Kentucky Fried Chicken box; five bottles of vodka formed a pyramid on a shelf alongside several really vile lads' mags and several equally vile gossip mags; and the walls had a poster of *The Graduate,* a panoramic photo view of New York, from Kate's last trip to see her mother, and a series of photos of Sean, Kate, and their friends stuck onto pinboards. At Kate's feet were two empty beer cans. Their eyes met and they burst out laughing.

"You know what?" Sean said, turning to her slowly. "You're right. I am glad I'm here instead, Katy." He took her hand and kissed it.

"Don't be sad," said Kate, and she gave Sean a hug.

"I'm not," he said, and he squeezed her tight. His hand cupped the back of her head. "Bless you, darlin'. It's just I thought she might be the one . . . you know? I thought she was the love of my life. So you can't help thinking about it."

"I know," said Kate, though she didn't. She had never thought Jenna was right for Sean. He needed someone . . . well, not like Jenna, that was all, and she'd been glad when Sean had come back for their final year single, truth be told. She felt cross, all of a sudden, like the conversation was shifting out of her control. She rested her head on his shoulder, breathing gently.

"Thanks, darling," he said, and she could hear his voice reverberating against her back. "I feel fine—God, it's years ago now, but you can't help having a little think when you hear something like that, can you."

"No," said Kate, stroking his back again, and feeling a little like Florence Nightingale, doomed to tend eternally to the romantically injured. "You can't." She stood up briskly. "I'm going to get changed, OK? We're going to get dressed up for the ridiculously themed fancy dress party, we're going to look like a million dollars, and you're going to have a great evening, I'll make sure of that. Get another beer. I'll be five minutes."

"Sounds perfect, darling." Sean settled back on the sofa. "What're you wearing?" he said.

"The blue and gold dress," Kate yelled as she ran down the corridor to her bedroom. "It's a special night."

"Sure is," said Sean, and Kate heard him cracking open another beer as she took the blue and gold dress from the hook on her bedroom door where it was hanging. She stroked it happily.

Kate wasn't a girly girl when she was a teenager, she was more into the old-fashioned, vintage dresses of years ago. She had her old stack of *Vogue* magazines from the 1950s and '60s that she'd picked up in secondhand bookshops and school fairs, and she still loved flicking through them, staring with envy at the girls in their effortlessly elegant cocktail dresses, in completely inappropriate settings: posing with a bough of cherry blossoms, or hopping off a suspiciously empty, clean double-decker bus.

On her nineteenth birthday, she and her father were walking through Hampstead. After Venetia left, they would often go for long walks through London, mostly on Sunday afternoons, ambling without aim through the deserted City, or along the river, or through the parks. They'd just come off the Heath, and were looking for a place to have a cup of tea. As they crossed a little cobbled courtyard, deep in conversation about what utter bastards Daniel's record company, who had just dropped him, were, Kate's eyes fell on a dress in the window of a rickety old shop. It was from the fifties, blue silk, embroidered all over with gold silk thread roses. Kate gazed at it helplessly. Her father, turning around and seeing his pale, lanky daughter peering shyly into the window, had looked at her quizzically, as if trying to work out why she was looking at the dress, why she would be interested in that. It was just a dress—Daniel had never been good at empathy. Then his expression had changed.

"My God. I did get you a proper birthday present, didn't I?" he said, suddenly remembering, panic streaking across his face in case there was a repeat of That Birthday Which They Never Talked About, the one where Kate had gone to school in the morning and come back in the evening to find Venetia had left.

"Yes, you did," said Kate loyally. "You got me the new lens for my telescope and that beautiful box of chocolates. It's OK, Dad, honestly."

(She had, in fact, bought the lens herself and he had given her the money, but to be fair, Daniel had actually bought the chocolates.)

Daniel breathed in heavily through his nose and pursed his lips, musing.

"Do you want that dress, old girl?"

Kate looked amazed. "Dad! But it's got to be a hundred quid!"

Daniel looked quickly at his watch and put his arm around her. "Who cares! It's your birthday, darling. Come on. Let's go and try it on. . . ."

Five years later, it was Kate's most treasured possession. When she was answering those quizzes at the back of the Sunday supplements, the reply to "What one item would you rescue if the house was burning down?" was always, always, the blue and gold dress. It once had been her telescope, but she was a bit over that now, and it lay, gathering dust, in the back of her cupboard in the Rotherhithe flat.

She only wore the dress on special occasions. She'd worn it to her mother's wedding, to her ball at university, and she was going to wear it tonight, for no other reason than that she suddenly felt alive with happiness. First Sue had given her the Editor's Letter to write, and now she was off to Zoe and Steve's housewarming party, and everyone was going to be there, and . . . who knew what might happen?

Kate was at her most beautiful that night, though of course she didn't realize it. She was twenty-three, still young but much more confident, more relaxed than she'd been even a year ago, her skin clear and unlined, her dark brown eyes shining with excitement, her cheeks flushed. She was smiling as she entered the sitting room forty-five minutes later, and as she cleared her throat lightly, and Sean sat up and tried to pretend he hadn't been asleep, she grinned at him, her evening bag cupped in one hand, the other hand holding the skirt of the blue and gold dress, and Sean whistled.

"Wow, Kate," he said, rubbing his eyes and standing up. "You look absolutely amazing, do you realize that?"

"Oh . . ." Kate rolled her eyes. "Be quiet!"

"I mean it," said Sean, still staring at her. He bowed and gave her his arm. "Let battle commence. You're going to hook up with someone tonight, I know it. I'm going to have to make sure no one takes advantage of you."

They moved graciously toward the front door and he held it open for her.

"Thank you very much," said Kate, stealing a glance at him. "You're too kind."

"My pleasure, miss."

"People are staring at us," Kate said as they moved slowly down the street toward the bus stop, Kate's high heels making steady progress tricky. People out on Rotherhithe High Street on a Friday evening were not especially accustomed to seeing men in black tie ambling down the street, accompanied by ladies in vintage silk and gold thread.

"I know," said Sean loudly. "Well, let them stare. I have a broken heart and you look ravishing. Hello!" he said brightly to an old lady in a thick purple coat who was gaping in openmouthed astonishment at them. "Good evening."

"Evening!" she replied. "Ooh. Do you know you take me back in time. Back to when I was twenty, you two."

"Madam," Sean replied, formally, in his rich American accent. "Surely that time can only have been a matter of weeks ago." He smiled wolfishly at her, and she laughed, delighted.

Kate laughed, too, and took hold of his arm again, and they continued their unsteady progress up the hill to the bus, carrying them north of the river again.

"So, Kate," Sean said as they turned into Zoe and Steve's road in the wilds of Kilburn over an hour later. "Are you looking for love tonight?"

Kate stared at the ground. "Maybe. I'm going to take it easy this evening, anyway."

"Still hungover?"

She stifled a yawn. "A bit."

"That Charly's a bad influence on you, girl," Sean said. "Aren't you feeling a bit rough?"

"A bit, now, yes," Kate admitted. The excitement of what had happened at work, the drinks with Charly, comforting Sean, rushing to be ready—all had buoyed her up, and now, nearly there at the end of the long journey across the city, she was starting to flag. She had had, after all, roughly four hours' sleep the previous night.

Sean watched her as she rubbed her face.

"You funny girl," he said. "Where's the Kate I know from college who used to wear her hair in a ponytail all the time and sit in her room all night, studying?"

She met his gaze, boldly. "She grew up."

Sean smiled lazily, looking her up and down. "You bet she did."

He was flirting with her; he always did this; it didn't really mean anything.

"How about you?" Kate said, bringing the conversation back on track. "You on the pull tonight then? Drown your sorrows?"

"Oh, you bet," Sean said. "I'm hoping to break my 'ninety-eight-exam party record."

On one heroic night after their finals, Sean had picked up the prettiest girl in the bar, and snogged ten other people—including the barmaid at the pub where they'd started off.

"You're such a tart," Kate said as he fell into step with her, her gold kitten heels clattering on the ground. "But—hey. Good luck. Here we are."

They stood at the gate to the house. Sean held out his hand solemnly. "Hey, darlin'. Good luck to you, too. May the best partygoer win. Who is Jenna, anyway?"

"Exactly!" Kate shook his hand firmly. "Definitely."

"And we're sharing a taxi home, whatever happens," said Sean. "I'm not doing that bus thing at three in the morning—we'll be taken to, like, Manchester without realizing."

Despite the fact he'd lived in the United Kingdom for more than four years now, Sean's grasp of the geography of his adopted country was somewhat shaky. He sort of thought that because everything was much smaller here than in the U.S., ergo it was literally five minutes away from everything else. That is, Edinburgh was a thirty-minute drive away, not an eight-hour drive away.

He released her hand. "Let's go in, Katy-Kay," he said.

She was a bit flustered, and fumbled with her bag, but he took her elbow, and as they approached the front door, it flung open and there was Zoe, dressed in a twenties flapper dress dripping with sequins, her glossy dark hair curled into ringlets.

"Hooray! You're here!" she cried. "Now the party can really start! Woo-hoo!" She called out to Steve. "Steve, love. Kate and Sean are here. Turn the music up! I'm going to get you two a cocktail each. We've got vodka in the bath. Hurrah, you're here! Come in!"

Steve appeared behind his fiancée, his dark eyes full of pleasure. "Well, well, well!" he said, clapping his hands together. "Man!" He slapped Sean's hand. "Kate, you look like—like a dream." He kissed her. "I could eat you." His smile was enormous. "Seriously, you two. I kept saying to Zo, the party won't really get going till you get here. And now you're here! Yes."

Sean and Kate smiled at each other on the doorstep, proud of their party-starting status, which was acknowledged and, in Sean's case, well deserved. Sean rubbed his hands together and Kate smiled. They were good, and they knew it.

"We'll see you inside," said Kate, and she pushed Sean toward the door again, wanting to get inside, and as she stepped forward, following him in, someone came in from the other side, and she stumbled across the threshold, into the house, almost falling into their arms.

"So this is the famous Kate," the someone said, holding her by the arm to support her. She gazed up at him, helplessly, in the dull glow of the swinging hall light's bulb. With his open, handsome face, his dark eyes, his ready, wide smile, he looked strangely familiar, and yet . . . she knew him, but she didn't know him.

"This is my brother, Mac," Steve said, a catlike grin on his face. "Finally! You've never met, that's really weird."

Mac. Of course. He looked like Steve, and yet he was totally unlike him. Steve was easy, open, laughed a lot, restless. Mac was taller, broader, his hair was the same light brown as his brother's, but closely cropped. He had lines on his forehead, laughter lines by his mouth. Kate suddenly had the irresistible urge to reach out, touch them with her index finger. She stared at him. She was glad Zoe had gone into the kitchen.

"No, we've never met," said Mac, still looking at her. He took her hand now, and shook it. "I know a lot about you, though. A *lot*," he said.

"Yeah, sorry about that," said Kate, recovering herself, her eyes still on him. His eyes were green, a strange, scrubby, sealike green color. "I know a lot about you, too." When she was nervous she talked too much. "You're a medical genius, and you live in Cricklewood, which is weird, because I never thought the two would go together, except we just did an article in the magazine about people who come from unlikely places. Did you know Cary Grant was born in Redland in Bristol and he was an acrobat at the Bristol Hippodrome?"

There was silence. Kate looked down at her feet, hating her high heels, which prevented her from fleeing into the night. She bit her lip, yelling at herself inside her head. *What? How?* Was she *mental*? *This,* this was why she hadn't had a date in six months, she told herself.

"I did not know that," said Mac, conversationally. "Did you, however, know that it took ten million bricks to build the Chrysler Building in New York?"

"No!" said Kate with pleasure. "That's—that's wonderful."

Their eyes met again; he smiled, she smiled, and that was it.

"Kate! Are you coming in?" Sean called from the kitchen. He sounded almost cross.

"Better come inside, then," said Mac. So she did.

Ten

*T*wo hours later, it was after midnight, and Zoe and Steve's house-warming party was an unqualified success. Zoe had made vodka jellies, of which Kate had had four. Steve was the music mixer, flipping between CDs and his LPs with the greatest of ease. They danced themselves stupid to Michael Jackson, all pretending they could moonwalk in the narrow kitchen. At one point there were thirty people doing the conga to Pérez Prado through the small, corridor-like flat, out into the garden, down the side entrance, and through the front door again. Then Steve—who was a brilliant host, who only wanted his guests to have a good time and didn't care about the carnage they caused to his new flat, as long as they were enjoying themselves—started making flaming B-52s, and Zoe stood on a chair and sang "Rescue Me" into a hairbrush, until she fell off and Steve had to pick her up. He threw her over his shoulder, slapping her on the bottom, and carried her out of the room, as she screamed and the others applauded.

Occasionally she would catch sight of Sean, who was drinking steadily, and wave at him or pat his arm, checking in to make sure he was doing OK. But otherwise she lost herself in a whirl of drinks, laughing, catching up. She kept looking over her shoulder to see where Mac was, kept thinking she saw him—had she just dreamt it?—as the party grew more and more raucous. In fact, it turned out the party was so good that when the new neighbors from upstairs—a married couple in their thirties—came down after midnight to complain about the noise, Steve thrust each a Moscow Mule into their hands and had them both dancing with Betty to Britney Spears in five minutes.

Betty was after Sean tonight, Kate could tell, and she watched her bat her false eyelashes at him with some amusement, impressed at the way she could be so subtle and yet so obvious with him. Kate was pretty sure Betty and Sean had slept together at university, and watching them, she was suddenly pretty sure that was the way it was going to end up tonight. She stood in the corner of the sitting room, taking a breather from the dancing, with her glass curled up against her, and she saw the way Betty touched her top lip with her tongue as she talked to him, her blond pigtails wagging on each side of her head, the way Sean watched her mouth as he answered her, the way they smiled into each other's eyes, moving slightly closer. They were both consummate flirts—Kate knew this about both of them—and suddenly the Sean of a few hours earlier, desolate at the news of Jenna's engagement, seemed far away. He was on a mission tonight, that was clear. Kate bit her lip, tasting blood on her tongue, and turned away, surprised at the intensity of her reaction. Yes, she thought. It's true. I do have a crush on him. Zoe appeared beside her, watching Sean and Betty.

"Great party, Zo," she said.

Zoe was hugging the doorframe, using it as support, her small hands clinging to the carved wood almost desperately. "Thanks," she said. "This bloody flat, you know what a nightmare it was getting it, I can't believe we're here now." She banged her head gently against the frame. "I think I may have to grovel to the neighbors tomorrow, though," she added nervously, glancing down the corridor into the kitchen, where through the French windows Kate could see Francesca and Steve was lying on the small lawn, singing something loudly.

"You're cute, though," said Kate. "They'll love you. We had a thing in the magazine last week, how to get on with your neighbors. Accept responsibility, go around to each of them with a box of chocolates tomorrow and just say sorry. It'll be fine."

"Did you meet Mac, then?" said Zoe suddenly.

"Yes," said Kate. "Well, at the beginning—" She looked around. "I don't know where he's gone."

Zoe shrugged her shoulders. "Don't know," she said. "He's working too hard. He looks exhausted. Don't you think?"

Kate hadn't noticed anything except how lovely he looked, and she'd never met him before, so she was hardly qualified to judge.

"Zo, Zo!" Steve yelled from the kitchen. "Zo! Come and see! If you put shaving foam in a Tupperware box and light it, look what happens!"

"Jesus!" said Zoe. "You are such an *infant,* Steve!" she yelled back, half laughing, looking down the corridor. "Oh, wow. That's really—" There was a loud bang. "I'm going to—"

"Go," said Kate, draining her drink. "I'm going to find another glass of—" she looked at her glass. "Don't know what that was. I'm going to find it, anyway."

She turned around in the tiny hallway as Zoe walked away.

"Hello," said a voice behind her, and Kate spun around. It was Mac. He was shutting the door to the spare bedroom.

"Hello again," she said, uncertainly. "I haven't seen you for a while."

He scratched his head. "I know. I fell asleep."

"You fell asleep? In the spare bedroom?" Kate was mystified. "Can't be as good a party as I thought it was, then."

"I'm sure it is," he said. "I heard Zoe singing 'Cabaret.'"

"Oh," Kate said. "Well—there was more, but perhaps you—"

"I like your dress," he said, interrupting. "It suits you." He caught himself. "I mean, I've never met you before so how would I know. But you look nice in it." He turned away to the wall and said something under his breath, before turning back. "Man. How— God."

Kate smiled; she was a bit bemused. "Thanks, though. That's really . . . *nice* of you." She repeated the word "nice" unconsciously and then realized what she'd done; they both grinned, relaxing a little more. "It was a present from my dad. It's old, like from the fifties, I think."

"Of course, your dad's Daniel Miller, isn't he?"

"Yes," said Kate, vaguely pleased he should know that, that there was this connection with them because of Zoe and Steve, even though they'd never met. It made it seem even more comfortable, the air between them.

"I heard him the other day, on the radio, talking about his new album. Some interpretations of songs by ABBA?"

"Yes," said Kate again. "Er, it's great apparently. It's just out, I haven't heard it yet."

"Well, I've seen him twice now. On the radio, and he was on some daytime TV thing while I was on rounds yesterday."

Daniel had a new publicist, Lisa, who was getting him all this recent coverage. She was responsible for Daniel's new, choppy haircut, his Ralph Lauren suits, the moody shots of him gazing out of the windows of dilapidated old country buildings. She called him "Danny," too. She didn't seem to like things like long evenings in basement kitchens drinking cheap red wine (red wine stains the teeth), walks on the Heath on cold days, or daughters who were close to her in age. Yes, Kate had met her. She wasn't wild about her.

"Yep," said Kate. "It's great, he'd been quiet for a while before that." She cleared her throat to change the subject as a shriek echoed from the next room. "God," she said, laughing. "Zoe's absolutely trollied."

Mac's expression was mock-serious. "So, what were the two of you like when you were little, then?"

Kate laughed. "Well, Zoe was very bright and bubbly, and loud. Very loud. And I was . . . clumsy. And a bit moody. And not as nice as Zoe."

He bent his head and lowered his voice. "Kate. I'm sure that's not true."

"Thank you," she said slowly. "But it pretty much is." There was a pause. "How about the two of you?"

"Who? Me and Steve?" He shook his head and crossed his arms, so his hands were wedged under his armpits. "He was the typical annoying little brother, always bright and perky and funny and loud. Bit like Zoe, clearly." Kate shook her head, moved closer toward him. She wanted to touch him.

"How about you, then?"

"Me? I was . . ." He was smiling down at her. "Well, I was quite awkward, and I liked staying in my room, reading books and writing terrible poems. And looking at things under my microscope. God, this is embarrassing." He grimaced. "And I can't believe I'm telling you this."

"A microscope?" She laughed, incredulously, and embarrassment flashed across his face till she said, putting her hand on his arm, wanting to reassure him, "Mac. That's weird. I had a telescope." Kate thought of her poor telescope, confined to the back of the cupboard. "In fact, you've just described me as a teenager. So there you go."

"Great minds think alike," said Mac, nodding. "Or perhaps not."

There was silence again, comfortable. He yawned suddenly. "Sorry." He rubbed his face; she remembered he'd only just woken up. "I've been . . . busy, you see."

She recalled Zoe saying how tired he was. "Is it work?"

"Something like that," he said. "Yeah." He hummed, and looked down at her; she was tall, but he was taller. "Let's get a drink, shall we?"

"Great," she said, her eyes flicking up to him again. She couldn't stop looking at him, not just because he was incredibly attractive, but because she felt she knew him, recognized him from somewhere, and she couldn't work out where.

"Good nap, then?" Steve called as they came into the kitchen. "Feeling better?"

"Yeah, bruv, thanks," said Mac. "Sorry about that. Kate, what do you want?"

"That looks good," said Kate, pointing at a bottle simply because it happened to have liquid in it. "Thanks." She stole a glance at him again, to find him watching her as he poured the wine into her glass. Strange, strange, she told herself. She had never felt like this before. So . . . in control of it, so . . . certain. She didn't know what was going to happen next, but yes, there it was—a kind of certainty when she looked at him, into those kind yet quizzical green eyes of his.

Mac clinked his glass against hers. The kitchen was nearly empty of guests—some were in the garden, shivering in the cold spring night, most were back in the sitting room or in the corridor, and the music was punching through the walls to where they stood. Steve watched them for a moment, scratching his face, and then he said, "Hey, Francesca, you've seen Mac, haven't you?"

Francesca was an ex of Steve's. She was the girl he'd been seeing right before Zoe appeared on the scene, and she turned away from her ex-boyfriend reluctantly and gave Mac a catlike, enigmatic smile.

"Of course I have, darling," she said. "Hello, Mac, how are you?"

"I'm fine," he said. She kissed him, patted him on the shoulder,

"What happened to the Edinburgh job?" she asked. Kate watched her, very curiously.

Mac shifted on his feet. "The one at Saint Giles's? It didn't—"

"Hey! Hey!" Zoe called from outside. "Oh God, I think he's about to be sick. Ugh! Steve! Steve, can you—"

Francesca turned away, watching through the French windows. "Oh no," she said, sounding bored, as Steve ran into the garden.

"You need me, bruv?" Mac called after him.

"No, man," said Steve, kneeling behind someone. "Urgh. That's horrible."

"Come on," said Mac, and he put his hand on Kate's elbow. His touch sent a jolt through her; his thumb was dry and warm on the inside of her arm. "I want to ask you something."

Kate followed him into the corridor again and stopped short. There were Sean and Betty, locked in a grappling embrace and oblivious to everything else, including someone reaching up behind them to get his coat off the bulging coatrack. Kate looked at Sean's face, what she could see of it, absorbed in chewing off half of Betty's, and smiled to herself. Why wasn't she surprised? Why had she thought something might happen tonight? Silly girl. He was Sean, wasn't he? Always the same.

Mac didn't notice; he was looking out into the garden again, to make sure the poor unfortunate outside was OK. His jaw was set, his posture tense. But as she gave a little sigh and shook her head, he looked down at her and said, "What do you think about getting out of here?"

"What?" Kate said, dazed.

He touched her shoulder, lightly. "Come back with me. Let's get out of here."

"But it's—" Kate looked at her watch, unsure of what to say next: it was two o'clock. "Oh." Then she looked over at Sean and Betty again, then back at Mac, Mac, who just met her gaze and nodded.

She nodded back at him.

"Yeah," she said. "Let's go."

It was dark in the corridor, by the entrance to the kitchen. He took her hand and pulled her toward him, and they kissed, their hands twining together. She could feel his stubble rasping against her skin, his tongue pushing inside her, his lips on hers, warm, dry, strong, like the rest of him.

"Kate Miller," he said when he broke apart from her. "The famous Kate Miller."

They walked past Betty and Sean; Kate had to tap him on the shoulder to let him know she was going, especially since she had a pact with Sean. "Hi," she said, picking a limb, hoping it was Sean's. Mac held her other hand, his fingers stroking hers. She felt warm, melting, swoony with him beside her, his hip touching hers.

Sean turned around, his eyes glazed, panting slightly. "Kate, hi," he said, and there was a note of irritation in his voice; Kate couldn't blame him. Behind him, Betty tried to casually look around, as if she were a prospective buyer for the flat, making a note of the ceiling moldings.

"I'm going," Kate said. She jerked her head, as if to indicate Mac, that this was the situation.

"What?" said Sean quickly. "Oh. Right . . ." His gaze left Kate's face and looked behind her, to Mac, who nodded politely and tightened his grip on Kate's hand. She swayed toward him, dizzy with wanting him, wanting to be alone with him. She cast a look back at Sean.

"I'll see you tomorrow, OK?" she said. "Don't—"

"It's fine, Kate," said Sean, and there was a sharp note to his voice. "See you tomorrow, babe." He took his hand off Betty's bottom and squeezed Kate's arm. "Have a good one."

She turned away, and she and Mac stepped out the front door and closed it behind them, and then it was just the two of them, alone.

Eleven

They stood outside on the sidewalk, looking at each other, the sky above them flecked with bright stars; it was a cold, clear night. The space between them was fraught; particles of tension, magnetic attraction that Kate felt was drawing her closer to him, closer and closer. And then Mac said, "Listen. There's something I have to tell you."

"Oh." Kate shoved her cold hands into her pockets. Even she knew that no conversation that started like that ever ended well. "What's that, then?"

"Look," Mac said, stepping toward her. "I just thought I should say it before this gets—"

Kate heard herself say, "No way. You can't dump me. We haven't even done anything yet. We only met three hours ago."

He laughed. She liked his laugh. It was a proper laugh, from deep inside him, a warm, chuckling sound. "No, nothing like that. You are funny. Why would I dump you?"

She ignored this and said, "So, what is it?"

He said, blankly, "Er, well—it's not a big deal, because like you said, we only met three hours ago. But before this goes any further, I thought I should say . . ."

"Say what?"

Mac spoke in monosyllables. "I'm leaving, in the morning. Edinburgh." Kate stepped backward. "That's why I'm tired. I've been packing all day. The flight's at midday."

"You're—"

"I'm moving there. Got a consultancy at Saint Giles's, in the city. It's—yeah, well, I had to take it. And Mum and Dad are there, that'll be nice, too."

"Oh, right," said Kate, deliberately keeping her voice light. "Well, right!"

"Yeah," he said, shifting his weight from foot to foot. "Like I said, Kate. Just thought I should say something, you know."

"Yes, of course." She didn't know why she was being so stupid. After all, they'd just met—it was hardly like . . . She smiled at him and stepped back again. "So why are you telling me? Do you want a lift to the airport tomorrow, is that it?"

"Come back with me," he said, even more softly. "You can still come back."

"I . . . I can't," she said.

"Why not?" Mac said, a note of impatience in his voice.

"Because . . ." She gestured weakly around her. "It's different."

"You have the most amazing face, did you know that?" Mac said.

"Face?" Kate laughed, bemused.

"Yes. It's totally heart-shaped, and when you're sad about something, or thinking about something, you're totally closed off, and when you smile—you're beautiful. Absolutely beautiful. Did you know that?" He spoke conversationally, looking around him, at Zoe and Steve's low front garden wall, into the sitting room, as he said all this.

"Mac—you're mad. And a massive flirt," Kate said weakly.

His faint Scottish burr was more pronounced; he said, grinning, "I'm not, that's the strange thing, my dear. I'm not a flirt at all. Normally can't think of a single thing to say to a girl I like. Never normally meet a girl I like."

"I . . ." Kate said. She shrugged her shoulders, helplessly.

"You're not coming, are you." It was a statement, not a question. "Oh well."

"It's . . . look, Mac, I don't know . . ."

He laughed. "Very eloquently put. Come with me. It'll just take a minute."

He pulled her out into the road, the middle of the road, and there in the cold night air he put his hands on either side of her head and, pulling her toward him, kissed her. So she kissed him right back, wrapping her arms around him, laughing softly as she did, feeling his tongue in her mouth, his beautiful, hard, tall body against hers, so strange and yet so familiar, and they kissed for a long few minutes, until Mac pulled himself away and said, his voice husky, "You're really not going to come back with me?"

She thought of Zoe and Steve inside, of not having said bye to them properly, of Sean and Betty entangled in the hallway, and she thought of how even though she was changing every day, growing more and more into herself, how still unlike her it was to go off with someone like this. It wasn't like this was the first time she'd gone off with someone, so why was she so scared? Scared—of what? Hurting herself, of disappointing Mac, and not sure why he'd picked her, thinking he must be drunk or mad or both.

"Seize the day," Mac said. "Never heard that expression?" He touched her forehead with his finger.

Kate couldn't help thinking of her mother when she heard that expression; it was almost her mission statement. "All the bloody time," Kate said. "I'm normally just no good at it."

"It's my last night in London," said Mac. He looked at her, that strange look she found so disturbingly familiar. "And I like you, you like me, I know it, you know it, too, don't you?"

"Yes," she said, honestly.

"Are you the girl who usually helps the other drunk girls home? I bet you are."

"Er," said Kate sadly, thinking of the previous week, when she had ended up on the night bus after Jo's postwork birthday drinks, with Sophie's slumbering form slumped over her lap like a sack of grain. "Sometimes."

"Come on, then," he said, and he stepped forward and hailed a passing cab, which Kate found extremely impressive, and then castigated herself for. She put her hand on his arm suddenly.

"You're really leaving London tomorrow morning?"

"Yes," he said, holding the door open for her. She stepped inside.

"Better make the most of it then," she said.

Kate had never run out on her friends before. She realized this, the next day, as she lay in Mac's arms, the spring light flooding into his dingy, gray, boy's bedroom, stripped bare of all his possessions, which had gone up to Edinburgh ahead of him. And she didn't care. Didn't care about a thing. She had given herself up to pleasure totally, not worrying about anyone else. And it had been totally, utterly worth it. She could feel happiness washing over her, into her, like she was bathing in it.

"You don't think it matters," she said, sitting up and stretching her arms out, yawning.

"What?" said Mac, his voice muffled, and he smoothed her hair back from her forehead, pulling her back down onto his chest, which was thickly matted with hair. He stroked her hair, and she turned her face toward him, so she was looking at him.

"That we didn't say bye," Kate said. "To Zoe and Steve. We just did a runner."

"Oh," said Mac.

She stroked him, ran her hand down his body. "Don't you care?" she said, half mockingly. "You're leaving them today."

"No, not at all," he murmured, enfolding her in his arm so she was just above him. She felt him growing hard again against her. "I'll call Steve, don't worry."

"When?" Kate said, kissing him. Her hair fell over him, surrounding the two of them. As Mac kissed her shoulder, her breast, her collarbone, she pushed her hair out of her eyes and looked at his tiny, bashed-up digital clock. It was six o'clock. "Your flight's in six hours."

"Oh," he said, and he turned her over so she lay beneath him, and he was over her. He stroked her hair and bent down to kiss her again. "We don't have much time, then, Kate Miller."

"No, but—"

She couldn't say any more. She felt so happy with him that she couldn't burst the bubble of this night. Like asking, "So . . . will you call me when you're four hundred miles away and working seven nights a week and never coming down to London?" As Mac pulled the duvet over both of them, enclosing them together again, Kate kissed him back and laughed happily, thinking back over the past twelve hours in befuddled, pleasurable amazement—but also a strange sense of certainty, one that she never got back again.

She went with him to the airport. After all, she told him, he was leaving London, he needed someone to wave him off. She stood in her blue and gold dress on the sidewalk, thanking the Lord she'd brought a black cardigan and her coat that she could wrap around herself to minimize the too-dressy-slash-I-am-a-prostitute look, and she watched as Mac locked up his bare flat, as he slung his suitcase into the back of the minicab. He stood back and sighed, looking up at the tall, redbrick house for the last time. It was strange, sharing all this with him, part of a life she'd never known that he was now saying good-bye to.

"Were you happy here?" she asked him.

"I was," he said, but he didn't say more. She didn't know what he meant and there was suddenly, now, constraint between them, he moving on, she staying here, both of them not really knowing each other. He held the door open for her; she got into the back of the cab, he climbed in after her. He looked rather desolate, his face tired in the morning light, and she pulled him toward her so his head was resting on her shoulder, his hand in her lap. She took it, held it tightly.

"Kate Miller," Mac said after a moment. His voice was serious. "God. I wish we'd met sooner," he said as the cab plowed silently through West Hampstead, long gray shadows flooding the streets, morning sunshine cutting through the gaps in the buildings. No one was around.

She said nothing, just squeezed his hand tighter. Kate still sometimes felt like a juvenile in a world of grown-ups, someone who didn't know the rules when everyone else seemed to. Here, in the back of the cab, racing through town toward the airport, she felt as if she knew what she was doing.

"I wish we had one more day, one more night," he said into her chest.

"Shh," she said, and with her other arm she pulled him in more closely. She kissed his rough hair, so strangely boyish, at odds with him when he was . . . such a man, compared to the other men she knew, those boys from university, those boys from growing up. Mac was—he was a grown-up.

That was why he was going away, she told herself, staring out of the window, her chin resting on his hair. His life was sorting itself out, he was three years older than her, he was simply a grown-up, and she felt as if she still had to establish the most basic facts about herself.

"I wish we'd met sooner, too," she said. She fought back tears, staring ahead as they rolled on. She didn't know how to say what she wanted to say. "It's like a bolt from the blue, this . . ." She gestured weakly, between them. "You know?" He nodded. "I didn't think *this* would happen last night." She shrugged her shoulders, smiling at the way she'd thought the night might go, at her own vanity. "Strange, how things turn out," she said.

Mac's fingers beat a pattern on hers. "You and your flatmate, eh?"

Kate was startled; she sat up straight. He laughed, amused at her shock. "What do you mean?" she said.

"You and—what was that guy called? Sean? Steve's friend?" Kate nodded. "I thought you were a couple when you arrived last night, when I saw you both on the doorstep."

"Hah," said Kate.

"I got that vibe off him, too." Mac shrugged his shoulders. "That's why I left you alone for most of the evening. Didn't want to annoy him. He looked like the sort of bloke who'd bite your ear off if you annoyed him."

Kate giggled. "He's not like that!" she said defensively. "He's like a great big puppy once you know him, honestly." Mac nodded somberly. "He's lovely," she said. "Really."

"Right," Mac said, without rancor. "Well—perhaps you should have got together with him last night, then."

Kate started. "I'm not saying—" she said, defensively.

Mac held up his hands. "I'm glad you didn't." He took her fingers again. "I'm just saying, I'm glad you didn't. Last night, anyway."

"You're both very different, anyway," Kate said, mirroring him. "And—well, I think he went off with someone else, anyway. Our friend Betty. Not that I want it to happen, anyway."

"Anyway," Mac said gently. "Stop saying *anyway*. You babble when you're nervous, did you know that? And you have the most beautiful eyes, Kate, they're black when you get cross. I love them." He kissed her. "And I don't want to talk about Sean. I want to talk about us. About how you've made me not want to leave, and it's only one night. OK?"

"Yes, OK," said Kate. "More than OK." She clutched both his hands in her lap. "Oh, man."

"I know." Mac looked out of the window.

"There's no way—?"

His hand tightened around hers. "Perhaps, you know?" He sat up straight. "But, Kate, I just don't think it's realistic. Is it?"

"Why? I'm not saying 'Oh no, why,' I mean, tell me just why it's completely out of the question," she said bravely.

"Perhaps it's not," Mac said. "But I'll be working five nights in a row most of the time, and I won't be back to London for at least three, four months—and I have to find a flat, and you have—" He smiled. "I don't mean this to sound patronizing, but it seems to me from what you say, and from what Zoe says, that you've got a pretty good thing going on in London at the moment."

They were turning off the motorway slip road into Terminal 1.

"No—" Kate began, defensively, and then she stopped, looking down at their hands, his holding hers. Her hard-won job, her friends, Charly, her flat. Sean . . . Sean—she wondered where he was. Suddenly she missed him, the security of their flat together. This—this was new and strange and . . . sad. It was just so damn bloody sad. She couldn't work out what Mac was trying to say, whether it was a gentle letdown or the truth. In any case, facts were facts. He was moving to Edinburgh, and it was just over two hours till his plane left. When she looked up into his face, he was staring ahead, his jaw set again.

He turned away from her to look out of the window, and then he said calmly, "We're here."

Perhaps she had been wrong. Probably she had. She raised his hand to her lips and kissed it. "Thanks anyway."

"No," he said. The cabdriver was opening the trunk of the car, loading suitcases onto a trolley. Mac's grip on her hand was painful. "Kate, no. Thank you."

She moved toward him, almost frantic to feel him against her again. He pulled her close. "This is stupid," she said in his ear. "Why is it like this?"

His breath was warm on her neck; her coat itched in the spring sunshine. "Because our timing's crap," he said. "Look, when I get there I'll call—"

"Don't say you'll call me," said Kate, and she put her hands on his cheeks. "Don't take my number, don't say you'll email me and we'll have jolly banter about the weather or how hungover we are, or whatever, each of us trying to inflate it with something. Just—let's leave it." A tear ran down her cheek; he wiped it away, gently, and then he slowly kissed her skin where it had been, as if she were the most precious thing on earth to him.

"Yes," he said. "I think you're right. Today. Not forever. I'll see you again, Kate. This isn't good-bye." She shook her head, fervently, and he said in her ear, "I don't know what it is, in fact, but it's not good-bye."

The cabdriver cleared his throat, and the spell was broken; Mac turned and handed him the fare, and took the trolley from him.

"I didn't think I'd spend Saturday morning at an airport with Steve's brother," Kate said, sinking her hands into her pockets, stepping back, trying to restore normality.

"That can be our second date," Mac said, looking down at her once more. She met his gaze and they stood utterly still, watching each other, for a few seconds more. And then he turned, saying nothing, and pushed the trolley away. The automatic doors into the terminal snapped open for him, and snapped shut again; and he was gone.

When Kate arrived home later that morning, having cried silently all the way back on the tube, ignoring the curious glances from her fellow passengers, Sean was there at home, waiting for her.

"She's back," he called as she opened the front door quietly. "The dirty stay-out's back. Yee-hah!"

The flat was still a mess; the hallway was littered with trainers, bits of Kate's bike that Sean was allegedly mending for her, old newspapers. As she stood in the hall, tiredly taking off her coat, Kate thought back to the previous evening, when she'd arrived back home from the pub, and how long ago it seemed. A lifetime, really.

"Hi," she called. "How are you?"

"I missed you, darlin'," Sean said. She could hear him shifting on the sofa. "I've been waiting for you to come back so we can go and get some lunch. What an awesome night."

"Not sad about Jenna anymore then?" Kate said, half joking.

"Who?" Sean's face was blank. "Ha-ha. You know what?"

"What," said Kate, longing for a bath.

"She seems a long time ago now. Like I've moved on." He shuffled on his feet, not looking at her. "Hey, so you wanna run and get changed? We can go and get some food and I wanna ask you what you think I should do for my birthday."

It was Sean's birthday the following Sunday; she'd completely forgotten. "We'll think of something," she called, taking off a shoe, rubbing her aching foot.

Sean appeared in the doorway, out of his black tie, back in his normal uniform of jeans, trainers, T-shirt, a light V-neck over the top. She felt even more ill-at-ease, standing there. "Wow," he said. "You still look hot, Katy." His eyes ran over her; his fingers drummed on the doorframe. "So I guess you did, then?"

"Did what?" Kate took off the other shoe, not meeting his gaze.

"Well, well," said Sean. A silence fell between them, then he said softly, "You dirty girl."

"You snogged Betty," Kate shot back.

Sean raised his eyebrows. "I didn't realize it was a competition," he said coldly.

Kate felt confused; she was tired, hungry, and sad. She wanted to crawl into bed and cry, cry over someone who wasn't ever coming back, who she barely knew anyway—it was ridiculous.

"Oh, just forget it," she said, passing her hand over her eyes. "Let's go and get some lunch." She smiled at Sean, giving him her most winning grin, and he recovered slightly and nodded back at her, his eyes twinkling wolfishly.

Twelve

Over the next few days, Kate didn't know why she expected Mac to call, she just did. But he didn't.

In fact, Kate Miller and Mac Hamilton didn't see each other again for nearly two years. In the intervening days, weeks, months, the night she spent with him was to become almost mythic in Kate's mind, until she came to see what it probably was—the night bridging her old life with her new life. Part of her didn't understand why he didn't call. Even though they'd said that was it, and the reasons for leaving what happened as one night only were still so clear to her, a part of her didn't believe it, didn't understand it. He would call eventually, she told herself a couple of days afterward, when she was missing him more than she could say. But he didn't.

A week later, with no news, Kate sort of knew by then he wouldn't contact her. It never occurred to her to call him; perverse logic told her he'd never want to hear from *her*—he'd just moved! It was in the past! She'd just make a fool of herself, when they'd both agreed to leave it. He had a new life; she had to get on with hers. And so she did. Kate was always good at following instructions.

· · ·

That Saturday evening, Sean had his birthday drinks, and that's when Kate finally shook herself out of the mood that had enveloped her all week. Sean knew, and Kate knew, that no one would come to Rotherhithe; instead, they and their friends went to the Punch and Judy in Covent Garden, which was loud and stuffed full of people, shouts of merriment bouncing off the flagstones and stucco walls of the covered market. Kate loved Covent Garden—it was touristy and full of silly shops and stalls selling plastic brooches that no one would ever want—but it reminded her of being young, coming into town with Zoe, going to the Bead Shop and buying ridiculous beads for earrings that would never be made, or sitting outside in the piazza, drinking coffee, watching magicians, feeling ever so grown-up and sophisticated. Covent Garden was like a film set; it never stopped being so for Kate, even though she was grown-up and (relatively) sophisticated now.

Just being out, being with her friends, watching Steve and Sean as they mock-wrestled in the courtyard, chatting to Zoe and Francesca, standing in a crowded, sweaty pub with a drink in her hand, Sean's arm around her shoulders, was more than enough to cheer her up. Here was where she belonged, she told herself, here in this city, with her friends—and screw anyone else who tried to make her doubt that. For damn sure! she told herself, trying to sound like a motivational trainer.

"You OK, babe?" Zoe said as Kate returned from the bar after last orders with a drink for her and Steve.

"Me? I'm fine," said Kate, wedging herself against Sean in the crush of the throng. "Why?"

"I just wondered," said Zoe, bellowing into her ear. "Thought you seemed a bit down this week. Wondered if everything was OK."

Steve was leaning in, nodding along with interest. "Yeah," he said loudly. He cupped his hands around his pint, the way he always used to do at college, as if it were a cup of tea; Kate watched him fondly. "Me and Zoe, yeah, we wondered. Didn't we, Zo?" Zoe looked at him in alarm. "What happened with you and M—ow! Damn!" He hopped backward in agony, squashing several people behind him, including Sean and Betty, who were talking intently, and knocking over several drinks in the process.

"What?" said Zoe innocently.

"You stepped on my foot! With your bloody heels!" Steve winced, as people looked at him in disgust, thinking he must be drunk. "My God, it's like a knife went through me!"

"He's such a girl," Zoe said, rolling her eyes impatiently. "Ignore him, darling."

"Zoe, you—ow!"

Kate was trying not to grin. She patted Steve's back, feeling sorry for him, as a harassed barman appeared with a towel, to mop up the drinks.

"It's drinking-up time, anyway," the barman growled loudly. "Come on, get moving." Steve set the glasses right again, back on the bar.

"Poor Steve. What did you want to say?" Kate said, innocently.

Alarm crossed Zoe's face; she put her arm through her fiancé's. "Right, then. You OK, Ste?"

She doesn't want to give me the bad news about Mac, Kate thought. That's why she's freaking out now. Like, he's got syphilis, or a girlfriend, or he's really a woman. She shook her head, realizing she must be drunker than she thought. He definitely wasn't a woman, she knew that much.

And she didn't really mind who knew, after all. It wasn't a big deal. She didn't care. She checked her phone again, pretending to look at the time, and then looked up to find Sean watching her, standing next to her. Behind him, Betty hovered in a hopeful way. He touched Kate's shoulders. "You OK?"

"Yup," she said. "You going on somewhere?" She was tired; it showed in her voice.

Sean paused for a moment. "Um. Not sure. What do you think, you up for it?"

"I'm quite tired—" Kate began.

"Me too," said Sean quickly. "Why don't we just head off. It's been a long week," he said, turning to the others. "I'm bushed."

"What?" said Steve. "It's your birthday, man!! You don't want to go on somewhere? How about the Rock Garden?"

"Oh my God," said Zoe. "No way. The Rock Garden? What are you, an American tourist from 1983? I want to go home. I've got to get up early tomorrow—we said we'd take the tiles off around the fireplace, remember?"

"Hm," said Steve. "No."

"Liar," said Zoe, hitting him.

"God, the abuse," said Steve, squashing her with a hug. "Stop assaulting me, woman!"

Kate watched them, swaying slightly on her feet; she was suddenly really tired, and Sean's arm came around her shoulders again. "Come on, Katy-kay," he said. "Let's get you home. We can have a bowl of cereal and watch my new video of *The Godfather*."

"Plan," said Kate. The barman was shouting again; Betty turned to leave, discontent written large over her pretty face. "Good plan."

They sat on the sofa in their pajamas, Kate eating toast, Sean with a bowl of cereal, the empty video case of *The Godfather* between them on the cushion, and a collection of beer bottles on the floor. It was late.

"You happy now?" Sean asked through mouthfuls. "You've been quiet all week, Kate."

"Yeah." Kate held the toast in her hand. "Just—you know. Stuff."

Sean shook his head, his eyes still on the screen. "Stuff. Right. Like—anything to do with you being a dirty stay-out last week?"

Kate watched him, curiously. Irresistibly, she was reminded of Mac's hands, how supple and thin they were, proper surgeon's hands, how they felt on her, holding her. She gritted her teeth. "Yes," she said.

"Thought so," Sean said, waving the spoon at her. He turned and looked at her, rather strangely. "Kate, I didn't know you were that kinda girl."

"Oh, shut up," said Kate.

"Was he good?" Sean said, still watching her. "Was it worth it?"

She didn't want to go over the details with Sean. "You know."

"I don't know," said Sean. His jaws were working again.

"Well, it's a nonstarter." Nice and vague. "Hey, how about you? What exactly happened with you and Betty, then? Were you a dirty stay-out too?"

Sean set the bowl down carefully on the ground. "I didn't go home with her, no," he said briefly, wiping his mouth. "I thought it might—" He shrugged.

"Yeah," said Kate, understanding that he meant it might have become weird. "You're friends . . ."

"Well, it was late, and we were all pretty drunk."

"Is it cool?" Kate said. "She seemed a bit . . . weird tonight."

"I hope so," Sean said. He put his head on one side, unconsciously considering, almost like he was preening himself. "She said, Is this OK, all that. I hate that kinda stuff. Clingy."

"You did the right thing," Kate said wisely. "Friends shouldn't sleep with friends, and that's why."

She patted her thighs, and made as if to stand up. But Sean caught her hand.

"Sometimes," he said. "Sometimes they should."

"What?" She turned, not sure she'd heard him right. But he shook his head at her, smiling provocatively, teasing her almost, and she smiled back, watching him, his eyes, his lips, thinking how well she knew him.

He raised his hand to her mouth, and ran his forefinger over her lips, staring into her eyes. "Kate—" he said. "God, Kate—"

She was kneeling, turned toward him. His hand was on her thigh; slowly, he turned, too, and pushed his knee between her legs. His hands moved, up her body, under her fleecy pajama top. She could smell him; he smelled of shower gel, of beer—of safe, familiar things. But his eyes were glittering over her; this was unfamiliar, strange, weird, and yet, of course, she told herself, it was not that much of a surprise, and as Sean slid his hand around the back of her neck and pulled her toward him, as they sank onto the sofa, kissing with fierce passion, their teeth clashing, their arms wrapped tight around each other, they said nothing, nothing at all—what was there to say?

On Sunday morning, when Sean woke up in Kate's room, their limbs entangled, hungover, exhausted but exhilarated, it just seemed simpler for him not to go back to his room. So he didn't. And he didn't that night, nor the next night, nor the one after that.

As Sean said that first morning, as they lay in bed together, surprised but not really that surprised, "I knew this was going to happen, didn't you?"

"Er . . . yes," Kate said. "I did, that's what's weird."

"I knew," Sean said, rolling on top of her again. "I knew last Saturday, especially after I heard about Jenna, getting engaged. I just didn't care that much. And on Sunday, after you came back from shagging Mac." Kate patted him, gently; she didn't want him to put it like that. "I wanted to kill him. That's when I knew."

"That's pathetic," Kate said, sliding her arms around his neck.

"No, it's human nature," said Sean. "And it's you, Katy. I don't know what you do to me, but I can't stop thinking about you. I've been wanting to do this for the longest time." He brushed her hair back from her face with one hand. "You feel it, too, don't you?"

"Well, yes," said Kate, pulling him toward her. "Yes, I do." She didn't know what else to say—it just seemed right. She looked up at him, smiling almost shyly. Sean gave a shout of delight, a cry that rang out in the small, sunny bedroom.

"God, this is a great start to my birthday, you know that?" He kissed her. "Now, wish me happy birthday properly, and then I'll make us some coffee and get the papers."

Thirteen

Kate had never been the sort of girl to ask for much: she was not a princess, the type who sat with her arms folded in a restaurant, ignoring her boyfriend because he hadn't noticed her new shoes. She was the girl who was used to sitting in the corner, watching her father as he told a story, his hands suspended in midair, fluttering like birds over the table.

She could remember her mother coming downstairs in the evening, ready to go out and meet him after a concert, for dinner, in wine-colored velvet, smelling deliciously sweetly of roses on a summer's night, smiling graciously at her daughter and their babysitter, Magda. People would clap when her parents walked into a room after a show, or into a restaurant, sometimes; all eyes were on them, softly talking, flirting after all these years or screaming at each other, slamming doors, throwing things.

None of it ever involved Kate, and she grew used to watching from the sidelines, through the banisters, silent at the other end of the table, lonely at the end of the garden, happy up in her room, always by herself. She was quite happy with it; it gave her time to think, to dream, to play with her dolls, or when she was older to read, to imagine things, to think about what she would do when she was grown up.

When she was eight she thought she would like to live in a big house with blue-painted windowsills, in the countryside. Wisteria climbing up the walls, a little round window by the front door, a huge garden, with the River Thames at the end of it. She would have a husband, called Mr. Brown, who worked in the City and carried a briefcase. And whenever she wanted, she would get a boat down the river and sail into London.

When she was sixteen, she wanted a flat, in town, with a roof terrace, a window seat, and a CD player—she desperately wanted a CD player of her own. She would play Ella Fitzgerald songs on it and listen to them, curled up on the window seat, gazing out glamorously at the London skyline. Someone who looked a little like Gregory Peck in *To Kill a Mockingbird* would be her lover; he would be desperately in love with her and would turn up, demanding to be let in, shouting glamorously, "Kate Miller, goddammit! I love you! Let me in!" (Why Gregory Peck was not allowed in wasn't a detail she troubled herself with.)

Now that she was, she supposed, a grown-up, Kate had never really thought about what she wanted, in reality, from her life. She was used to everything being easy for other people; going to parties, chatting to people, kissing boys, falling in love. Kate had never found it easy. So when she properly, wholly, totally fell in love, once she let go, it changed her life. When she realized she loved Sean, that that was what she was put on earth to do, that everything over the last couple of years—their getting a flat together, him becoming friends with Steve, even further back, him deciding to come over from Texas to England to study, even Kate's night with Mac, which had kickstarted it—had led to this, well, it all made sense to her and she ran toward it wholeheartedly, and the next few months passed in a haze of pleasure.

"Worrtah."

"Wewrrterrr."

"No. Worrtah."

"Wawwterr."

"Sean. No. Listen."

"I don't want to listen. I want to do *this*."

"Don't be disgusting. We're in public."

"In a park. In Battersea Park. Doesn't count. Can I feel up my gorgeous girlfriend without anyone noticing? Ah, yes, I can."

"Worrtah."

"Can I have some worrrtah please," Sean said, in a perfect English accent, kissing her languorously as they stretched out on the rug together. Kate reached behind her and threw the bottle at him.

"Ouch! You witch," he said, rolling over on top of her.

They stayed like that for a while, giggling quietly as people walked past. Kate looked at her watch. "Oh," she said, sitting up. "I should get back."

"No you shouldn't." Sean pushed her back down again so she lay facing him. "You should lie down and stop checking the time. It's a Sunday. You don't need to do anything today."

"But I've got to finish that article and Sue said . . ."

"Sue said nothing. You'll finish it. Now finish off what you started here. Have another beer."

His fingers traced her jawline; staring up at him, framed by the wide blue afternoon sky, Kate gazed into his eyes.

"I'm so happy," she said quietly.

"Are you?" Sean said, mock-curiously. "Why?"

She felt a rush of honesty overtake her, a desire to stop playing it cool, to tell him everything she was feeling. But there were no barriers between them anyway, hadn't been when they were friends, and now that they were together, there was nothing but honesty between them. They were alone as much as possible, from waking tangled up in each other to rushing back from their other social commitments—drinks after work, cinema outings with friends, catch-up meals in desultory, cheap pizzerias—to their gorgeous, grubby flat, sinking into each other. Sean had not slept in his room since the night of his birthday. In fact, the only time he went in there now was to get new clothes or to dump some of his dirty clothes back in there from Kate's room, especially when they had friends coming around.

Though she was a daydreamer, in daily life Kate was a practical girl, for the most part. It blew her away, the feelings she felt for Sean. As spring flowered into summer, they didn't go away. It got stronger and stronger, and they both grew more confident, and happier.

They started telling their friends: Betty and Francesca were amazed, and a little appalled; Steve and Zoe were fascinated, dumbstruck, and then very happy for them. Sean's friends at work barely cared—in the world of IT, falling in love was akin to killing people: socially unacceptable. The one friend Kate hadn't told, the one cloud on her horizon, and it was so silly she couldn't believe she was worrying about it, was Charly. She didn't know why she hadn't. She didn't want to hear what Charly would say, hadn't seen much of her lately, either, not just because she was spending all her spare time with Sean, but also because, if she was honest, she knew what Charly was like sometimes, and she didn't want to be on the end of it. She felt guilty about it, hated making excuses about it to Charly. It was Charly, after all. She didn't know why it bothered her.

Thinking of this now, Kate frowned and bit her lip.

"Are you going to tell your dad, then?" Sean said. Sean loved Kate's dad. He thought he was a real dude, a great guy. They got on pretty well, on the rare occasions Daniel Miller had made it down to Rotherhithe.

"He's in Jamaica, recording his new album, with that horrible new girlfriend," Kate said glumly.

"Who?" Sean said, almost joyously. He slapped his thigh.

"Your dad, man! He's crazy! Always some new girl on the scene—it's like a revolving door. Sorry." He corrected himself as Kate gave him a withering look. "So . . . who is she? Is she a stayer?"

"Oh, I don't know," said Kate. "It's that PR from the record label, Lisa. Remember, she was at his birthday dinner thing."

"The short thin one with the massive—" Sean gestured expressively with his hands. "Yeah. I remember."

"Dad's mad about her," said Kate crossly. "He even bought her a *watch*. To say thank you for what she's done for him." Sean raised his eyebrows; Kate flicked him. "Don't. Ugh." She shook her head. "It's a holiday fling, that's all. I give it a couple of weeks. I'll go and see him when he's back and tell him about us. It'll cheer him up after he's dumped her. He likes you."

Sean grinned. "I like him, man. Lisa! Well." He shrugged his shoulders.

They fell silent again, Kate lying with her head in Sean's lap, watching the sky, listening to the people around them playing in the park. She breathed in slowly, catching everything, how she felt.

"What shall we eat tonight?" she said lazily.

"Can I ask you something?" Sean said then, kissing her on the nose. A bee droned dangerously close to Kate's ear; she squirmed and sat up suddenly, bashing him.

"Ow," Kate said, rubbing her nose. "Ow. What?"

Sean rubbed his face; she thought it was because she'd hit him. It was only afterward that she realized it was because he felt awkward.

"I think . . . Gosh, I don't know how to say this."

"What?" said Kate, feeling the breath tighten in her throat. She leaned against him. He looked into the distance, up toward Primrose Hill. Kate followed his gaze. She could see a kite in the sky, its red and yellow tail fluttering in the breeze.

"You know the lease on the flat's up next month?"

"Yes." Kate nodded, too vigorously. "Er, yes. They're raising the rent, I told you—"

"I've been thinking," said Sean, cutting her off. His voice was awkward. "I think we should stop living together." He breathed deeply and sighed, like it was a weight off his shoulders. "I think we should move in with other people."

"Why?" Kate said, trying to swallow, fighting down the panic washing over her. "Don't you—don't you love me anymore?"

It sounded so weak, compared to what she was feeling.

"Of course," Sean said. "I'm in love with you, and I want to ask you to live with me at some point."

"Oh," Kate said. "I see." But she didn't.

"Kate," he said. He took her hand solemnly and kissed the tips of her fingers. His forehead, under the short thatch of yellow hair, was a little pink from the sun; so was his nose. She looked at him in amazement, still not quite believing he was here, and that this might all be about to end. "I'm in love with you. This is all I want. But I want us to start our life together properly. Like it's special. I want to date you, take you out to dinner, stay the night at yours sometimes and *then* move in together. Not just go from being flatmates in some dingy flat who got drunk and had sex one night and then never moved on. I want us to be . . . special."

Kate blinked at him, a smile spreading across her face, like sunshine warming her up again.

"There," he went on. "You see what I mean. Do you?"

"I do," Kate said.

"Does it make sense? That we need some time apart if we're gonna be together?"

"Well . . ." She thought of how much she was going to miss him. She saw him every day, spent every night with him, he was her world, totally, and panic suddenly gripped her as she thought about making her way in the world without him.

As if he were reading her mind, Sean said, "Hey, babe. Look

at me." He lifted her chin with one finger so she stared into his eyes. She clutched his finger with hers, like a little baby clutching an adult's hand. "This is a good thing, OK? We'll be glad we did it. I promise."

She knew he was right, but she clung to him, not wanting to let him go, as the shadows lengthened in the park. Only after a while did it occur to her, when she was drunk with wanting Sean, as they swayed home together, wrapped around each other. Charly. She would move in with Charly! She gave a little shiver.

"OK, babe?" Sean asked her, wrapping his arm around her a little tighter.

"Absolutely," she said softly. "Great."

"You're a weird girl, Katy-Kay."

"I'm not!"

He pulled her up so she was sitting on his knees, and she wrapped her arms around his neck, then he kissed her, all over her face, her ears, her neck, her eyes, till she stopped crying and was laughing, shrieking, pleading with him to let her go. He could always win her around like that, could always make her fall in love with him again, all over again.

Fourteen

"*You?*" Charly said the next day, when Kate ran into the office, eyes shining. "Why the hell d'you think I'd want to move in with *you?*"

"Oh," said Kate slowly. She put her bag down on her desk and took out the floppy disk with the Editor's Letter she'd written hastily the previous night, after she and Sean had got back from the park.

"I mean," said Charly, sinking into her chair and pushing herself away from the desk with one long, shapely leg, "you're a bit of a loser, Kate." She started counting with her fingers, long nails passing over each other. "You own Ace of Base's debut album. And *Fields of Gold* by Sting."

"I bought them with a coupon—"

"You think little gray cardigans are the answer to all the world's fashion dilemmas," Charly went on, lifting and then dropping the edge of Kate's beloved Whistles gray cardigan, currently the most expensive item in her wardrobe, bought with the money her mother had given her for Christmas. "You like *Coronation Street,* for God's sake. Like an old granny. *And* you like garden centers. I can't live with someone whose idea of a good weekend is picking out trellis plants and then rushing home for another gripping installment of what happened to Derek and Mavis."

"Derek died in 1997, and Mavis has moved to the Lake District. They haven't been in it for years," said Kate, trying to fight back. "Get your facts straight. And garden centers are . . . cool! You can buy all sorts of stuff in them."

"Jeez." Charly stood up. "Look, if it'll help you out, I'll move in with you."

"What?" said Kate.

"God." Charly rolled her eyes, looking totally bored. "I'll live with you, Miller. OK?" She put her arms around Kate and hugged her. "You know I'd like to."

"Really?"

Charly squeezed her. "Look." She sounded embarrassed. "You're my best friend, ain't ya?"

"Right!" said Kate, pleased not just that Charly was going to live with her, but also that she'd called her her best friend. "Yes!" She hugged Charly back. "Oh my God, this is so great! Do you seriously want to . . . ?" She gazed anxiously at Charly, who sighed again.

"Man, I said I did, didn't I?" she said crossly. Charly didn't do overt displays of emotion.

"Great! Great!" said Kate. "I'll just give this to Sue"—she waved the Editor's Letter at Charly—"and then let's start calling up places, shall we?"

"Go on then," Charly said in a childish voice. "Give your little head girl swotty letter to Sue. Hey—you never said, by the way. What's happened with the Tex Mex Sex Machine? Why aren't you guys living together anymore? Finally got bored of waiting for him to snog you, did ya?"

"Oh, that," said Kate, humming nervously, and turned back toward her, running the piece of paper through her fingers. "Well—um."

"What?" Charly looked at her suspiciously. She could smell intrigue a mile away.

"Yep," said Kate. "Look. There's something I have to tell you."

"No way," said Charly. She stood behind her desk, arms akimbo. "You're doing your flatmate. I can't believe it. Kate Miller. How long?"

Kate swallowed; she could feel her eyes bulging. "How the hell did you know that?"

"I'm not stupid. You're shagging Sean. Sean the sheep. Sheep shagger. Hey! You're a sheep shagger!" Charly clapped her hands. "Woo-hoo!"

"Charly!" Kate said sharply. "Zip it."

Sophie and George, who sat a short way away from Kate and Charly, looked around to see if they could work out what was going on. On the other side of them, Claire and Phil, reunited once again, studiously ignored them. Relations on their side of the office since his encounter with Charly the previous year had not been great.

"Sorry," said Charly. She narrowed her eyes and was silent. "OK," she said, after a moment's pause. "You screwed him."

"Charly." Kate felt helpless; she forgot, always forgot what Charly was like when you showed vulnerability.

"Oh my God," said Charly, stepping around her desk and coming and standing next to Kate. "Has he dumped you? Is that why—" She looked into Kate's face, searching, and Kate felt the power of Charly's gold-flecked tiger eyes sizing her up, seeking her out. "No way, no way. What's going on? Don't tell me you like him, Kate."

"I love him," Kate said, trying to sound calm, and like it was normal, not extraordinary. "He loves me. Our lease is coming up, so we're moving out so we can start over properly, go on dates and stuff. He's moving in with our friend Jem. And I want to move in with you."

"Uh-huh." Charly nodded. She was silent again, her eyes taking in Kate once more.

"So that's the situation," said Kate, firmly.

"So you've got a boyfriend," said Charly. "This is shit. You're going to be a real pain in the neck, having dinner out of cookery books with other couples and talking about property. God."

"Yeah, right," said Kate.

"You'd just better not have anything like that in *our* flat," said Charly. "Otherwise I think I'd rather stay in Leigh-on-Sea with Mum. Got it?"

"Promise," said Kate.

"And no fucking Radio Four in the mornings, either," said Charly. "I'm depressed enough already in the morning. I don't want to have to listen to John Humphries going on about Kosovo or the rain forests before I've even had coffee. Got that, too?"

"Fine by me," said Kate.

"And another thing—" Charly began, but Sue appeared in the doorway of her office, looking rather more flustered than usual.

"Kate! Have you got the thingy?" She waved her hands vaguely and pulled down the jacket of her executive suit. "Editor's Letter. I need it for—"

"Yep, sure, in a minute," said Kate, looking down at the crumpled, sweaty printout of the Editor's Letter, which she had crushed in her hand. She looked at Charly. "What else?"

"I'm pleased for you," said Charly. "He's a really nice bloke. OK?" She turned back to the desk as Kate smiled with pleasure. "And you're in luck. I had a fling with a real estate agent in December. I'll give him a call. And the beat goes on. Now, off you go to buy some matching monogrammed dressing gowns, OK?"

Kate ignored her and sat down to print out the letter again, as Charly picked up the phone. A minute later she was talking to an ex-boyfriend she'd dumped only last month and who just happened to be a real estate agent for a lettings agency in Killburn and West Hampstead. By lunchtime they had five different flats to see. Charly was, as she reminded Kate, really, really good in the sack.

• • •

"You're going to share with Charly?" Sue didn't look up from her desk, but she swiveled from side to side as she read Kate's piece, chewing a pencil, her cropped blond hair never moving an inch as her head bobbed. "This is good, Kate. Great. I thought you had a boy you lived with? Isn't he your boyfriend?"

Confused by this nonsequential speech, Kate said, "Thanks. Yes, he is now, actually. Er . . ." She scratched her head, trying to keep it simple. "We were flatmates when we got together, so we thought it'd be best to live apart for a while, make sure we're doing the right thing."

Sue wasn't that interested. "Hm, hm . . ." she said, looking up at Kate over her article. "Thanks again, dearie. You know . . ." She stared into space. "You're an interesting girl. Did you know? You Are An Interesting Girl."

Kate moved from one foot to the other, not sure how to respond; she never did with Sue, who was capable of great insight and total, crushing rudeness at the same time.

"Interesting," Sue said again. She tapped a pencil on the table, her small, busy fingers drumming a beat. "How long have you been here now?"

"Nearly two years," said Kate.

Sue nodded. "I'm thinking about something. Forget it. It's just—you."

Kate raised her eyebrows hopefully.

"You, Kate. You're such a funny mixture."

"How?" Kate asked, suddenly impatient.

"Well. Of reserve and openness. You're so shy, you wouldn't say 'Boo!' to a goose"—she made the "Boo!" extremely loud, and Kate jumped—"but at the same time you're a very intuitive girl. You get what people want to read about. What they're interested in. Always have done. I worried you were this shy little freaky thing with her head full of books. And I'm glad I was wrong." Sue flicked her eyes over her. "And you look good these days, too, now that you've found black and stopped experimenting with tartan miniskirts. That's all. Thanks."

"Er . . ." said Kate, brought up short. Sue waved her away, imperiously, with the pencil.

"I'm thinking about you, that's all," she said. "Wait to hear more."

"What does that mean?" Kate couldn't help asking. "Sorry."

"OK," Sue sighed, and looked around conspiratorially. She was clearly bursting to tell. "Have you heard about this start-up magazine Broadgate's financing? Have you heard of . . . *Venus*?" She said it in a whisper, like it was a hallowed name.

Kate shook her head slowly. "Oh. Well . . ."

She had, of course, heard loads about *Venus*, but since the world of magazines was rife with gossip, and since Sophie, Jo, and George were the worst gossips in the world, wildly unreliable and apt to overembroider to the point of Bayeux Tapestry lengths, and since Charly loathed "industry" gossip, as it implied an interest in one's job, Kate had tried to ignore most of what she'd heard, as it was impossible to separate the wheat from the chaff. Besides, for the last couple of months she hadn't really cared either way, had just worked as hard as possible so she could get home as soon as possible to Sean.

But *Venus* was the secret obsession in the office. It was going to be bigger, faster, glossier, trendier, younger, more beautiful than anything that had gone before, they said. New offices, by the river, they said, were being designed right now and the interiors were being done by Philippe Starck. *Venus* was going to be revolutionary, they said, a fortnightly glossy for young women, with fashion and celebrity and gossip and interesting articles, too. They said more was being spent on its launch than the combined revenue of *Your World!*, *Lovely Life*, and *even* the mighty *Great!* in one whole year. They said . . . well, they said lots of things, all in hushed voices, in corners, which gave the already supersecretive enterprise an even more momentous air.

"You like your job, don't you?" said Sue after a moment.

It was an unexpected question. Kate looked at her curiously. "Of course I do."

"Do you like magazines? Working in magazines?"

Kate said simply, "More than almost anything. I can't believe how lucky I am."

"You want to stay at *Your World!* for the rest of your life, then?"

"No," said Kate frankly. She wanted Sue to understand. "But, you know, I love it. I mean, I love working here, with everyone, but I love the magazine, too. I like answering the readers' letters, and working out what they want to read about, and talking to people, and giving people a slice of their lives. You know, the good slice." She realized she was talking too much; she babbled when she was nervous—she knew it. Suddenly Mac's face, saying the same thing, flashed into her mind. How strange. She shook her head, as if exorcising his image, willing it away.

"Yes," said Sue slowly, and Kate wasn't sure if she thought she was crazy or not. "Thanks, Kate. Thanks a lot." She tapped her pencil impatiently on the desk. "And good luck with the flat hunt. I think you're mad to move in with Charly. You'll have no liver left, no boyfriend, and no money after six months. She'll steal them all. But each to his own."

"You could be right," said Kate happily, but the phone rang, and suddenly Sue wasn't listening anymore.

The next week, Kate and Charly found their flat, a sunny but tiny two-bedroom at the very top of a tall Victorian house, in between Kilburn and Queen's Park, near Zoe and Steve. The agent said they should say they wanted it now. It was a busy time of year, and the market was crazy. It was all happening fast, too fast for Kate. Only a week ago she hadn't known about any of this and now . . . ? But Charly had been galvanized into action by the thought of leaving Leigh-on-Sea and having her own place, a place with Kate. "Two crazy single girls out on the town," she said when they signed the lease.

Kate wanted to say, No, that's not it. But on her first night in their flat, after Sean had helped her pack up their old flat, taken her to the new place, lugged her boxes up the stairs and then regretfully, sadly, kissed her good-bye and gone off to meet his new flatmate Jem at the pub, Kate found herself standing on the steps of the spindly redbrick house that was now her home without any idea how she'd ended up there.

She turned back, opened the front door, and started up the stairs wearily. As she did, she heard a loud bang from her floor, up in the roof, and looked up cautiously—what had Charly done now? Was it always going to be like this? Loneliness clutched at her again, and as she got to the second floor she thought of Zoe, wished she could take advantage of their new neighbor status to pop around to their home, a real home. But she and Steve had left that morning to visit Mac in Edinburgh. Zoe had told her they were going a few days ago, in a very soft voice, as if she were worried about how Kate might react. Kate wasn't sure what Zoe was worried about—that she wouldn't be around for Kate's first night in the flat, or was Mac still verboten as a subject between them, even now? She shrugged, thinking about this as she climbed the stairs. Coolly, she told herself she rarely thought of him now; she didn't need to. To remember him—it—what had happened, how she had felt . . .

She blinked. Surely that was all behind her now—she had her life, he had his, and there was no further proof needed of the fact that their night together was way in the past than this—her new life, what she was doing now, climbing the stairs to her new home.

As Kate finally reached her floor, panting slightly, she squared her shoulders and pushed open the door. Time to get on with it, then, she told herself, and she forced herself to smile, faking a cheeriness she didn't feel.

Wheeeeeeeeeeeeeeeeeeeeeeeeeeeeeeeeeeee! came a high, whistling noise from inside, and as Kate came into the sitting room, not knowing what to expect, she found Charly, a small silver party hat sitting lopsided on her silky tawny hair, blowing a streamer whistle, with a just-opened bottle of champagne—the source of the loud bang, Kate realized—in her hand.

"I thought you might need cheering up," Charly said, smiling at her. She handed her a glass, shaking her head, as if laughing to herself about something, and she looked happy, happier than Kate had seen her in ages. "Welcome to our new home, Kate."

"Hey!" said Kate delightedly. "That's so—you're so sweet!" They clinked glasses. "Welcome to yours!"

"To new beginnings," said Charly. She nodded wisely at Kate. "Who knows what the future holds, eh?"

Kate nodded, and they each took a sip, framed by the window in the early evening light as the setting sun streamed in across the rooftops.

"Who knows," she said, but she was thinking only of Sean now, only of the life that lay ahead of her with him, and she crossed her fingers with one hand. "Who knows."

Part Two

Fifteen

LONDON
2007

*K*ate woke feeling like she'd been hit by a hammer. She banged the clock radio, ineffectively, trying to turn it off, emerging from the kind of deep sleep where you feel your limbs are melding into the mattress. She blinked wearily, trying to work out where she was, fragments of dreams and memories and actual events all crowding into her mind. Coming home. Dad—Mr. Allan—the coffin. Dani's pink pajamas. She'd seen Zoe. Zoe—Mac—Sean—Charly's letter.

Sitting up slowly, Kate rubbed her eyes with fumbling, clumsy hands. Her limbs felt as if they were full of lead. Her head ached, her throat was a little sore, and she didn't really feel rested at all. She looked around slowly, taking in the contents of the room, how weird it was to be here again. The gray painted chest of drawers, the long blond wood wardrobe that was to have housed her and Sean's grown-up business attire. He had put up the creamy Venetian blind; you could still see the black holes in the wooden window frame from the previous blind that he'd taken down.

No. No more of this. To her own surprise, Kate stumbled out of bed, pulled up the blind, and opened the window. Outside a bird sang enthusiastically, chirping loudly against the faint hum of traffic, and it hit her weary brain then: she was definitely back in London. She could even smell it. Coffee. She needed coffee. She stumbled through to the kitchen, remembering how the floorboards squeaked just so, how she and Sean had discussed carpets.

Kate shook her head and started hunting for something to put her coffee in. She loved opening the cupboards in her kitchen again, rediscovering the old mugs she'd left behind: the orange striped penguin mug that said 'Pride and Prejudice,' the spotted set from Habitat her dad (or probably Lisa) had bought for her birthday, the ones with pictures of the Moomins, the old chipped mug that said "Central Perk" on it—she'd been so proud of that one when Sean had given it to her, a month after they'd got together. She opened the tiny door onto the minuscule balcony, no more than a windowsill, really. Fresh air flooded into the kitchen and she took a deep breath.

"So you're back," she said aloud. "It's OK. But you've got to—"

Got to what? She looked out around her, drinking in the wet London, petroly, grassy smell, and went back inside the kitchen again. She didn't know what she had to do. Then she caught sight of the Central Perk mug.

"Got to make it work. So you sort everything out. Don't leave feeling like you're slinking away."

The kettle switch flipped off. She took it as a sign and nodded firmly, ignoring the stare of the man in the flat opposite her. She felt properly awake, and suddenly full of purpose.

She was going to see her father later, but she had to time it right, didn't want to tire him out—or make him angry. He was not a good patient. Lisa knew enough, too, to keep Dani out of his way for a large portion of the day. That was for after lunch. In the meantime, what else was she supposed to do? Kate poured water into the cafetière, thoughtfully.

She could go and see Zoe again, or call Francesca. She hadn't spoken to her since she'd been back. But Francesca would have a go at her, ask her questions Kate didn't want to answer. She couldn't quite face it, not just yet. She couldn't call into the office and make sure everything was going OK; they wouldn't be there for another six hours. And she'd only left on Friday; what was the point? Then it struck her with force that apart from anything else, there was nothing she needed to check on, anyway. Jersey Lorraine could do that job standing on her head. Better than Kate.

Silence crowded in on her, standing in the kitchen, as she realized the strange situation of her own futility. Out there was London, the city she loved, friends she knew, and Kate felt removed from it all, in an ivory tower. And then she heard a noise from upstairs. Someone was moving around, shuffling slowly across the floor.

She felt the pull of the city suddenly, like it was talking to her, telling her to come outside, walk around again. There was spring on the breeze, and outside she could hear someone singing in the street. She had to get up, go out, keep moving, she had to embrace this or else just not bother, slink back to New York again and give up. She made the coffee, cradling it in her hands till it got cold, looking out of the open window until she realized her bare arms had goose bumps and she was shivering. She had a shower, got dressed, and shut the door. She knew where she was going.

"Hello Kate," he said.

"Hello, Mr. Allan," Kate replied. She handed him the daffodils she'd bought the previous day and kissed him, squeezing his arm briefly. "How are you?"

He moved out of the way to let her in, nodding his head in a kind of motioning movement. She walked down the corridor, so like the one in her flat and so utterly different. In the corridor, in the light pretty sitting room, books and records lined the walls, shelf after shelf of them, with another wall devoted to CDs. A breakfast bar, with stools, was cut into the wall between sitting room and kitchen, and an old speckled blue fruit bowl sat on it, a denuded bunch of grapes its only inhabitant. Everything was too tidy somehow. The two of them stood in silence, looking alternately at the floor or out of the window, and Kate wished she was back downstairs again, not trying to be a good neighbor.

On the walls, lining every spare inch, there were album covers. Blue, red geometric shapes, faded black-and-white photos of lanky young men. "Chappell Quartet Plays the Tin Pan Blues" proclaimed the framed album nearest to Kate.

"Is that you?" she said, pointing at the second of the lanky men in the row.

"Yes," said Mr. Allan, plunging his hands into his pockets. "That was me. West Berlin, I think was where that photo was taken. Well, by then Jimmy had left, so . . ." He trailed off.

"You've come about Eileen, I expect," he said after a long pause.

Kate was thrown by this. She looked down and saw that she'd put her hands in her pockets, unconsciously mirroring her host. Mrs. Allan had usually done most of the talking.

"Um. I came to say hello," she said.

"Right." Mr. Allan nodded; he didn't venture anything further, or ask her to sit down. "I'm so sorry," Kate said firmly.

Mr. Allan nodded again. He said, without looking at her, "I thought that was why you'd come."

He blinked; his receding white hair moved up and down slightly as he frowned and then widened his eyes in rapid succession.

"When's the funeral?" Kate said.

"Thursday," said Mr. Allan. "But we're actually having a cardboard coffin, not that one she left in. We both want cardboard coffins, it's more environmental." He said this flatly. "You saw her yesterday, didn't you? When you were getting back."

Again, Kate was irresistibly reminded of a Pinter play. "Yes—I didn't know if you'd seen me. I nearly knocked yesterday—" Mr. Allan bowed his head.

"I didn't want any visitors, really. Just wanted to be on my own. Get used to it for a while."

"Right, right," said Kate. "Well, I'm sorry for—"

He batted her apology away with his hand. "We were together for fifty years, you know. So it's strange. We always knew one of us would be alone, you know." He blinked again, and looked around the flat. "We're having people back here afterward," he said suddenly. "You missed Sue yesterday."

"Sue . . . Sue!" Kate said, contexts slotting into place, her brain whirring. Sue—of course. Sue Jordan, her beloved boss at *Your World!*, was married to Alec Allan, Mr. Allan's nephew. It was she who had mentioned the flat below Alec's uncle and aunt was for sale at auction, four years ago. "Oh, how lovely. I haven't seen her for . . ." She trailed off. "Ages."

"Yes," said Mr. Allan. "And she's looking forward to seeing you, Kate. She wants to know how you are."

Kate thought of Sue: brisk, comforting, hard as nails, always encouraging, always demanding the best. She wondered what Sue would say if she heard what Kate had spent her last week at work doing (sorting out paperclips and booking Anne Graves's flights to Bermuda for her holidays). She would be cross with Kate, and rightly so. Kate shook her head, looking back at Mr. Allan. "I've missed her."

"I'm sure. Now, she said you'd be able to help me." Kate nodded. "Would you mind telling me something?"

"Yes, of course," said Kate.

"Where can I get some food, crisps and things?" He said this as if they were extraordinary delicacies. "You know, if people come back after the service." Agitation was working its way across his face. "You see, Eileen is—was the one who did all that sort of thing. I was on the road, she was at home. That's how it worked.

The shops at the end of the road—would they be best, do you think? I'm just not sure."

"Yes, and the supermarket and stuff," said Kate. She crossed her arms and rocked back on her heels. "Look, Mr. Allan, why don't I take care of all of that for you?"

To her relief he didn't protest or make excuses. He opened his eyes and said, "Thank you, Kate. That really would be extremely helpful." He looked out of the window and was silent for a while. "It's a lovely day outside, isn't it? Spring really is here."

"Gorgeous, I know," said Kate, following his gaze. "Actually, that's why I came up here. Apart from—well, you know I wanted to . . . er . . ." She cleared her throat. "I was wondering. Would you like to go for a walk?"

"A walk?" he said, slowly, as if she'd just suggested joining the circus.

"Yes," she said. "Like we used to, remember? I need to get out of the flat. Clear my head a bit. I thought you might want to, as well."

"Well, yes," he said. "Of course. I'd forgotten. You're only just back, aren't you? How long has it been?"

"A day," said Kate.

"No, my dear," Mr. Allan said. "How long has it been since you left?"

"Oh," said Kate. "Nearly three years."

"Has it really? You never came back, did you?"

"I've come back now," said Kate, looking out of the window again.

"Eileen always said what a shame it was," Mr. Allan said. "She thought you were such a lovely girl, my dear."

"I don't know about that," said Kate, embarrassed. "She was a lovely woman, though, Mr. Allan. I am sorry."

"Well, well, well," he said, shaking his bowed head, and a tear dropped to the ground. She looked away, embarrassed, not wanting to see his grief. He looked up. "I'm not ready to talk about her as—as a dead person yet. So, please don't be sorry. Is that all right?"

"Yes, of course," said Kate hurriedly. Mr. Allan continued as if uninterrupted, "She'd be sorry to have missed you, you know. We often used to wonder how you were getting on."

"I know. She wrote and I never wrote back to her," said Kate. She felt as low as can be. "She sent me newspaper cuttings, bits and bobs, you know."

"Yes, I know."

"I never replied." She shook her head. "It was so rude of me. I'm sorry."

"No, it was natural, after everything that happened. We just wanted you to be happy, dear."

"Bless you," Kate said, giving him a small smile.

Mr. Allan strode across to the coatrack and picked up a long raincoat. "So how's New York? I want to hear all about it."

Kate jangled her keys in her pocket. "Not really much to tell."

"Well," he said, and he let her help him on with his coat. "Let's get going, then, and you can tell me all about it."

The daffodils were out all along the roads up to the park, in window boxes, in clumps on the ground. They walked through St. John's Wood, toward Lord's, through the heart of London's apartment-block land, every street lined with charming Victorian flats, with balconies, brass plaques fitted with bells, perfectly manicured gardens. The hum of the first mowing of the lawns echoed around them as they walked farther, through the wide, quiet streets, past the private hospitals, the synagogues, the little rows of shops underneath the flats, and down St. John's Wood's High Street. It was Monday morning, and the roads were almost empty in the cold spring sunshine; pensioners, middle-aged couples emerged from their blocks, slowly moving down the street, talking animatedly to each other.

Mr. Allan walked fast, which Kate liked; she wasn't a stroller. For a man of his age he was extremely fit: tall and sinewy. They talked for a while, he asking her questions about how she'd been, she replying and asking him questions in return, but after that they fell into silence. He didn't say much, neither did she, but it was almost as if they didn't need to. After twenty minutes or so like this, he suddenly stopped abruptly.

"Oh, we're here," he said. "We have gone far. We've reached the park. I was miles away, I'm afraid."

Regent's Park. She could see it unfolding ahead of her. To their left was the zoo; ahead, the tangled bushes at the edge, rolling away toward the rest of the park; gorgeous, glorious Regent's Park. It seemed so strange to her, all of a sudden, so . . . *English*. She hadn't realized how much it would affect her, how overwhelming it was, now, here, to be back home, and how strange it must be for Mr. Allan. Last week he wouldn't have known, couldn't have imagined in his worst nightmares that this would be his Monday morning, the day after his wife died. They were both silent.

Without meaning to, Kate said impulsively, "I miss New York."

He looked up, amazement written on his face.

"You miss New York? After twenty-four hours? Oh, come on. Look at this!"

He waved his umbrella at the scene in front of them, then at her. "Come on, Kate. This is London! How can you say that?"

"Er . . ." Kate was embarrassed. "I don't know, I just do."

"Rubbish," Mr. Allan said firmly. He was quite animated. "I've lived here all my life, apart from when I was touring. I went everywhere, all over the world, Kate, we were playing when British jazz was up there, having its Golden Age. And do you know something?"

Kate shook her head.

"Always missed it. Always glad to be back. To see Eileen, to do our walk to the shops, to go into Soho and meet my old bandmates. To walk across Hyde Park, to see Johnny Dankworth in concert—Eileen and I used to do that when we were younger, you know, or we'd meet in Soho, in a cafe, pretend we were on a date, not a boring old married couple.

"You're the same, Kate. I remember seeing your father in concert at the Festival Hall, and this little girl leaving with him at the end, you were jumping up and down and holding on to his hand and to your mother's, too. Between the two of them. Your mother, she was so beautiful. Red hair?" Kate nodded, and he said eagerly, "Do you remember that evening?"

"No," said Kate, smiling. "I don't think so, anyway. That's so funny. I never knew that."

"Brahms's violin concerto." He shook his head. "Ah, he was wonderful."

Kate could, in fact, vaguely remember the treat of that evening, of being allowed to come and see her father. It was a rarity, she hadn't often gone. Her mother and father had argued about it, badly. She must have been about eight. She remembered then not liking the South Bank, it wasn't a London she was used to—like an alien landscape. She sucked her lower lip into her mouth and bit it, whistling through her teeth, the cold air stinging them.

"He's not very well," she said incoherently. "That's why I've come back."

"Ah," said Mr. Allan. He stared at her briefly. "What is it?"

"Kidney transplant. He was very . . . he was very lucky." Kate didn't trust herself to say more.

He nodded and patted her arm, as if she were a little girl again. "I am sorry. We both have our sadness, then. Let's cross the road."

Suddenly Kate felt strangely at home again, standing on

the side of a road overlooking the park with her neighbor. Mr. Allan—he was one of several people she hadn't allowed herself to miss since she'd gone. Concern for him flooded over her once again, on this strange and awful day for him, but as she turned to ask him something, he interrupted her brusquely.

"Miss New York," he muttered. "I'll show you what a foolish thing that is to say. Look. There. The Regent's Canal," he said, waving his umbrella in the direction of the bushes. "Now that is something to admire. Perhaps we should go to the bank and see, eh?"

There was the canal; there behind it was the London Zoo. Kate stood still and heard the faint cry of something—a chimp, perhaps.

"There," said Mr. Allan. "There's a boat. My goodness."

There was a narrow boat just pulling into a little docking station outside the zoo. It was so strange, Kate thought, that she had never known about or seen this before. Mr. Allan made a sound, like a cough, and Kate turned to look at him.

"I'm sorry," he said. "Eileen loved the canal. We used to get this boat up to Camden Lock, from Little Venice. At least once a month. She really did just love it." His voice trembled. "This is . . . Oh dear. Everything's awful. That's all."

Kate didn't know what to say. She took his arm. "Oh, Mr. Allan." She squeezed it and they stood there, on the canal bank, in silence. The daffodils were out in force; sun flickered on the water. It was a beautiful day.

"Last call for the boat trip, please!" the ticket master shouted. Suddenly Kate heard her little sister's voice: "I wanna go on a boat trip!"

"Mr. Allan," she said. "Why don't we get the boat back home?"

So they sat there, with the tourists, and the strange old man with a camera who took notes, and a moody girl reading a book, as the narrow boat sedately glided through the water, past the vast white stucco houses with private launches and perfect gardens, through Lisson Grove, where three people were trying to start a barbecue on their old, rather dilapidated boat, through the long, dark tunnel cutting underneath Maida Vale and bringing them out in Little Venice, past the cafe, and the spot where Nancy Mitford used to live, and finally they arrived at the lake where the Regent's Canal met the Grand Union Canal, and got out.

"This is called Browning's Pond," said Mr. Allan as they stood on the little bridge crossing over the canal, watching the moorhens slide through the water and the Canada geese screeching overhead. "Do you know why?"

"No," said Kate.

"Robert Browning. He lived there." He pointed to the houses overlooking the canal. "See that blue plaque there? That's for him. The house is demolished now. But they named it after him."

"I didn't know that."

"Lots of things you don't know," Mr. Allan said. He crossed the road, and they walked next to the canal. Kate glanced up at the houses, the sunshine bouncing off the creamy white stucco, the blue grape hyacinths and yellow daffodils bobbing happily in the gardens, and felt a sort of calm within her. She laughed quietly as they turned the corner and crossed the road again.

"What's so funny?"

"Nothing, really," she said. "Just . . . I didn't expect to be doing this on my first day back. I don't expect you did, either."

"No," Mr. Allan said. "Kate, I didn't. But I'm glad you're here. Thank you."

She patted his arm. "I'm glad I'm here, too."

They walked in silence a little while until Mr. Allan said, "Are you writing anything at the moment?"

Kate wrinkled her forehead, slightly taken aback by the question. It had been a longish walk; she was surprised he wasn't more tired, but he seemed absolutely fine. "Er . . . no. Why?"

"I mean to say, what are you doing in New York?" Mr. Allan said. "Didn't you get some wonderful job out there? That was what we heard from Sue."

"Ha," said Kate. She had to be careful, she realized. This was the scenario she practiced for, being back in London and answering questions about her job. "I'm working at a literary agency."

"Working with writers, you mean? At the agency?"

"Something like that." Kate neatly sidestepped a cracked paving stone. "Be careful."

"Yes, yes." They were on Warrington Crescent, walking back up toward Elgin Avenue. The sun went in suddenly. Kate looked up; gray clouds scudded, from nowhere, across the blue sky. She shivered.

"So it was worth leaving for," Mr. Allan said. "Eileen and I always thought you'd win a Pulitzer prize one day. Or the Booker Prize. Weren't you going to be a magazine editor before you left? Sue always said you would."

This was the thing with old people, Kate reminded herself. Their version of the past was totally unreliable.

"No," she said. "I loved *Venus,* but I needed to get away after everything that happened." He was watching her. Time to roll out phase two. "And, you know, I wanted to see Mum—she left when I was fourteen, and I'd never really spent much time with her, you know. . . . It seemed like a good time to go then."

This was her stock answer, and it always worked. It was vulnerable enough to guilt people into accepting it, and it had the merit of being true, although that was far from being the whole story.

Mr. Allan said, "I'm sorry. So you're back to see your father, and that's fine with your—your employers, I suppose?"

"Yes, yes," said Kate. "Someone's in covering my job while I'm away, while Dad's ill. I'm only here for two, three weeks, and then I'm back there."

"Two weeks," Mr. Allan said, sinking his head onto his chest. "I see." He blinked. "What will you do about your flat?"

"I don't know," Kate said. "Get someone else in, get an agency to rent it out, I expect. I'm not staying. I don't really live here anymore, you see."

"Of course, of course," he said, and then they were both silent, walking in pace together until they were almost home.

"That was quite a walk," said Mr. Allan, taking off his deerstalker hat while Kate unlocked the door and let him into the lobby of their building. "Phew."

"I'm knackered," said Kate. "Well done, us. We must have walked three miles!"

"Goodness gracious," said Mr. Allan. He rolled his eyes and then smiled at her. They walked upstairs to his flat and Kate waited as his hands jangled the keys in his pocket.

"Dear Kate," he said as he unlocked the door. "Thank you so much."

"Not at all," said Kate, almost laughing, "Thank you—I'm so sorry—"

He brushed her condolences aside again. "No, no. Thank you, dear girl. It was a wonderful morning. And—ah. Thursday?"

"I'll buy the food," Kate said. "You don't need to worry about a thing. Now," she said bossily, "what are you doing for the rest of the day?"

"Alec's coming around soon, and Sue." Alec was Sue's rather unlikely husband, a scholarly, quiet man who worked on the finance side of the magazine publishing business, quite unlike his energetic, firecracker of a wife. "They're bringing lunch, we're talking about—about arrangements, you know."

"Right," said Kate, not wanting to meet his eye, embarrassed. "Well." She pushed her toe along the ground, gingerly, not wanting to leave him on his own, not wanting to be on her own suddenly.

"Don't suppose you'd want to pop up for a cup of tea later—they'd love to see you, I know."

"I can't," she said hurriedly. "I'd love to see them, too—but I'll be at my dad's."

"Of course," Mr. Allan said. "Well, they'll be gone by six thirty; they have theater tickets. How about after that, maybe a glass of wine?" He made a gesture like a maître d', welcoming her to a restaurant.

"Sure!" Kate smiled. Mr. Allan smiled back. Her unease vanished, and she kissed him on the cheek and went downstairs to her welcoming but echoing flat. She opened the door, humming a tune Mr. Allan had been singing.

As she was taking off her coat, her eye fell on something on the floor. A letter—someone had pushed it under the door. No address this time, just

Kate Miller
by hand

And inside Charly had written:

Here's my mobile number, Kate. Please give me a call. Did you get the letter I posted you? I'm having a little girl. I wanted to tell you. I need to see you, please get in touch.
CHARLY :)

Sixteen

*I*t was Wednesday evening and four days since Kate had been back in London. It seemed to her as if the first twenty-four hours had passed in a flash, and from then on it was almost scary how easily she fell into a routine. Like the first few days at a new school, when after less than a week a need for normalcy makes it feel like you've been there for years, not days. She'd visit her father at home in the morning, usually when Lisa was out with Danielle. On Tuesday Lisa had given her a key so that Daniel didn't have to answer the door. She'd come back to the flat and pottered around for a while, making lists of things—*buy new pots for balcony* and *need more teaspoons*—small tasks, never big things. She didn't call the lettings agent, she didn't call Zoe again, though she knew she should. In the early evening, she'd go upstairs for a cup of tea with Mr. Allan, and he'd tell her about Eileen, about their life together, and they'd sort things out for the funeral. Kate wasn't sure how much of a practical help it was, but as he said, it was good to talk. She'd speak to her father again, and then go to bed, early.

She didn't go into town, didn't explore farther than she'd walked with Mr. Allan. She went to the supermarket, to get the food for Mrs. Allan's wake, but that was about it. She was back in London, but she might as well have still been in another country. She didn't ring any old friends, or email anyone from the laptop she'd brought back with her. Francesca called several times but never left a message, and Kate simply let her phone ring and ring.

On Monday evening she had rung her mother, but that merely served to unsettle her.

"Darling, so what have you been doing?" Venetia had asked brightly. "Lots of fun superb things? Catching up with all your friends? How lovely."

"Oh," Kate said uneasily, "er, well . . . I saw Zoe."

Venetia sounded insanely overenthusiastic. "Lovely! How is she?"

"Oh . . . fine."

There was a pause. Kate felt, as she did so many times, that she had never worked out how to show her mother her best side.

"How are the party plans for Oscar going?" she said after a moment.

"Oh, they're exhausting," Venetia said. "I've booked us both into the hairdresser for Saturday morning, I'm going to have rollers, you can have what you want—do you want a blow-dry? That's probably best, isn't it?"

"Um," said Kate. "Not sure—can I—"

"I don't need to let them know for a while, but if you could have a think about it."

"Sure," said Kate, biting her little finger and trying not to laugh, because her mother was funny, especially from a distance. "And the party? All under control?"

"It is going to be ah-may-zing," said Venetia fervently. "Nearly three weeks to go, my God. But you'll be back before then, won't you!" Her voice rose a little.

"Of course I will, Mum." Kate tried not to sound stern. "I said, right from the start I've always said, I'll be back in lots of time. I wouldn't miss Oscar's party, would I?"

"I know," said Venetia, sounding chastened. "It's just—well, you know how I feel about London."

She made it sound as if London were a war criminal on the loose, persecuting her. "Mum, you know, I'm really glad I came back," Kate said, hearing a certainty in her voice that she did not feel. "It's been so great to see Dad—"

"Well, exactly. And how is darling Daniel?" Venetia interrupted fondly, as if darling Daniel were a particularly beloved old friend of hers, or her pet dog, not her ex-husband with whom she had parted on the most painful terms, and whom she used to refer to at dinner with her New York friends, after a few glasses of wine, as "that bastard Miller."

"He's OK," said Kate. In truth, Lisa had told her that day, with a semi-exasperated sigh, that the doctors thought he wasn't doing as well as he could be. He was a bad patient, that was the trouble. Nothing to worry about, the nurse who came to see him each day had said, but the transplant operation had knocked him for six—and they still wouldn't know for a while whether his body might reject the new kidney or not. It was a waiting game, and he was no good at waiting for something over which he had no control—especially his own body.

On Tuesday, she called Perry and Co., to check in with Bruce Perry. For some perverse reason she wanted her boss to know she wasn't on holiday, that she was back in London for a reason. She wanted him to think she cared about her job, didn't she?

"So it's all going OK?" she asked him.

"Sure thing!" Bruce's tone was breezy. "We miss you, Kate! But we're just about managing here, you know. Don't you worry."

"So is everything OK with Lorraine? You don't need . . ."

"Hey, hey. Kate." Bruce's voice grew louder, as if he were closer to the phone. "Lorraine isn't you, please don't misunderstand, OK? But she's great!" His voice grew distant again, as if he were announcing this to the office. Kate could hear someone laughing in the background. "She brought doughnuts in today for everyone! Krispy Kreme, no less. What a gal. And she's changed a few things, it'll make your life so much easier."

"Uh-huh . . ." Kate said. "Like what?"

"A few corrections to the filing system, and she's called a couple of authors to introduce herself. Personal touch. It was Doris's idea."

Kate kicked the baseboard in the hallway viciously, then hopped in agony. God, that dwarfy helmet-haired Doris! She was a . . . witch! She took a deep breath.

"That's great," she said. "What a great idea. Hey, I've got to go, Bruce, but I'll call you on Friday, OK?"

"No need, Kate!" he said. "No call for it! You just focus on your dad, OK? And we'll see you soon."

Yes, they were fine without her, just fine. No, she told the voice that said loudly in her head, "They're not missing you at all, are they?" That was the bargain I made with myself when I went to New York. A quiet life, no ties, no commitments. A life I can walk away from if I need to.

She just hadn't realized how easy it would be to walk away from it. To be forgotten, melt into the background.

And it went on. On Wednesday morning, she visited her father once more and on her way back she went to the shops at the edge of Elgin Avenue, to buy a few more final things she needed for Mrs. Allan's funeral tea the next day and a newspaper. She marched up to the desk and deposited her wares on the counter.

"Hi," she said brightly, and she realized it sounded almost desperate. She *wanted* to talk to the shopkeeper, wanted some human interaction.

But he just nodded and shoved everything into a bright blue plastic bag, and when Kate said, "I don't need a bag," he looked at her coldly, as if she'd just been sick on the floor.

Kate said, feeling insane, "How are you today?"

In New York he would have known her name by now, smiled with utter delight when she walked in, had everything piled up and in her own bag in three seconds, and engaged in mundane but satisfying small talk while he made change. The strip lighting above the till hummed. A car outside revved loudly, and silence reverberated in the shop as the man behind the counter nodded politely, but said nothing.

"Well . . . bye," said Kate. "See you later!"

She walked out, her bag swinging by her knees, feeling mad, wanting to talk to herself, shaking her head. Suddenly the spell of the last few days was broken. Wednesday evening stretched ahead of her, lonely hours spent in the flat she'd thought would be her first married home, and the only respite conversation with two old men, one sick, one grieving; one her father, one her neighbor. She opened the front door with a heavy heart.

And then Francesca rang.

"So, stranger," said the voice on the phone as Kate slid over and sat upright, as upright as she could get, on the sofa. "What. You've been back for practically a week and you don't call me. How kind. What's up?"

"I think I'm going mad, Francesca," Kate said. "I need a drink." She paused. "How are you? Are you well?"

"Fine," said the reassuring voice, so cool and collected. "I'm still at work. Give me thirty minutes. I'll meet you at Kettners, in the bar. Eight p.m. OK?"

"Er . . ." said Kate, suddenly getting cold feet. That was the center of town. She hadn't banked on having to go into the center of town.

"That's my best offer," said Francesca. "Take it or leave it. I'm not schlepping over to you. I'm in Clapham, remember, or is your geography shot to hell now that you're a New Yorker?"

"Shut up," said Kate indignantly. "Of course it's not. Hurrah. I'll take it. Eight p.m. See you in a bit. Bye."

But Francesca had already put the phone down.

• • •

This, then, was it. The center of town, the tawdry, pulsing, utterly confusing center, filled with sights and smells and sounds. She had missed the pretheater chaos; coming out of the tube at Piccadilly Circus, Kate almost smiled at how awful it was, this center of her beloved home city. The Trocadero, Eros, Shaftesbury Avenue—all marooned in a sea of traffic; swelling tourists; horrid, feral pigeons; and the hotdog stands, with the ever-present smell of reconstituted pigs' eyelids, fried and sweating, next to rancid onions. In New York the streets were wide—Times Square may have been Disney-fied but it was clean and friendly and open all night, and the adrenaline rush of walking through it was incomparable. There was order there, she never understood people who said New York was chaotic. This—this, she thought, as she walked up Shaftesbury Avenue, dodging caricaturists, lounging men in cheap leather jackets, angry white van drivers, gaggles of tourists with backpacks bigger than them, as she turned into the bottom of Wardour Street—*this* was chaos.

As she turned off and stepped into Soho, the traffic eased off, and the tourists and pedestrians slimmed down. She walked past the little school and the church with its graveyard, so unexpected, down Old Compton Street, where a few brave souls were sitting out in the night air, celebrating the relative warmth of another sunny March day. Nostalgia was nudging her, the memories of evenings at Pulcinella's, or the tapas place around the corner, the Mayflower back across the road, or the Dog and Duck on Bateman Street—she had spent vast amounts of her twenties in each of those places, it seemed. And Kettners.

Kettners hadn't changed, she was relieved to see. It still kept its old-world, almost frowsy charm, a certain faded elegance mixed with a buzzy atmosphere, old-fashioned waiters who were proper waiters, not out-of-work actors who wanted to let you know they were great at every available opportunity. No, Kettners was old-school. It had been one of Kate's favorite places in London. She smiled at the girls in the cloakroom and turned right, into the bar by the restaurant, where an old guy sat at a piano, singing "Someone to Watch over Me"—it was always "Someone to Watch over Me." Memory and emotion flooded through her, and she paused on the step, momentarily disorientated.

"Oi," said a voice in the corner, and Kate looked over to see Francesca slumped on a sofa, her suit jacket bunched up, the shoulder pads standing up inches higher than she. Her long dark hair fanned out about her shoulders. She smiled at Kate, and patted the leather cushion.

Kate knelt on the sofa and hugged her, remembering as she did so how thin Francesca was.

"It's great to see you," she said.

"You, too," said Francesca. "About bloody time, too. Do you know it's been . . ."

"Over two years," Kate said, smiling down at her. "I know. I'm sorry."

Francesca said unexpectedly, "I know you are. Let's not get into all that." She cleared her throat and said dryly, "Not until we've had a few drinks, anyway. There's a bottle of champagne on its way."

The house champagne at Kettners was famous—it was cheap and good. A dangerous combination.

"Great." Kate rubbed her hands, the excitement of being out finally hitting her.

"So. How've you been?" Francesca said as a waiter gingerly placed an ice bucket on the table and two glasses.

"No," Kate said firmly. "How've *you* been. I'm sick of myself—tell me how you've been. You look great, Francesca."

"Screw that," said Francesca. "Kate, the mystery woman, comes back all of a sudden, and I'm going to spend the evening talking about loan structuring and how much I hate London Bridge, and how my boss is a total pig? Idonthinkso. Come on, Katy. How the hell have you been? Tell me."

And, as if watching herself from the ceiling, Kate heard herself say, "I don't think I should have gone back."

"Gone back to that flat?" Francesca nodded, and poured the champagne. "I did wonder, you know."

"Really?"

"Course," said Francesca. "*I* wouldn't have, that's for sure. Why couldn't you stay with someone else?"

"Zoe?"

"Well, yes—"

"I know," Kate said weakly. "She's just got so much going on. And what with everything. I didn't want to . . ."

"Yep," said Francesca. She handed Kate a glass. Kate took it. She took a huge gulp of it, and the fizzing bubbles stung her nose, but she let them. It reminded her, as it always did, of something— what was it?

"How's she been?" Kate said, not wanting to hear the answer.

"You've seen her, though, haven't you?"

"Yes, yes," Kate assured her. "I may be crap, but I'm not *that* crap."

"Hm." Francesca raised her eyebrows, and then she smiled, her serious dark eyes crinkling with warmth. "Maybe you're not, darl. Zoe." She took a sip of champagne. "She's OK. You know she's back at work now?"

"She told me," Kate said.

"It's—how long since Steve . . . died?" Francesca said. There was silence.

"Two years and nine months."

"Of course," said Francesca. She ran her palm, flat, over her forehead, and Kate remembered that Francesca had loved Steve, long before Zoe had appeared on the scene. She had been his first girlfriend at university. Kate nodded at her, eyes narrowed.

"Hey!" Francesca said sharply, and she brought her palm square down onto the low table in front of them. The other drinkers looked around in surprise. Francesca said in a low voice, "Look, I know Steve. I knew him. Remember? I went out with him for a whole blinking year, until you introduced him to that young harlot, Zoe—" She smiled. "What happened, happened, OK? It wasn't your fault."

Kate shook her head, the pain of tears already stinging at her eyes, in her nose. She smiled grimly. "Too heavy. I'm sorry."

"I know." Francesca laughed hollowly. "Man. Nice start to the evening, eh? I get out of work and come to meet you and it's like an evening with Verdi."

"In what way?" Kate said innocently.

"God, you're so literal. I mean . . ." She leaned over and hit Kate on the arm. "Look. Cheers, darling. It's just so nice to see you. You look different, you know?"

"How?"

"Grown-up."

"That's what Zoe said," Kate said, remembering. It didn't sound like a particularly great thing to be. "Don't feel it, myself. Anyway. How are you? How's the job, how's the house? How's . . . everything?"

"Job, crap. Far too hard." Francesca sighed. "There's a squeeze on in our department. They do this every couple of years. Just fire a whole load of people, get some new, better people in, then do the same in two years' time. So they know they've always got the best. We're in the middle of it now."

"Are you . . . ?" Kate said.

"Please," said Francesca. "I made them millions last year. London's their most profitable office."

"Wow," said Kate.

"It's just—you know. It's hard." Francesca blew air out from her bottom lip so it ruffled her bangs, as if she were trying to cool down. "It feels like there's—there's nothing left over."

"After work?" said Kate, not sure what she meant.

"Yep," said Francesca, nodding in agreement. "You know what it's like." Kate nodded uncertainly; she only vaguely remembered what it was like. Francesca went on, "Work, work, work. And then—what? Everyone else is settled down, living out in—" She waved her arm vaguely. "Cheam. I don't know. Places outside town. I don't want that. It's just—" She gulped the rest of her champagne down, poured some more in. "I didn't sign up for this. When we were younger—you know, it's even depressing I can say 'when we were younger,' too—well, when we were younger, I didn't think this was the way it was going to be. Look at us now. At our friends. You remember Zoe and Steve's housewarming party?"

"Of course," Kate said. She smiled. "Funny, we were talking about it on Sunday. Me and Zoe."

"I remember that evening so clearly," Francesca said. "Mainly because I couldn't drink that much, I was on antibiotics. I remember just looking around the room at all of us, thinking how great everything was." She laughed bitterly. "Look what's happened to all of us since. It just didn't work out how we thought it would. Zoe, *Steve,* Mac, you, me—even Sean . . ." She dropped their names in like stones, hitting the palm of her hand with her fingers each time, and then she gestured around the room, and Kate shuddered, involuntarily, remembering Charly's letters, which she still had done nothing about. She took a deep breath and blinked, pushing it all away, down inside her, which is what she normally did.

"You heard from Mac lately?" Francesca said.

Kate started. "No. Mac? Why?"

"No, it wasn't him. Someone said they'd seen you. Perhaps it was him. Was it him?"

"I'm in New York," Kate said. "It can't have been me. He's—I haven't seen him for ages."

"Perhaps it was Betty who saw you," said Francesca.

"I saw her last week, before I left." Kate took a sip of her drink. "You must be thinking of her."

"Yep," said Francesca. "We're scattered all over the place now, all of us, aren't we." Her face clouded over, then she laughed. "Honestly. Look at us. Tell you what, let's stop being maudlin. You're back and it's wonderful to see you, babe. Tell me about New York and I'll tell you about my new bathroom. It's got heated floor tiles. If that doesn't cheer us up, nothing will."

"My God." Kate recovered herself. "You're living the dream."

"It's true," Francesca said. "I'm the only landlady in Clapham offering heated floor tiles."

"How's your flatmate?" Kate couldn't remember her name, a whey-faced girl Francesca had worked with.

"Sara? She moved in with her boyfriend, a couple of months ago. I had to get someone else. Oh my God, I forgot to tell you, Kate darling—at the moment I'm lucky because I've got—oh yes? Hello. Thanks, another bottle."

Kate nodded fervently in agreement as the waiter moved away.

"Where was I? Yes. Let's play Who Would You Do?" Francesca said. "It's been far too long." She shook out her hair decisively. "God, this is nice."

"Who Would You Do?" Kate asked.

"Him," said Francesca, nodding at the man next to them, who was extremely short, with thinning, all-over sparse black hair, who was grunting slightly as he worked his way through an elaborate cocktail.

"You wish," Kate said.

"He's your boyfriend."

"He's *yours*."

"How about you?"

"Who Would I Do . . . ?" Kate mused. She looked around surreptitiously. "Him. Actually, seriously, I would."

They swiveled round together, again incurring the curious stares of their fellow drinkers. There, in the doorway, was an actually remarkably good-looking man, bulky, tall, something of a rugby player about him, close-cropped curly dark brown hair, an open, handsome face. He was looking around the room and smiled at them briefly, before being claimed by a rather cross-looking, short girl who leaped up and waved, her fingers wiggling in the air.

"Dom! Dom! Over here! *Dom!*"

Kate and Francesca looked back at each other, chastened.

"All right, calm down," Francesca muttered crossly. "Don't get your knickers in a twist, dear. Ah, second bottle. Right, my turn."

"Who Would You Do?"

"Him," said Francesca, pointing again at the gorgeous Dom, and both of them collapsed in laughter.

Seventeen

*A*fter the second bottle of champagne, everything was a bit of a blur. In the file Kate kept in her brain called Things I Must Remember When Sober (a file that is neurologically impossible to access, unfortunately), she filed the fact that Francesca paid the bill, insisting she should, and the fact that she thought the waiters probably hated them both as they got more and more helplessly giggly. And the fact that it was great to be out, to be back, to see Francesca, to laugh and have a drink and gossip and talk about things: important things, silly things—just talk. That, she remembered, though the particulars of their conversation weren't so clear.

She didn't, however, remember the following things:

What else they talked about
What time they left.
How they got home

The next day, she thought wearily that the difference between New York and London was that in New York it was impossible to get anyone to behave like that, whereas in London it was impossible to meet a friend like Francesca for "a" drink and not get knee-walking, eyeball-bleedingly drunk. It *should* be possible, it just never was.

She remembered that they decided to go back to Francesca's, because Kate wanted to see the heated bathroom tiles, suddenly she was desperate to see them. This she remembered. She also remembered:

> Francesca's front path had black and white tiles leading up to
>   the front door.
> They stopped at a cash machine on the way back. It was
>   blue.
> She asked Francesca if she knew how she could find out where
>   Charly was now. Where she was living.

But she couldn't remember the answer.

So the next morning, Kate woke up, and she was chewing her own hair, and it was half strangling her, half choking her. Her mouth felt like she'd been using it to store vinegar. She rolled around in bed, her mind a total blank, trying to remember where she was, what she'd done the night before. For a brief, hangover-induced moment, she thought with panic that her mind must have been wiped during the night, like a broken iPod. She looked up, around her, at the pale, ascetic walls, at the bare trees with buds outside, and then she looked at the wall next to her. There was a photo, and she recognized herself, Zoe, Betty, and Francesca, all in fancy dress, the night of Zoe's housewarming party all those years ago. Her arms were slung around Zoe's and Betty's, she was bent double, laughing at something Betty was saying, pulling the others down with her in hysterics . . .

Kate blinked and stared at the photo again. Yes, that was it. She was here, at Francesca's, in her room, wearing a strange small T-shirt and some baggy boys' boxers—but where was Francesca?

Downstairs, someone was moving about in the kitchen, and Kate rubbed her eyes. She felt dreadful. She swung her legs out of bed and picked up a dressing gown hanging on the back of the wooden door. She raked her hands through her hair, clutching her scalp as she did. It felt warm. Was her blood actually boiling through the amount of alcohol in her brain? Was that it? Kate stumbled downstairs, holding her head, her hair.

"God, I feel awful," she said to the figure rustling the paper loudly, too loudly.

The figure looked up.

It wasn't Francesca.

"Mac?" Kate whispered.

"Kate."

Mac was looking up at her from his paper, his eyes locked on hers. He didn't move. He looked as if he'd seen a ghost.

"What are you doing here?" Kate said softly.

"I live here," he said. His jaw tightened; he opened his mouth to say something, then shut it. His voice was deadly quiet. "I might ask you what *you're* doing here."

"You don't live here," Kate said, confused. Her champagne-scrambled brain was turning over in itself, desperately trying to remember what Francesca had said last night.

"Sara? She moved in with her boyfriend, a couple of months ago. I had to get someone else. Oh my God, I forgot to tell you, Kate darling—at the moment I'm lucky because I've got . . . Thanks, another bottle."

He hadn't forgiven her for what she'd done. Had he? Kate forced herself to look at him. She looked at his hands first, how one of them was clutching the side of the paper so hard it was in a fist, the paper crumpling around it, like a rosette, and he threw it on the table and stood up. He was tall, she always forgot how tall. She took a step toward him, not allowing herself to look at him. The two of them stood there in silence. Memories of the last time she'd seen him came flooding back to her—but she pushed them away. No, she didn't let herself think of it anymore.

Vaguely, somewhere else in her head, Kate heard the sound of the shower, in another corner of the house. It brought her to her senses, and she finally looked straight up at Mac, and it was then that she felt it. She was almost felled by the venom in his eyes, the anger, the disgust that he felt for her. Kate backed away, quailing under the force of his stare.

"I do live here," he said. "Temporarily. I'm looking for a place." He collected himself, as if he didn't want to give too much away to her. "Anyway. Why the hell are you here?"

She couldn't think of an adequate reply. "I didn't realize you lived here. I was out with Francesca last night. Sorry . . ."

"Fine." He looked out of the window, collected himself for a moment. "Francesca's in the shower. Do you want some tea?"

"Oh, yes, that'd be—"

"Kettle's just boiled," he said, and went back to the paper.

"Thank—thanks," Kate said, and she went forward timidly to the kettle. Her head was pounding, and her heart was beating. Ghosts everywhere, she thought. Can't escape them. She looked up at the clock. It was eight o'clock. She'd told Mr. Allan she'd be with him at nine.

"Shit," she said.

Mac ignored her.

"I've got to go," Kate said, retreating back up the stairs to the sitting room. "Something's—I'm supposed to be somewhere."

"Sure you are," he said, looking up at her briefly. His tone was careless, almost conversational. "You'd better be off. You're good at that, aren't you? Running off."

Kate felt something inside her release, with a ping.

"I didn't mean to," she said, turning toward him, all fear gone.

"What?" he said, surprised. His head jerked up and she noticed the gray hairs at the sides of his head, at his temples.

"It wasn't my fault, Mac." She was calm. "I mean, it was my fault, but—I've paid for it. I know you hate me. I know I screwed up." She cleared her throat.

"What are you talking about?" he said.

Kate stared at him, almost with exasperation. "Mac! You know what I'm—"

"No, I don't," he said, his voice almost vicious. "You see, Kate, you've screwed my life up not just once but—yeah, actually, a couple of times. In every way. So when you troop in here and say you're oh so sorry, I'm not sure for which of the several ways you've managed to ruin things you're apologizing."

She tried to swallow, but she couldn't. "Listen to me. I didn't mean . . ." she began, but he started laughing.

"Oh, that's a big consolation to me," said Mac, still holding on to the newspaper. His eyes were cold, cold green and unflinching. "You didn't mean to. Wow. Is that supposed to make everything better? Look, Kate, just forget it. I don't want to have this discussion with you. OK?"

"It's not OK," said Kate. "You—me—we . . . that . . . everything that happened." She pulled the paper swiftly out of his hands. It sliced one of his fingers, such was the speed with which she did it. Mac breathed in sharply and stood up. He moved toward her, and Kate actually thought for one moment he was going to hit her. "Everything that happened," she said, walking toward him. Fight it. Fight fear with fear, she told herself, dragging up some strength from she didn't know where, suddenly conscious of her dressing gown, her shorts, her skimpy top. They stood facing each other, the tension almost palpable.

"I'm never going to not think it was your fault," he said simply. He pressed his finger to his other palm; she saw blood where she had cut him. "That's all. It was you, Kate. After everything that happened, we could have made it better, you and me." For a brief second she saw tenderness in his eyes, and she knew he remembered it the way she did, and it hurt her so much more than she'd thought it could. "But you went and broke it all over again. And that's why I'll never, ever not think it was your fault."

She hit the side of a cabinet, her bones smacking hard into the wood. She winced, and he fractionally winced with her.

"You don't know what you're talking about—"

Mac ignored her, carried on as if she hadn't spoken.

"You ran away *again*," he said, exasperation on his lean, tired face. She thought how much older he was looking. "God. God!" He half turned away. "You never even wrote."

"I did write, Mac, I did," she said, justifying herself, and it sounded so weak.

He waved it away and turned to her, his eyes so full of pain she could hardly bear it. "My God! It's like a nightmare. All of this is a nightmare, and it's because of—"

Francesca appeared at the top of the stairs leading down to the kitchen. "Ah," she said casually, doing up the buttons on her black city jacket. "Morning—Kate. I'm hideously late. Gosh, you look awful."

"Francesca—" said Kate, but Francesca carried on, saying, "Look at this nice surprise, eh? I meant to warn you who my—"

"She's going, anyway, don't worry." Mac flicked his fingers dismissively at Kate. "She's got things to do." He took a deep breath and winced, and then he turned back to his paper.

That was when Kate snapped, backing away from him, sudden tears sprouting and streaming down her face.

"Why don't you understand?" she screamed. "Do you think it was easy for me? Mac, there was *nothing else I could do*!"

Running up the stairs, pushing past an astonished Francesca, she fell into the bedroom and pulled on last night's clothes. Barely a minute later, she ran down the stairs again. Francesca was standing in the hallway.

"What on earth's going on?" she said.

"I've got to—" Kate sobbed, her eyes puffy. She wiped her nose. "I'm going, please don't—sorry, darling."

"You and Mac?" said Francesca, her brow furrowed. "Wowsers. I always wondered. When did—"

Mac appeared in the corridor, his bulk blocking the light from the kitchen. He touched Francesca lightly on the arm, his eyes never straying from Kate's face.

"Let her go," he said bleakly. "Please, Francesca."

"Just wait, Kate, I'll walk to the—"

"No, no," said Kate, breathing in and trying to smile like it was all OK. "I'm late, I really am, I have to go—"

And she ran out into the street, pulling the door shut in Francesca's and Mac's face. It slammed loudly behind her. It was cold and gray outside, the sky a uniform blanket of cloud. Ghosts. The ghosts in London were everywhere.

Eighteen

Kate blinked back fatigue and a hangover. The Allans' sitting room was hot and crowded, and with the exertions of the morning—getting back from Clapham, running around trying to get everything ready by the time the mourners returned from the crematorium, chatting, pouring drinks, soothing, handing things around—she hadn't stopped rushing and moving since she'd left Francesca's, four hours before, and now she was ready to drop, heartsick, champagne soaked, and miserable. Especially after she'd seen darling Mr. Allan enter the room from the crematorium, pulling his black trilby off his head, pushing his fluffy white hair back from his face, which was crumpled with grief. Pain—screaming, horrible pain—was etched into every line, it filled his eyes, and he suddenly looked much, much older than Kate had ever realized him to be. He had smiled at her, just a little smile, and said, "Dear Kate. Ah. Here we are back again, then."

She'd poured him a glass of wine as his family started streaming through the door, followed by the Allans' friends, his old jazz buddies, creaky-looking musicians in checked shirts and cords, neighbors from the building—Kate realized with a start how few people she'd ever known here, how she and Sean had never really bothered to get to know anyone apart from the Allans.

Now, an hour later, the room was full, stuffy, and throbbing slowly with the buzz of good conversation and emotion hanging over the assembled throng. Kate was feeling worse and worse. Why had she put on a woolly top? She swayed slightly, trying to focus on those around her, and turned to find a serious, rather elongated man staring at her. She blinked and looked again. She knew him—how did she know him?

"Ow!" Fred Michaels, singer with the Chappell Quartet and Mr. Allan's oldest pal, was wailing in the kitchen. "Oh! Look, I think my finger's burned"

"Oh, Mr. M, I'm sorry," Kate cried, squeezing past the throng and rushing into the kitchen. "You should use *oven gloves*," she said loudly to him.

"I'm not bloody deaf," said Fred Michaels. "Keep your voice down. It's a wake for the deceased, not an Iron Maiden concert," he added as the old man next to him sniggered.

"Good one, Fred," he said.

"Thanks, Frank," Fred replied. "Ho-ho."

"Leave her alone," said Mr. Allan, coming into the kitchen. He put his arm around Kate. "She's doing a brilliant job, absolutely brilliant."

"Er, thanks," said Kate. She tugged her straggly ponytail tighter, rather distractedly.

"Where are the plastic cups?" Mr. Allan said.

Kate handed them to him. "Are you OK?" she said.

"No. But I will be," Mr. Allan said. He blew air out of his cheeks in a low, whistling sound. "Oh. My sister's just asked me to go on holiday with her."

"She mentioned it to me," said Kate, nonchalantly flicking at the kitchen surface with a tea towel. "So—are you going to go, do you think?"

He waved his hand toward the window, where it was gray outside. "Think I might, you know. Just for a couple of weeks. The only question is," he said, his arm tightening around her, "are *you* going to be OK without *me*?"

She could feel his comforting, bony arm around her, his fingers pressing into her shoulder, and the kindness of the gesture took her by surprise.

"Well," Kate said, looking at the ground so he couldn't see how close to tears she was, "If that's your only question, then you should definitely go, don't you think?"

"Hm. Maybe." He kissed the top of her head. "Thanks, sweetheart." He nodded, and then poked Fred. "Are you ready to do some singing?"

Fred nodded. "Absolutely."

Frank said, "I'll just go and get the sax."

"Sh, please," Fred said, five minutes later, and the crowd that was packed into the room became silent, and the only noise was the faint roar of traffic from outside the open windows.

"This is for Eileen," he continued. "Gram, do you want to say anything?"

But Mr. Allan simply shook his head.

"I want to say," said Fred, and his voice was very quiet, so that Kate had to strain to hear, "I want to say that I was there when they met, I was there by their side when they got married, I was there to see them through years of happiness together, and, Gram"—he turned to his friend, who had his head bowed, holding his trumpet lightly to his chest—"I'm glad we're all here now with you. Here's to Eileen. This is her favorite song. This was her favorite song."

He nodded to the rest of the group. Kate leaned against the kitchen door, her hands in the pockets of her apron, resting her tired head against the wooden frame, and he started to sing quietly "That's All."

When Kate went back downstairs at about six o'clock, her face was swollen and aching with the effort of not crying, of smiling kindly, of soothing, patting arms, clearing up. Suddenly her sitting room looked huge with just her in it, where his had been packed to the rafters with people, friends and ghosts, and memories. Here all was white and safe and clean and it was different, weird. She looked around the room, undoing her apron tiredly. She sniffed loudly.

"Hello?" came a voice from nearby and Kate jumped. The voice was from the other side of her front door.

"Hello?" it said again. "Kate, are you in there?"

It was a woman's voice. A woman's voice she knew.

"Hi. Kate?" said the voice again.

"Who is it?" she asked cautiously.

"Kate, it's Sue. Sue Jordan."

Sue Jordan—of course. How could she have forgotten. Kate flung the door open as fast as she could.

Sue's face broke into a smile at the sight of her, but she didn't move. She simply nodded.

"Here's the reason the circulation of my magazine's a disaster."

"Why?" Kate said, stepping forward and hugging her.

"Went downhill after my star girl left, didn't it?" Sue said, squeezing her briefly.

"I'm so sorry," Kate said.

"For what?"

It really was Sue Jordan was standing in front of her, like a package from the past. She hadn't changed much since the day she'd interviewed Kate for the job, eight years ago. She had a neat sandy bob, was dressed in a sensible gray suit, with a large, stiff black handbag over her shoulder. She had smile lines at the corners of her eyes; Kate had always noticed that because Sue never smiled at work—well, hardly ever. She used to think it must mean Sue smiled a lot at home.

Sue was smiling at Kate now. "You'd forgotten all about me, hadn't you," she said.

"No—" said Kate. "Of course not, it's just—"

"The context. I know," said Sue. "Completely out of context. I knocked on your door on Monday after we'd been to see Graham, but there was no answer."

"I must have been with Dad," said Kate. "Sorry."

"Don't be sorry, silly girl," said Sue, and she stepped forward, breaking an invisible wall of some kind, reached out and gave Kate a hug. Just a quick one, but a hug nonetheless, and the unexpected physical contact from her, from Sue, brought a lump to Kate's throat. "I'm sorry I didn't see you in there"—Sue jabbed a finger upward—"I was late, had to stay at the crematorium to sort a couple of things out. I could see you, talking to people, and handing that lovely food around, you are wonderful. But I kept missing you, and it was so crowded—I thought I'd do best to come down after it quieted down and catch you then."

"Come in, come in!" Kate said.

"I won't, actually," said Sue. "Alec's in the car with Graham, we're taking him out for a meal in town. At the French House. It was his and Eileen's favorite. His idea, you know."

"Aaah," Kate said. "Well—it was—"

"Kate." Sue stepped back and looked at her shrewdly. "You're back now, aren't you?"

"What?"

"For good, I mean. You *are* staying this time, aren't you?"

"No," Kate said, shaking her head. "Just a couple of weeks, till my father's better. I've got to get back to New York after that."

"Hm," said Sue. "So you're not interested in getting back into magazines, then."

"What?"

"Well, you remember Sophie?"

"Yes," said Kate. "Sophie, of course."

"Well, she was writing a column for *Venus* for me. 'Girl About Town.' 'Intrepid girl struggling through the concrete jungle,' kind of thing." Sophie was a hearty, walking-boots kind of person. "But she's just announced she's fallen in love with some bloody Moroccan geezer from Essaouira, and she's moving there to live on the beach and sell seashells, or something ridiculous."

"Sophie?" said Kate, pleased. How unexpected people's lives were, especially those you hadn't thought about for so long.

"Kate," said Sue. She cleared her throat and faced up to Kate. "Listen. Write me five hundred words. About what you love about London. Say you've just come back to live here." Her eyes shone. "That's even better. Girl returns to the Big Smoke after three years living in New York. Her impressions, all that. What she likes about London. Yes. And come in for a chat with me about it. Tomorrow. No, not tomorrow. Um, let me think. Tuesday." She rolled her eyes. "Look, I want you to do it."

"Her column?" Kate was being slow; her brain, she realized, was dehydrated, exhausted. She could follow Sue's ideas, but she was about a minute behind them; she'd forgotten how fast she thought.

"Yes. Her column. Like I say—" Sue repeated herself, slowly. "Write me five hundred words, email them over on Monday. It's a sign, all of this—" She waved her arms, briskly, and cleared her throat again. "I always thought you were the best. You are the best. I want you back, Kate."

Kate swallowed; the lump in her throat was giving way to a feeling of tightness in her chest. "But I've got a job," she said, smiling at her old boss politely. "Sue, that's—wow, that's amazing, but I've got a job."

She hoped this would knock it on the head. But Sue fixed her gaze on her and plunged her tongue into her cheek. There was silence between them.

"No you haven't," Sue said eventually. "I don't know what you're doing over there, but don't call it a job."

"Actually it's—"

"You're the assistant, Kate."

It had been a long day—a longer night and day. Kate hugged the doorframe, tapping the wood with her fingers. "What's wrong with being an assistant, Sue! That's a dreadful thing to say!"

A car horn sounded outside. Sue wrapped her scarf around her neck. "Look," she said. "You're my girl. You've been my girl since you were that baby giraffe with long legs and big brown eyes looking terrified at your interview, what was it—eight years ago? Now, I know what happened to you was shit, it was awful, and it must be awful being back here. But you belong here, Kate. You just have to get used to it. Can't you see that?"

"I don't belong here," Kate said. "And I certainly don't belong in magazines."

"That is the biggest rubbish of all," said Sue. "Look at you—your life is straight out of a magazine! You've got enough material from your life to be still writing copy fifty years from now! Don't you understand, Kate, every girl is basically like you. Every *Venus* reader, especially."

Kate laughed. "I bloody well hope not, for their sakes."

"Not that." Sue shook her head, impatient that Kate didn't get it. "They all think they're useless, or they've screwed their life up, or their relationship with their parents is awful, when are they going to have children, they don't know what they want to do with their lives. They should have married X. They let Y get away. They don't have enough money for Z. We're all the same, you know, it's just different versions of being the same." She looked Kate up and down. "Except you've always been skinny. I kind of hate you for that." She buttoned up her coat. "Right. You'll have a go at it, then?"

"Yes," said Kate. "Yes, I will. I'll email it on Monday." Her eyes were shining. "Thanks, Sue."

"Thank me next week, Dollface," came the reply. "Now I'm going. But thanks for today, you're a star."

Kate shut the door behind her and, irresistibly, started to

laugh. She didn't know why, but she couldn't stop. And then she stopped laughing and stood up to her full height, thoughtfully. Squaring her shoulders, she went into her bedroom to unearth her old stack of *Venus* copies. They were there, underneath her beloved telescope, fifteen or so of them, and at the top, the first issue, with its classic, fifties-style type, its pretty and stylish shades, the girl on the front running to catch a bus on Piccadilly, wearing TopShop's newest spring bell-shaped raincoat in apple green linen. She had loved that cover, loved everything about what they were trying to do. Kate gingerly moved the telescope out of the way and crouched down, thumbing through the slippery, shiny covers, marveling at them, what *Venus* represented to her. Where had that Kate gone?

Nineteen

May 2003

"*B*ut I mean, come on, he's *gorgeous*!" said Juliet, the fashion editor, stroking the silk on a top she'd brought in to show the meeting that polka dots were on their way back in. "He's like an older Marco Pierre White. Except not mad. God, I love him."

"Did you see him comforting that shit flute player girl from Italy last night?" said Jo, the art director.

"I know!"

"Who is he?" said Sue Jordan, and Priscilla, the supersucky news editor and deputy editor said immediately, "Daniel Miller. He's on that TV show *Maestro!* It's like *Popstars.* He's gorgeous, Sue."

"Daniel Miller?" said Sue. From her lofty position at the head of the table she called down to Kate. "Hold on. Let me just ask our lovely new features editor something—Kate, isn't he your father?"

Kate, who had been staring out of the great glass windows, looking out down the South Bank, across the river, during this conversation, turned back toward the group. She smoothed a fleck of imaginary dust off her gray Joseph suit, her most expensive clothing purchase ever.

"Um, yes." She scratched her head with a pencil and hummed nonchalantly. "I suppose he is."

"What?" said Tom Price, the publisher of the magazine. "Daniel Miller's your father? My God!"

"Are you shitting me?" said Juliet. "Kate Miller. Daniel Miller. Oh my God!"

"Wow!" said Priscilla, trying and failing to look pleased for Kate at her genetic heritage, which had given her these inadvertent brownie points.

"He's your *dad,* man?" said Nicola, the deputy features editor. "Why didn't you *say* so!?"

Kate thought back to eighteen months ago, before the show had been commissioned, and how close Daniel had come to having to sell his house and move into a flat in Acton. "It didn't exactly come up."

"Why doesn't he like being sent chocolates?" Nicola demanded. "There was an interview with him in *Good Housekeeping* and he said he hated being sent chocolates. That's so weird! But sexy of him!"

"He's diabetic," said Kate in quelling tones. "He can't eat sugar. It's really bad for him. People are always sending him presents after recitals and so forth. Right. Shall we move on?"

And so forth? When was the last time she'd said "and so forth"?

"Wow," said Priscilla. She drummed her square nails loudly on the glass surface. "This is great, Kate. Can you get us an interview with him? And tell him not to go with anyone else? Oh my God!" Her eyes lit up. "He's divorced, isn't he? I read it in *Hello!* last week," she told the assembled faces around the table, who were gaping with interest. "His wife ran off with someone. Isn't that true?"

"She's my mum, Priscilla," Kate said sharply. "And she didn't *run off* with someone. She—" She was extremely thankful when Nicola interrupted.

"Well, I know he was devastated! Is he looking for love? Perhaps that's the angle! We could fix him up with someone!"

"Hm," "Mmm," "Ooh, that's a good idea," various people

murmured, not without bitterness, as if Kate had organized all of this merely to advance her career.

Kate clutched her big square notebook, hugging it to her. It was quite funny, really, to think how the fortunes of the Miller family ebbed and flowed, resulting in this completely ridiculous conversation. She was almost laughing; she wished Charly or Zoe was here to hear it. Sean wouldn't get it, she thought to herself, bless him. He'd be outraged on all their behalfs. "Right," she said, feeling sympathy for the very first time with celebrities who complain about how misrepresented they are. "First, that's my mother you're talking about, and she didn't run off with someone else. She left Dad because it wasn't working."

"Why?" said Priscilla, fascinated.

"Oh." Kate was flummoxed. "Well, I don't know why, actually. It just wasn't working." They looked at her blankly. "I was fourteen," she offered. She didn't say, "It was my birthday, and I didn't see her for over a year afterward."

"Mmm."

"Plus, it was thirteen years ago," Kate pointed out. "It's long-passed water under the bridge. They're the best of friends now."

Since last week her father had referred to her mother's request for him to send her their wedding album (she'd just got into scrapbooking) as "another demand from Satan's minion" and then roared loudly, "*God!* I hate her!" this was not at all true, but for now, here at this meeting, it would have to suffice, because she certainly wasn't going to go into the whole long drama with them. It made Wagner look a bit thin on plot.

"And what about your poor dad?" Juliet's eyes were like saucers. "That's sad for him, though. Is he still on his own?"

Kate thought of the sopranos, the violin students, and fans who'd littered his bedroom and the rest of the house after Venetia left, whom Kate had had to fight past on her way to school in the morning. It was like running the gauntlet every day—one never knew if Natalia from Moscow or Briony from Colorado might be trying to be domestic in the kitchen, making coffee for their hero, and catch her on the way out, plying her with insincere compliments, pumping her for information, how best to snare her father. Kate had to be polite to them, but it made her uncomfortable. She much preferred the constant stream of good friends, old compadres, who filled the house, always had done, flooding it with music and laughter and expensive red wine, late into the night. The question was ridiculous, in any case. Her father, on his own! It was almost laughable.

Then she thought of his life after he'd met Lisa, how all of that had gone, how her home, the spindly house in Kentish Town, had been sold, how order and beige colors had entered his life. Someone had written of Daniel Miller in the *Observer* a couple of weeks ago that he was a marketing exercise now, not a musician, and Kate couldn't help but agree, secretly. It had taken Lisa six months to move in, a couple of months after that to get pregnant, ten months to get her old friends from GMTV, where she'd worked, to meet him, and a year later he was back in the studio, recording *Daniel Miller Plays Glenn Miller*. And now he could afford a wedding where his wife wore Temperley couture and the guests were each given a small silver violin charm engraved with Lisa's and Daniel's initials and the date as a memento. Kate shook her head.

"He's not on his own, no," she told the assembled meeting. She coughed. "It's his second wedding tomorrow, actually."

There was astonishment around the table. This was news. "Wow," said Tom, still unnaturally fascinated. "Is someone taking the photos? Have they got a magazine deal?"

"No," said Kate, holding her pencil. "At least, I really, really hope not. Otherwise I'll have to wear a yashmak."

"Don't you mean a burqa?" asked Priscilla, faux-kindly.

"No." Kate put her pencil back down on the table.

"Sure you do, Kate."

"A burqa's a whole garment thing. A yashmak is just a veil, er—it's mainly worn by Muslim women, usually Turkish," Kate heard herself say, and then she groaned inwardly.

"How *do* you know this stuff!" Priscilla trilled. "You're like a fat old man in a pub quiz! Oh, Kate. You are funny."

"What, because she knows something beyond how much weight the Spice Girls have lost this week?" said Juliet unexpectedly, and Kate looked at her in surprise and smiled.

"Right, right." Sue patted the glass desk with a gesture of finality. She nodded kindly at Kate. "That's all for now, then," she said. "Let's meet on Monday as usual and, Kate—enjoy the wedding."

As Kate gathered up her things—her Filofax, her ideas book, the latest issues of the magazine—Sue followed her out, toward her office.

"You OK about tomorrow?" she said as Kate reached her desk. "Just wondering."

Sue was not given to sentiment or overt displays of affection, and Kate turned back to look at her, smiling with gratitude. She was features editor only because of Sue, and it was the most unimaginable, thrilling, exciting thing.

After the weeks and weeks of interviews and the secrecy surrounding the whole thing, she had finally left *Your World!* to be deputy features editor in time for the launch of *Venus* in early 2002. But the original features editor, Alice—who was more of the fashionista school and believed in claiming every single cab, and once even her own husband's birthday dinner, as business expenses—had not lasted until the launch, and so, just before Christmas, Kate had been promoted to features editor.

Thinking of this now, Kate lightly patted Sue's arm—the two of them were rare in the *Venus* offices for not going in for displays of affection. There was a lot of surplus air-kissing; Sue didn't like it much. Nor did she like anorexic models; hugely expensive photo shoots in Miami to get a shot of a model against a white wall; overpaid, irrelevant columnists; or fashion itself, really. It was why Broadgate had hired her to head up the magazine. They wanted someone with a fresh eye, someone who could keep costs down, and someone who could assemble a team of young people who *did* know all of that.

"It's going to be great," she told Sue. "It's not like I can't wait and it's the best day of my life, but, you know . . . I'm really happy for Dad. Lisa's turned his life around."

"I'm so glad," Sue said. She looked around Kate's small glass office. "It must be weird, that's all."

"Yeah, it is a bit." Kate was honest with Sue. "But Sean's coming. And Zoe and Steve—our best friends, you know. They got married last year—you remember you got that wedding company to provide the free sugared almonds?"

"Little Zoe, with the black hair." Sue was pleased. "Ah, lovely. How is she?"

"She's very well," said Kate. "She's pregnant, in fact, so she's really well."

"Well, it'll be good for you to have a gang of your own there."

"And Charly's coming," Kate added, mischievously.

Sue looked mock-horrified. "Right. A gang, indeed."

"She's wearing black, and she told my mother on the phone last night that she'd scream 'No!' during the speeches if she wants her to."

Sue genuinely looked horrified this time. "Oh dear God, she is something, isn't she. What did your poor mother say?"

"History doesn't relate," said Kate, laughing. "But I expect, knowing Mum, she'd love it if it were all about her instead."

She could tell Sue didn't know whether to laugh or not at this, and Sue waved good-bye and scurried, relieved, back to her own office. Kate turned back to her desk and picked up the phone. Sean was staying at hers tonight before the wedding, and she wanted to make sure he'd remember to bring everything. He hated staying over, much preferred it if she came to his, and would doubtless forget something. On her desk were the layouts for the next issue's quiz: "Who's in Charge of Your Relationship? You or Him?"

"Hah," said Kate, putting her heels up on the desk as Sean's phone rang. She swung herself around a little so she could see out of the window again, and caught her reflection. That was her, that girl in the gray suit with the smooth hair and the office. How weird. She sighed with something like happiness waiting for Sean to pick up the phone and gazed out across the river. The spring view of the city from her office window really was lovely.

Twenty

*T*he next morning, the day of the wedding, Kate climbed back into bed, handed Sean a cup of tea, and said happily, "It's going to be a lovely day. Not a cloud in the sky; it's already warm and it's not even eight!"

"So why are we awake, then?" Sean grumbled, putting his mug of tea on the side table, turning over, and pulling the duvet over his head.

Kate sat up in bed and sipped cautiously, testing the heat of the tea, letting her cold feet warm up a little under the duvet. She hooked a foot over Sean's leg and took another gulp of tea.

"Aah," she heard herself say, as if she were sixty and not twenty-seven. "Ah."

There was silence.

"Sean, is your shirt ironed?" she said, tentatively.

"Yes," Sean rumbled, deep underneath the duvet.

"Because I could always just run over it again with the iron."

"It's ironed," Sean said. "Shh."

Kate wanted everything on her side to be perfect. She was Daniel's daughter, it was up to her to keep the Miller family end up. She didn't want people looking at her and smiling, whispering to each other: "His daughter, the one who had the mullet and was obsessed with Sylvia Plath—she really did turn out rather strangely, didn't she?" No, she wanted her father, all his many friends and colleagues, and all of Lisa's family to be proud of her. Briefly the thought crossed her mind: What if she'd had to go on her own, single, or go just with Charly, Zoe, and Steve. What if she didn't have Sean? Truly horrible to have to go alone to that, your father's glamorous second wedding to the mother of his new child. Thank God for Sean, she thought again, and she put down her mug and snuggled down next to him.

"Sorry," she whispered, pulling the duvet up and around her. "I'll let you sleep." She was tired, too; her new job was exhausting, juggling it with everything else. She put her arm around Sean, but he was snoring lightly, and even though she wanted to sleep again, too, she couldn't. Instead Kate lay there for another hour, blinking, staring up at the ceiling from underneath the duvet, thinking.

After a while she started to hear strange noises—banging, clattering, furious muttering—coming from the sitting room and the kitchen, and she winced every time one was particularly loud, not wanting it to wake Sean. The noises grew louder and louder as the hour wore on. Charly was up, and getting ready. It was a big operation, requiring a lot of noise, and a lot of equipment, at the end of which (Kate always thought but never said out loud) Charly looked *exactly* the same, only more terrifying, and less sweet-faced than she looked when she was in her pajamas, wolfing down toast, and swearing at the TV, or in hysterics over a video, or lounging around chatting on the phone. That was when Charly was at her most beautiful, Kate had come to see, but Charly had no idea.

There was a loud bang and a muffled, expletive-laden rant began.

"What's that?" said Sean, blearily, turning toward Kate. She pushed herself against him, hoping he'd pull her into his big, warm morning embrace, but his arms were crossed on his chest and he was still half asleep.

"Only Charly, sorry," said Kate. "She's so noisy. Don't worry. You should be getting up soon, though."

"She's doing it deliberately, stupid cow," Sean said. He rubbed his face. "Blaghh." And with that he dozed off again, and Kate sighed. Of course she wasn't. Probably. . . .

Because Charly couldn't stand Sean. Kate tried her best, but it was too much like hard work after a while, too awkward.

"I just don't get you," Kate said to Charly later that morning, after Sean had gone out to pick up Zoe and Steve, and the two flatmates were left to get ready. Anticipation and irritation made Kate bolder with her than she would normally have been. "Do you really think he's that awful?"

Charly was sprawled out on the sofa, which was covered with an old batik cloth. She was dressed from head to toe in black, even black boots. It was the height of summer. Her long, tousled caramel-colored hair hung over the arm of the sofa. Kate looked at her in the mirror as she was drying her hair. Charly's perfect tilted nose wrinkled.

"Look, Kate, darling," she said, in her husky Cockney voice. "I know he's not the devil. Or a kiddie fiddler. OK? I just don't like him. Got it? I don't bloody have to, do I ?"

She lit another cigarette and ran her fingers through her hair.

"But why?" Kate said in a small voice, holding the hair dryer in her hand.

"I just don't." She exhaled, and then turned to look at her. Her voice softened. "Look, darling. I'm sure he's fine. I just think . . . he's . . . well, he's such a *boy*." Her voice was contemptuous.

"A boy?" Kate said, thinking of how big Sean was, how he dwarfed everyone and everything, how small she felt when she was with him, in his arms. "Are you mad? He's the size of a house, for starters. He rowed for his college!"

"I'm sure, babe," Charly said. "But he's still a little boy." She paused and looked at Kate from under her lashes, obviously considering how far she could go, whether she'd already gone too far. "That's what I think, anyway."

"So you think he's a bit childish." Kate persisted, hoping that now she'd got her talking, she'd tell her more. "Has he pissed you off? Was it when he came as a baby to our fancy dress party?"

"Yeah, right," Charly said drily. "He pissed me off by dressing as a baby at our party. No, look, darling." She sat up on the sofa, blowing her bangs out of her eyes, and curled her long, coltish limbs up underneath her. "I'm just being a cow. I'm sure I'm just jealous or something. OK? He's nice, I'm very happy for you."

"He's nice," Kate repeated slowly.

"He's nice," Charly said again. "But I don't see you with him forever." She said slowly, "I'd have thought you'd be living together by now, and you're not, are you?"

"That's—" Kate fluffed out her hair. "We need to talk about it."

"Right," said Charly. "It's been over two years now, dollface. What's holding you back?"

"Shut up," said Kate, determined not to let Charly annoy her today. "I like being your flatmate too much, that's what's holding us back. He keeps begging me to, and I just can't face life without you."

"Oh, ha-ha," said Charly, waggling her legs in the air. She seemed more cheerful. "OK. I'll try with him, I promise. I hope you'll be buying some god-awful house in the suburbs sometime soon. Is that it?"

"OK," Kate said. She didn't want to say what she was thinking, which was that she kind of pitied Charly, actually, for simply not getting it. She didn't know how to explain it to her. But Charly's glare told her the discussion was over, and Kate kind of loved her for admitting she was a cow, that she was jealous. Perhaps, after all, that was all it was.

The doorbell buzzed. Charly swung her legs onto the ground

and stood up. "Come on, Katy," she said, throwing her arms around her. She took the hairbrush out of her frenzied grip. "Your hair's fine. Let's go, OK? We're going to be late for Mr. Lover Man. I promise I'll be nice. Why would I spoil the Millers' big day, eh? It's going to be great."

Kate wasn't so sure. Not long after she had arrived at Holland Park, Kate realized her father's wedding wasn't so much a celebration of the sanctity of marriage as an excellent networking opportunity for all of her dad's acquaintances and the spurious semicelebrities he'd met now that Lisa was by his side, managing his second climb up the slippery slope of fame. From the moment they arrived at The Orangery, the restaurant where the reception was being held, and got out of the car, Kate was assailed by old friends of her father's looking for other old friends of his.

"Kate, darling! Where's Boris, have you seen him?"

"Hello, Kate! How are you, dear? Have you seen Elizabeth?"

"Do you know if it's true she's moved to the BBC?"

"I hear Michael Ball's coming, is that true?"

"Woo," said Charly as they tramped across the still-soft grass in the blazing April sunshine. "Michael Ball, how will I contain myself."

"This is hilarious," said Steve, who had his arm around Zoe. "Kate, all these years of me thinking you were the world's squarest girl and now look at you. You're the daughter of a celeb. You're going to be in *OK!* talking about your boob job soon if you're not careful."

"She's not square," Sean said, loyally defensive. "She's gorgeous."

"You are a bit square," said Zoe, not unkindly.

"Thanks, oldest friend," said Kate. "That's nice."

Zoe smiled at her. "I didn't mean it. You know what I mean." Kate looked down at her friend, tidy and chic in a green dress that made her bump look, for the first time, pretty significant. Zoe smoothed her hair behind her ears.

"Where did that come from?" said Kate, pointing to her stomach.

"I know," said Steve, turning his hands palm outward, as if in total amazement. "Seriously, last week her stomach was almost entirely flat, and now—look at it!" He stroked his wife's bump. "I think it's a boy."

Anything Steve told you was always pretty unreliable; they all laughed. "I'm sure it's a girl," said Zoe.

"Me too," said Kate. Sean shifted his weight from one leg to the next.

"I do too," said Charly. She lifted her hair with one hand and threw it carelessly behind her back, as if it were a separate entity. "You're carrying quite low. That's what that means." Kate looked at her quizzically. "Yes, I do know what I'm talking about," Charly snapped. "OK?"

There was a pause; they all nodded, as guests drifted by. Steve clapped his hands together. "Anyway! So, Kate's really square. I remember, the first time I met Kate in our college bar, and—"

"This story is complete rubbish," said Kate crossly. "You always tell it and it's rubbish! I never said that!"

"She told me that she was only going to stay for one drink, because she had to go back to her room and rearrange her cassette collection," Steve finished triumphantly, smiling fondly at Kate. He rubbed his face with delight, his green eyes flashing mischievously, and Kate shook her head at him.

"God, you look just like—" she began, and then stopped, quickly.

"Who?" Steve said. He was looking at Zoe, his hand still protectively on her stomach, as someone pushed slightly against them.

"No one," said Kate. Sean nudged her.

"Go on, who?" he said, curious.

"Nothing," said Kate. She noticed Charly, opening her mouth and shutting it, and felt desperate gratitude. "Anyway. I deny that story ever happened, and, Charly, I certainly don't need any input from you on this."

Charly nodded. "Yeah," she said, smiling at Steve. "Do you know we won the intercompany pub quiz two years in a row when Kate was on our team? There was this question about some totally obscure medieval poet or something, and no one had ever even *heard* of him, but Kate knew when he'd died!"

"George Herbert was Elizabethan," Kate said. "And he isn't obscure."

"Oh my God," said Charly as Zoe and Steve laughed. Sean came to her defense.

"Hey," he said crossly, not quite looking at Charly. "Don't be mean. I don't have a square girlfriend."

"Hello, hello, hello!" came a ringing voice from behind them. "Well, what's all this!" Daniel appeared between Sean and Charly. He slapped Sean on the back. "Welcome, welcome!" he cried cheerily. Several people turned toward him and smiled.

"Hello, Daniel," Charly said politely, kissing him. "Congratulations."

"Ah, thank you, Charly," said Daniel appreciatively, running his eyes over Charly's sexy black form. Kate rolled her eyes. "How's my beautiful girl?" He kissed Kate.

"Dad," she said, kissing him back. "Bless you. What a lovely day."

Through the great glass windows of the restaurant, the sun poured in as the guests spilled out onto the lawns and manicured gardens nearby. Around her, men in linen suits and women in little jackets, their best chiffon, and high heels chattered, laughed, drank—it was like something out of a lifestyle magazine, Kate thought; she could have used all of it in the magazine, no models required. Most of the people here were perfectly coiffed. And if they weren't, they looked "distinguished," like they could get away with it.

Sean shook Daniel's hand and Daniel slapped his back smartly and slipped into his wedding patter.

"Ah, Mr. Lambert. Sean! Good man. Good to see you, thanks for coming."

"Thank *you*, Mr. Miller," Sean said, slapping his hand in a bearlike grasp.

"Sean, I've told you before. It's Daniel."

"Of course, Daniel," Sean said, smiling. "Sir." He slid his arm around Kate's waist, and she caught his hand in hers. Daniel watched them.

"So proud of you, darling," he said, with a catch in his throat, and Kate thought how far they'd come, and what he might be thinking of on this day, and she kissed him again.

"I'm proud of *you*, Dad, darling," she said.

Kate watched Daniel, smiling at someone over her shoulder. His thick, graying dark hair was swept back like a lion's mane, his great hulking body tailored and tucked in a navy blue suit, immaculately cut, with a pink silk tie and pink rose buttonhole. He looked exactly how Kate knew he'd want to: sleek, sophisticated, attractive, young for his age—nothing like the poor little Polish boy who'd arrived here after the war, who frequently went without shoes (or so he claimed), who changed his name to escape persecution from his peers at school. Kate watched him with pride, trying to feel happy for him on this day.

After the ceremony, and as the day wore on, Kate realized she was having fun, and she blessed Lisa, for once, for her thoughtfulness in letting her bring some of her own friends. There was one cloud on the horizon, though: that afternoon, a few drinks down, Charly really did make an effort to talk to Sean, but Kate could tell it was a lost cause. Kate realized, as she watched the two of them inside The Orangery, that the reason she didn't like him was simple—Sean didn't like her. And Charly was used to everyone liking her, especially men. She fought them like a cat, treated them like dirt—but they still wanted her. Kate was used to seeing men's eyes light up when they saw them together, and it was never because of her. Charly's pert little breasts, her tousled hair, her snub nose, her look of disdain: they fell for it like so many toy soldiers.

But Sean just didn't get it. So as Kate and Sean rejoined Charly and Zoe and Steve, Charly flicked her hair and tried her best to charm Sean. She even told some of her best jokes about the magazine, where she was still working, including the one about the lady who'd turned up with her collection of knitted dolls stuffed with fluff, embroidered KATE on the front.

"She'd been writing to Kate, ringing her up, she was a complete nut job, and only Kate was nice enough to speak to her. . . . And there she is, with these stuffed dolls, and Josephine, that's the new editor, just said, 'You'd better take care of it, Charly. She's *your* best friend after all. When's Kate's birthday? You can give it to her as a present!' And—"

But at this juncture Sean laughed politely and turned to Steve, asked him to explain something about cricket, which was his new obsession. Charly was left standing there, talking into midair. Steve noticed, broke off from his answer to Sean, and said, "Ah, Charly. So how the devil are you? I haven't seen you since your party."

Steve was a flirt, always had been. Zoe raised her eyebrows at Kate and they both smiled as Charly melted under his gaze.

"I'm all right, Steve. How are you, Indiana Jones?"

She shifted her hips slightly so she was facing him.

Steve smiled, and blinked lazily. "Good, thanks, good. Well remembered."

"How could I forget," Charly said, lowering her voice.

"You too," said Steve. "You were mightily impressive that night."

"Good grief," Zoe said under her breath, rolling her eyes, and Steve laughed and stepped back. He put his arm around Zoe, who patted his chest, and they walked away. Charly watched them, her eyes narrowing, an indefinable expression on her face, and Kate knew how much it hurt her, other people's happiness. Because being Charly was a great thing, of course it was, it had to be, but sometimes it must be pretty damn miserable.

Kate had thought about it a lot, especially since she'd moved in with her. She thought Charly must get pretty lonely at times. She wasn't as hard as she liked to think she was. Charly herself didn't realize the ways in which she was strangely kind—making endless cups of tea and bullying Kate into wearing clothes she wouldn't normally dare, or strangely funny—her impressions were uncannily accurate, and she had a pitch-perfect recall for people's idiosyncrasies of speech, which made Kate helpless with laughter. It was weird these days, though. Charly was still at *Your World!* and Kate didn't know the people she talked about sometimes. They had less in common, less to talk about, than before. Sometimes it felt as if their bills at home were what bound them together most, that they were growing apart, and Kate hated that.

"Kate!" Charly hit her on the arm.

"Sorry, I was listening," Kate said. "What did you say?"

"I said, he's nice, isn't he?" she said, jerking her head at Steve.

"Yes, very nice," said Kate severely. Sean's hand snaked around her waist, and she leaned into his embrace. "Very nice indeed."

"Oh, get over it," Charly said crossly. "He's totally vanilla. I wouldn't go there, Kate." She tossed her hair, remarshaling herself. "Hey, you two? Fancy some champagne? I'll get us some more drinks."

She went toward a waiter, but turned back, a smile frozen on her face. "Kate!" she hissed. "She's coming!"

There, gliding over to them in a haze of cream chiffon and silk, was Kate's new stepmother, Lisa, with a smile like a Cheshire cat and a forehead smooth as a new apple, entirely wrinkle-free.

"Hellooo," she said graciously, holding out one hand to Sean, who took it, rather bemused. "Hi, Kate," she said more quickly. "Having a good time?"

"Yes, thanks," Kate said. She kissed Lisa on the cheek. "Congratulations, Lisa."

"Ooh," Lisa said, stepping away. She batted Kate lightly with her hand. "Don't get makeup on me! Look at my ring!"

Steve rolled his eyes in amazement at Zoe, who hit him sharply on the arm. He turned toward Lisa. "Hey, Lisa. You look absolutely beautiful."

"Thanks, Steve!" Lisa said, pleased.

"Thanks a lot for having us," Steve said, in his easy, polite way. "It's been so great."

"Well, congratulations to you, too!" Lisa stroked Steve's shoulder; he looked a little alarmed. "I haven't seen you both since you got married. Bringing back memories, eh?" She looked across at Kate, then back at Steve and Zoe, whose mouth was set in a straight line but who was nodding fervently.

"Well," Steve said. "We got married in a registry office and had a bash in the pub around the corner, so not really. The whole thing cost about fifty quid. So for us this is like a dream wedding."

Absolutely none of this was true, but he couldn't have said anything better. Lisa looked absolutely over the moon. She grasped Kate's hand, and Kate took her cue from that.

"Congratulations," she said, admiring the peanut-sized diamond on her finger with the new band next to it, studded with smaller diamonds.

"It's white gold," Lisa said proudly. "It's very original."

"Yes, very," Kate said.

"Ooh, look. There he is!" she cooed, and Kate looked up to see her Dad approaching.

"Hello again, darling," he said to his daughter.

"Darling," Lisa said. She fingered his tie, and then patted it proprietorially. "Want you to come with me and say hi to Gabi.

She's here with Cole, you know, from Funicular, the production company? She says you've ignored her all day. . . ." She ran her hands down the front of his shirt, stood up on her tiptoes, and bit his bottom lip, and Kate gazed at her, literally speechless that she thought it was OK to do that in front of her, in front of everyone.

"Sure," said Dad, squeezing her bottom, creasing the silk in his hands. He turned away amiably. Kate shook her head at her friends.

"Man . . ." Kate began, but Zoe, rubbing her friend's back, said quickly, "Shush. No point crying over spilled milk."

Kate watched her father and his new wife walk across the lawn, he genially following her as she held him by the hand. Lisa's sister, Clare, who was the babysitter for the day, handed Lisa sixteen-month-old Danielle, decked from head to toe in white taffeta and lace, like it was her own wedding day. They stood under a tree, the three of them, and some people started snapping photos, this perfect little family unit, so happy and beautiful, on this lovely day. Kate knew it would hurt in a little, small way, but she was surprised by how winded she felt as she watched them. She recalled her parents' wedding-day photo, the one she still had, her mother so fresh and free, her father so tall and virile, both of them looking so young, as if they were on their way to dinner, not to the registry office. It was so easy to imagine the whole thing had never happened now. That her mother, that she, had never existed. That this was the real wedding, the white wedding, and she, Kate, was a ghost girl.

"You OK?" Sean said softly in her ear.

"Yes," she said, turning to face him. He wrapped his arms around her.

"I love you," he said. "You look beautiful."

"Thanks," she said, wishing they were alone again, but as Sean pulled her toward him and they stayed like that, clinging to each other, she was watching her father and Lisa, with Danielle.

Twenty-one

Charly and Kate climbed the stairs to their flat wearily. Charly was carrying her shoes in her hand, and Kate was more than a little unsteady on her feet. It was one thirty, and Kate reckoned they'd been drinking for nearly twelve hours. She stabbed at the lock with her keys, and the two of them fell into their sitting room. Kate put the door on the latch, breathing in as the smell of the dusty flat, filled with sunshine all day, washed over her. She sneezed, flopping onto the sofa.

"There's a message," said Charly, grabbing a sticky old bottle of Limoncello from the fridge. She neatly shut the door with her bum and sashayed back into the room, carrying two glasses as well. "Whoa," she said, pressing PLAY on the flashing answering machine with her elbow. "Here you go."

She handed her a drink. Kate lay horizontally on the sofa. Her eyes were tired. They felt sticky. The cotton of her dress was creased; it fluttered on her stomach as Kate breathed in and out. She watched it.

There came from the machine an indistinct crackling sound, then murmuring, then the sound of people talking, glasses clinking, all very Ambassador's Reception.

"Darling. . . . Darling Kate, hello, darling. Hello!" A whisky-smooth, low woman's voice floated across to her on the sofa.

"Oh, no," said Charly, moving back into the kitchen. "First-wife alert."

"Sssh," Kate said wearily, sitting up.

"Darling girl. It's your . . . What? No, Oscar. I won't sing. You are awful! Darling. Stop it! I'm talking to Kate. No, no more to drink for me, thanks, Dick. Oh, go on, then, just one."

"Argh," Kate said, running her hands through her hair. "Argh. I can't bear it."

"Darling, how are you? It's your mother, wanting to know how you are."

"Why does she refer to herself in the third person?" Charly said. She was leaning against the kitchen door, swigging Limoncello and trying not to laugh. Kate smiled fondly at the answering machine.

"Why does she call me 'darling girl,' too. I haven't seen her for nearly a year and I'm twenty-seven. Bless."

"I remembered it was your Father's Second Wedding today. I thought you'd find it hard so I thought I'd just give you a call. I love you, darling! And hope it went gorgeously well, darling. Call Mummy tomorrow. I guess you're not back yet. I'm at Dick's! We're having cocktails with Vance and DJ! Oscar sends love! Come visit New York soon, darling, I miss you."

There was thirty seconds more of background chatter, then silence.

"She's mad," said Charly. "God, your parents are both mad."

"She's not mad," Kate said. She wasn't in the mood for Charly's needling. She took a sip. "She's just a bit—well, she's a bit tipsy for starters. It is Dad's wedding day, after all. . . ."

She shrugged her shoulders slightly helplessly, trying to work out how to explain her mother to a stranger, how you could love someone who brought you up and then abruptly left you, who you honestly believed loved you more than anything, but who was capable of just shutting you out when she wanted. Still, she was the only person, other than Zoe, who could understand what today had been like for her, Kate. Suddenly Kate missed her desperately. She knocked the sweet, viscous liquid down her throat in one go. It had been a long day.

"God," she said. "I'm knackered. I might—"

Suddenly there was a noise in the hall, and Charly screamed. "Oh my God! The door's open! Who the hell's that—"

Sean appeared in the doorway.

"What on earth?" Charly demanded. "How did you get in? What are you—"

She looked at Kate, accusing.

"I left the door on the latch," Kate said. "He's staying tonight, hope that's OK."

Sean had gone by Zoe and Steve's to collect a laptop that needed looking at. Kate could have sworn she'd mentioned to Charly he'd be coming around. It wasn't *that* much of a shock, anyway, for God's sake. He was around all the time.

"Hi," said Sean, unperturbed.

"Oh," said Charly. She stared at him, disdain so clearly written on her face that Kate withered with embarrassment. "That's fine."

She stepped forward, and Kate thought she was going to leave, but then she reached for the bottle. "Have a drink," she said. She filled her glass and handed it to him, biting her lip as she did, staring up at him again.

"That's OK." Sean waved his hands at her. He looked down at Kate, on the sofa, and came over, crouching down. He ran his hand lightly over her stomach, pushed her hair back, kissed her forehead. "Big day today. You tired, babe?"

"Yes," Kate said.

He shook his head at her and mouthed, *No.* Kate sat up.

"I'm going to bed," Charly announced, and put her drink down hard on the table. "Night, Kate."

"See you tomorrow," Kate said, still looking at Sean.

"God, she's a bitch," said Sean, and he kissed her, pushing his tongue insistently into her mouth. "Why's she such a bitch?"

Kate pushed him away, bit his ear, wanting to bite all of him, eat him up. "She's not," she said softly. "She's just . . ."

Sean's hand was inside her dress, on her breast, touching her. "You're gorgeous, babe. Kate . . ." He trailed off, then said, as an afterthought, "She needs a man. She needs a good shag."

Hazily, as he stroked her, as he kissed her harder, undid her dress, pulled her up, Kate thought of the stream of men, mostly unknown to her, who appeared in the sitting room the morning after a night with Charly. Spanish exchange students. Burly plumbers. Posh, polite boys. Angry, surly men from the magazine, who lusted after her for ages and realized they'd been used and were about to be dumped. She often ran out and left them. Kate had to make them breakfast.

"She doesn't, believe me," Kate whispered. "But . . ."

He pulled her into her room, and Kate knelt on the bed, and he pushed the door shut violently. His eyes were glazed, slightly impersonal, almost, and Kate realized they were both a bit drunk.

"I wanted to ask you something," Sean said suddenly. "I've been thinking about it for a while." He bit her shoulder. "Oh, Kate . . ."

"What?" said Kate, looking over the room to where a pile of clothes lay. She ought to tidy them up. God, it was huge, and she didn't even recognize half the clothes in it. She was tired, she wanted to sleep, and she knew that was a bit crap. *Venus* had a problem page, but it didn't have the answers to the problem of when you were a bit exhausted and not in the mood for it.

Dear Marie. I love my boyfriend, and we've been together for three years, and honestly I can't imagine life without him, but you know sometimes you just can't be bothered to talk to him and you don't want to have sex with him. Is that normal? Does that make me a terrible person? No, *Venus* went more in for the answers to questions like *Dear Marie. I'm thinking of getting my clitoris pierced. Do you have any safety dos and don'ts?*

". . . marry me?"

"Hm," Kate said, still chewing her lip and looking at the washing. Damn it, half that pile of clothes was Charly's! *Lazy cow.* Kate sighed crossly.

"Kate, are you listening to me?" Sean said, pulling away from her and staring at her.

"Oh . . ." Kate blinked. "Yes, yes of course I was."

"Were you really?" he said, smiling kindly at her. "I don't think you were, were you? What did I just ask you?"

"Um . . ." Kate said. "Something about the wedding?"

"Kind of," Sean said. He rocked back so they were both kneeling, facing each other on the bed. He took her hands and clasped them. "Kate. I just asked you to marry me."

"What?" Kate said, her eyes flying open. "What did you just say?"

Sean coughed, and closed his eyes. He took a deep breath; she saw he was shaking.

"OK . . . I said, you silly, gorgeous girl, will you marry me, and make me happy, and carry on being crazy shy beautiful Kate with me for the rest of our lives?"

"Oh—my God," said Kate. "Oh my God—Sean . . ."

She clutched his hands tightly, staring into his face. It was weird, she thought. Every girl spends her whole life wondering what her proposal will be like, and when it comes . . . it doesn't feel like a proposal, like the most amazing moment of your life. It just feels like . . . well, two people having a bit of a casual chat. Perhaps she should get Marie to do a column about it in the next issue of *Venus:* "How It Feels When It Feels a Bit Underwhelming." Of course, it wasn't underwhelming, though. It was Sean, of course it was the most amazing moment of her life, so Kate leaned forward, leaned in toward him, and she kissed him and said, "Yes. Yes, darling. Of course I will."

He sighed, breathing out deeply, and she realized how tightly wound up he was.

"I talked to your father just now," he said. "Caught him before he went off with Lisa."

"I bet he was grateful to you, holding up his wedding night," said Kate.

Sean frowned. "Hey! Don't. I knew I wanted to do it today, you know?"

"Oh, Sean," said Kate.

"I saw you . . . you and your dad, you talking to him, and you looked so beautiful, standing there with a glass in your hand, being yourself, your amazing self, and I was so proud of you," he said, his eyes burning with emotion, liquid with unshed tears. "Kate, I knew I was gonna do it. Your dad was hilarious."

"I bet he was," said Kate. She was trying to picture herself as the girl Sean had watched and to whom he had known he was going to propose. She had felt like a stranger in someone else's life all day, and it was strange that he had felt the opposite. But then, she knew that was how she and Sean worked, that he made her feel part of the world, less of a loner, a fruitloop. He showed her the life she should be having, opened the door to things for her, and she loved him.

"Is that what you came here tonight to say?" she said, almost shyly, not knowing what came next in situations like these.

"Well—yes," he said, speaking softly into her hair. "Of course it was. And now it's done. All over."

All over, all done, of course.

Twenty-two

*K*ate didn't want a big white wedding. And she certainly hadn't wanted an engagement party, but Sean had been really keen on it. Afterward, neither she nor Sean could remember why they had selected a bar on a cobbled side road off Old Street, clear across town from (a) their respective flats, (b) their friends' flats, (c) where they went out, (d) everything else. But at the time it seemed like a good idea, the upstairs room of a bar-cum-pub with new dark shiny floorboards, fuchsia flock-patterned wallpaper on one wall only, a steel and glass chandelier, and a host of stroppy bar staff who were anxious to let you know that they were really training to be an actor/studying film/ working toward a degree/recording an album. They did this by looking askance at anyone who ordered a drink and by loudly dropping names to each other as they turned to the wall to make the drinks.

"They said it was like Almodóvar."

"I'm meeting this guy who knows this girl Pam who worked at the National Film School."

"Apparently it's too metatextual. Yes, what do you want? A mojito? We don't actually do cocktails. Have a look at the bar list please."

Kate was wearing emerald green silk T-bar shoes, which were making her uncomfortable but happy, and a caramel-brown silk shift dress with huge pockets at the sides, which Juliet, the fashion editor at *Venus,* had been sent the day before. She'd given it to Kate with a kiss. "Wear it tomorrow!" she'd said. "It was made to be worn, not hanging around our sample cupboard for weeks on end. Come on! It's your night."

As she waited to be served at the bar, Kate thought of how kind Juliet had been, how kind everyone was, and she looked around her, at the crowded room, humming and buzzing with people she loved. There were Zoe and Steve, Betty, Francesca, Bobbie, Jem, and her old gang from *Your World!* Sophie and Jo and George, in a corner with Charly who was holding court, and Sue Jordan and her husband, Alec, and all the lovely new people from *Venus,* Claire and Juliet and Tom—even Priscilla was being nice. Perhaps it *had* been a good idea, after all.

It was like a wedding reception, really, and Kate was pretty unsure about the idea of receptions, cakes, big pouffy white dresses, and all that in general. They had decided they weren't getting married for at least a year, until they'd found a place and Sean had left his job and found something better. Kate had ummed and aahed through the summer, through all of her friends' congratulations, as other things took precedence. Sean had rung his mother in Texas about her engagement ring, which he wanted to give Kate. Zoe had her baby, Henry, always known as Harry, and she and Steve bought the flat upstairs, meaning they owned a House, and had a Baby, both of which were great, but really scary. Betty got a job in New York and had a going away party, which took the pressure off Kate, she'd thought, except everyone at the party sided with Sean and kept saying, Why aren't you having an engagement party?

Then Sean was given the perfect piece of ammunition because in early September, Venetia rang, and announced that she and Oscar were coming to London in a couple of weeks. One of Oscar's musicals was closing on Broadway and opening in London and they were spending a month in town. Was she having a party, because then would be the perfect time?

So . . . they were having the party. And now here they were, together again—and Kate never got to say these words, it was weird, rolling them around in her head—*her parents*. Her father and Lisa, her mother and Oscar, and it made her love Oscar more than ever that he, normally content in the shadow, was taking the conversational lead, gently flirting with Lisa, his hand always present on Venetia's back, just letting her know he was there.

Lisa was laughing at something Oscar had said, sliding her fingers carefully between the blow-dried locks of hair that framed her face, when Daniel leaned forward and said something to Venetia in a low voice. Kate watched, absolutely fascinated, as Lisa caught Daniel's hand and held it behind her. He clutched it tightly. But he was looking at his ex-wife, and she at him, and they were smiling into each other's eyes like a couple of teenagers.

Kate hadn't seen her mother since she and Sean had visited her in New York just before she'd started her job at *Venus*. She always forgot how beautiful Venetia was. Kate didn't look anything like her, despite Oscar's frequent avowals. "You could be *sisters*! Sisters, I tell you! Venetia, I can't believe you have a grown-up daughter!" It was true that Venetia looked much younger than her ex-husband, however—but that was because she was, and it shocked Kate to see them next to each other, to realize just how big the age gap was between her parents, how young her mother must have been when she married her father.

The last time Kate had seen her parents together was on her fourteenth birthday. She leaned on the bar and felt very grown-up, for a moment, as she watched them. It was strange, thinking they were her parents, when it had been so long since she'd thought of herself as part of a family, member of a unit. Very strange. It made her feel funny; like she didn't know herself again. She looked around for her *fiancé*—what a weird word, again, all these weird words she was having to say, *parents* and *engagement* and *fiancé*—and found him in the corner of the room, laughing loudly with his buddies in that trumpeting way men in groups have.

His eyes met hers and she looked mock-annoyed with him, then shook her head as he waggled his fingers, motioning something and mouthing, *Do you want me to come over?* But she was quite happy here, she realized, standing on her own at another corner of the room, relatively unwatched, anonymous, for a few moments at least.

"Yes, what can I get you?" An unsmiling barman flicked a glance at Kate, jolting her back to reality.

"Did you just tell someone you weren't doing mojitos?"

"Yes, that's right." The barman looked hugely, hugely annoyed to be questioned in this manner.

"Um—sorry. You're supposed to be," said Kate. "When we booked the room they told us we could have three different cocktails. That was one of them."

The black-haired barman didn't blink. "We can't do them now. It's just beer and wine."

"But we paid for free cocktails for everyone."

"Well, there isn't any."

"Any what?" said Kate, staying calm.

"Mint?" he said, a sneering tone in his voice.

Kate turned so she was facing him and rested both her elbows on the bar. "Here's the booking confirmation, and here's my credit card," she said, and she smiled politely at him. "I'm sorry if you don't have any mint, but either go out and get some, or give me the deposit back. Otherwise I'll go downstairs and talk to your manager."

He didn't even snarl, he simply accepted the will of the greater force, in the dog-eat-dog world of new London, turned, and went downstairs. Kate breathed out, and wished he'd got her a drink before he left.

"My God," said a voice behind her, in an amused tone. "Look at you. Who the hell are you?"

She knew that voice. She would know it anywhere.

"Mac!" Kate said, with genuine pleasure. She stood on tiptoe, flung her arms around him, and he hugged her tightly. She could feel her heart hammering in her chest as he clutched her to him, briefly. She hoped it wasn't obvious. *Don't be flustered,* she told herself. *You knew he was coming.*

"Hey," he said, releasing her and stepping back. "Thanks for letting me come." He rubbed the back of his neck. "I'd booked the flight already, didn't realize it was tonight—you know." He looked awkward.

"Don't be silly!" She smiled at him, assuming the easy, carefree tone she had told herself she was going to adopt with him. It was easier that way. "You're staying with them, you could hardly have just sat in by yourself with Harry and the babysitter."

"I could have, actually, but he's with my parents—they're the babysitters," he said. She watched him as he spoke. "God, how on earth are you, Kate? I haven't seen you since—when was it?"

"Since Zoe and Steve's wedding," she said. "Nearly a year."

"We only seem to meet on momentous occasions," he said. "Housewarming-cum-engagement parties, weddings—and now look what's happened since I've been away."

The bartender took this opportunity to appear again, slamming a mojito down on the counter with an injured air.

"Mint's on its way; I'll add it in a minute."

"Thanks," said Kate. "Thank you very much." She smiled politely at him as his eyes narrowed in suspicion. "Cheers," she said, raising her glass. Mac clinked it with his, looking curiously at her.

"The Kate Miller I used to know would never have done that," Mac said, leaning on the bar so he was facing her. He touched her arm lightly. "The Kate Miller I knew hardly used to say boo to a goose."

"Rubbish," said Kate, and she laughed. "The Kate Miller you knew you knew for one night."

"That's not true. We spent the morning together as well, if I remember rightly," he said conversationally. Kate looked around anxiously, not wanting anyone to hear. He followed her gaze and shook his head, smiling. As if he knew what she was thinking.

He had no idea, really, though. No idea how, when she had heard Mac was down in London for the weekend, *this* weekend, and had to be invited to the party, how it had shaken her to know he'd be there on this night, the very night she'd resisted having for months. He had no idea that she sometimes thought of him, late at night, lying in bed alone when Sean wasn't there, or when he was next to her, breathing heavily, moonlight falling into her tiny bedroom. That she wondered what might have been—not every day, of course not—but she wondered. That she wondered how he was, was he OK, was he happy, not working too hard? Strange, so strange, to feel such tenderness, protectiveness toward someone you hardly knew. And he had no idea, she hoped, how it felt to see him standing in front of her now, tall and rangy, with his cropped brown hair, his bitten nails, his deep green eyes.

Kate shook her head, willing away the thoughts inside of her. Keep it light, remember what you told yourself, she said, looking around easily again, checking for Sean. "Do you think anyone ever worked it out?" she asked curiously. "Us, I mean."

"I never told anyone," he said quietly. "Did you?"

She was silent for a moment. "I didn't," she said. "Well, Sean. But he doesn't count."

"Doesn't he?"

"You know what I mean," she said. "It was—it's in the past, isn't it." She sounded rather prim, like a schoolteacher, and she hated it. She felt uncomfortable.

"Heartless woman." Mac banged his fist theatrically on the wooden surface of the bar. It broke the tension. She stared at him helplessly and laughed. "You started going out with your flatmate and now you're marrying him, just to prove a point to me. Whereas I had to move to a cold inhospitable city with no friends and hear all about how much in love with Sean you were. It's all about the point scoring with you, isn't it, you heartless woman. I know the real reason for this farce of an engagement party."

"Oh dear," said Kate, laughing again, and standing on one foot, then on the other. "I'm sorry, Mr. Hamilton."

"I'll forgive you," he said, with that old, strange stare of his that she remembered. Silence enveloped them as they stood together. "Everything else OK, though?" Mac said quietly. "Sounds like it."

"Brilliant, thanks," she said, her face alight. "Just brilliant."

"I'm so glad," Mac told her. He squeezed her arm, his big hand wrapping itself above her elbow. "It all worked out for the best, didn't it?"

"I think so," said Kate. "I think so." She allowed herself to stare at that wide, generous face, the hint of stubble on his jaw, the shadows under his eyes. "How are you? Zoe mentioned you might be moving, is that true?"

"Back down here? Not sure. Just had an offer from a hospital in South London."

"Wouldn't you miss Edinburgh?"

"In some ways," said Mac. "Not in others. I haven't decided yet, that's why I'm down this weekend seeing them again." Kate nodded. "I love it up there, but I'm a bit lonely sometimes, you know? Since Alice and I split up."

"Alice?" she said stupidly.

"My ex." Mac turned suddenly to the barman.

"Your ex. I didn't know—"

"What," he said. He turned toward her suddenly, his eyes searching her face. "You didn't know I had a girlfriend? Ever? There have been others, you know, Kate."

She didn't know why his tone had changed suddenly. "I know, Zoe told me—"

His eyes flashed at her. "Ah, did she? And you've been eating yourself away with jealousy, I know."

Kate shifted her weight from one foot to the other, feeling uncomfortable. "Um," she began, not really knowing how to continue. "Well, I hope you move down," she said.

"I'm not sure," he said, finishing his drink in one gulp. He wiped his mouth with the back of his hand and stood there, looking at her. "I'm not sure it's the right move yet." He paused. "God, Kate, I'm sorry. But it's so good to see you."

"You too," said Kate, her heart racing again. "Really—you too. I'm glad, you know—it was awful that we never did . . ." She trailed off, not knowing how to go on, afraid to go on. The cozy world she was cocooned in, this bright and friendly party, her parents and their spouses talking easily over there—all of it seemed skewed, false, unreal, all of a sudden. She didn't know why, didn't know why. Gathering herself together, she took a deep breath.

"I'd better go and find Sean," she said.

"Yes," said Mac.

"So I'll see you later."

"I'd like that," said Mac. He cleared his throat. "Hey. I really need a drink. Mojito, large, lots of mint, when you've got a minute, please," he said to the barman.

"Coming right up, mate," said the barman, and Kate slumped back against the bar.

"God," she said.

"What?" Mac asked.

"I hate you," Kate said. "He didn't listen to me, he completely ignored me. I have no bar presence. And you come along and say 'Jump,' and he says 'How high.' "

"You're doing just fine," Mac told her. "I heard you. You sorted him right out. That's why he's scared witless," he said, and he nudged her, so she turned and stood next to him, watching the barman frenziedly chopping mint and crushing ice before he swiveled around to hand the drink to Mac, who took it with a nod. "Thanks, mate," he said.

"No worries," said the barman. "Madam, can I get you another one?"

Kate hesitated, looking sideways toward Mac.

Mac smiled, blankly, like the moment was over, and said, kindly, "Go off and find your fiancé, Kate Miller. I'm going to stay here." He pushed her off and she tottered, staggering slightly in her high heels, toward Sean, who stretched his arms wide open when he saw her.

Twenty-three

*T*hree hours later, the bar was still rocking, the mojitos were still flowing, and Kate was not sober. She had smoked a cigarette, which she never did. She had kissed Sean in front of everyone, which she also never did. Most important, she had extracted a promise from Sean that they would buy the engagement ring together, and that she wouldn't be wearing his mother's. Sean had a rather sweet, slightly dubious idea of giving Kate his mother's engagement ring, which Gerda Lambert couldn't wear anymore now that her fingers were so bloated with water retention. Kate didn't want her engagement ring to be hers as the result of water retention. She felt there should be more of a quest for it. Not Lord of the Rings–scale quest, but still, a bit more.

And there were still all these lovely people there. Her mother and Oscar were working the room, chatting to all her friends. It was so great to see it, to be in the same room with her again. She missed her mother. And Lisa was sitting on Kate's father's knee, whispering into his ear, like they were teenagers. Jem and Bobbie were in the very obvious stages of presnogging, Kate could tell—all around them was love, love and nice things.

She hadn't seen Charly for a while; she'd said hello when she'd arrived with the others from work, and then gone off to a corner with

them, where she had ensconced herself. Kate's eyes roamed around
the room, searching for her. She couldn't see what she was up to,
but that was probably a good thing, so she went back to her drink.
It was empty.

Sean was behind her; their backs were touching as they talked
to different people. She could feel his warm, comforting bulk behind her, the side of his hip nestling in her back. With an effort
Kate stood up straight and wandered back to the bar for another
cocktail, knowing she had probably had enough, but what the
hell. It was her engagement party, after all! she told herself, and as
she looked up she saw Mac, weaving his way toward her.

"Hey!" she said.

"I was looking for you," he told her, his expression grim.

"Why?" said Kate. "Come with me, come and get another
drink." She was suddenly heady with euphoria. Feeling free, invincible, like nothing could harm her, she shook her head, smiling directly at him, too close to him, looking into his eyes, knowing she'd
had too much to drink, knowing she was flirting with him and she
shouldn't be; it was her engagement party, for Christ's sake. She
pointed at Sean, who had Francesca pinned up against the bar and
was making her scream with laughter at something, and turned
back to Mac, who was watching her intently. She met his gaze. It
was oddly unsettling, knowing him so well, not knowing him at
all, and the way his suddenly flinty eyes bored into her, coldly.

"Don't marry him," he said.

Kate blinked. "What?" she said.

"Don't marry him, Kate. He's not right for you."

"Mac!" Kate didn't know what to say. She shifted her weight,
the emerald green high heels gleaming in the dark of the bar as
dimly she registered how much they were hurting her.

"I'm just going to say this once, and I'm sure you'll hate me for
it," Mac said, looking around him, as if he were checking out the
bar, the other people in it.

She suddenly felt totally sober. "Perhaps you'd better not say it, then."

"I have to," Mac said. "Don't marry him. You're doing it for the wrong reasons."

Kate blinked, mystified—it was like he was speaking a foreign language. For the past few months, all she'd heard was congratulations, expressions of joy—getting attention that, for once, she liked, that she sought out, basking in the warmth of the approval and pleasure that their engagement news brought them. She even liked discussing the wedding now that she'd got used to it. Dressmakers, caterers, estate agents, registrars, shop assistants, solicitors: an army of people was being mobilized into place to see to this next stage of Kate's life, her grown-up life with Sean.

And here was someone saying all of this was wrong, and she could barely recognize the words, let alone process them. Kate stared at Sean, who had his arm around Francesca. As if he knew she was watching, he turned around slowly and smiled at her, moving his hand onto his heart.

"And what makes you say that?" said Kate, trying to sound like Lady Bracknell. He looked at her and said nothing. "Seriously, Mac," she went on, softening her voice. "I don't know what you mean." She felt as if she were trying to reason with a lunatic.

"Congratulations again, darling!" Lisa appeared, pushing Mac slightly out of the way; he stood aside, smiling politely but still looking intently at Kate. Lisa pressed her cheek against Kate's, a glass of champagne clasped to her chest. "Great party!" she trilled. "Daniel, here's your daughter! The bride-to-be! Ooh, Kate. I've got so many questions I want to ask you!"

Kate had never seen her so warm or genuine, and again she was confused. She smiled gratefully at her stepmother and clasped her hand. "Oh, Lisa, that's lovely—thank you, but—" She looked around for Mac, not wanting to let him get away from this conversation, wanting to put him straight. "Give me one minute, will you?" Mac looked back at her, unsmiling. The party had an unreal air, the color, the drinks, her shoes, the laughter—it was like a fairground ride, everything distorted, nothing what it seemed, and she suddenly hated it, wished she weren't here.

"Of course," said Lisa, beaming at her. "We're over here—your Dad's waiting for you, remember! And your mother—I love your mother!—I think they're going in a minute. . . . Ooh, look, there's Sean come to say hello—Hello, Sean—"

Her voice receded into the background chatter as she tripped away and Kate and Mac stepped together again as if she hadn't been there.

"You were saying . . ." said Kate, her voice low, her head suddenly clear.

"Look, Kate, this isn't a cloak-and-dagger meeting." Mac sounded impatient. He pushed a cocktail stick along the surface of the bar. She watched him. "I'm not . . . I'm not doing this to be dramatic about it. I'm being honest. Do you get it? Don't marry him. Just trust me."

"Why shouldn't I marry him?" Kate was bewildered.

"Do you honestly think he's the man for you," Mac said, his voice close in her ear as he swooped suddenly low, and she felt her stomach tip over, full of the doubts and desires that she kept hidden away. "Do you honestly think so, Kate. Because if you do, then I'll just go away, but if you . . ." He trailed off and their eyes met.

She put her finger to the lapel of his jacket, gingerly. "That night we met . . ."

"Yes."

Her heart was in her mouth. "I thought . . . I felt like I'd known you for years."

"Did you?"

"Yes," said Kate recklessly. "I thought you were . . ." She looked straight at him. "I thought you were perfect. I thought I could fall for you."

"Me too," said Mac, his voice low.

She took a step back. "And then you—you casually went on your way, moving to a different *country* the next morning." He was here, she was really saying this to him. "I—I kind of hated you afterward, you know."

"I know. Our timing sucks," he said. "I nearly called you half a dozen times. I couldn't stop thinking about you."

"Why the hell didn't you, then?" she said, almost hissing.

"Believe me, there's not a day goes by I don't wish I had," he said fiercely, close to her ear. "You didn't call me, either, you know." She shook her head, closed her eyes, because he was right. "But it just seemed so—random, so out there to call someone you've only met once and tell them that you think that they're—"

She stopped him, and gently put her hand on his. *The love of your life.* "Yes," she said simply. "I know."

"And then a couple of months later I found out you'd been having a thing with Sean anyway, and I wasn't that surprised, I thought it was in the cards."

"I know," she said again.

"I wish you hadn't."

"I know."

"I should have called you."

She breathed out in a rush. "Oh, Mac. Maybe. Maybe you should." She wished she hadn't said it.

"It's too late, isn't it."

Now Kate breathed in, closing her eyes, which were suddenly heavy. The smell of him—the feel of his skin on hers—his face, his arms, the two of them together, entangled in each other. How intense it had been, almost terrifyingly so, and then how normal, strangely normal. . . . She opened her eyes, slowly.

"It's too late. . . . Mac, I love him."

"Don't do it, Kate." He caught her wrist, and poison was in his voice. She caught it and it scared her.

"I wish you could tell me why," she said. "Be more . . ."

"Specific?" he said, almost laughing. "Kate. Come on." He turned away, bowing his head, and was still for a moment. Kate looked up to see if anyone was watching her, and there were Sean and her father, clapping each other on the back, and she wished with all her heart that she was there next to them, not in the middle of this.

"Oh God," she said quietly, not sure what to do next.

Suddenly it was as if the tension had been cut, had slackened. Mac shook his head, and said something softly to himself. She turned to him.

"This was wrong," he said. "I'm going to go." He kissed her on the cheek, and she breathed in quickly. "Kate, I'm sorry. I shouldn't have said all that." He stopped. "Do something for me, will you?"

"Of course!" said Kate, already sounding cheery, though she felt anything but, and she wished she could sit down with him and talk, talk properly.

Behind them, Bobbie screeched as someone spilled part of their drink over her. It was Charly, sashaying over to Sean and Steve, a smile on her face. She touched Sean on the shoulder.

"Hey."

"Hey, Charly," Sean slurred.

"Just wanted to say congratulations," said Charly. She peered up at him, making an effort. "OK?"

"Sure," said Sean. "Thanks a lot."

"I'll see you soon. Yeah?"

"You will," said Sean.

"Are you off?" said Kate, turning to her friend.

"Yeah," said Charly, a fake smile of regret plastered across her face. "I'm going to meet Jag in town; we're going to a club."

"Cool," said Kate, who had no idea who Jag was. "Look, thanks for—"

"No worries," Charly said awkwardly.

Steve said, "Are you getting a cab, Charly?"

"Yeah," Charly said, flicking her long bangs out of her face.

"Zoe's gone already, so I'll come part of the way with you if that's OK. Cool." He downed his pint and coughed slightly.

"Smooth," said Sean, smiling at him, turning toward him so they blocked Charly out.

"I'm going now," said Charly.

"OK!" said Steve faux-dramatically. "Keep your knickers on!" He kissed Kate good-bye. "Darling, that was a great, great party. You're a star, you know that? Zo said if you had one you'd love it." He slapped Mac on the back. "See you later?" He didn't ask him if he wanted a lift. "Right, come on, dollface, let's be off."

Charly scowled at him.

"Bye, Charly," said Sean, and he stalked off to the other side of the room as Charly pushed her way out, with Steve following, leaving Kate standing alone again. She turned back to Mac and saw him watching her intently, his expression more serious than it had been.

"Sorry, Mac," she said. "What was it?"

The question sounded harsher than she'd expected.

"Look," he said, and he jerked his head over at Steve's disappearing form. "It's . . . It's Steve and Zoe. Look out for them, will you?"

"Um, sure," said Kate. "I do. You know that."

"Zoe, yes. I mean both of them. Spend some time with them. Just do it. Especially Steve."

And with that gnomic utterance, he kissed her again.

"Take care of yourself, Kate Miller," he said, and walked over to some other people. She watched him go, her mind racing.

Of course, there was no doubt that Sean was the man for

her—of course—but if she had to choose, as the magazines she worked for or read were constantly asking her and women like her, would she choose that one night with Mac again or a lifetime with Sean and what she and Sean had together?

Kate shook her head at the thought, watching the scene around her, her friends so happy for her and Sean. Ridiculous to even ask the question, and that was what sometimes irritated her about her job and the world of magazines. She spent all day working on the illusion that women could have it all, when the reality was much more complicated. Making promises, an easy sale for £3.20, the new body, new man, new job, and new house that you wanted were all yours for the cover price alone.

Her eyes were on Sean and he turned around, almost as if he knew she was looking at him. Kate snapped out of her reverie with a start.

"You OK?" Sean mouthed, flexing a hand toward her.

"I'm OK," she said, nodding at him. She watched Mac at the end of the bar, saying his good-byes to people, saw him push open the door into the dark, rainy night. She was glad he was gone, and she felt angry, too. How could he say that to her? The more Kate thought about it, the ruder it seemed, in fact, and she threaded her way through the crowd, people smiling kindly at the bride-to-be as she made her way toward her fiancé. Yes, that was what it was. Her engagement party. Her fiancé. Her life.

Twenty-four

*P*lanning a wedding, Kate discovered, was—like so much of life—not quite how it seemed in the magazines. In her time she must have written at least ten articles on the subject of being a blushing bride and how to organize the perfect wedding, but now that she was planning one of her own, well, it was all rather different, and she didn't quite know what to think about it.

For starters, she didn't *feel* like a bride. Kate wasn't the sort of girl who'd grown up dreaming of a big pouffy white dress, a cake, bridesmaids decked out in cherry pink, coordination and happy families. For starters, her family had been effectively obliterated when she was fourteen. The limelight was left for her father and his genius, his fans, his amazing, wonderful life, and her mother and her beauty, her grace in every situation, her hysterical dramatic gene. And like basic genetics, the combination of these two people had produced one child, a daughter who actively ran from the limelight, to whom the thought of doing a first dance in front of two hundred people was as terrifying as having to sing karaoke in front of people. It never occurred to her that she might have inherited anything from either of them.

That was what she liked about Sean: the limelight was his when they were out. He was the genial, loud, funny one, the storyteller, the buyer of drinks. When they were alone it was different, they were the two of them, but out together he was the center of attention. Kate liked it. She had her friends, she had a job where people listened to her. So what if occasionally she wished Sean would let her tell the story about the time they were on holiday in Crete and an unexploded mine went off in the garden next to their hotel? She'd been in the hotel at that moment, not him, she was the one who . . . Anyway, that didn't matter, it was great.

The wedding was going to be in September of the following year. They'd finally set a date, and with a lump sum Venetia had given them as a wedding present, they'd found the perfect flat, in a redbrick mansion building in Maida Vale. Alec, Sue's husband, had an uncle and aunt in this building, and he'd happened to mention to Kate that there was an auction about to take place on the flat below, as it had been foreclosed on. It was on the second floor; it had big bay windows, shiny parquet floors, and the lobby was imposing and cavernous, with a great big black door that squeaked loudly on huge, old wire hinges. They moved in five days before Christmas 2003, unable to believe they were finally there, in their own place. On their first night they drank champagne, each sitting on a cardboard box, looking around at the bare but strangely cozy flat.

Sean clinked his glass against Kate's. His legs were between hers. With his other hand he tugged the dusky pink scarf wrapped around Kate's throat.

"We did it," he said. "Can you believe it?"

"No," said Kate. She grinned. "I can't. At last. At last!"

He knelt on the floor in front of her, looking up at her with his impish, big generous smile, his arms on her legs. "This time next year," he said, resting his head on her chest. "We'll have a big tree, and presents underneath it, and we'll have been married for four months. We'll be an old married couple by then."

"It's weird, isn't it."

"It's not weird, that's what's so cool. It's great." Sean kissed her. "Look, we'll have all our Christmas cards lined up on that big windowsill there. And we'll have the sofa here, with a big otto— What's it called?"

"Ottoman?"

"That's it—a big ottoman to put our feet on. And we can build some shelves here, what do you think?" Kate nodded, watching him with pleasure and trying not to cry at the same time. She didn't know why. She was tired.

"We can put photos on the shelves, us on our wedding day. And you with your dad when you were little, and me and Doug on the baseball team. And we'll have the computer here, and a desk for all your important office stuff, and the dining table can go here, and we'll have all these dinner parties, you know?"

His enthusiasm was infectious. Kate could feel her face lighting up as she looked at him, the way she always did. "Go on," she said. "What else?"

"What else. Hm..." Sean frowned. "Well, next Christmas—on Christmas Eve, maybe—we'll have Steve and Zoe around, with Harry and the new baby." Kate nodded, a cloud momentarily passing over her sunny world as the champagne suddenly tasted vinegary. "Perhaps Betty'll be back from New York. Francesca and Pav—"

"If they're still together." Francesca was enjoying an overwhelmingly obsessive, secretive relationship with the trader next to her at work.

"If they're still together." Sean patted her knees, moving closer in toward her, so she could feel his breath on her neck. "Who else?"

"Charly," said Kate carefully. "You forgot Charly."

"Screw Charly," said Sean, almost viciously. "I don't wanna talk about Charly. Not tonight." He squeezed her shoulders, hard, and stepped back from her, tension suddenly thick between them.

Kate watched him angrily, hating the fact that their perfect night was being spoiled with this. The newly familiar feeling of hating things, hating Charly, this girl who had once meant so much to her, was inching its way into her mind again, and it was horrible. She didn't want to feel like this, in their safe, beautiful new home together.

They were perfectly still in the center of the room, a beam of light from the shadeless bulb hanging over them. Sean opened his mouth to say something, then didn't, and Kate was afraid suddenly.

"I need to tell you something," she said, her voice small.

Sean nodded. "Mm-hm. What, honey?"

"It's about Charly."

His face darkened. *He knows,* she told herself. *He knows what I know about Charly. About what she's been doing.*

It had happened three days ago, and even admitting she held the memory seemed deceitful, as if she were lying to Zoe, deceiving her herself. . . . Kate and her ex–*Your World!* colleague Sophie had been visiting Georgina and her baby. Georgina had, to everyone's surprise, not least Claire's, married Phil from the office (Charly had definitely not been invited to *that* wedding), and they were living in Hampstead, in a beautiful little house just off Keats Grove, behind the shops near the Heath. Sophie was a hearty type, now working for an off-the-beaten-track guidebook publisher that specialized in holidays through bits of the Amazon that no human had ever been to before. It was she who'd suggested they walk across the Heath toward Gospel Oak station.

"Fresh air," she'd said briskly as they emerged from the once chilly, now frazzled Georgina's house into a baby-free zone and each breathed an internal sigh of relief. "Do us good. Phew." She blew her short brown hair off her face. "Glad to be out of there, aren't you?" she said, as if they'd just emerged from battle.

Georgina, a superefficient dynamo in the office, didn't seem to understand why Ned, her sweet baby, didn't want to organize himself in the same way her computer did, and wouldn't stay silent when she wanted him to. All in all, it had been a rather disheartening hour or so, and Kate and Sophie had both felt they were in the way. They were discussing this and skirting up by the ponds, when Kate suddenly clutched Sophie's arm.

"What?" said Sophie.

"Nothing," said Kate. "Thought I was going to slip, that's all. Sorry."

Her heart was beating, she was red hot, she pulled her hat off, unwound her scarf, and pretended to be listening as Sophie carried on telling her how *she* would deal with the apparently very simple demands of having a baby. But she wasn't listening. No, of course not.

There ahead of her, standing by a bench facing each other, were Charly and Steve. She knew it was them; of course it was. He was holding her elbows as if trying to restrain her, contain her, and she was yelling at him, her face angry, dirty with rage. Her beautiful brown hair was underneath a black crochet hat, a matching scarf wound around her neck, her long, long legs still in her Charly wardrobe of high-heeled boots and jeans.

Kate watched as Charly broke free of his grasp and angrily kicked at the metal leg of the bench. She didn't know what to do; they were walking toward them.

"Oh my God," said Sophie suddenly. "Shit."

"What?" said Kate.

"It's Charly. Having some massive argument with some bloke. Oh God." Sophie turned to Kate. "Look, I know she's your friend and everything, but . . ."

"What?"

"I really can't face her—seriously, not while she's in the middle of that, too. No way." She grabbed Kate's arm. "Let's cut through the ponds, go around the side. We'll miss them." She shuddered. "Sorry, Kate. I'm being horrible. Do you mind?"

"No," said Kate hurriedly. "Of course not."

Steve was talking back to Charly. He tried to take her hand, to pat it, and Charly broke away, sobbing. He gripped her shoulders; Kate couldn't see his expression, but she knew his voice, could hear its pale undertones floating over to her. She tried to hear, but she couldn't. And she knew what the conversation was, anyway. Of course she knew. She'd known Charly for four years. And then she heard Steve's voice, just a snatch, a horrible, terrible confirmation of her worst fear as Sophie pulled her away, tugging her hat down over her face so she wouldn't be seen.

"It's got to stop, Charly. I'm sorry."

The thing that was still haunting Kate three days afterward was Charly's expression, of total, utter, blind—what was it? Intoxication? Obsession? She didn't know. She only knew that here, crying like a madwoman, was Charly, and at home, looking after eighteen-month-old Harry and pregnant again, was Zoe. They were her two dearest friends. They had been.

Tears were running down Kate's face as she finished the story, and Sean wrapped his arm around her, enfolding her in his big, bear-like embrace. He kissed her hair.

"Don't worry, darlin'," he said, his voice soft. "It's nothing to do with you, honey—"

She broke away. "Of course it is," she said angrily. "Sean, they're my two best friends."

"I know," he said. He wiped his hand across his forehead. "And Zoe—little Zoe. Man."

Kate's voice cracked. "Steve's your *best man*, for God's sake—what am I supposed to do?"

"Nothing," he said, putting his arm around her again and drawing her close till her breathing subsided. "Nothing at all."

"I can't just do nothing," Kate said, pulling away from him, turning around the room.

"I'll talk to him," said Sean, holding out a hand to her. "It's gonna be fine, Katy. It's nothing. I know it's nothing. I don't want you worrying about it, OK? Come here."

There, in the cold but brightly lit Christmasy flat, Kate suddenly felt fear for the future, a sensation she hadn't felt since she'd got together with Sean. As if the house of cards she—and Sean, and all her friends around her—had erected was just that: card, flimsy, impermanent. Kate had spent years searching for structure, order, security. Here, in her new flat, in her husband-to-be's arms, a John Lewis catalog on the table beside them, she suddenly felt in the midst of chaos, as if the wallpaper might start peeling off the walls, the china jump off the counters and smash, and the lights suddenly go out.

Twenty-five

"Steve's got a day off today, you know," said Zoe, sitting with her feet up on another chair outside a café in Smithfield. "He said he might go around to your place, see Sean."

"What?" said Kate, startled. She put down her menu, blinking at Zoe in the sunshine.

"Do you know where Sean is?" Kate's face was blank, and Zoe said patiently, "The bathroom tiles in your flat. Sean's doing them today, isn't he? Steve's helping him."

Kate stared at Zoe. It went into her head, this nugget, another little piece of information. Kate wished she could connect them all in some way, but her brain didn't seem to be working lately.

They weren't doing the bathroom tiles for another couple of weeks, Kate knew. The tiles were delayed, some problem with the manu-facturers in Italy, due to Sean's incredibly precise tile requirements, which had driven Kate practically up the bathroom wall itself. Plain white from IKEA was absolutely no good; no, they had to be from some tiny artisan shop near Modena, cut to the same design as some Japanese designer from the sixties. Kate just couldn't have cared less. Having grown up with parents who barely knew one end of a hoover from the other, Kate had learned to be practical to survive, and it surprised her to realize just how good she was at organizing their finances, sorting out their tax returns, organizing the wedding, though actually that didn't interest her as much as other things did. Sean laughed at her; he thought it was funny he was marrying a girl who was more interested in tax returns than bathroom tiles or fonts for wedding invitations. He quite liked all of that, he told her.

He did, too. It surprised her to realize what a homebody Sean was, to see how subtly both of them were changing. He wanted to be an old man with his pipe and slippers, sitting by the fireside. Kate couldn't see big, strong Sean in slippers at all—he was always doing something, always up before her, out getting supplies from somewhere, and yet more and more he wanted to stay in. He was out so often during the day for work, going to other offices, in meetings all over town, so when he was off he wanted to be with her and he liked her to be there with him—though these days Kate's job took up a lot of her time, and it was sometimes a real struggle to get away from the office, from the parties, the launch for a new fragrance, the preview of a new film. As she did better in her job, she became less of a homebody; the opposite of Sean. Sean had enjoyed doing up their flat so much, she found it really quite touching, though his zeal for home life was sometimes a bit overpowering, as if he'd tried on the coat for size and found it was too big but wanted to keep it anyway.

"We should think about moving out of town in a year or so, though," he'd said a few nights ago, as Kate was sitting on the sofa in her pajamas, tapping away at her laptop, making some last-minute changes to an article she'd done.

Kate peered at him over her glasses. "What?" she'd said, not really taking it in.

Sean was squatting on his haunches by the fireplace, a palette knife in his hand. He'd found some antique ceramic tiles that exactly matched the period of the flat, and had removed the dull seventies gray-green tiles around the fireplace to replace them with these, old, burgundy, florally delicate, charming ones. Now she watched him fondly.

"I said"—Sean heaved himself up—"we should really think about moving out of London in about a year or so." He put the palette knife in his tool belt; Sean loved his tool belt.

"Why?" said Kate, trying not to sound rattled. "We've only just moved in here."

"We don't want to raise kids in the city, though, do we?"

"What kids?"

"The kids we're going to have, Kate." Sean sat down next to her. "Hello?" He patted her arm. "Don't freak out."

"Oh," said Kate. "Those kids. Yes, but—Sean, I don't want to move out of town."

"I'm not raising kids here in the city," said Sean. He sounded affronted. "Do you really want to do that? Wouldn't it be better to be in a house? In a cul-de-sac? They can ride their tricycles and . . . and stuff?" he finished, rather vaguely. "Wouldn't it be nice to live in an actual town?"

"We already live in an actual town," said Kate. "I thought you liked it here. You've never said . . ."

"Darling, calm down. This is way in the future," he said, putting his arm around her and pulling her close. She could hear his heart beating as she rested her head on his chest. "We won't be in this apartment forever, will we? Or are you saying you want us to stay here for the rest of our lives, never move, never change anything, live here for fifty years, just like the Allans upstairs?"

He always did this—got her to agree with him by making fun of her, driving her arguments into the ground with gentle hilarity. She couldn't argue with him, never had been able to. He was like the Teflon man—nothing stuck to him, he just got on with it and did his own thing. Usually she loved that about him.

"I'd like to be like the Allans," she said. "They've got a great life."

"No, they've got a stupid life," said Sean, sitting up. "They should have realized the profit on their place years ago. Don't they realize the market's going to bottom out and they could have got a great little cottage in the country somewhere?"

"I've never asked them," said Kate, moving away from him. "But maybe you should run up there *now* and make sure they're aware of that." She poked him gently. "Calm down! Last week you wanted us to start going to the local church, now this. Is it the wedding, is that what's making you freak out and act like Mr. Suburban all of a sudden?" He swung around toward her. "It doesn't matter," she said softly. "I don't need a house in Epsom somewhere to be happy with you. I'm happy here now."

He frowned, looking annoyed. "Kate, that's not what I mean. You know that."

"I don't—"

"Hey. *You're* the one freaking out about the wedding. Ever since we got engaged, you've become Ms. Career Girl in the City."

She inhaled sharply. "What the hell do you mean by that?"

"It's, like, you with your job these days. It's, like, it's the only thing that matters to you. 'Ms. Miller? Ms. Miller?' " he said, imitating a receptionist on the phone in a high, silly voice.

"This is stupid."

"That's what Sue's assistant called you when she rang about the car to the airport. 'Is Ms. Miller there?' Since when were you a 'Ms.'?"

"I don't know!" Kate ran her hand through her hair. "You're being ridiculous! Who cares if I'm Ms. or Miss or Mrs. or whatever? Why should it matter?"

"Because you're marrying me," he said. "You're going to be Mrs. Lambert."

"I know, but—" Kate sketched something with her hand, a helpless gesture. "Sean, don't be like that—" She reached forward; he had stood up, and she caught his leg. "I can't wait to be Mrs. Lambert, honestly."

"Really?" he said, turning around and looking down at her. She met his gaze solemnly. "It just feels like—it's your job first with you, then organizing the wedding, then Zoe, then the flat and stuff, and I come about fifth on the list."

She didn't know how to reassure him; all of those things were true, because she did them all for him. He had urged her to work that hard, to make them the money that would keep them afloat, that would pay for not just the tiles from Modena, but the honeymoon in the Maldives, the car outside, and one day, the house in the commuter belt, with a driveway to park the car in and a mantelpiece to put the framed photos of the honeymoon in the Maldives on. They'd got onto a treadmill and, Kate realized, they didn't know how to get off.

"Sean—" she said, moving her hands up his body, pulling him toward her. "Sit down, darling." He sat down. "You are first with me—you know that, don't you? Always first."

"Of course I do." His face softened. "It's just—"

"Let me finish," she said, holding up her hand. "Look, I want to be with *you*, I want a marriage to *you*, not so I can say 'my husband's over there' to people at parties. That's why we're doing this, isn't it? Because we want to be together."

She said it in a funny voice, like the old Prudential ad, but Texas-raised Sean didn't get it, and he looked blank for a moment. "Sure," he said. "Forget about it." He leaned in toward her and kissed her, moving her arms, breaking up her defensive body language. "We are together," he said after a moment, his voice muffled in her hair.

Kate sighed. She was so tired, after a long day on the magazine, where there was a new drama every day. She wasn't sleeping much,

stymied by various things. She hadn't called the caterers to final-
ize the menu, nor spoken to Lisa about Danielle's little dress (Lisa
was insisting on Daniel's new album of Westlife ballads being
played at the reception and Danielle being a bridesmaid. They'd
compromised on the latter). And always, at the back of her mind,
was Charly. Steve and Charly. She had absolutely no further evidence, no sign that anything was amiss. Was she going to upset
pregnant Zoe over what Sean was convinced was just a misunder-
standing? Threaten everything, lose Steve's friendship—because
how could it be otherwise—when she wasn't really sure?

The trouble was, she couldn't stop thinking about it. Her
mind ran in a circle, around and around, always coming back to
the same thing: Was that why she hadn't seen Charly for months?
Was that why Sean and Steve didn't play their weekly game of
pool anymore? Was that why Zoe seemed strange with her now,
like she was on her best behavior? Everything led back to it, and
it seemed to Kate as if she were the only person who could do
something about it, and yet the only person who shouldn't. She
was like a rat caught in a trap, with no way out, and she honestly
didn't know how much longer it could go on like this. Her brain
wasn't working properly. She was losing weight, too much weight.
People kept saying it was prewedding nerves. She knew it wasn't.

"Did you speak to the photographer?" Sean said softly, running his hands over her shoulders, his lips on her jaw.

"No," said Kate, twisting toward him, hoping to distract him
further. "I will tomorrow. Forget about that now."

"OK."

"OK."

Remembering this night, only three days ago, Kate shook her
head, as if the thoughts inside it were buzzing loudly, and looked
around her. She and Zoe were by Smithfield Market, sitting outside in a cafe that overlooked the vast wrought-iron building.

They could hear the shouts of traders, finishing up for the day, echoing behind them as they sat in the sunshine, smiling politely at each other.

"So the tiles are going up today, are they?" Zoe said, recalling Kate to the present.

"I suppose so." Kate shook her head again, trying to work out what was bothering her. "I thought it was later, but . . . perhaps they arrived early. That'd be cool."

"Nice of Sean to give Steve the key. I wouldn't trust him with . . . anything," said Zoe happily as she patted her tummy and lifted one foot up onto the slatted chair opposite her. "Look. Harry does this when he's hungry." She made circular movements on her rounded stomach. "God, I'm starving. Shall we order?"

"Yep," said Kate. "Let's. Let's do that." She gazed around, suddenly feeling sick. Sick to her soul with something that was beyond her control. It couldn't be true, could it? *Could it?* Steve wouldn't . . . Charly wouldn't . . . Kate tried to focus.

"So," Zoe was saying. "What have you got left to do?"

"For the wedding?"

"*Yes,* for the wedding," Zoe said. "I know you're the least bridal bride in the whole world, but you must have *some* things left to do."

"Not really," said Kate. "Dress, fine." She was going to wear a beautiful dress she'd found in Fenwicks. It was pale blue. "Registry office booked. Venue booked, band booked." Lisa had taken care of the venue, a disused church hall around the corner from their flat, on Shirland Road, and her father had, very kindly, after the CD debacle was cleared up, offered to find a good band for the wedding, coming up trumps with the Frank Walden Band. There was two months to go, anyway—Kate didn't see what the fuss was about, personally. She kept thinking she should be in a flap, but it was like she was watching it from a long, long way away, and she simply couldn't get worked up into a mound of stress about it. It'd be a party, she and Sean had decided. A great big fantastic party. Sean was more nervous than she was, she thought. His family was coming over, whereas she had virtually no family. And he was more one for the big occasion. When the registrar had, attempting small talk, asked which of them was going to cry, both Kate and Sean had pointed at Sean and said, in unison, "Him." As the registrar simpered, batting her eyelashes at Sean, who was nodding and smiling, he'd added, self-deprecatingly, "I'm just a real sucker for the whole thing. I . . . I can't wait, you know?"

"And I'm dead inside," Kate said to Zoe. "She looked at me like I was a total witch."

"Rubbish," Zoe said briskly, putting her menu down and squinting at her friend. "I can tell you, Harry is really, really excited. I think he thinks a wedding's something to do with the police. He keeps shooting imaginary things when I talk to him about it, I don't know why."

"Hah," said Kate, pretending to study her menu.

"Steve says he's got an unhealthy interest in weddings for a year-and-a-half-old child. Well, he says *I've* got an unhealthy interest in weddings, too, and he's right, Kate, but, oh, I'm just so excited! He'd rather fiddle around with tiles in your flat, stupid man."

A waiter walked past; a pigeon landed near them; a car hooted in the background. That was when it suddenly hit Kate. It wasn't a flash from the skies, a thunderbolt; it was one ordinary moment passing into another, but it changed everything. She put her menu down, staring thoughtfully at Zoe, not caring if she was being odd. This was her best friend in front of her, the girl she had grown up with, who had been more family to Kate than her actual blood relatives, really. She had to know what was going on, had to take control. She realized that now. No more of little Kate in the shadows, waiting for Sean to sort everything out for her, for them both. He had failed her in that, she had to admit it. It was time for her to do something, though it terrified her.

She stood up.

"I've got to go," she said suddenly. She picked up her bag.

Zoe looked up at her in astonishment.

"What?" she said.

"I've—a conference call," she said, recent memory giving her inspiration. "The Americans. I forgot. Shit, I'm late," she said, unconvincingly. She met Zoe's eyes, bent down and kissed her. "Don't get up, darling," she said, patting her best friend on the shoulder. "Stay there. It'll be OK."

"Kate!" Zoe was shouting. "Kate? Come back!" Her voice was incredulous, almost amused, worried. "Kate!"

She ran off through the cobbled Smithfield lanes, down Cowcross Street, past the boys in leather jackets and the girls in ponchos, past the coffee shops and little restaurants, gathering pace as she went, brushing City boys out of the way, running now as she slammed her pass against the ticket gate and ran onto a train, not caring about work, about Zoe thinking she might have gone mad, just knowing now she had to get back to the flat, to stop them, because she suddenly knew that's where they'd been meeting, and it was down to her to stop it. Her alone.

Half an hour later, as Kate ran up the stairs at Maida Vale, panting, and ran across the road toward the flat, she was no clearer about what she would do when she saw them, and doubt was starting to crowd in on her mind. *Come on, Steve isn't a cheat!* He wouldn't do that to Zoe, to Harry, to the baby. He just wouldn't!

And then she saw it, outside her and Sean's building. Steve's car, a little red MG, which he had bought over Zoe's protestations, her arguments that they needed a family car. There it was, like a little shiny cliché, parked slap bang in front of the front door. Kate almost gasped at the audacity of it, and rage overtook her, rage and bile. Her clumsy, shaking hands stabbed the key in the lock.

She slammed the door and ran, taking the stairs two at a time.

She slowed down as she got to their flat, caution getting the better of her. Stealthily, smoothly, with murder on her mind and her teeth gritted, she slid the key in smoothly, opening the door so quietly she knew anyone inside wouldn't have heard her.

Perhaps there was no one in there, she said to herself. *I must have got it all wrong, stupid me.* And just as she thought that she heard something, heard a noise from the bedroom, the door of which was ajar. Kate took a step forward. The muscles in her throat had closed up.

Steve . . .

Oh God. No. No, no, no.

There she was, on the bed, moving slowly up and down, her hair falling about her shoulders, down the creamy, pale skinny back. Kate would know her anywhere. She was moving up and down on top of him. Kate stopped short at the door. But she still didn't see it. Then he sat up, pulling her down toward him, his face greedily gobbling between her breasts. He groaned, shaking his head. She moved against him, tilting her head, and Kate saw his face.

It wasn't Steve.

Twenty-six

Steve's voice came behind her as she stood at the door. He was out of breath, she registered it vaguely. She could hear him, as if he were underwater or far, far away.

"*Kate . . . Kate, it's . . .*"

It wasn't Steve in bed with Charly, her best friend.

It was Sean.

Sean's hands pressed on Charly's hips as he exploded into her, with a great, bellowing moan. Steve grabbed Kate's hand and pulled her away, but she wouldn't move. Why couldn't they see her, why didn't they notice, why didn't they *stop*.

"*Shit*," Sean said suddenly, and Kate looked at him, realizing he'd seen her, standing in the doorway. "Kate. *Kate*." He groaned again as Charly ground herself against him furiously.

"It's *Charly*, you *twat*," Charly spat into his ear as she collapsed again. "Charly."

He pushed her off him—she tumbled backward gracefully onto the bed, turning around and looking up lazily, breathing deeply, her tousled hair falling over her perfect naked body. She stared up at Kate.

"Oh God," she said, her eyes dilating. And then she breathed in again and closed her eyes, shuddering slightly, running a hand through her hair, grabbing onto it. Sean got up, pulling his boxers on.

"Kate, Kate," he said, stumbling toward her.

It was so strange, seeing him awkwardly naked, having just come inside Charly a few seconds before, fumbling with himself, his clothes: Kate backed away, like he was an embarrassing drunk on the street. She bumped into Steve, who caught her.

"Come on," he said. She turned around in his arms.

"I thought it was you," she said.

"I know," said Steve, his face red, his green eyes watching the figures behind her. He breathed in, squeezed her arm. "Zoe called me. I guessed you must be coming here. I was on the phone to her in the car and you ran past . . ." His eyes were full of sympathy. "Oh, Kate."

"I thought it was you," she said again, as Charly pulled the duvet over her body.

"I know you did," Steve said. "But there wasn't much I could do about it, was there?"

She pointed at him. "But you've been seeing her—I saw you—"

"I've been seeing her to get her to stop doing it, stop both of them," Steve said, shaking his head. "It's me, Kate! How could you think I'd do that—"

"Oh my God," Kate said. Bile rose in her throat. She swallowed it back, but it choked her. Sean pushed her into the bathroom next door. Her bathroom, with the tiles they were waiting for. "Get away from me," she said, backing away from him. She turned, and was sick. Sean and Steve stood at the bathroom door, watching her. It was bright and sunny in there, her huge beautiful bathroom that she loved so much. Kate frowned, thinking abstractly to herself, as she heaved and was sick again. Stupid thoughts flew into her mind, silly questions. What would happen to the bathroom now? She couldn't come back here again, she was sure of that.

"Kate, I'm sorry," Sean said when she stood up, a few seconds later. His hair was standing on end, almost comically; he was rubbing the back of his neck. "You— I'm sorry. I love you. This means— Oh shit, seriously. I don't know how it happened."

How to stand, to face him, to behave in this awful, ungodly situation? She didn't know, couldn't work it out. And Charly— she was still in there, in her bed.

She stood up straight. She wiped her mouth, breathing as calmly as she could. Her neck, throat, chest felt constricted, like she might pass out. She would stay there, she wouldn't leave.

But she couldn't.

"Get out of here," she said. "I don't want to see you again." She looked down the corridor to the room where Charly was still lying there, curiously expressionless, and that's when Kate lost it. She could feel herself losing it as it happened. It was a most strange experience. She marched into the bedroom, aggressively upright, standing straight, and she walked over to the bed. She grabbed Charly by the hair, by her long, tossable hair, wanting to hurt her, kill her. Murderous rage swept through her as she dragged Charly off the bed.

"Get out," she cried. "Just get out, you evil, *evil* bitch!" She was waving her hand up and down, and Charly's head, imprisoned by Kate's steel-strong fingers, was waggling around underneath her. "My God, Charly, I always knew you were cheap, but . . . this! *This!* You *cow!* Get *out!*" And she flung her away from her as far as she could, to the other side of the room. Charly tumbled onto the floor.

"You bitch!" Charly screamed, suddenly alive, scratching at Kate, her long talonlike nails scratching Kate's arm, but Kate felt invincible suddenly. She marched over and grabbed Charly again, not thinking, not feeling. Charly was tripping over herself, bashing into the doorframe as Kate swung her from side to side, wishing she could swing her around the room, rip out her hair, break every bone in her body. Adrenaline pumped into her, coursing through her veins, making her feel light-headed. She could have killed her. She could have killed him. And all the time Charly was screaming at her, screaming torrents of abuse, filthy, black-hearted words in her ear, as she scratched her, clawed at her like an animal. Kate opened her front door and flung her, still naked, out into the landing, and Charly screamed as she banged against the banisters and fell back, over the stairwell. For a second she hung there, as if she were going to fall, but then she bared her teeth, her dark eyes glittering at Kate, and smiled, righting herself.

"I always knew he was mine, darling," she said clearly. Kate shut the door in Charly's face just as she rushed toward Kate and leaned up against it, breathing hard. Sean and Steve watched Kate in horror, rooted to the spot, as Charly started banging on the door.

"Let me in!" she screamed. "Let me in, you silly, stuck-up, pathetic little bitch! He's mine! He has been for months, years even. I can have *whoever I want*, Kate, you *stupid* little girl. Why didn't you see that years ago? Why didn't you ever see that?"

Sean was slumped in the hallway, his head in his hands. He didn't even look at her, didn't seem to be able to. Kate started shaking. She had to get out of there, but she didn't know how. Steve pushed her out of the way, gently, and as he opened the door to let Charly in, Kate dodged past her, her feet flying down the stairs, down, away from that flat, away away away. She heard Charly's hiss, and the patter of footsteps behind her.

"Kate!" Sean shouted suddenly. "Come back!" No, Charly wasn't going to catch up to her. No no no. Kate ran into the downstairs hall, flinging the door open. She daren't pause for breath, had to keep going, had to, had to. The footsteps behind her were getting louder, closer, and Kate ran out onto the street, hair flying behind her like a crazed madwoman, like the hounds of hell themselves were after her. She could feel Charly gaining on her all the time, and she kept on running, toward the shops, toward safety, she didn't know where.

She kept on running as she reached the road, and there were footsteps behind her, pounding louder and louder, and it spurred Kate on, more and more. The lights were green, she could see them, but the lights were green for the traffic, not for her, and she couldn't see it.

There was a loud sounding of horns, people jamming their hands to stop her, and the screeching of brakes, and Kate came to and slowed down in panic, just as someone started shouting.

"Kate! Kate, get out of the—"

She could see a great big bus approaching, and as she turned someone pushed her with all their force, so that she flew across the road and fell to the ground, facing upward, and she saw what happened next. She saw the bus driver's look of horror, she saw the bus desperately braking next to her as Steve, who had pushed her out of the way and saved her life, was hit.

Kate's leg and arm were covered in blood where she had fallen to the ground and skidded. She ran back over, as people starting piling out of cars, rushing over to the man lying in front of his bus, his neck at an unnatural, strange angle, his body sprawled out in the middle of the crossroads. They watched her, almost not daring to come too close.

"Steve?" she croaked, in a hollow voice. "Steve? No. No. *Steve?*"

Twenty-seven

Should Harry come to the funeral? was the question everyone asked. He was eighteen months old. He wouldn't really understand what was going on; he was simply too little. Would Steve have wanted him there? It was the question everyone asked because it was an issue about practicality, and in those black, empty, horrifying days before the funeral, when there was nothing to do and everything to do, and there were no answers to why this had happened, practicalities were what kept everyone in some kind of sanity.

Zoe didn't know. She said she wasn't sure. When Kate asked her, looking into her face for some kind of direction, some sign that she was absorbing this, what had happened to her family, she saw nothing, only a sort of blankness, as Zoe rubbed her pregnant tummy and shook her head.

"I don't know. You decide."

Kate couldn't decide, though. She turned to Steve's mother, Mary, who had arrived that morning. "What do you—"

"I think we'll think about it later, dear," said Mary in her soft Edinburgh-accented voice. "Zoe, why don't you go and lie down? You must be tired, what with all the arrangements this morning."

Zoe hadn't slept since Steve had died, three days ago. Because even saying Steve had died was so horrible, so totally alien; it was words that didn't go together. But she was docile, easily led now. She raised her hands in silent protest, as if to say, This is pointless, and got up heavily from her chair in the kitchen. Kate followed her through to the sitting room.

"Do you want some water, a cup of tea?" she said, looking around the room as Zoe sat down on the sofa. There were photos of them together everywhere, photos of Steve and Zoe on their wedding day, Steve and Mac laughing, their arms around each other. One of his ties was hanging off the banisters. Kate wanted to make Zoe go outside, stand on the front doorstep for five minutes so she could tidy all of it up, remove every trace of him from the house so Zoe wouldn't have to see his presence everywhere, how recently he'd been with them. An ice-cream van trundled slowly by out on the street and Harry, out in the garden, called out in pleasure at the noise. Kate rubbed her eyes, wondering again how things could be so prosaic, how life could be carrying on in its normal way when this had happened. Things kept striking her, like how Steve would never see his new baby. She would never know her dad. Harry would forget things about his father that he knew now because he was too little to carry them with him. A trail of sweat trickled down Kate's back. It was so hot, disgustingly hot. It shouldn't be like this now; it should be snowing, or raining— winds should be howling. They shouldn't be wearing T-shirts and flip-flops while they discussed what kind of coffin Steve should be buried in. Everything was the wrong way around now, everything. Kate didn't know where to even begin, and that's why they focused on the practicalities. Who was going to make the sandwiches for afterward? Should Harry come to the funeral?

Interrupting Kate's thoughts, Zoe said quietly, "Actually, can I have a glass of water?"

"Of course," said Kate hurriedly. "I'll get it now. Do you want some food? You should—"

"No," Zoe said.

"But you haven't—"

"I don't want food," Zoe repeated, with that edge of steel that Kate had seen in her these last few days. "I'll eat later. Not now. OK? Can you make sure Harry's OK, Kate?"

"Yes, of course," said Kate, going into the kitchen. "Just stay there."

Mary was staring out of the window into the garden, watching her grandson playing with his grandfather and uncle on the lawn. She turned as Kate came in.

"Does she want some food?" she asked.

"No," said Kate. "She says she'll eat later."

"Right," said Mary. "Right, then." She turned back to the window, her fingers stroking the glass. Kate poured the water. "What are we going to do?" Mary said quietly, almost to herself. Her eyes were hollows, sunken into her face, her skin a pale, papery color. She looked old, all of a sudden. "Tomorrow. After it's over. What are we going to do?"

Kate nodded, because she didn't know what to say.

"Perhaps we should stay down here." Mary nodded to herself. "Move down and help Zoe. Oh my God. What will she do?"

Kate came over and stood by her side at the window. She touched her arm, gently. "Her mum's here, and I'm here, Mary. I know it's—"

But Mary wasn't listening to her. "Mac's saying he should have taken that job. He says he should move back here now, get a place nearby," she said, almost conversationally. "Perhaps that would be best."

Kate watched Mac, out on the lawn, and he looked up as if he could hear them, and stared straight at them. He pointed at them to Harry, who waved, unsteady on his feet. Mac clutched his nephew's arm and they both looked at Kate and Mary. They were, in that moment, so like Steve, the same quick glance, the same hair color, shape, that it struck Kate like a blow and she steadied herself, holding on to the kitchen surface. She thought she was going to be sick. A mug rolled over into the sink with a clatter.

"Are you OK, dear?" Mary said briefly, flicking a glance at her before staring out at the window again.

"Fine, sorry," said Kate. "Just—yup." Her arm was hurting, the injuries down one side of her swollen, bruised body throbbing with pain.

They were silent again, and then Mary said, "I need to talk to Jim. I just don't know what we should do."

Kate said gently, "Don't think about that just at the moment, Mary. Wait till it's over tomorrow, and then see how you all feel."

Mary turned back then and looked at her sharply, and Kate knew she'd said too much. "Thank you," she said, almost curtly. She lifted the water glass away from Kate. "I'll take this through to her, then."

They were all grown-ups now. Funny, she'd thought they were the young ones. Kate carried on looking out of the window, swallowing, breathing slowly. She looked down at the sink, full of mugs, and ran some water as the kitchen door opened.

"Hi," said Mac.

"Hi!" said Harry, who was holding on to Mac's hand. "Mum!" he said, pointing into the sitting room, and he ran off toward her.

"Hello, baby!" came Zoe's voice from the other room. She sounded so tired, her voice cracking. Kate turned the tap on full blast. The hot water hurt her hands.

"How are you?" said Mac, turning the kettle on. "Need a hand with the drying?"

"Thanks," said Kate, handing him the tea towel. He stood next to her and picked up a mug, glancing at her as he dried it.

"You all right?" he said, nudging her. "You're very pale."

Kate swallowed again. "I feel a bit sick, that's all. It's nothing."

He looked her over appraisingly. "You should take it easy, Kate. Your body's had a shock. Those are nasty." And he gently touched her arm, which was scribbled over with deep, brown-red grazes, bruises, half bandaged up. "Don't try to do too much."

"It's fine," she said, gritting her teeth. She didn't want any sympathy, from anyone.

Mac watched her. "So, is Sean moving out today, then?" he said, in a low, easy tone.

He uses this tone with his patients, Kate thought to herself. Gently, quietly, kindly, make them feel secure, make them feel better even when it'll never be better. He had arrived early on Saturday morning and she had not seen him cry, not seen him anything other than composed, organized. He had taken charge of the funeral arrangements, he had sat by Zoe and stroked her hair as she went to sleep, he had held his father when yesterday he'd broken down. She didn't know how he could do it. How can he be asking me things when his world has fallen apart, completely collapsed. She stared at him.

"Sorry," he said. "You probably don't want to talk about it."

"It's not that," Kate said, shaking her head. She moved toward him. "Mac, how can you be so—"

Mac looked down at the sink. "Don't ask me about that," he said. She bent her head, trying to see his face. "I mean it, Kate. Please."

"Sure." She nodded, and touched his arm, fleetingly. "I'm sorry."

He shook his head back at her. "No, I'm sorry. I want to do it this way."

"Yes," she said. She took her cue from him. "Sean, yes. He packed up yesterday. I'm not sure how he's getting his stuff out."

It was as if they were talking about a wardrobe being delivered. "You haven't seen him?"

"No," Kate said. "I didn't want to . . ." She trailed off. Sean had called—four, five messages on her phone each time she checked, alongside all the others from everyone else, each one sadder than the last. She had to listen to her messages—it might be friends calling about the funeral, about Zoe. But mostly they were from Sean, imploring her to listen, begging her to see him, crying about what had happened. But what could she say to him? She couldn't even cling to him, or comfort him. He was the one person she blamed more than herself: she couldn't see him. She shook her head. "He's ringing all the time, he wants to know what's going on. It's pathetic of me but—"

"Hey," said Mac softly. "It's OK."

"No, you don't understand—" Kate began. Tears welled up in her eyes. She could feel something in her chest, a physical pain that hurt her when she thought about why this had happened, how it had happened, and wondered why she was still here when Steve was dead. Steve's hands, pushing her out of the way, pushing her over onto the ground, so that she was alive now, standing here.

Why was she alive? Why was Sean alive? Why was he allowed to live when Steve was dead, his body cold, lying in the morgue in the hospital down the road? She didn't know. She didn't know where Sean would go now, where he was. Zoe needed her here—to field the phone calls, make the sandwiches, play with Harry, run to the shops. So that was where she'd be. Kate didn't need to be at home. After all, it didn't matter what happened to her now. She shook her head, willing the tears away.

"I'm sorry, I shouldn't have asked you," said Mac.

He was so kind. She wished she could put her head on his shoulder, give in to it, but she couldn't. "It's my fault," said Kate. She cleared her throat and gritted her teeth before she spoke. "Sean's been in the flat today and yesterday. I think he's moving in with—with her. He doesn't have much stuff. He's canceling everything, too."

"Your wedding."

"Yes," said Kate. The idea of a wedding now, *her* wedding, seemed farcical. She turned toward Mac. He was holding a mug in his hands, twisting the towel over and over around it, looking down at her. "Can we not—"

"Of course," he said. "I understand. When are you going back there? Later tonight?"

"Yes," said Kate. "Zoe's giving Harry his bath in a bit. I'll go then. We should get an early night, all of us."

"Yep." Mac nodded. His mouth was set. "It's going to be a long day." He shook his head, smiling at the mundanity of his words. "Jesus Christ."

"Oh, Mac," she said.

He gazed at her, his eyes glazed, drunk with pain.

"I can't stand it," he whispered suddenly, closing his eyes, and he bent over, as if grief was crippling him. She put her arm around him, in the sunny, bright kitchen. He put his hands on his knees and made a low, choking sound, his body shaking. Kate rubbed his back, not wanting to break the comfort of physical contact, not knowing what else they could do, any of them, now, other than hold each other and try to make it through the next hour, and the hour after that. Then the next day, then the day after.

It was Zoe, calling from the sitting room, who broke the moment. "Hey, can you come through? I mean Mac, can you come through?"

"Sure," Mac said, clearing his throat. He stood upright again, his tall, broad frame blocking out the sun from the garden, and wiped his eyes with the balls of his palms. Kate went ahead of him, to give him a little time to gather himself.

"Hi, darling," she said. Zoe was on the sofa, with Harry lying next to her, his eyes wide open.

"Where's Mac?" said Zoe.

"Just coming. Do you need anything?"

"I wanted to ask him something," said Zoe.

"Right," Kate said. "Are you hungry yet?"

"For God's sake, Kate, stop asking me if I'm hungry all the time, OK?" Zoe ran a hand through her lank, lifeless hair. "I'll eat when I want to."

"I'm sorry," Kate said, stepping forward. "Zo, sorry, I just want to make sure you're—"

Zoe said blankly, "Look, Kate. It's great you're here and everything, but you can't make it better, OK?" She nodded. "So don't try."

"I'm not trying to make it better, I just want to look after you."

Zoe gazed at her, biting her lip. "Especially *you* can't make it better, Kate." She spoke slowly, like she did to Harry. "That's all."

"Yeah, I know." Kate nodded her head vigorously. There was nothing else she could say. She turned. Mac had appeared behind her and was watching them. Harry sat up. "I'll take him, shall I?"

"Thanks," said Zoe, looking up at her gratefully. "Hey, Harry, go with Auntie Kate for a bit, darling. I want to talk to Uncle Mac."

Harry stumbled off the sofa, his small unsteady legs wobbling as he trundled toward Kate. She picked him up. "Garden," he said, with pleasure.

"Sure," said Kate. "What do you want to play?"

"Robot." He waggled his arms, squealing with delight, and she hugged him to her, hard.

Kate left them an hour later. As she had done every day since it had happened, she walked to the bus stop and waited for the bus, marveling again at how unreal it was to be doing this yet again, another day gone by like this, dealing with his death, the collapse of everything around them. The bus arrived five minutes later, and she got on and sank into a spare seat. The bus was always full of people at this time, adults coming back from work, children from school, people heading into town. She wanted to stand up and tell them what had happened, what grief and pain she had left behind in the little house down the road. She wanted to ask the people on the bus if they could make sense of any of it, of how it could have happened. But she couldn't. It was the same route that the bus that killed Steve had taken. On the first day she had walked for a while—she couldn't bear the idea of getting on that bus. But she realized it just didn't matter what she did or didn't do, and no one was going to see or care about it, anyway.

She felt as if she were becoming invisible, as if parts of her life were becoming invisible. When she got off at her bus stop, she looked around for a sign, terrified that she might see them again. The trees were still in the evening light. There was no other traffic on the road. She got back to the flat and climbed the stairs, trying not to feel dread, but praying he wasn't still there.

He wasn't. His stuff was gone. Four years together gone in an afternoon. The flat was exactly as she'd left it, no tidier, no messier; it was just that half the things in it were missing. Half the clothes in the wardrobe, half the books and DVDs and CDs. No second toothbrush in the bathroom, no dressing gown on the back of the door. And it didn't hurt. As Kate gazed around her flat, she tried to make it hurt but it didn't, not compared to everything else now in this strange new world they were all coming to terms with.

She almost didn't see the note; it was on the mantelpiece, which had been cluttered with invitations, photos of them all, before this happened. It was written on an envelope, on the back of a bill, and this somehow made Kate angrier than any of the rest of it, that Sean would say good-bye to her like this, scribbling a few words on an electricity bill.

KATE

BELIEVE ME, I AM SO SORRY FOR WHAT HAS HAPPENED AND THE WAY IT HAS HAPPENED. I NEVER MEANT TO HURT YOU. I STILL LOVE YOU—BUT I DON'T EXPECT YOU'LL BELIEVE THAT.

LOOK, IT'S BEEN MADE CLEAR TO ME THAT I SHOULDN'T COME TO THE FUNERAL SO THAT'S WHY YOU WON'T SEE ME THERE. BUT I HOPE I SEE YOU SOON, TO EXPLAIN SOME THINGS. IN THE MEANTIME, I'LL BE THINKING OF YOU ALL TOMORROW. YOU KNOW HE WAS MY BEST FRIEND.

S x

Twenty-eight

At nine o'clock the next day, Kate came out of the flat, blinking in the harsh light of yet another relentlessly sunny day. The funeral was at noon. Mac had said he would pick her up to take her to Zoe's. He waved to her from the car as she stood on the doorstep checking for her keys and she waved back, as two figures appeared in front of her, their outlines almost black in the glare from the early morning sun. She was hot already, even though it was early. She was wearing long sleeves and a long skirt to hide the injuries on her arm. She didn't want people to see them, nor the cuts on her legs, over her shoulders. Underneath the black cotton, her skin smarted with pain and sweat.

"Hello, dear," said the first one. "Oh, good. We're glad we caught you."

It was Mrs. Allan. She caught Kate's hand.

"Oh, hello," said Kate. Mr. Allan kissed her on the cheek.

"Are you just off to Zoe's, then?" he asked. She nodded. "We spoke to Sue yesterday. It's the funeral today, isn't it."

He was holding the *Guardian* and the *Telegraph* under his arm, and Mrs. Allan was clutching a string bag with some tomato juice and milk in it, the promise of a normal, ordinary day in their flat, reading papers, eating toast, being with each other, like they had done for decades and decades.

Mrs. Allan stroked Kate's cheek, her silver bobbed hair bouncing as she did, and she said softly, "We're here all day today. Just so you know. All right? You be off now, but we'll be here later."

"That's—" Kate began.

"I know you might not want to see anyone when you get back, or you might. All I'm saying is," she said firmly, "Graham and I are here all day."

Mr. Allan pointed at Mac, sitting in the car behind them. "I suppose you'd better go. I'm glad we saw you. We haven't seen much of you since it happened. I came around to the flat yesterday and Sean was there, clearing up." He looked at his wife. "He said you'd been at your friend's most of the time since it happened."

Kate nodded, not knowing what to say. She was almost glad to know he had been there, that she hadn't dreamt that note, the only sign of him she'd had.

"Let's go for a walk tomorrow," Mr. Allan told her. "We haven't been for a walk for a while. I'll come and find you. Sue said she'd signed you off work for as long as you needed."

Work. Kate blinked, trying to see Mac in the car across the way. Work seemed like a different universe. The idea that people went to work, that she had her office and a desk and a view over the river, that she had a job she went to, a life before all of this? It was mad, unbelievable, like everything else. She looked to where Mac was waiting patiently to take her to the funeral. And the idea that this funeral marked a point in time after Steve's death, that things would change again now, suddenly hit her.

"OK," said Kate. "Thank you. Thanks a lot."

"We're here, that's all we wanted to say," he said again.

Mrs. Allan hugged her. "You'd better go."

She smelled of parma violets, of wool—comfort, security. Kate

hugged her back, not wanting to let go, but she did, waving good-
bye as they opened the door to the flats behind them.

Kate walked down the steps toward the car.

"All OK?" Mac asked her as she got in.

"Thanks," she said. She looked at him. He looked like he
hadn't slept at all. He was so pale, the circles under his eyes so
blue, they looked almost ghostly. He was suited and his short hair
was neat. He was impeccably shaved, except for a longish cut on
his jaw. She pointed at it.

"You OK?"

He touched it, quickly, and nodded his head. He put the car
into gear and they drove away. Kate saw the Allans on the steps
of the building. They were waving, and she couldn't understand
why.

The church in Willesden was full to bursting, the noise of subdued conversation rustling through the building like dry leaves
in the wind. As Kate walked to her seat, people she knew, had
known for years and years, people she and Zoe had grown up
with, people she and Steve had been at university with all stared
at her curiously. She heard someone say in a whisper, "That's her."
Kate kept walking; she did not look around.

She was on her own, having left Zoe and Mac outside. He was
a pallbearer, and she was walking behind the coffin. They had
their roles. They had talked to the vicar about it—about when
and where and how, on this summer's day in North London, in
a church that no one apart from Zoe had ever been in. Kate sank
into her seat and someone took her hand. She looked up in surprise. It was her dad; she'd forgotten they were coming. He kissed
her. Lisa, who was next to him, reached over and grabbed her
hand.

"Babe," she said.

"Darling," Daniel whispered in his daughter's ear. "This will be awful. Don't try and fight it." He put his arm around her and squeezed her tight. "I'm here, Kate."

Kate sank against him as the main doors at the back of the church swung open and the vicar called out behind them, "Could you please all stand."

She knew she would have to turn around, to see them coming down the aisle, Mac and Zoe and Steve's parents. Mac stared ahead, the coffin on his shoulder, as the procession came slowly down toward the altar. His jaw was set firm, but his Adam's apple was bobbing up and down with the effort of swallowing, and a film of sweat covered his forehead. Zoe seemed calm, but halfway down the aisle, she looked ahead for the first time, at the coffin, seeming to see what it really was. Kate watched her in alarm as her face froze. She stumbled, almost tripping, and there was a gasp, as Mary and Jim Hamilton held her up, and Zoe's mum, behind, stepped forward to hold her. Her face crumpled, her composure gone, and it was unbearable to watch.

When they had set the coffin down, Mac slid into the seat next to his sister-in-law, and he pulled her toward him, her head on his shoulder as she sobbed quietly, and the vicar started talking about Steve. In the row behind, Kate watched them, saw how Mac's fingers dug hard into Zoe's bare arm, trying to contain her as she sobbed, her shoulders heaving.

"It's OK," he said into her hair. "It's OK."

But it wasn't, of course, it wasn't.

Mac gave the eulogy. They didn't know who else to ask; his parents' friends didn't know him as well as they all did. Steve and Zoe had loads of friends, but it was too much to ask one of them to perform this, this horrible task. Steve had spent so much of his life, from eighteen to twenty-eight, with Zoe, just the two of them, and she couldn't do it.

As Mac got up and walked to the front of the church, he left a gap next to Zoe, so she was on her own, on the end of the row, totally by herself. She was so small, her stomach so big, sitting there on her own at the front of the church, her husband's coffin ahead of her. Kate reached forward and held her hand, and Zoe clutched it, her nails digging into Kate's palm. She was humming quietly as she cried, and the sound filled the silence of the vaulted ceiling as Mac fiddled with his notes, composing himself, his jaw set. Eventually he looked up at the congregation, with what seemed like an almighty force of will.

"Our hearts are broken today," he said simply. "Steve died last week. He was far too young, and all I can say, on behalf of Zoe, Harry, my parents, and myself, is that it's broken our hearts. I don't really know what else to say because I still don't believe Steve is gone, and so to talk about him in the past tense seems completely crazy. He was my little brother, who stuck a pea up my nostril when I was five because he wanted to know what was up my nose. I had to go to hospital to have it removed. He stole my bike when he was thirteen and trashed it, and then tried to pin the blame on me. He stayed up all night with me the night before I got my A-level results and I couldn't sleep. He came all the way up to Edinburgh for four hours just to have a pint with me last year because we hadn't seen each other for a while. He made me an uncle." He paused. "He was my little brother, but he was a bigger man than me, than most people. He was my big brother really, I suppose.

"And he and Zoe—their life together, the home they built, their family—it was just a pleasure to see it, to be a part of it. They didn't just have the best parties, they had the best life."

Zoe bent over as far as she could, rocking in her chair and sobbing piteously. Kate looked around, looked up at Mac, and then she got up out of her seat, pushed past Zoe's curled-up form, and sat down next to her in her row. She put her arms around her, and Zoe put her head on her shoulder, tears literally flowing down her cheeks.

Mac nodded, looking at her, and he took a deep breath and then went on.

"So, I don't know what to say to you all today, now that his life has gone. Now that their baby daughter will never know her dad, now that Harry will grow up without his father. And for all of us, who thought that Zoe and Steve, their house together, their life, represented everything they most wanted. It represented home to all of us, even if it wasn't our home. That's all over now, and I honestly can't ever see how we will ever smile again." He was about to break down. His fists clenched at his side.

"So perhaps we—Zoe, Mum, Dad, Harry—perhaps we have to take refuge in remembering him with pleasure, and being grateful that we had him in our lives, grateful that he met Zoe, that they had Harry, who's the spitting image of his dad. Grateful that he was here at all.

"But to be honest, I can't see a way to do that yet. Because, like I say, our hearts have been broken."

Twenty-nine

*I*t was Betty who planted the idea in her head. She had come back from New York for the funeral. They stood by the French windows looking out at Zoe, talking to Mr. and Mrs. Hamilton in the garden, her hand on her back, as if it were aching, Harry sitting at her feet. Mac stood next to them, tall, rigid, watching Zoe all the time. Kate could just make out Mary's soft voice rising gently above the hubbub that rippled through the house.

"They seem so lovely," said Betty quietly. "I can't believe I'd never met them before."

"I know," Kate said. She watched the group, unwilling to tear her eyes away from them. "Oh, Bets," she said.

Betty's hand slid into hers. "Babe," she said.

"How's she going to cope?" Kate said bleakly. "I just don't know what you do with something like that."

"I don't know either," said Betty. "She's Zoe, though. She will cope. I suppose if you have children, you have to."

"Yes," said Kate, realizing there was truth in this. She held on to the wooden frame of the door.

"Hey, Katy." Betty's voice was still soft. "How about you? How're you doing?"

"I'm fine," said Kate. "I'm not, but I'll be fine." She pushed some cakes toward Betty. "Here, have one of these."

"I don't mean like that," Betty said. "I just think this must be much harder for you than most people realize, darling."

"I don't know," Kate said through her tightened throat. "I don't think about it like that. It's not about me."

Francesca was standing next to them, talking to an old family friend of Steve's parents. Betty looked at her with surprise. "Right." There was a pause. "Only, sorry, I meant because he saved your life. Because he pushed you out of the way." She closed her eyes, shaking her head. "Sorry, that's so crass of me."

Francesca turned toward them at this point. "Betty, don't," she said under her breath. She nudged Betty. "Hey, Kate, those cakes look nice."

Kate looked from one to the other of them, then down at the plate of fondant fancies, which she had bought that morning. They looked gaudy, celebratory almost, stripes of yellow and pink, chocolaty and sweet. Her skin crawled, nausea swept over her, and heat. The wounds on her body stung; she prickled, ached in the heat. She wished she could tear her top off, scratch the scabs away.

"You OK?" Francesca asked.

Kate looked around the room, filled with people, all making desultory conversation, all watching other people over their shoulders. She whispered, almost to herself, "I feel like—like I'm disgusting."

"Look—" Francesca began.

"You mustn't feel guilty," said Betty.

Mrs. Allan had said that to her the day after Steve had died. She'd brought her down a cake, made her yet another cup of tea, held her hand. Her father had said that to her the previous night on the phone, when he'd rung to tell her he and Lisa were coming to the funeral. Even Zoe had said it to her, the day after it had happened. Kate still shuddered to think that Zoe had felt she had to say it.

"I don't feel guilty," said Kate. She clutched her left arm, where the cuts were worst. But it wasn't true. Things were starting to come together in her tired, battered head.

Watching her, Betty said, "Perhaps you should get away for a bit. You should come to New York, visit your mother maybe. Have you thought about that?"

"I don't want to leave Zoe," said Kate.

Francesca stroked her hair. "You can't be there for her the whole time," she said. "She'll have to get on with it. Mac's here, isn't he? And her mum, and his parents." Kate's eyes rested on the group in the garden again, and her throat rasped with the pain of not crying.

"I kind of think maybe you need to leave her alone for a while," Betty said after a pause. "You know."

"Oh." Kate nodded. "Perhaps you're right," she said.

"I think that's a good idea," Francesca said, nodding, like they'd already discussed it and thought it was a good idea.

"Come and stay with me," Betty said. "Or with your mother."

"What about my job, and the flat?" Kate said slowly. "I can't just leave them and go away."

She watched Betty closely, wondering if she realized just how much she wanted her to have the answer to all of this.

Betty said, "Oh, babe. They've signed you off work for two months. Don't you remember?"

"Oh yes," said Kate, wondering how she could have forgotten. She smiled at Betty, trying to let her know she wasn't mad.

"I spoke to your mother this morning," Kate's father said, clinking his glass gently against hers. Kate started.

"Really?" she said. Her parents never spoke, normally. But this was not normal.

"Yes," Daniel said. He stared down into his drink. She thought how much older he looked suddenly. When had he grown older and when had she not noticed? "She phoned first thing. You know, she was thinking of coming over for the funeral, to be here for you. She loves Zoe, you know that. And she was so fond of Steve." He nodded.

"She didn't need to come over," said Kate. "It would have . . ." She trailed off, thinking of her mother suddenly, how lovely it would be to have her near, to see her. She remembered her very clearly now, stroking her hair, reading her stories, laughing delightedly at her when she was little, how comforting she was, how Kate knew everything would always be fine when she was around, until suddenly she wasn't. She had never really felt it again with her mother, after she left—the wound she left was too deep. But there in the hot, sunny sitting room, with everyone dressed in black, Kate missed her mother with a force she hadn't known she possessed. To see her there, her long red hair, her warmth, her smile . . . She looked at her dad and clutched his hand, not able to speak all of a sudden.

"So he moved his stuff out, then?" Daniel asked grimly.

"Yep," said Kate. "The rest of it was gone when I got back yesterday."

"And what have you agreed about the mortgage?"

"Dad!—I don't know," said Kate. "I don't want to talk about it."

"How long will you be off work, do you know?" Daniel asked gruffly.

Kate watched him, wanting only to stay calm. "Look, Dad— it's too soon to think about all that stuff. It's not about me, about Sean and everything, at the moment. It's about Zoe."

"I know, darling," Daniel said. "But—"

"Please, Dad, let's not talk about it."

"I only want you to start thinking about yourself now," Daniel said. He sounded stern. "I'm your father. Your father, Kate. So

I worry about you. You have a flat you have a mortgage on and you're signed off work for however long, and you have a fiancé who's done the dirty on you and buggered off. And the funeral's over now. It's a week since—since Steve died. I'm just saying, you need to think about these things. Not now," he said, holding up a hand as Kate's eyes flashed and she started to speak, "but you need to think about them at some point."

"No," said Kate. "I'm only thinking about Zoe at the moment. Her and Harry, and the baby."

Daniel looked at her. He put his hand on her shoulder and turned her slowly so she was looking out into the garden, where Zoe and Mac were talking together and Mary was holding Harry. He looked so like his father, Kate took a deep breath.

"Kate, listen to me," Daniel said quietly. "You can't stay here with Zoe and make everything magically better. It's not like that. It won't mean Steve didn't die. It won't mean it wasn't your fault." He corrected himself. "It wasn't your fault, in any case. But you have to let them get on with it. You can be the best friend in the world—but you'll only ever be a friend. You're not Mac. You're not her baby. You can't bring him back, either. And you have to consider—"

"What?" Kate said.

"Nothing, nothing," Daniel said, and he kissed his daughter, patted her shoulder. She winced as his hand settled on her bruised skin. "Here's Lisa. Darling, we're going now, got to pick little Dani up. I'll phone you tonight. Do call your mother."

"Yes," said Lisa unexpectedly. "Call her." She turned to Daniel. "We'd better go and say bye to Zoe."

People watched in vague curiosity as they made their way across the room—Daniel was recognizable to a variety of people now. Kate gazed unseeingly at them, too, watched as they smiled at Zoe, as Mac and Jenny, Zoe's mother, appeared at her side, as Lisa and Daniel kissed them all, holding hands as they did. She was alone on the other side of the room and even in the heat of the day, suddenly felt extremely cold.

There is a sense at a wake that some people are clinging onto it as the last stage in a recognizable process. Because after that, the period of unreality is to some extent over, and you have to get on with your life in some way. People lingered at Steve's wake for ages, until the evening, until it was getting dark. The group of them who had spent their twenties in this house, first the ground floor flat, now the whole house, stayed the longest. Betty was staying at Francesca's that night, Jem and Bobbie and the others were just down the road, and as the packed throng thinned out, Kate found herself in the kitchen again, unloading the dishwasher with Zoe.

Zoe had been upstairs for a nap, but she hadn't slept and had come back downstairs again. Her mother had put Harry to bed and he was fast asleep, alternately bewildered and excited by the events of the day.

"There's some soup in the fridge," Kate said. "Do you think people will want—"

Zoe looked out from behind a cupboard at the group of people left. "Give it a while. If you're all still here in a bit I'll heat it up."

"I can do it, don't worry."

"Let's see," said Zoe. "I'm pretty tired now anyway, so hopefully everyone will have gone soon."

Kate shut the dishwasher. "Do you want me to get people moving?" She wiped her hands on a tea towel, and hung it carefully on the hook by the sink. Zoe was watching her as she did it.

"It'd be great if you were all off soon, to be honest." She wiped her hand over her forehead and gave a great, ragged sigh. "I'm not going to go hysterical again. I'm just really, really tired. I'm sick of all these people being here."

"Of course," said Kate. "You must be. It's just we don't want to leave you on your own, you know?"

And Zoe looked at her directly. "Yeah. But actually, Kate, I'd quite like to be on my own at some point."

Kate took the hint. "Look, I'll have a quick word with everyone. Are Mac and his parents—are they staying on?"

"Yes," said Zoe. "Just everyone else." She flung her hands up in the air and gave a little defeated moan of despair. "Is that OK." It was a statement, not a question.

Since she knew the contents of Zoe's fridge better than anyone at the moment, Kate said, ticking off things with her fingers, "Zo, you're low on milk, and cheddar, and veg, and those little yogurts Harry likes. Shall I pick some up tomorrow and come over first thing? We can—"

"No thanks," said Zoe, quite loudly. She corrected herself instantly. "I mean—sorry, Kate. I don't need you to come around tomorrow. Steve's parents are leaving and we'll have stuff to sort out."

"Oh, right," said Kate. "I'll call you in the afternoon, then. Perhaps I can—"

As if it was in slow motion, Zoe shook her head. She didn't say anything, she just looked at Kate, and a tear ran down her cheek as she rubbed her stomach again. Her eyes were shining with tears, her hand was on her back, and she stood there silently, shaking her head as Kate watched her, understanding dawning.

Eventually Zoe just whispered, "No, OK? Please, Kate. You need to leave me alone for a while."

Kate stepped back and nodded. She knew. She kissed her best friend's cheek, her heart cracking as she turned away. "Of course. I love you. OK. But soon. I'll see you soon."

Zoe nodded, too, not meeting her gaze.

Five minutes later, they were all outside on the sidewalk. The others went to the pub to carry on the wake, talking about Steve, remembering the good times, like Mac had said. But Kate went home. She tore off the black cotton dress, the long cardigan. There were spots of blood on her skin where the scabs had shifted, opened up again. She ran her fingers over the knobbly, rashlike bumps they formed over her tired, bruised skin as she sat on the sofa in her sitting room, staring at nothing in the darkness for hours. She had seen the look on Zoe's face, heard the tone in her father's voice. She knew now that what she had said to Betty and Francesca earlier— well, it was probably true. She was to blame, she was disgusting, she should not be here, she should not be here at all.

Thirty

So that was how it happened that Kate left London. One sunny, dappled day in September, just as the leaves were beginning to change color and the sky above New York was so blue it seemed to bounce off everything around it, Kate found herself pushing a trolley through the airport terminal at JFK, past the baggage claim and passport control, where a moustachioed customs officer said with a strangely kind expression on his face, almost like he knew the importance of it, "Welcome to New York, miss." She smiled at him blankly, unable to believe she was there, that she had made it this far, that she was away from the flat, away from the piles of paperwork, away from her friends' questions, her work's sympathy, the sly looks of neighbors in the hall, the horror on people's faces when she went outside before the scabs had healed, revealing her arms cut up, shredded. All of that was behind her now.

The automatic doors into the main terminal shuddered open and she emerged into the big glass atrium. Kate looked around, but she should have known that she wouldn't need to. Because there, standing in front of her, waving a placard that said MY DAUGHTER KATE!, was her mother, and as Kate ran toward her, pushing the trolley out of the way as she embraced her, she started crying, and once she started, she couldn't stop. Venetia pulled her into her arms and kissed her. "My little girl," she whispered. "You're here now. It's OK. It's OK."

When Kate woke up, it was late the next day, nearly ten o'clock. She looked around the pretty white bedroom perched on a corner of the apartment. It was strangely quiet except for the noise of the birds singing loudly outside—she'd forgotten how loud they were, how many there were. She sat up and looked out of the window. On the other side of Riverside Drive was the park. A man was chatting to a friend, both out walking their dogs on this glorious September afternoon. Other than that it was silent. She felt nothing. She stared out of the window, and then around the room. It was clean, small, empty, blank. She thought of the possessions she'd boxed up and put away at her flat, of the new person living there now who would call it her own home. It was three o'clock in London. Juliet would be sitting in Kate's old office now, doing Kate's old job. Gemma would be moving into Kate's flat—perhaps she'd have unpacked even now. And Kate felt totally at home for the first time in weeks. Perhaps months.

In the other room, Oscar started playing the piano. Kate listened. It was "I Remember You." She did. She always would. She lay back on the bed, watching the ceiling, just listening to the music, simply enjoying the feeling of calm that washed over her. She was safe. She was at home, she was away from London. She didn't even have to think about going back. Perhaps she would never go back.

When, a month later, Zoe had her baby girl, Flora, Kate sent a baby bag and a hamper and a card, and Zoe never replied. Kate told herself that it was because she was busy with the baby, but she wasn't quite sure.

But Zoe did email her a couple of months later. She was chatty, sweet. Flora was fine, Harry was fine, they were all fine. Francesca said she was doing brilliantly. Mac, with whom she was in contact most frequently, kept her posted, sent her pictures, told her little snippets. He never reproached her, never made her feel bad about running away to New York. He never really commented on anything at all, nor could she expect him to. Her father was an infrequent correspondent, but he came to New York occasionally and she saw him then, which was almost better.

For over two years after she left London, it was almost as if Kate Miller had hardly existed there at all. It was her hometown, her life was there, but now it was all gone. She tried to pretend she didn't miss it but sometimes—like once when she was in the Frick Collection, and she turned to see the Turner scene of the Thames at Mortlake Terrace, or when she heard Venetia laughing at comedy programs from Radio 4 on Oscar's computer, or just sometimes, when she was walking down the gray, chaotic, tarry streets of New York, chewing on a bagel, drinking her coffee, and she thought of home, of the green parks and the gray skies and the people she loved most of all—sometimes it was almost unbearable.

She didn't consider herself damaged. She thought she'd coped with what had happened, and what happened afterward. Kate had come close to the edge, and she couldn't let it happen again.

Part Three

Thirty-one

*K*ate rang the doorbell of her father's house, smoothing down the fabric of her dress, nervously. It was just after eight, and she was due at the *Venus* offices to see Sue at ten. She shivered on the front doorstep in the cold March morning; it was a week now since she'd come back to London, and in that time she'd been around to her father's every single day, but it still felt weird, each time.

Lisa appeared in the hallway, and Kate watched her through the glass. She didn't make eye contact with Kate until she'd opened the door.

"Hi, Kate," she said, kissing her stepdaughter on the cheek. "You're here, then. I was wondering where you'd got to."

"Hi," said Kate, refusing to get ruffled. She was too exhausted to rise to Lisa's bait; the previous day she had written and rewritten her five hundred words for Sue so many times her brain felt like it wasn't working properly. She had finally emailed the piece over late the previous night, but she had slept badly, her dreams full of scenes she wanted to bury, her mind woolly, thoughts circling inside her head like they were trapped there. She had woken up while it was still dark; someone had been shouting at her. It had taken Kate a while to realize it had been her, calling out in her sleep. She was glad Mr. Allan wasn't there; she knew he would probably have heard her otherwise.

Early the previous evening, Mr. Allan had left to go on holiday with his sister. "Break a leg," he'd told her as he climbed into the cab. "I'll see you in two weeks, dear girl. Two weeks! What will I do without you?"

Kate hadn't wanted to say that she'd probably miss him a lot more. Besides her father, he was the one constant in her London life, the one person she'd seen every day. Now it was just Dad—and Lisa and Dani, of course, but it was her father she came to see. And somehow Mr. Allan's departure and her completing the article had thrown all of this into even sharper relief. She felt awkward, uncomfortable again, like she had done a week ago. It was just nerves about this morning, she told herself, and she stepped over the threshold.

"You look nice," said Lisa tonelessly.

"Oh, thanks," said Kate. "I've got a meeting—"

But Lisa had already turned and walked toward the kitchen. "Your father's through here," she said briskly.

There was an Atmosphere in the kitchen as Kate entered behind her stepmother. Her father was there, and she was surprised to see him fully dressed, sitting at the table impatiently whipping through the pages of the *Times,* an untouched pile of toast by his side.

"Hello, Dad." Kate bent down and kissed him. He smiled politely, and Kate looked inquiringly over at Lisa, who began loading the dishwasher.

"He's fine," she said calmly. "He's been like this all morning. He's not hungry and he won't eat anything. He wants to go out. I've said it's far too soon."

Daniel looked up and ran a hand through his thin hair. "I'm not a child. Don't talk about me as if I weren't here," he said in a clear voice.

"Hey, Dad. It's great you're feeling better, though," said Kate.

"Thank you, darling. Thank you for coming to see me."

"That's OK." Kate tapped the kitchen table. "Hey. Dad, I've got a sort of an interview today—"

Lisa slammed a cupboard door shut and dropped something in the sink with a loud clatter, and Daniel winced.

"Now, listen, Lisa—" he said, trying to contain his irritation, but Lisa turned around with a sneer on her face.

"Daniel! We're not having this discussion! I'm not doing this for my own amusement, believe me! You are Not Going Out, and that's that," she finished, slightly hysterically, and stormed out of the kitchen.

"I was going to ask you to keep it down, dearest," Daniel said loudly after her, his voice high and cold. "God, that girl," he said, turning to Kate, shaking his head, and she was worried to see the expression on his face. "You know, she's wonderful, but my God! So temperamental, so . . . bloody . . ."

Kate wanted to say a variety of things, but instead she said, "I expect she's just tired, you know. She's had a lot on her plate, with Dani, and you being ill and everything . . ."

"I know," said her father sadly, and it made her suddenly want to hug him. "I'm awful. I've been awful to her. She's so good, and I've been . . ." He trailed off, looking out of the window into the handkerchief-sized garden, where the wind blew roughly, shaking the tree perching on the corner of the neat lawn.

A small disloyal thought flashed through Kate's brain, that her father was actually enjoying all of this, enjoying the suffering and being maudlin and the center of everyone's attention once again. She shook her head and slapped her hands onto her thighs. Feeling like the supervisor in an old-people's home, she said, in a loud, cheery voice, "Well! So how are you feeling today, any-way?"

"Fine, fine," said her father, brushing her away with his hand. His tone was still irritable. "Just bored, that's all. No one's been to visit me, not a bloody soul. It's as if I'm dead. Shows you who your friends are, doesn't it? And I've got work to do, arrangements for the Manilow album. No one cares."

"I care, Dad," said Kate carefully. "And I've been to see you, haven't I?"

"Oh." Daniel nodded kindly at her. "Yes, that's true. You don't really count, though," he said. "I mean, outside the family. You know, *others*."

Kate said patiently, "Hey, I'm sorry, Dad. This is the worst stage, I think. You're feeling better but you're still not that well. Shall we sit down in the other room and just chat?"

His eyebrows waggled together, undecided how to play this offer, but eventually he said gruffly, "Sure. Yup, sure, let's go through."

They climbed the two steps up to the living room-cum-dining room, Daniel moving slowly, and suddenly Lisa appeared from the large, spotless cellar, where the surplus fridges and freezers for their house were stored, clutching Dani's lunch box. She looked flustered.

"Look, Dan, I just thought of something," she said. "Why don't you and Kate walk Dani to school? Kate can make sure you're OK, and I can run to the dry cleaners." She said this last sentence in a rush.

"Why do you need to go to the dry cleaner's?"

"Um. I forgot to pick up your dinner jacket," said Lisa, avoiding her husband's eye.

"What?" Daniel said sharply. "But, Lisa . . . I . . ."

"I know you do," said Lisa. "I'm sorry. I forgot, I forgot, OK? With everything that's happened."

"I asked you to pick it up last week, before the operation. I never know when I'll need it. Lisa, you *must* remember things like this!"

"Oh, don't sound so bloody patronizing," said Lisa, and she ran her hand across her brow, baring her teeth at Daniel. "It's not like you're going to be needing it any time soon, is it?"

Kate watched her, alarmed at the expression in her eyes, and tightened her grip on her father's arm.

"I will!" her father shouted, in a weak voice, petulantly. "Shut up! You don't know anything, anything! I will!"

"OK, Dad, OK," said Kate, patting his shirtsleeve. She remembered with a flash her mother doing the same thing. Patting his arm, talking him back down to normality, telling him it was OK, she was sorry.

"I'm sorry, darling," said Lisa, seeing he looked really alarmed. "Look, it's no big deal. I'll run and get it now. You two take Dani to school. You can have a little walk. It'll do you good, don't you think?"

There was a rumble upstairs, and a thundering sound, and right on cue Dani ran furiously downstairs, hanging on to the banister with one small hand. She jumped the last step onto the ground and looked faceup at her father, beaming, then at Kate.

"Hey there!" she said loudly. "Kate! Hey there!"

"Oh," said Daniel. He turned away and said grumpily, "She's doing it again. That stupid voice. She's doing it again."

"Hi, Dani," said Kate, feeling sorry for Dani, having to live with these two. "How are you? I'm going to walk you to school with Dad, is that OK?"

"Sure! Sure!" Dani jumped up and down and grabbed the lunch box from Lisa. "Let's go!"

"Bye, darling," said Lisa, holding her wriggling daughter's head in her hands as she bent down and kissed her hair. "Be good for Kate. I'll see you later, yes? Have a lovely morning. Good-bye, Daniel." She looked at her husband, a curious expression on her face, something like triumph. "Do you have anything to say?"

"Why should I?" said Daniel, still secure that the balance of power was his. "I'll see you when—"

Lisa turned away. In a low voice she said, "Just forget it. I'm sorry about the dry cleaning, darling. Just be careful."

Daniel was mollified. He furrowed his brow. "No, darling,

I'm sorry. I'm a horrible old man. And you're wonderful to put up with me."

"I know I am," said Lisa. She crunched her keys together. "Oh, darling." She kissed her husband softly on the cheek.

"Have a nice day," Dani said, hitting the banisters and the wall alternately with her hands. Lisa opened the door and they trooped out in single file, Dani first, Kate second, Daniel last, and Kate felt like singing, "The animals came in one by one, tra la," out loud, but she quelled it and took Dani's hand.

"We have to walk slowly, for Dad," she told Dani. "You OK, Dad?" she said, looking back at her father.

"Never better," Daniel said, grinning. "I'm so sorry for being such a bastard this morning. I just find it very frustrating, you know?" He pushed a lock of hair out of his eyes.

"You must do," said Kate. "Will you get Lisa a present? Should we stop and get her some flowers?"

But Daniel wasn't listening. "Ah, it's wonderful to be outside," he said, breathing in deeply. He coughed. "The old lungs, still not quite up to scratch yet." And he thumped his chest, hard. "Aah."

"Dad, be careful," said Kate, but Daniel was enjoying himself. He spread his arms wide, on the quiet street, and nearly stumbled over a cracked paving stone before correcting himself.

He said casually, "So, Kate. Tell me, how's your mother?"

"Ah," said Kate, taken aback. "She's—she's fine. Dani, what have you got there?!"

Dani was fumbling in the big plastic wallet that passed for a school satchel, and from this she removed a blue plastic cartoon shark, its teeth bared, its face contorted in an expression of hatred.

"It's my Migmog," she told Kate. She patted the toy and made a soft cooing noise. "She's my friend."

"Ohhh-kay," said Kate. "Oh. He's nice."

"*She!* She's a *she*!" Dani boomed, waving the shark alarmingly close to Kate's face, and Kate veered toward her father, feeling like she was jackknifing between two lunatics, both of whom were her blood relatives, she realized to her surprise.

"Sorry!" she said irritably. "*She!* OK!"

"Is she . . . well?" said Daniel, continuing as if nothing had happened. "Is she happy?"

She didn't really know how to answer this question. Of course her mother was well, of course she was happy. She was relentlessly positive, upbeat, a show-off showman, with the starring role in the miniseries of her own life, with the devoted Oscar at her side, living in a beautiful apartment in the most exciting city in the world.

Tramping slowly alongside her father, back here in London, Kate didn't quite know how to explain it to him. For she had come to see, in the time she'd lived with her in New York, that her mother was more of a mystery than she could have supposed. She still didn't know lots of things about her, really, little details like what her favorite film was or big things like why she'd left her husband and daughter, why she'd run away—and Kate knew she *had* run away, just like her daughter had done sixteen years later. And now, glancing quickly at Daniel, shuffling along beside her, his breath visible in the cold morning's air, she couldn't see them together, couldn't remember what they'd been like. He seemed so much older, so . . . thin in spirit somehow, whereas Venetia was overflowing with life, and energy, and lots of other things Kate didn't really understand. It seemed mad they'd ever got married, had a baby. Had her. They were her *parents;* it was strange. Kate blinked rapidly, her mind whirring.

"Well, you know what Mum's like," she said after a while. "Always the same old Mum." She shook her head, smiling at the memory of Venetia's beautiful face as she stood and raised her glass to Kate, her still-thick glossy red hair falling around her shoulders as she solemnly recited "May the road rise to meet you" the night before Kate had left them for London. Oscar had merely looked on in wonderment. "Isn't she the best?" he'd said reverentially when she'd finished and sunk gracefully back into her chair, as if she'd just sung the title role in *Aida,* not read a poem out loud.

For a moment Kate was back there, in the warm, quiet apartment overlooking the Hudson, the fire crackling in the corner, the books lining the walls. Safe, tranquil, easy. She shook her head at the memory, smiling. "She's wonderful, just the same as ever. The life and soul of the party. You know what she's like," she said again.

Daniel looked surprised. "Oh." He furrowed his brow.

"Oh?" Kate was curious.

"I don't remember her like that at all," he said, and he looked old, confused for a moment, and fear flashed through Kate. She clutched tightly onto Dani's hand, feeling the soft plump fingers tighten in response. She wished they weren't talking about this, and sought to tie up the conversation again.

"You know, though. Mum's so—" She cast around for the word. "Well, she's such a free spirit, isn't she? Always has been." She chuckled, as if to involve her father in the gentle joking, the way she did with Oscar back in New York, for Oscar saw through his wife's faults and loved her for them anyway.

Daniel said strangely, "She wasn't like that when we were together. . . ." He trailed off, and said after a while, "Perhaps she was—perhaps I remember that in the beginning." His pace slowed and he shook his head, looking down at the pavement. "She wasn't, really, though, not when you were growing up, when we were still together." He flicked a glance at Dani. "But it was very difficult by then."

Kate tried to remember something of her parents together but, as ever, she drew a blank. She could remember the house, her exercise books from school, the Nativity play when she was small, but she couldn't remember her parents together, what they were like, how they *were* with each other. It was somewhere in her brain— she just couldn't get to it. The only memory she had was from Mr. Allan, of her leaving the Royal Festival Hall with her mother and father, she eight years old, happily holding on to each of her parent's hands. Them together: it just seemed hilarious, impossible.

The last time they'd seen each other was at her engagement party, four years ago, and they'd behaved like old friends. A little *too* much like old friends, in fact. Lisa had spent the whole week Oscar and Venetia were over looking like she was sucking a lemon. Kate often remembered the way they'd looked at each other that night: like they got each other. Simple as that. Like there was no one else in the room. She'd never looked at Sean like that, she knew. Knew it now, hadn't known it then. Oh, she'd loved him, but she'd never really understood him the way she knew her parents understood each other. But when she thought about it, how understanding someone, like the way they got each other, the way she and Mac got each other, proved nothing, really. Got you nowhere.

So she said nothing. And Daniel said, matter-of-factly, "You know, Kate, all this makes me think."

"Think what?" Kate said, looking around her, trying to see if they were near the school.

"About your mother." He cupped his hand into a point. "Bah. Never mind."

"What?" said Kate.

"I said never mind. Did she even ask how I was?" Daniel pushed his hair out of his face.

Kate thought back to her conversation with her mother last night. "I expect he's malingering, like he *always did*," Venetia had said, and at the time Kate had thought that was a rather harsh judgment call on a man recovering from transplant surgery, but now, having seen her father this morning, she could kind of appreciate her point. She thought she'd better change the subject, and looked down at Dani, who was completely silent, chewing her plait. She bent down toward her. "Where's your school, Dani?"

"It's just across the road, Kate, we're nearly there," Daniel said, a little faintly. Traffic whizzed past them, and Kate turned to him. "Why don't you sit here, Dad?" she said, gesturing to a bench. "I'll drop her off. Just wait a second."

She and Dani crossed the road and stopped outside the school gates; people looked inquiringly at Kate. She crouched down, looking into her sister's face.

"You've got really blue eyes," she said in surprise.

"Blue eyes," said Dani. She patted Kate's cheek.

"What color are my eyes?" Kate asked her.

"Brown eyes!" Dani said with pleasure.

"Yes. Yours are beautiful," said Kate.

Dani tugged Kate's skirt. "But I'm tall. I hate being tall," she confided suddenly.

Kate felt her heart contract, at this little thing thinking she was tall. "You're still small," she told her sister.

"I'm not," Dani said, shaking her head firmly. "I'm the tallest girl in my class. The boys call me daddy longlegs, I hate it."

"Well," said Kate, thinking for a moment. "They just wish they were tall like you, that's all. I was very tall when I was your age, all tall and spindly, and it was very useful, do you know why?"

"Why?" said Dani.

"My mum could always spot me in the playground," said Kate. She wasn't sure this was going to seal the deal for Dani, who looked unconvinced, so she added, with more zeal than she meant, "And Dani, I promise you. You'll grow up and you will be so glad you're tall. It's the best, honestly. You can wear boots and baggy tops and you don't look like a dwarf. Or a woodcutter."

"Ah?" said Dani, looking utterly confused.

"Never mind," said Kate hurriedly. "I *promise* you, please trust me. Aren't supermodels tall?"

"Yes!" Dani looked more cheerful, to Kate's chagrin, and she bent down and kissed her sister again.

"Wish me luck for my interview today," she said.

"Good luck," said Dani. "Can I have a present, please?" She

held her skirt and put her head on one side, trying to look coyly adorable. Kate stood up.

"Humph. Don't push your luck, love," she said, and she kissed her sister again. "See you soon, Dani. You go into school now, OK?"

"There's Olivia. Bye!" Dani said, and then, with the remarkable callousness of extreme youth, turned around and ran inside shouting, "Hello, Mrs. Bateman!" as she did, having entirely forgotten about Kate.

Kate brushed her skirt down again and watched her sister disappear through the doors of the school, feeling strangely bereft, and she looked at her father, waiting for her on the other side of the road. He looked tired. She ought to get him home. She checked her watch; it was just before nine. She felt strange, being so dressed up so early on this cold, windy day. Strange and nervous. What if Sue hated the piece—what would she do then? She'd done it now, she told herself. No going back, and she didn't really want to.

"I'm coming, Dad," she called as she waited to cross the road.

Besides, she had something to prove to herself. She was pissed off. Finally. In her bag she had the letter she'd got that morning. That made three now.

Kate

It's been over a week now. I don't know why you haven't called me. Look, I know you hate me. Just wanted to ask you though, didn't you ever see you had it coming to you? So smug and grown-up with your FIANCÉ and your FLAT and your amazing wonderful bloody job. You left me behind in the dust, darling, didn't you? I thought we were friends and you just ditched me when you found something better.

I know you think I must feel guilty. I DON'T. OK? The reason I keep writing is, look, Kate, I just need to tell you something. So get in touch. We need to sort some things out.

CHARLY

Thirty-two

"Shall I tell you what's wrong with this, then?"

The great glass office was the same; the ornaments on Sue's desk were the same. There was even the same poster up in the kitchen, a yellowing Health and Safety notice about what to do if someone was choking. Underneath it someone had written *Leave them alone. They're probably bulimic.* Kate never knew if they were serious or not. The layouts for Sue's approval were the same, piled high in her tray; Kate could see the marks scribbled all over them. But still, everything at *Venus* felt different, Kate most especially. She couldn't remember being in those meetings, telling people what to do, and she most especially couldn't remember leaving that life, going home to Sean in their flat. Kate sat in front of Sue, who was holding a printout of her article. Her bangs were falling into her eyes; she blew them away nervously.

"Go on, then," she said, torn between being completely humiliated and suddenly, inexplicably, wanting to laugh.

"Right," said Sue, grinding her jaw. "Here goes. 'It was the advent of the canals, which, coupled with the arrival of steam-engine power to England, hastened the Industrial Revolution and helped enable the greatest—and most controversial—empire since Roman times.' " She fixed Kate with a baleful glance. "And that's one of the more interesting bits. The rest of the time it's all about the good old days during rationing! *Rationing,* for Christ's sake! This is a fun, informative lifestyle magazine for young women. This is supposed to be a charming, funny column about one young woman's experience of London. It's not a slide show evening with Isambard Kingdom Brunel and Dame Vera Lynn!"

"I like Dame Vera Lynn!" Kate protested.

"Honey, I love Dame Vera Lynn," said Sue. " 'A Nightingale Sang in Berkeley Square' was the first dance at my parents' wedding. I love the woman, I have nothing but love for her. That's not the effing point, OK?"

"Don't swear about Dame Vera Lynn," Kate said.

"Kate." Sue shook her head. "Can you not see what I'm talking about?"

"Yes." Kate bit her lip. "I know, I know."

"You're a young Londoner. Act like one."

Kate was shaking her head. "Sue! I'm thirty, I'm not that young."

"Oh, for God's sake, ridiculous girl. You see, that's the trouble." Sue was practically banging the table in frustration, half leaning over toward Kate. Kate couldn't decide if she was going to slap her or hug her. "Kate, Kate. You're young, you're still really young. Half these op-ed pieces or lifestyle columns or whatever—they're written by forty-five-year-olds pretending to be thirty." She calmed down a bit; her voice softened, and this time Kate really did brace herself. "I was wrong, after Aunt Eileen's funeral, what I said to you."

"What was that?"

"I told you to grow up. I was wrong. You don't need to grow up. You need to stop behaving like an old lady. You bought *doilies* for Eileen's wake, you were handing around miniquiches! And those disgusting wet crisps. Oh, I could cry. Look. Eileen hated doilies! So does Uncle Gray! So do you!" Sue was practically screeching. "Kate, when I poached you to come to *Venus* with me it was because you were everything a modern girl was supposed to be! You knew the key pieces from every prêt-à-porter collection that year *and* your favorite book was *Middlemarch*! You were the modern girl par excellence!"

Kate, fascinated at this description of herself, was nodding along, rapt by the staccato rhythm of Sue's speech. "You're not a doilies girl!" Sue calmed down a little. "It's like you've stopped bothering to engage with the real world around you. Do something wild for once. Sleep with someone you shouldn't. Dance on a table! Stay up all night! You're becoming an old lady, and you're still a young woman."

Kate raised her hand, as if in a classroom, to make an Important Point. "Er—"

"You are. Let me finish." Sue waggled a pencil at her. "Living with your mother and stepfather, for example. What's that like?"

On the verge of defending herself, crossly, Kate was suddenly, irresistibly reminded of her last Saturday before she'd left, when Oscar had held an impromptu piano party, and Mrs. Da Costa and the Cohens from down the hall had come, and Maurice, the doorman, (practically, she was realizing, her best friend in New York) had popped by to say hi and sung, brilliantly, "Makin' Whoopee," and they'd all had gin fizzes made by Venetia, and Kate and Oscar had duetted to "Baby, It's Cold Outside."

"Oh my God," she said, the scales falling from her eyes.

"And what have you done since you got back? Seen anyone your own age?"

I don't like people my own age, Kate wanted to say. Instead she said crossly, "Of course I have. Don't be so silly. I've seen Zoe—and—"

"Zoe? The one on her own with the kids?"

"It wasn't like that, Sue, we needed to catch up, and—"

"Well, whatever. Woman in a semidetached making jam and wearing a tabard—that doesn't count, all right? Anything else?"

"Um—I've seen Mr. Allan," said Kate.

Sue's eyes were twinkling now. "Yes, of course. But he's almost younger than you, dear. He's gone off to Mallorca. Most likely he'll join a band and stay there, playing to tourists. Who else?"

"Well, I see Dad and Dani most days. And Lisa—"

"Who's Lisa?"

"My stepmother."

"How old?"

Kate considered this. Lisa was mysterious about her age, but Kate remembered her fortieth had been mentioned as having possibly taken place a couple of years ago. "She's about forty-two."

"Right," said Sue. "So, apart from me and my recently widowed uncle, and the mum with the kids, the person closest to you in age you've been hanging out with is your stepmother. And *that's* why this article doesn't work."

More than just the article. Kate's head sank to her chest, but then suddenly snapped up again.

"Wait, wait!" she said. "My friend Francesca. I saw her."

"OK," said Sue, her eyes lighting up. "What's Francesca do?"

"She's a banker."

"Cool. Where did you go?" said Sue, practically rubbing her hands together.

"Er . . . we went to Kettners."

Sue looked crestfallen. "God. Established 1964 or something. This is depressing. And that's it?"

Well, no, Kate wanted to say, *I also saw Mac, who I think is very likely the love of my life, but he told me he actually kind of hates me, and then I ran out screaming into the streets like a madwoman and that is why the food at the party was not particularly well prepared, must you keep going on about it?*

Oh, plus, Charly, your old assistant, remember her? Well, she's writing me letters that keep turning up delivered by hand to my flat. And they're scary.

If you knew what I'd seen the day Steve died, if you'd spent the last three years knowing you were responsible for his death, if you'd been told by his widow, your best friend, that it might be best if you leave them all alone and go—if you knew all of that, perhaps you'd understand why I like hanging out with Mr. Allan and hearing about the night he played with some old legend at the 606 Club, or singing Dean Martin songs with my stepfather, or walking my four-year-old sister to school.

Kate reached across the glass table and took the article back. She tore it up and threw it in the bin.

"Point taken," she said. "I'll rewrite it. You'll have it by the end of the week."

"That's my girl," said Sue. She stood up and shook Kate's hand. "Now go out and get yourself drunk. Or go to a club somewhere. Pick up someone."

Kate laughed. "Jeez, Sue! If I still worked here, I could have you done for harassment, you know."

Sue ushered her out of the door. "You don't work here," she said, handing something to her assistant. "Book Orso for lunch, will you? Thanks." She pushed Kate gently in the back. "I'll walk you to the lifts."

As they walked through the white and gray, light and airy offices of *Venus*, Kate noticed how much busier it was, filled with more things. Backlist issues lined the shelves; filing cabinets were scuffed; she recognized hardly anyone's faces. The magazine was three years old now—it was practically a senior citizen in the marketplace.

"Look," said Sue carelessly. "That's Rachel." She pointed toward Kate's old office.

"She does my old job?" Kate said, looking at the small, perky blond girl gesticulating to someone on the phone. She looked up, saw Sue, and waved.

Sue waved back. "No, darling. You did her job. Once. So get back to your desk and get on with it. You can do it." They were at the lifts. She kissed Kate briefly on the cheek. "I'll look forward to getting the piece again," she said. "Let's sort this out this week—otherwise I'll need to look at other options."

Kate nodded. "Fair enough," she said. She stood up straight, feeling like someone was challenging her for the first time in years. "That's great. I won't let you down, Sue." She put her hand on her arm. "Thanks a lot."

"All right, all right," said Sue, backing away. "This isn't a Céline Dion video. Don't get yucky on me. Just email me when you've done it. Tomorrow?"

"Definitely," Kate told her.

"And remember. Enjoy yourself."

Kate walked across Waterloo Bridge, the wind whipping her hair around her face, ignoring the thoughts jostling for position in her head. The Thames was gray and choppy underneath her, the sky above matching it, and she turned and looked out at the South Bank and the Millennium Wheel, across to the Houses of Parliament and the white Shell-Mex House with the huge black clock above a balcony where Churchill used to stand during the Second World War, watching the German bombers tear up his capital city. She stood for a while, thinking. About the meeting, about her dad. But mostly about the letters from Charly, how angry she was with Kate. It was weird. Kate had never really realized it before, that someone who appeared to be that strong and beautiful, so in command of her own life, could actually be so—was *weak* the word? No, probably not. She didn't know what it was with Charly. But weirdly, she realized as she looked out across the river, she didn't really care that much anymore. When she thought about her dad, Zoe, Dani—making things right with Mac, even—the lives and loves of Charly and Sean didn't concern her in the way they used to. She turned and walked across the bridge. When she reached the other side, she pulled out her phone and dialed.

"Hi, Francesca," she said. "It's me. Kate."

"Mysterious Kate Miller," said a wry voice on the other end of the phone. "Last seen running out of my house in hysterics a week ago. She lives."

"Sorry to call you at work. Can you talk?"

"Sure, for a minute," said Francesca. "I'm glad to hear from you. I was starting to think you were D.E.A.D. dead. What happened last week, for God's sake?"

It was a high-risk strategy, but Kate decided to go for insouciantly forgetful. Barely a couple of words in she realized it was a mistake. "What, oh, after we went out? The next day at yours?" Her voice was getting higher. "Oh, you know, don't you remember? I had to go, my neighbor's wife died and—"

"Good grief," said Francesca, her smoky voice sounding amused. "You're as bad as he is."

"Who is?"

"He. Mac. The two of you."

The two of you.

"Oh, really, why?" said Kate, trying to sound politely interested. "What's he said?"

"He's said nothing," said Francesca. "Said he wouldn't discuss it and I wasn't to ask him about it. Thanks for making the few free moments of leisure I have at my home full of tension and stress."

"Oh God, Francesca," Kate said. "I am sorry, you know that. And I should have called you. I've been a bit crazy, and—you know."

"Well, I don't know," said Francesca. "That's the point."

"Look," said Kate. "It's in the past. It's to do with old stuff. I promise it's nothing for you to worry about and I shouldn't have behaved that way. It was . . . childish of me. Old lady with doily-ish, maybe."

"Eh?"

"Nothing," said Kate, hurrying on. "Nothing. Look, are you around tomorrow night? I've got a freelance job."

"That's great, Kate!" Kate could hear the pleasure in Francesca's voice. "For who?"

"Sue again," said Kate. "It's for *Venus*—look, I'll tell you all about it. I've got to do it tonight, for tomorrow. Can we go for a drink, then, to celebrate me finishing it?"

Even walking down the street, Kate could hear the hesitation in Francesca's voice.

"Um," she said after a while. "Look, I was supposed to be seeing Zoe, and—"

"Well, that's fine," said Kate. "Isn't it?"

"Yeah, it's just—I was going around to hers for supper."

"Oh," said Kate, not sure how to play it. She was crossing into Covent Garden, her feet wobbling on the tricky cobbles, passing the Punch and Judy, where Sean had his birthday all those years ago. "Well—"

"Look, I'm sure Zoe'd love it if you came, it's just—Mac might come. I mean, he says he can't, he's working, but he was going to maybe pop by. Perhaps I should tell him not to—"

Kate was suddenly a bit cross at Francesca assuming this way and that. How did she know what Zoe would or wouldn't love? Zoe was her best friend, wasn't she? And she and Mac were grownups, weren't they? Uncertainty made her defensive.

"Francesca, look, I'll talk to Zoe," she said firmly.

"Does she know? About you and Mac, I mean?"

"No," said Kate. "It's complicated. I mean, I don't want to talk to her about it. I mean . . . he may have told her, I haven't." How she wished she could tell them both.

"I thought you told each other everything," said Francesca. "Oh."

Kate opened her mouth to say something and then didn't. The truth was, she and Zoe didn't talk about anything much these days: both before, when she was in New York, and now since she was back. She'd seen her a couple of times since she'd been back, since that first night at her house. It was fine, of course it was fine. But it wasn't great. Somehow she'd thought, naively, that it would be when she came back. But she didn't want Francesca knowing that.

"Listen, I want to see you, and I want to see Zo again—I haven't for a few days. Me and Mac, it's in the past, it's fine. If he turns up, it's fine. Honestly! I promise you we can be in the same room without it being awkward. And"—she corrected herself—"anyway, he's not an ex."

"That's almost exactly what he said!" said Francesca. She sounded almost impressed at their psychic synchronicity.

"Did he?"

"Yep," Francesca said firmly. "Tomorrow, then. That's great. I really want to see you again." And then she added, "But, God, Kate. What did you do?"

Kate stopped and a car hooted at her. "I—what do you mean?" She ran to the other side so she was in the Piazza, under the shelter of the church.

Francesca's voice was kind, but she said, "To make him hate you that much. What on earth did you do?"

Kate stared out across the square, where a magician was rather gloomily plying his trade to some unenthusiastic schoolchildren. She turned away from them, toward the door of the church. "Good question," she said quietly. "I messed him around. You could say I broke his heart."

There was a pause. "When?" Francesca said. "God, I knew it. When?"

"It's a long story—I'll explain it sometime."

"You don't have to explain anything, babe," said Francesca. Kate could hear typing in the background, and she knew her slot with her was coming to an end. "See you tomorrow."

"Thanks," said Kate.

"What are you going to do today?"

Kate thought of Charly's letter, one last time. *You always were a bit of a loser*. Screw her. "Oh. I'm going home to work. I'll give Zo a call, too. See you later."

Thirty-three

"*I hadn't been on the canal since I was eleven,*" Zoe read aloud carefully. "*And now that, after a walk in Regent's Park and then a nice cup of tea by the canal, would definitely be my idea of a great day out in London. Perhaps you could hop in a cab and go to Fortnum and Mason's for tea. Even though I'm grown-up, I think it's the simplest things that often provide the most satisfying memories. I like this day out because it's perfect if you're by yourself, if you've got children, or if you're visiting London for the weekend, or even if you're on a romantic date, and when I was in New York it was what I used to dream about. I'd love to know what your suggestions for your own great day out in London would be. Until next time, love from Girl About Town.*"

Zoe lowered the paper. "Very good," she said. "Wow. I never even knew about the canal boat ride. Or that those men in the clock are Mr. Fortnum and Mr. Mason. How did you know that?"

"You know me," said Kate. She tapped her head. "I'm a repository for useless information."

"The only person who enjoyed General Studies at school. I'd forgotten." Zoe put the article down. "Well, you're brilliant. Look at me now. I am a Satisfied Customer. There you go."

"Girl About Town doing her job, you see," Kate said, taking a sip of wine. They were sitting in Zoe's back garden waiting for Francesca, pretending it was July and not April, as a watery sun shone onto the lawn and Flora and Harry kicked a ball around. The garden was denuded still of greenery, but everything was in bud, and the daffodils and grape hyacinths were out in force, spiking up through the black earth. A bird sang a lazy evening song in a bush nearby, and across the fence Kate could hear another family chatting loudly, the kitchen door swinging open and shut as people raced in and out.

"So you wrote this in . . ."

"A day and a half."

"And when do you hear back from Sue?"

"Tomorrow."

"So you've only been back for two weeks and already you've got yourself a job. Wow."

Kate loved Zoe's gloriously positive spin on everything. "It's not a job," she pointed out, leaning forward to offer Zoe another crisp. "She'll probably hate it. It's one column."

"So will you do more?"

Kate thought of the job Sophie had had, the retainer fee Sue had mentioned to her, twenty-six columns a year plus ten articles, more money if *Venus* went weekly, which they were currently aiming for. It wasn't big bucks, but she had worked out—just casually, back-of-an-envelope sort of thing—that it would be enough to cover her mortgage and bills, and she'd have enough left over for the occasional glass of wine and trip to Zara. If she was going to stay here, which she wasn't. But if she was, she could. She had options. That was weird, all of a sudden.

She was lucky, she knew it now—that was luck. But when she thought about it, how it had happened—because Mrs. Allan had died and had a funeral and so she had seen Sue again—a cloud passed over the sun. She said, "I don't know. I think I'd like to. It's just weird." She took a deep breath. "I wish it hadn't happened because of Mrs. Allan."

"Oh, Kate," said Zoe as Harry appeared, holding a muddy bulb of some description. "You have to learn to take the good— Hey, Harry, that's great! Have you been gardening?"

"Yes," said Harry. "Look." He held the bulb up even higher so it swung around, bashing Kate and Zoe in the face and spraying them with mud.

"Well, I'm proud of you," Zoe said, half to Harry, half to Kate. "Hey. Love. How's your dad?"

"Better and better. They say he can drive in a week or so. He's getting dressed and going out every day now. Just for a little bit, you know, but it's good."

Taking another crisp, Zoe cracked it loudly in her mouth. She looked at her watch. "Francesca'll be here in a minute. I'll put the supper on. Tell me, is Loosa still driving you mad? How's Dani? Still a bit awful?"

Kate felt an ever-increasingly familiar stab of loyalty to Dani and Lisa. "They're fine," she said. "Actually Lisa's not that bad, you know. And Dani—she's pretty sweet."

She had played with Dani that afternoon, in the communal square in their pretty little road, soaking up the sunshine, enjoying the warmth. Dani had gotten filthy, and Lisa hadn't even complained, saying it was good for her to get out of the house. It was a beautiful spring that year. It came early, shining through the windows first thing in the morning, pushing the buds into leaves, gilding people in sunshine and warmth. Kate couldn't remember a spring like it; she had forgotten how green, how spacious and leisurely London was, how white and graceful its buildings, how nice it was to walk around. She thought it was funny when Londoners complained about the pace of the city, how frenetic it was. Yes, it was a huffy, self-important place, yes, London was messy and chaotic and often depressing, but compared to the nonstop anonymity and adrenaline of New York, it was a welcome respite. She hadn't realized it before; she knew it now.

And London in springtime was beautiful, especially this spring. Later it would rain for all of June and July, the weather humid and unreliable, and people would snap at one another and be miserable about it, but now, when it was April and the skies were beautiful and clear, and the temperature warm, with the blossoms frothing on the trees and daffodils and forget-me-nots in the parks, now it was a happy, refreshing place to be.

It had changed her, she realized now. She'd been back for eleven days. She was sleeping well, for hours and hours, sunshine pouring onto the parquet floors of her flat. More and more she felt increasingly at home there, pottering around by herself. She put flowers in jugs, opened the windows, whistled as she made her tea in the morning. She checked the post for Mr. Allan and watered the plants in his flat, she saw her father every single day, she sorted out the rubbish in the kitchen and the old chest of drawers in the sitting room, and she had sat at her bureau desk and written the article, writing and rewriting, scratching her head till she was happy. Sue was right, she was an old lady. She ate carbs and drank wine and did other things she would never have dreamt of in New York, where everything for her had to be under control, her own world.

Still she left things untouched. Still the letters from Charly, three of them, piled up unread, still the letting agents remained untroubled by her, and still she did not call Perry and Co. She said to herself that now the article was over, she'd do it tomorrow, the very next day, and contact the letting agents, and she'd ring Charly, summon all her strength, and tell her to go to hell, that she didn't want to see her, that she didn't wish her any harm but that she didn't want to know that her child was coming into the world, the child of a person like Charly. Watching Zoe's children running around on the lawn, Kate nodded to herself, reminding herself of why it was so, why she couldn't—

"Oh, Mac rang earlier. He is popping over tonight," Zoe said suddenly, standing to get some more wine.

"What?" said Kate, sitting up with a start.

"He wasn't going to." Zoe was picking up stray bowls of crisps; her back was turned to Kate. "Don't know if Francesca said he might be coming or not. Well, he is. He wants to see the children. He's got a present for Harry."

"Why?"

"He's their uncle, Kate," Zoe said slowly to Kate, as if she were a mental patient. She flicked a look at her friend and stood up straight with a sigh. "Oof. I'm knackered. Do you think those vitamins you take to make your skin better actually work? I'm chowing down about fifty a day and I'm still always getting this spot right here on my chin, right—can you see it? Right here. Look." She jabbed at her chin with her finger. "What's the blimming point?"

"Yep, yep," said Kate, waving her concerns aside. "Keep taking the vitamins. Great for you. Zinc in particular. Er—Zo? Does he know I'm—me and Francesca are coming over?"

"Yep, course he does," said Zoe. She stared at her. "He asked. He's only popping over, he said he won't stay. We'll just have to persuade him."

Kate nodded, trying to look enthusiastic about this while mentally bemoaning the fact that "popping over" was an entirely British phenomenon. You didn't "pop over" to someone's apartment in New York. God, no. You met at a restaurant or a bar nearby. You were organized about it. Even if you were hanging out with someone, you organized where and when you'd be hanging out together. Why couldn't Mac have said right from the start that he was either *definitely* coming or *not* coming? Why was she still unable to think about him, at this very minute, on his way toward her without feeling like someone had literally laid her heart on a table in front of her and sliced it in two?

"Uncle Mac coming!" said Flora, poking Kate solemnly in the leg.

"Yes, he is," said Kate. Kate was almost pathologically fond of

Flora, having only met her for the first time a week ago. She was like a very small version of Zoe, and was already pretty small, from her black hair down to her big, determined feet, which were rarely encased in shoes and, like their owner, had a mind of their own.

"Yay!" said Flora, raising herself onto the balls of her feet and then down again, which was her version of jumping.

The doorbell rang, and Zoe went to answer it. "That'll be Francesca," she said. Harry ran toward Kate and Flora ran back onto the lawn, like a relay race. Kate watched them playing in the garden—they both looked like Steve, so much it hurt.

Francesca appeared in the kitchen and waved. "Right, let's go in and wash your faces, so you're ready for your uncle," Kate said.

"Why does he want us to wash our faces?" said Harry, clearly not sure whether to trust Kate.

"He . . ." Kate chewed her lip and took Flora's little hand in hers. "He thinks that should be part of the law, too. Having a clean face or else. Um . . . ask him about it when he gets here."

"Are you going to wash your face, too, Kate?" Harry asked.

"Very much so, of course," Kate said. "Come on, then."

They went back into the house, all three strangely subdued.

"God. Buses," Francesca was saying as they entered the kitchen through the French windows. "I hate them." She pulled her dark, silky hair out of the neck of her coat and then took her coat off. "Ouch! Fuck! That hurts."

"La! La-la-la!" Kate sang loudly, grasping the children's hands. "Oh, la-la-la!" she shouted, practically running past Francesca with them.

"It's OK," Zoe intervened as Flora and Harry peered in front of Kate's legs and looked at each other as if to say, *Help, everyone here is insane.* "Harry, you know what Francesca said was a bad word, don't you?"

"Yes," said Harry. "Really bad, you should not say it."

"I know," said Francesca, nodding at him. "Tell me something else, Harry. Where's the wine?"

"OK," said Zoe, shaking her head at Harry. "Ignore Auntie Kate and Auntie Francesca. Auntie Kate is pretending to be Mary Poppins, and it's scaring the bejesus out of me, and Auntie Francesca gets cross when she doesn't have wine nearby. She is an old lush."

"Hm?" said Francesca, picking at a thread on her suit jacket.

"I'm going to put *The Little Mermaid* on," said Zoe, and the children shouted with glee. "You can watch it *for thirty minutes* while we talk, and then I'm going to put you to bed, and Uncle Mac will come and say good night to you. OK?"

Flora nodded, but she'd nod at anything.

Harry said, "Yep, OK."

When the DVD was playing, and the three friends were sitting around the kitchen table a few minutes later, Francesca produced a bottle of champagne from her rucksack, clad in a chiller jacket.

"I had a big deal today," she said. "Finally went through. So let's celebrate."

"Wow," said Zoe, getting up to fetch some glasses. "This is great! Congrats. What was it?"

"Germans," said Francesca briefly. "There." She eased the cork out of the bottle without so much as a murmur. "Zoe, take that— Kate, that's yours." She poured herself some, too. "Ladies. A toast."

"Yes," said Zoe.

"To each of us. Here's to me," Francesca said, her dark eyes glittering above the champagne glass. "I deserve every last drop of this beautiful fizzy liquid." She took a sip. "Wait. Now, to you, Kate. To your article and you being back here. You're not going back to New York, we're going to start a campaign to keep you here. In fact, this is the campaign's first meeting."

"OK," said Kate, nodding and smiling, watching her glass, bubbling gold.

"And finally, Zo, here's to you. Thanks for having us over. And here's to you especially because you're wonderful." She smiled. "Now, I know you've probably told Kate all about it, but you'll have to tell it again because I want to know. How was the date?"

Zoe made an urgent shushing noise.

"The *what*?" said Kate, reeling.

"Didn't you tell her?" said Francesca, pointing her champagne glass at Kate.

"You went on a *date*?" said Kate. "And you didn't *tell me*?"

"It's not *that* big a deal," said Zoe crossly. "Stop staring at me as if I've got two heads. It was a date. Big deal."

"Do the children know?" said Kate. The other two turned to look at her.

"Have you lost your mind?" said Francesca. "Why are you being so weird? Now," she said, turning back to Zoe. "Did you wear the blue and gray wrap dress?"

"Yes, and you were so right about wrap dresses being my thing," said Zoe excitedly. "Thanks a million. I always thought, with my boobs and stuff—you know—bad idea, but they're perfect, aren't they! They just keep everything—"

"Hold on!" Kate said. "What the hell is going on! You had a date! Who with?"

"He's—" Zoe picked up her glass and took another slug. "He's called Diggory. He's a landscape gardener. He works at the nurseries with me."

"He's called what?" said Kate.

"Diggory. Like the boy in *The Secret Garden*," said Francesca helpfully.

"Seriously?"

"But his friends call him Digg."

"One *g* or two?"

"God, I don't know!" Zoe rolled her eyes impatiently. "That's not the issue, ladies!"

"So did you snog him?" said Francesca.

"Wait," said Kate. "Back up. Where did you go?"

"Well, we went to a pub near work, off Primrose Hill." Zoe's eyes sparkled; Kate watched her uneasily. "It was funny, actually, because there weren't any seats." She laughed at the memory. "Ah."

"Then what happened?" said Francesca, who was starting to look bored.

"Oh, then we got some seats," said Zoe. "A couple left. By the window. So—"

"I don't care about the frigging seats," said Francesca. She banged her hands on the table. "What was he like? What was it like? Was it weird being on a date?"

"Superweird," said Zoe. The others nodded sympathetically. "But, you know, I just told myself it would be weird going on a date with anyone who wasn't Steve. Of course it's weird. But I just pretended it wasn't weird, and tried to get on with it. Not let it take over the evening."

Kate sat down suddenly. "Wow," she said, running her hand through her hair. "That's huge. Good on you, Zo."

Zoe sat down beside her, her face pleading almost. "Oh, Kate, I'm sorry I didn't tell you, I really wanted to, to ask your advice and all that, I just—I just didn't want to make it into a big deal, and if you tell people it becomes a big deal. You understand, don't you?"

You told Francesca, Kate wanted to say. *I wish you could confide in me.* But instead she said brightly, "Totally, of course!"

"So?" said Francesca. "Then what happened?" She poured them all more champagne; Kate knocked hers back as fast as she could.

"Well, we stayed there for ages, just chatting—you know, about work and stuff. It's really easy when you've got things to talk about already," said Zoe, and her sweetly serious face was heartbreaking. "Diggory spent lots of time in Australia, he's got all these really interesting ideas for irrigation systems, as that's going to be the next big challenge in garden design in the next few years, of course."

"Of course," said Kate and Francesca, nodding.

"And then—well, I was a bit reckless, and I got a cab home."

"Zoe Hamilton!"

"Did anything happen?" Francesca said.

"Nooo," said Zoe. She looked from one to the other. "You know. Not yet."

"Sure, sure," they both said.

"Not yet," Francesca added.

"Well, good for you, Zo," said Kate. "That's great. Did you say you'd see him again?"

"Oh, er . . . yeah," said Zoe. "We're going to Hampstead Heath this weekend with the children."

"Fast work," Francesca muttered.

"Well, no. It's someone at work's birthday and they're having a picnic on the Heath, so there'll be lots of people we know there, and lots of children—you know. It'll be great. He's met them before, at Jool's wedding party, a few months ago, anyway."

Zoe had always looked the same to Kate—a little, energetic, determined, unassuming ball of energy and fun—but it was only since she'd got back that Kate had thought she was starting to look tired. Run-down. Weary of the hand life had dealt her. Now, looking at her friend, she saw a sparkle in her eyes that she hadn't seen since—well, since that fateful day they'd had lunch, nearly three years ago, when Zoe was still working at the law firm, pregnant with Flora, and Kate was engaged to be married. Look at them now, she thought. Look at Zoe, having to go out on dates. It was still wrong, she would never not think that. Kate cleared her throat angrily.

"Look at us now," Zoe said, like she'd been reading Kate's mind. Their eyes met and they gazed at each other in a moment of clarity, and Zoe shook her head at her friend. Something shot through Kate like a bolt of electricity. It made her want to bang the table and shout that life was bloody unfair.

Francesca, sensing the mood needed lifting, got up and got a bottle of wine from the fridge.

"Mac'll be here soon," she said, in a not-so-subtle reminder to both of them. "Is he eating?"

Zoe jumped up. "The food!" she said, smacking her head. "I've got to start cooking!"

"Thank you," said Francesca as Zoe rushed out and ran down to the cellar. "We could be here all night otherwise. I can't stay late either," she said. "I've told Mac I'm going early."

"Right," said Kate, still staring into space.

"So I'll be leaving before Mac, is what I mean," Francesca added.

"I get you," Kate said.

"So Mac'll be going home on his own," she said.

"Yes," said Kate. "Thank you. I wish I could work out what you were saying. It's all smoke signals with you."

"Shut up," said Francesca aimiably. "I'm only trying to help."

"I know you are," said Kate. "Sorry."

"Go on," said Francesca as the sound of crashing and muffled curses drifted up from the cellar, where Zoe was trying to locate something. "While she's gone. Tell me what happened between the two of you. She doesn't know, does she?"

"No." Kate bowed her head.

"Can't believe that."

"Like I said . . ." said Kate. "There's a lot of stuff we don't talk about anymore." She gestured vaguely. "Look at Diggory. *Digg.*"

Francesca ignored this. "So what happened?"

"I stole his stethoscope and he was furious."

"*Kate.*"

"*Francesca.*"

"I give up," Francesca said. "All I'm saying is, you don't hate someone that much without still feeling something for them. The opposite of love isn't hate, it's . . ."

"Indifference. I know," Kate said.

Thirty-four

The doorbell rang at eight. Zoe was hunting for a spare knife and Francesca had Flora on her lap; she made to put her down and stand up, but Kate was quicker than she.

"I'll let him in," she said. "I'll say hi. You stay there." She brushed Flora's cold, baby-smooth cheek with her hand and went inside.

Mac registered no surprise when she opened the door. "Hello," he said. He bent forward and kissed her.

He was dressed in a suit and tie. When she'd seen him at Francesca's, he was in trousers, an open-necked shirt, which was how she always thought of him. He looked formal now, buttoned up. And tired.

"Francesca told me you were back because of your dad," he said unexpectedly, his soft Scottish accent hitting her in the solar plexus. "I'm sorry. I didn't know he'd been ill."

"Thanks," she said. "He's much better now. The operation was a couple of weeks ago. It's looking OK, touch wood."

He nodded. "That's usually enough time to know. That's good. How are you?" he asked, loosening his tie and putting his satchel-style briefcase on the floor. His voice was pleasant. She watched his hands.

"Oh, er," Kate said, not sure how to contain her surprise at this, a semicordial exchange. "I, I am well, thanks. And you?" She felt like a character in a Dickens TV adaptation. "Are you well?"

Mac looked at her in some surprise. "Yep. Fine."

"Good. Good!" Kate said as she shut the door. "They're this way." And she gestured toward the kitchen, which was the only direction one could possibly go anyway.

"Thanks," said Mac. A smile flickered across his lips. "This way we go, then." And he followed her into the kitchen.

"Hey, Mac," said Zoe, who was licking her fingers.

"Yo, flatmate." Francesca waved her wineglass at him over Flora's semisomnolent head. "How are you?"

"I'm fine, fine," said Mac, suddenly awkward in the halogen lights, still in his trench coat. Standing next to him, Kate could smell the fresh air of outside still on him, in the warm fug of the kitchen.

"I brought some wine," Mac offered, and he handed it to her, watching her, and Kate took it and said, "Thanks. I'll . . . put it in the fridge." She smiled at this faux-domestic scene—it wasn't hers—and he smiled back, and the ice was broken a little further. He was going to be nice; he'd obviously made up his mind. Very well, good for him, she told herself. She would happily do the same.

He took his coat off. "Harry's upstairs?"

"Yes," said Zoe. She nodded at her daughter. "This one won't go to sleep." She saw he was holding a bag. "Is that for Harry?"

"It is. It's a doctor's kit. We do them at the hospital. He wants to be a doctor."

"Just like his uncle."

"Absolutely," he said, and he looked away.

"Mac?" called a small voice from upstairs. "Hello!"

"Hey, Harry," Mac said, slightly raising his voice. "Be up in a minute."

"Have some wine," Zoe said. "I'm going to take madam here up to bed."

"Ooh, I'll come with you," said Francesca suddenly, as Zoe scooped Flora into her arms, and the three of them set off upstairs.

"You know where everything is, Mac," said Zoe over her shoulder.

"Sure," said Mac. He moved toward the cabinet on the side, pulled open a drawer, and took out a corkscrew; he knew his way around this house. "You want some wine?" he said.

"Sure," said Kate, watching him, unable to believe the luxury of being in the same room as him again.

He took a bottle of chilled wine from the fridge and it was a screw-top; he smiled again, the corkscrew in his hand, and it broke the ice a little further.

There was silence in the kitchen, then. It was just the two of them, standing on either side of the corner of the table. Kate put her hands awkwardly in her jeans pockets. He did the same.

Clearing his throat, he said, "Look, Kate. I don't want to get into it again, but—just to say, I'm sorry about last week."

Because Kate thought about him all the time, she couldn't instantly recall what was different about last week. "What?" It took her a moment to process what he was saying, and she blinked, slowly. He watched her.

"I thought you were supposed to have a brilliant journalistic brain," he said. "Last Thursday, whenever it was, at my house. I was vile to you. I'm sorry, Kate. I wasn't expecting to see you, that's all. Whatever's happened between us. I'm sorry. I shouldn't have spoken to you like that."

Kate bowed her head. "You should have," she whispered. "I deserve it."

"No you don't," he said, moving slightly toward her. It was so quiet in the kitchen, she could hear Harry and Flora upstairs, Zoe talking to them soothingly. He took her wrist. His skin was warm on hers. "You don't deserve it, Kate, you've—you've been through enough already."

Kate didn't allow herself to cry much these days. She wasn't an attractive weeper anyway. Tears didn't tremble on the edge of her glossy black lashes and drop to the ground as her big dark eyes filled with water, like they did in novels. No, her nose went red, her eyeballs became bloodshot, she got swollen lids that wouldn't go down for days, and rough, raw patches underneath her eyes. Partly because, on the extremely rare occasions when she did properly cry, she really went for it. It was silly. He was only being nice to her. But the niceness was the very thing she'd been missing and she could feel her throat swelling up, tears pooling in her eyes.

"Don't," Kate said, and she smiled. "Otherwise I'll start to like you again."

"Not much chance of that at this end," he said, and though it was a joke, it came out sounding cold.

His hand on her wrist was suddenly tight. He dropped her arm as if he were holding a poisonous snake, and picked up two glasses of wine. The tension between them was as strong as ever, and as Kate went over to the sink, spotting a knife and washing it, all the time she was aware of him behind her; she was apprehensive.

"Anyway, I am sorry," Mac said with his back to her. "It made me think. We should talk about it. About last year."

"Not now," she said as Zoe's voice was heard from upstairs.

"When, then?" said Mac wearily. "*When,* Kate? That's the trouble with you and me. Mainly you, I have to say." He smiled, grimly, but she couldn't smile back. "Our timing bloody sucks." He rubbed his face; she saw again, with concern, how tired he looked. She wanted to get him to sit down, make him supper, take care of him. But she mustn't. She couldn't do that to him again, even if he wanted it, which it was clear he didn't.

They heard Zoe and Francesca on the stairs.

"Later," said Kate. She set her jaw, turned to look at him, and he was standing under one of the spotlights in the kitchen. She clutched the back of the chair.

Don't get a taxi home with him, she told herself. *Don't* sleep *with him. Don't open all of that up again, don't hurt him, don't hurt yourself.* She turned around, as if he'd spoken those words out loud to her. He scratched the sandy-brown stubble on his cheek. His face was expressionless, but his eyes were on her, flinty gray-green, stormy.

"Ah, Kate," he said simply. "Damn you." And leaning back on her hands, against the chair, watching him, too, Kate knew. She was terrified, exhilarated, at the power he still had over her, at how much she wanted to give in to it. She couldn't.

"Mac, Harry's asking for you, if you—" said Zoe, slightly loudly, as she came into the kitchen.

"I'll go now," he said instantly, and went upstairs.

Zoe made pasta bake and they sat in the kitchen and ate, leaving the French windows to the garden ajar so they could hear the birds singing in the trees outside. Mac was upstairs for a while to say good night to Harry and give him his doctor's kit.

Then the four of them stayed around the table till ten, when it was time for Francesca to go—she had to be up early for a meeting at eight.

"I'm going," she said, standing up, pushing herself away from the table. She looked at Kate significantly. "I'm going to leave you to reminisce over times gone by."

And then it was just the three of them, late into the evening, long after they'd cleared everything away and were left with wine-glasses, and the French windows were closed against the night. They talked of everything—but mostly they talked about Steve. How he'd mended Kate's desk chair at university, and the next time she'd sat down on it it cracked beneath her. How on their wedding night he had had a nightmare about Zoe trying to kill him and woken up screaming, "No, Zoe, no!" How he had broken Mac's calculator-ruler, by flicking rubber Disney characters off it till it snapped in two, then put it back in Mac's drawer, hoping he wouldn't notice. Just saying Steve's name was hard for Kate, and at first she found it impossible. She never talked about him. Who in New York had known him? Hardly anyone. She had liked it that way at first, and now, here, these last few days with her friends, she'd started to realize that she might have been wrong, like she was starting to wake up again, from a long sleep.

Still, long after Harry was asleep again, Flora would not go down, and she sat up in her small person's chair, staring around impassively and munching bits of crackers she'd crushed with a spoon. As Flora banged her spoon and tried to stick some cracker pieces into her eye, eventually Zoe said, with resignation, "Oh, Flora, love—don't do that."

Flora banged her head on the tray that lay on the table. Her face scrunched up and she screamed.

"Oh God," said Zoe. "She's gone. I'm sorry," she said, scooping a wailing Flora into her arms. "She's really, really tired. I should put her to bed—"

Mac stood up, pushing his chair out. "Let me help."

"No," said Zoe firmly, pushing her hair back with her hand and trying not to look harassed. She smiled brightly. "Honestly, it might be best if she sees you going—she'll understand the night is over. God, she's awful." She clutched Flora closer to her; Mac watched them both, and then said, "Of course. Anyway, Zoe, love. We'll put the stuff away and— God, it's late." He looked at his watch. "Let me just—" He put his wineglass by the sink.

Kate looked at her watch; it was twelve thirty. "God, I'm sorry, Zo. I had no idea it was so late."

"Neither did I," she said, holding the wriggling Flora in her arms. "She just won't sleep like other children—she likes the nighttime. Just like her mummy and her daddy, I'm afraid. Look, you two, just go, OK? I should put her down now, and I can put the plates and the few wineglasses in the dishwasher afterward."

"Well—" Mac looked uncertain, but Zoe shooed him along. "Come on, seriously."

He bent down and kissed his sister-in-law and his niece. "Bye, girls," he said, his voice soft. He grabbed Zoe's arm lightly. "I'll see you on Sunday. Thanks, Zoe."

She looked up at him, grateful, her eyes sparkling. "Oh, Mac. Thank you . . ."

Kate had hung back but stepped forward then and kissed her. "Bye, Zo. Thanks so much, so much, it's been a lovely evening." And it had been. She squeezed Flora's arm. "Bye, Flo. Be good."

They were almost pushed out by Zoe, and as the door shut quietly behind them they shivered on the street, the two of them alone again, in the cold, clear night.

She knew that she was going to go home with him. It was inevitable, the way it always was. She had known it from the moment he touched her wrist, how powerful the connection between them was. But neither said anything as they walked toward the main road. Kate could hear Mac's breathing. She turned quickly and saw the black outline of his profile in the moonlight. She wrapped her arms around herself and stepped a little way away from him, so they were walking in parallel, a meter separating them, along the quiet street with its cracked pavement slabs jammed with cars.

Did he remember this was where they first kissed, all those years ago, after the housewarming party? It had been spring then, too. Did he remember this was the exact spot they had caught the taxi back to his flat? Did he replay it in his mind, did he know how often she had? They stood in silence, waiting for a cab to arrive, and when it did they both stuck their hands out.

"Where to?" the cabdriver said.

Kate didn't look at Mac. He held the door open for her.

"Maida Vale, then on," he told the cabdriver, who nodded as Mac shut the door.

They settled down in the cab and silence fell.

"So, how is work, Mac?" said Kate. Perhaps an interesting conversation about the merits and demerits of the National Health Service might help smooth out the spiky atmosphere.

She felt his eyes on her in the darkness, knew he was smiling at her, and she turned to meet his shadowy gaze.

"You always were terrible at awkward silences, Katy," he said.

"But I'm not."

"You are. You always crack first."

Don't kiss him.

"Well . . ." The wine was going to her head; she sat up straight against the hard leather of the cab seat, trying not to smile. "It's an only-child thing. Social pressure, you know."

"Hm," he said, moving toward her. She could see his face in the gray night. She was cold, hot, every part of her was tingling, and now she was smiling as his lips were next to hers. "You shouldn't worry about that," he said, and he kissed her. "Oh, Kate." His voice was hoarse now. "I don't like you for your conversation, you know."

His lips on hers, how she remembered them, the rasp of his day-long stubble on her cheek, his strong, supple hands on the back of her head. Kissing Mac had been her downfall before because kissing him was overwhelming, as if she'd never been kissed before. It always was, and the strength of her physical response to him floored her, like it always did, and they were back in the old game again, and to give herself up to it, to simply enjoy him, was a pleasure the like of which she hadn't had since she'd walked out on him before.

She pushed him away. "I can't," she said. "I really can't."

He held her head in his hands. "Come on, Kate," he said. "It's one night. You're going back in a week."

"But last time . . ."

"I'm over it," he said. He brought her hand to his mouth, kissed her fingers gently. "Aren't you over it? Come on. Haven't you been working hard, don't you deserve this?"

"Not if it's going to . . ." she began, but he kissed her again.

"I want you," he said. His breath was hot on her eyes, her lips. "And you want me. Don't worry about the rest, Kate. It's all in the past."

She knew that at the end of the cab journey was her front door, her hallway, where he would push her against the wall and press himself against her so she would cling to him in the darkness, her arms wrapped around his neck, to stop herself from falling down. That beyond that was her bedroom, where she would see him naked again, feel his body on top of her, pushing inside her, and then wrapped around her at the end of the night so that she might wake up in the early hours of the morning and turn gently to see him asleep, the harsh lines that crisscrossed his face wiped away by unconsciousness.

One more night with him. Never mind the realization that how much she missed him would be almost more pain than the pleasure that lay ahead of her now. Just once more, as they kissed in the cab, making its way silently and sedately through the moonlit streets of town.

Sue's words the day before rang in her ears. Do something wild. Stop behaving like an old lady. But for the first time since she'd come back to London, Kate had that feeling she'd had so long ago: of standing at the edge of a precipice, about to jump off, bringing destruction with her as she fell. The idea that Mac was with her was extraordinary—Mac, with whom she shared a secret history that only the two of them knew about, that they kept from their friends, it wasn't over.

"OK," she said, and she kissed him back. They were nearly home. *Yes,* she told herself, as his hands moved over her, as he kissed her more insistently, as she desperately wished they were alone. *Just enjoy this one night. Don't think about the past. Don't think about that past. Don't think about that last lie, the last betrayal.*

INTERLUDE

THE PREVIOUS SUMMER

"*K*ate?"

She was sitting at a table in a pretty French café just north of Grosvenor Square, pushing the padded paper coaster around with the tips of her fingers. The quiet Mayfair bustle of a summer's afternoon, fading into evening, was soporific. Kate stared at her arms, thinking how brown they'd become, which was strange because she was outdoors so little these days. The bangles on her wrist jangled as she shook more sugar into her cup of tea. She breathed in the smell of rich heat rising from the ground, tarmac, cars, and sweet, harsh, pollen.

The U.S. Embassy was closed: of course it was. July Fourth—why hadn't she realized? So stupid of her; a sinking, metallic feeling of dread had assailed her as she'd drawn closer to the square and looked for the line of people that usually ran down the side of the unlovely humorless building.

"Come back tomorrow, miss," the scary guard had told her, clutching his AK-47, his face expressionless.

"But—" Kate began. "I'm only here for two days, I've come specially for this. I've got to get back to the States. They promised they'd stamp my visa again and I could come straight home again."

"Miss, you'll have to come back tomorrow. I'm gonna have to ask you to step away now."

Kate was used to the humorless precision of American security now, after twenty-two months there, nearly two years, she knew it exactly. But here, on this beautiful English summer's evening, the trees dipping and whistling around the long, elegant square, it seemed totally incongruous, and she had smiled at him, without really knowing why, and stepped away, as requested.

One more day, she told herself as she trailed up toward Oxford Street. *One more day here and you can get back, and no one will know you're here.* Her mother and Oscar were up in the Hamptons for two weeks; they would never realize she'd gone. Luckily Perry and Co. was closed not just for July Fourth but for a week, most unusually, while Bruce escorted their cash cow, Anne Graves, back to Ohio, to receive an honorary degree from the university and to spend some time at her cabin there. Bruce had closed the office as a reward to his loyal coworkers, he had told them all, not because he was a control freak who hated not being there if others were there. Kate wondered what he thought he'd be missing if he left them all to it for four days; more of Doris's interesting stories about her husband, Mikey? Megan's weekly complaint about her book club's choices? The tension wrought by Perry and Co.'s temperamental air conditioner?

One more day here, she thought as she sat down for a coffee, gratefully resting her tired limbs. No one knew she was here except Betty, who had driven her to JFK, told her she was crazy, but was going to pick her up in two days' time, when this visa mess was sorted out. In, out, clean, precise, and no one need know she was here.

No one.

"Kate? Is that you?"

She heard the voice again, but still she didn't move. She looked down. It couldn't be him, surely. Perhaps he'd just walk on, leave her here, alone, unseen, perhaps she could still get away with it. . . .

"Kate." A tall figure looked down at her. "My God. It really *is* you."

She glanced up, shielding her eyes against the sun, knowing what she would see.

It was him. It was Mac. Shock ran through her, instantaneous; her heart started thumping. She put her hand to her collarbone, pushing her chair away from him, at the same time astonished at her own visceral response to the sight of him. He laid a cool hand on her arm.

"Don't go."

"I . . . I . . ." Kate swallowed, mastering herself again. "My God."

She stood up awkwardly, facing him. He was so tall, she'd forgotten that. Everything about him was so familiar; it was like opening a locked door stuffed full of memories, all bursting to come out. She didn't know what to say.

He stretched his arms out briefly, as if he were going to hug her, and as she took another step back, almost frightened, he shook his head and folded his hands under his armpits, defensively. He didn't realize he was doing it.

"It's been a long time," he said softly. "Kate, where did you go?"

Kate cleared her throat, wanting to speak, but nothing came out. She looked around at her fellow patrons, who were watching with ill-concealed interest. How different from New York, where she and Betty last month had had a loud, drunken shouting match in the Village about Betty's useless boyfriend, Troy, and no one had appeared to notice them, let alone see them.

"Sit down," he said, his voice gentle. He touched her shoulder with one finger, and she sank gratefully back down into her seat. Mac was looking at her, his eyes searching her, as if he couldn't quite believe she was really there. Kate blinked slowly, terrified of what he could say to her, not knowing what to say herself, and he followed her, pulling up a chair.

She stirred the teaspoon around in her empty coffee cup. "So—so you're down here now?"

"I moved back, got a residency at Saint John's. To be closer to Zoe. You know."

"Yep." Kate nodded, staring, without seeing, at the ground.

"Why are you here?"

"Visa," she said. "I had to leave and come back. I'm only in town for a day."

He flashed a glance at her. "Right."

He ordered a coffee; they sat in silence for a while. Then he said, "You stopped answering my emails," he said.

"You stopped sending them," Kate said.

Mac rubbed his palms together. "I didn't think you wanted to hear anymore. I don't blame you. You're Kate, though. You just pushed it all away instead." He said this without emotion.

"I didn't," said Kate hotly, though he was telling the truth—she knew it. "I didn't know what else to do. I couldn't stay."

"Why not?"

Zoe's words still echoed in her head. *Please, Kate. You need to leave me alone for a while.*

"I just couldn't," she said. She said, honestly, "I was to blame. I still think I was. And I know Zoe did, too, then. I had to get away. I didn't know what I was thinking then, really."

"You were to—" He shook his head. "Oh, Kate. So you left and never contacted her again," Mac said, drumming his fingers on the aluminum table, looking at the ground. She noticed the gray collecting at the temples of his sandy brown hair. "Or me. I just don't understand how you found that easy to do."

She looked up at him swiftly, tendrils of hair falling about her face. "Don't say that," she said, her voice sharp. "That's a ridiculous thing to say."

"Couldn't you have talked to someone else, then?" Mac said, his voice low. He put his hand in her lap, steadying her writhing fingers. "Talked to someone, without running away like that."

There was a pause, a break that spooled into a silence between them, so long that Kate could hear sirens in the background, roaring down Park Lane, that sound of sirens that she'd probably never forget. She took a breath, trying to explain, and then slumped down into her seat again. Her eyes were stinging, and she was so tired.

"What?" he said.

"There wasn't anyone, was there?" Kate said. "No one, really. Well, Francesca—but she was so upset about Steve, she couldn't help me. And it wasn't fair to put all of that on her."

"Come on," said Mac, impatiently. "Your father?"

"Dad," said Kate. "Yep, right." She tried to imagine what would have happened had she really tried to talk to her dad about it all, in those ghastly, endless days after Steve died and Sean left. Somehow, being with them, her father's new family, highlighted how dreadfully alone she was, and she'd realized after several awkward, disjointed conversations and offers of help, halfhearted offers of accommodation, that she'd rather face up to it by herself than blanket it in the new, neutral, perfect house in Notting Hill into which they were about to move. Except it wasn't facing up to it, it was running away, but again, fight or flight: she had chosen flight.

"Excuse. Miss."

Someone was tugging at her sleeve; she looked around to see a Japanese tourist, wearing glasses and a sun hat wedged firmly onto his head, his wife standing next to him, opening and shutting a guidebook in Japanese.

"Diana palace nearby?" said the husband. Kate looked at Mac, who shook his head impatiently, not understanding.

"Oh," Kate said, recognition dawning. "Diana's palace. Where Princess Diana lived?"

They nodded. "Please." The wife jabbed her fingers at the guidebook.

"It's called Kensington Palace, and you need to get on a bus, or a tube, and go to . . ." She trailed off, realizing they had no idea what she was talking about. The people at the next table stared at her. Mac stared at her, amusement crossing his usually unreadable features.

Kate gave him a sharp look. It occurred to her that she was a tourist, just like them, after all. She took the guidebook out of the woman's hands and the woman tensed, looking nervous, as if she thought Kate might steal it. She found a map at the back of the book.

"Here," she said, and she took a pen off the table and drew a cross by where Kensington Palace was. "Bus. Top of road." She pointed in the direction of Oxford Street. "Numbers? You know numbers?"

"Bus," said the husband, nodding enthusiastically. "Bus, yes."

"Ten," Kate said, pointing again. "Ten. Bus number ten." She was almost shouting.

"She was a beautiful lady," said the wife carefully.

"Diana, yes," said Kate, nodding. Mac looked alarmed.

The woman's face lit up. "Beautiful lady. Queen of Hea—"

"Yes, she was, thanks," said Mac impatiently, patting the husband, to whom he was nearest, on the arm. "Good luck!"

They moved away, saying thanks as they left, and Mac turned back to look at Kate, shaking his head.

"I'd forgotten that about you," he said.

"What?" she said, smiling.

"You're like a girl guide. A grown-up girl guide."

"Charming," said Kate. "That's not very sexy."

"Oh, it is," said Mac, raising his eyebrows, and laughing. She joined in, shaking her head, but then he said, suddenly serious, "So, you were about to tell me why you ran off."

There was a cool breeze blowing down the street, refreshing and calm. Kate let it wash over her, calming her down, and she looked at Mac.

"Look, I had to go. That's the truth. Don't bother hating me for it. You couldn't hate me more than I hate myself."

He was silent for a long time, looking at her, and still he held her hand in her lap. It was so comforting, the kind of solid, kind comfort that Kate hadn't really felt for months and months. She knew Mac must despise her, blame her, loathe her, but somehow still, there at the table, her hand in his, in the shade of tall Mayfair red brick, she felt safe.

"You poor thing," he said after a while. "You poor bloody thing."

"We'll just walk, then," he said, checking back to make sure they'd left nothing behind. She liked that about him, his precision in everything, the way he managed to do it without fussing. It was a process, part of a process, like giving an anesthetic or removing a tumor or mending a tear.

"Don't you have to—" she asked.

"I don't have to be anywhere," he said. "Neither do you, so why don't we just walk for a bit? Where are you staying?"

"Hotel in Bayswater," she said.

"You're not staying with your dad?"

"He's away." She was lying; she didn't know why. "No one knows I'm here. Mac, I don't want—"

"Sure, sure," he said softly. "It's fine. I think you need to tire yourself out if you're going to sleep tonight, anyway. Let's just . . . walk, shall we?"

"OK," said Kate. "Where shall we go?"

"The park," he said. "Let's go to the park."

• • •

"So tell me what you've been up to, then," he said as they walked into Hyde Park, and Kate saw the vistas of paths open up before them, of trees and buildings far in the background.

"It's a pretty short story," said Kate. "A boring story."

"OK," he said easily, and he shot a look at her and then carried on walking. She could hear the shouts from Speaker's Corner. There were the people just out of their offices, relaxing in the evening sun, resting their heads on their backpacks, reading papers and books. There was the long, yellowy green meadow, never built upon, never constructed and molded into a park out of rock like Central Park. This was the parkland that Henry VIII had hunted on, that Lady Emma Hamilton had ridden over, where sandbags had been laid in the First World War. She smiled, thinking what a very tacky, non-British thing to think that was.

It was just that she knew it, she knew that over there was the Serpentine, with boats floating on the still surface, and the Albert Hall, and the Albert Memorial, spun out of gold and marble, ridiculously overshiny, and she knew that over there were the formal gardens, Kensington Palace, and the spot where Tyburn stood. She knew all this because she'd grown up here, and it was her home, and she missed it, she missed it so much that it hurt, and she missed *this*—walking along with someone, just chatting. About things that mattered.

"Tell me how Zoe is instead," said Kate. "And Flora. How's Flora?"

Zoe and Steve's daughter was now eighteen months old. Mac smiled. "Beautiful. Looks just like her mother. She likes things with mud," said Mac as they walked down toward Park Lane.

"Mud?" said Kate.

"Yes, eating mud. Harry keeps striding out to the garden and trying to shove handfuls of earth into her mouth. Zoe's in despair, she doesn't know what to do. She ate a worm last week." She turned toward him. His green eyes were full of laughter, though his expression was as serious as ever. "Flora ate a worm, I mean."

"Obviously."

"Does she know . . ." Kate trailed off.

"About her father? She's too little," Mac said, gazing into the distance, where a group of friends was playing a noisy and erratic game of Frisbee. "Harry remembers him. He asks where Steve is."

"What do you say?" Kate asked him.

"It's tricky. You have to be honest, but not too honest. Zoe's been amazing. . . ." He trailed off. "She's incredible, that girl."

She's my best friend, Kate wanted to say. *I know. I know.* But she had forsaken that right, the right to an opinion about Zoe, or any of them.

"She tells him that Dad's not coming back, that he's gone to heaven, but he's watching them all and he'll always love them."

It was so simple.

They walked in silence for a while, until they reached the Serpentine.

"You know," Mac said suddenly. "They've got each other. They're still a family."

Kate nodded gratefully, unable to speak, and he watched her. She stared out at the wind ruffling the water, the cars trawling slowly across the white stucco bridge, at the landscape of London sloping out in front of her.

"Love. That's what they've got. Lots and lots of it. Sounds corny but it's true. They may not have a dad, but there are so many people who love them, you mustn't worry too much."

She reached toward him and squeezed his hand in silent gratitude for telling her about them, for falling back into silence again, and they walked on, down to the south of the Serpentine, over the bridge toward the entrance of the park. They walked in silence, past ice-cream vans, children playing, tourists enjoying the sun.

The shouts from unsteady novice sailors echoed across the water, and the afternoon sun flashed and glittered on the surface. They were small, insubstantial, in the large, open space where the green met the sky.

They kept their hands joined, their fingers entwined, still saying nothing, asking nothing from each other, not knowing what was going to happen. But walking through the park as the shadows lengthened, as the day turned to summery, sunny evening, Kate felt more at peace, happier, more herself than she had since the day Steve died.

That night, after he'd dropped her at her dusty little hotel in the backstreets behind Paddington, unlooked for and unloved, she had let herself into her tiny room, little wider than its double bed, and got undressed, knowing she would never sleep. Under the sheets, Kate clutched the duvet cover, which was too big for its duvet. Lying there in the darkness, she could hear the sounds of London around her. She was less than a mile away from her old flat, her old life with Sean, her old happiness here, and now a girl called Gemma was living there and she was here, in this hotel, waiting for tomorrow, when she could get her visa stamped and get out of here. She was only a couple of miles from her father, her stepmother, and her sister. What were they doing on this summer's evening? She hadn't seen them since before Christmas, the last time they'd been in New York. Kate was inclined to agree with her mother, whose version of their marriage was that Daniel wouldn't notice her unless she was standing in front of him waving, but still. . . . Sudden guilt ate into her, mixed with fear of discovery, that she was losing control of the plan she'd thought was so tight. Perhaps she should just go—

And yet in her mind was the memory of Mac, rooting her to this place. His tall, broad frame, his clear eyes on hers, his serious face, so often dark, smiling at her in her distress. Mac, who would be picking her up from the embassy and taking her for a late lunch before he went off on holiday the next day. Mac, who was her only friend in London, who had held her hand, who . . . understood. Better than anyone, though she couldn't explain why. And in the midst of these contradictory thoughts Kate, who was more exhausted than she had realized, simply drifted off to sleep, and in that tiny, shabby room, badly soundproofed and unloveable, she slept through the night, a deep and dreamless sleep.

"So, you live with your mum and Oscar—and you see Betty and the people at the office. And that's it."

"Yep." Kate bent down to pick up a stone from the gravel path in St. James's, where they were walking.

"That's *it*?"

"Well, and friends of mum's and Betty's. And sometimes we have a work event." Kate realized she was sounding defensive. "It's just that . . . that's the way I want it."

"Of course," said Mac.

She looked at him, marveling yet again at the restfulness she felt when she was with him, so extraordinary when she thought about him, what they had been through together.

"It's lovely here," Kate said, sighing. She threw some gravel back onto the ground and looked around. They were walking down the Mall, which was strangely quiet in the summer's evening, the only real traffic that of knots of tourists, making their way down the red road toward the palace. Along the wide avenue, the trees swayed in the wind. Up ahead of them were the white backs of the private clubs of Pall Mall, each its own palace of privilege. Kate had never walked here when she'd lived in London—you generally didn't, really—and looking up at the man next to her, she still couldn't quite understand what she was doing here.

"Do you ever hear from Sean?" Mac said suddenly.

"No." It surprised her how quickly the reply to the question came. As if she'd been expecting it. He stopped and looked at her, and Kate stopped, too. "Never. Do . . . do you?"

He said easily, "They've moved to East London. He emailed me, about a month ago."

"Oh, right," said Kate.

"Do you know what Charly's doing?"

"I don't, no," she said, and her voice was a little wavery, a little uncertain, but she was doing it, saying it, talking about these things without freaking out, and that was something, she supposed. "I wouldn't have been in touch at all, but I had to send Sean some money, you know, when we bought him out of the flat."

"We?"

"Dad." Kate gave him a half smile. "Dad and Lisa. They bought Sean's share. Bless them. Turns out the Daniel Miller album of Westlife ballads was a great idea. Shows what I know, eh."

"That was kind of him."

"Very kind," said Kate. "They were great about it. Lisa said she knew I should never have gotten engaged to him." She laughed, shortly. "Hindsight's twenty-twenty, isn't it."

"Yes," said Mac reasonably, "but no one wants to hear it at the time, do they."

"It's true." Kate watched a seagull, circling above St. James's Park.

"Oscar said the same thing to me that evening, you know."

She didn't understand. "What evening?"

"The engagement party." They crossed the wide road, leaving St. James's Park behind them. A bike appeared from nowhere, out of one of the side alleys leading onto the Mall, and zoomed toward them. Mac's hand shot out and he grabbed Kate by the arm. She pulled away from him, angrily.

"Sorry," she said. Something crossed Mac's face, like irritation, exasperation. Kate saw it, knew it for what it was, and couldn't blame him. Perhaps this had been a mistake, she told herself, and started planning exit strategies to get back to her hotel, go to sleep.

"What did Oscar say at the engagement party?" she asked.

Mac looked around him. "The same thing I said."

"I—what?" Kate shook her head. "I don't remember."

"What?" Mac said, mockingly. "You really don't remember?" And he took her by the elbow, gently guiding her into Marlborough Road, the small street that led away from the Mall past St. James's Palace, up toward Piccadilly. It was quiet, no tourists, and suddenly they were in the shade. She blinked, unaccustomed to the darkening light.

"Oh," she said, recall of the evening rushing back to her now.

"What did I say, Kate?" he said, and there was amusement in his voice, something else, too, something she couldn't define.

"You told me not to marry him." She had said it.

"Ah." Mac nodded, as if she'd just pointed out an interesting statue. He shoved his hands in his pockets. His expression was unreadable. "Oscar told me he didn't like him, and he was allowed to say that because they were fellow countrymen. I love your stepfather. They may be fellow countrymen but I've never seen two more different people."

Kate wanted to get back to the matter in hand. "So—"

"Well, we had a chat about it. I was a little the worse, or the better, depending on which way you look at it, for the alcohol, you know. But he seemed to me to be making perfect sense. I agreed with him."

"Well, you were right," said Kate.

"I was," Mac said. "I think I actually told you not to marry him."

"So you did." She turned her hands upward, palms open. "You see."

"I do see," said Mac. "I did tell you that."

It was hard to ask, but she had to. "Did . . . did you know?"

"About Sean—and Charly?"

"Yep," said Kate. She never knew, because she had never wanted to know. "Did you know?"

Mac stuck his hands in his pockets. He looked deadly serious. "I knew . . . they'd been sleeping with each other. Steve had asked my advice about it. Sworn me to secrecy. He didn't know what to do."

"Oh," said Kate.

"Sean was obsessed with Charly, you know?" Mac said gently. "It wasn't love. It was—infatuation. It was a physical thing, that's all. Steve was trying to persuade him to give it up. Give her up. But he was obsessed with her."

Kate didn't want to hear any more. "OK."

"Just one thing," Mac said. "Honestly, I think he loved you. He did really want to marry you. I just think he was in too deep, and he didn't know how to get out. Until—" He shrugged, and smiled a painful, twisted smile. "I have to believe that, don't know why. Otherwise it's as if Steve had been completely wasting his time, and that bastard ruined the lives of all the people I love, in one day."

There was a pause.

"I know," Kate said, desperately wanting to hug him. She breathed in deeply, and looked up at him, then over his shoulder, breaking the tension between them. "We should go."

"Kate—" he said, his voice low.

"Excuse me," a voice behind them called. "Can you please tell me where is Princess Diana's palace?"

A small family was standing behind them, the father waving a badly folded map. LONDRA was written on it in large letters; the wife was wearing a T-shirt that said PARIS.

"Oh my God," said Mac under his breath. "Over there," he

said shortly, pointing toward Buckingham Palace. He turned back to Kate. "Look, Kate—"

The father was not convinced. "There?"

"Yes," said Mac.

"Rubbish," said Kate. "Look—"

"Is this where she lived when she died?" the wife asked Mac, looking anxious.

"Yes," said Mac firmly. "Kate. I wanted to say something to you," he said, turning back to her.

"Wait," said Kate, unable to help herself. She was watching the wife, whose expression was near fanatical. "No. Not really. It was Kensington Palace."

Mac looked at her, his eyes wide open, and shook his head.

"Here," said Kate, pointing to the map. "That's where."

"Is this where the flowers were?" said the woman, nodding emphatically.

"Yes, where the flowers were," said Kate.

"Did you see her?" the husband said.

"Er, I did actually, once," Kate said, memory flooding back to her.

"You saw Princess Diana!" The woman clasped her hands.

"Yes," said Kate with enthusiasm. "In High Street Kensington." Mac groaned quietly by her side. "In Marks and Spencer. It's a shop." The woman nodded furiously.

"She—she was very beautiful."

"Oh, she was," said Kate, clasping her hands. "You know, I think she was probably a bit mad, but, gosh, she was lovely."

"Queen of Hearts," the woman told her fervently.

"You know, I watched that interview in a pub," Kate said, stepping toward her. "And it was—"

"Right!" said Mac, taking her elbow. "Have a lovely time," he said, bearing Kate off in the other direction and smiling at the tourists, who called "Thank you!" loudly after them. They walked in silence a little farther, a constraint suddenly upon them. They stopped outside St. James's Palace, which glowed almost rose pink in the sunset, and a slight breeze blew across Kate's face, her neck, through her hair.

"Ah," said Kate. "I hope they find it."

"Mm," said Mac, looking wrathfully at their retreating backs. "They should pick their moments better."

"We're here, aren't we?" she said honestly. She put her hand on his. "We're here. That's all that matters."

She turned away from him for a second, looking up at St. James's Street, the great Regency stage set up toward Piccadilly, so that he was standing directly behind her, and they were quiet, though Kate could feel his eyes on her.

He bent and kissed her bare shoulder, and she felt his lips on her skin. He slid his arms around her waist and he kissed her again, kissed her back and her hair, gently. She held his arms, wrapping her own around his, so they were snaked together in the shadow of the palace and no one—not the passing tourists, not the guards standing to attention outside, not the couple in black tie hurrying toward Pall Mall—paid them any attention as they stood there in silence, holding each other, both watching the evening scene in front of them.

Eventually she loosened herself from his grasp and swiveled around to face him, to meet his eyes, his face, the face of the man she knew so well. He opened his mouth to say something, but Kate knew she had to speak first.

"You're lovely," she said, her hands on his chest as he pulled her tightly toward him. "I've missed you."

"Eloquently put," he said, and kissed her on the mouth, and she wrapped her arms around his neck and kissed him right back.

At four o'clock the next morning, in her tiny, rabbit hutch of a room, he ran his hand over her stomach and pulled her toward him. Pushing her hair out of her eyes—for it had wrapped itself around her face, like candy floss—he kissed her again and said, "Would it be all right with you if I didn't go on my holiday?"

The strange thing about Mac, Kate felt, was how none of it was really a surprise, a revelation. With Sean, she'd never really felt she'd known him, even through the mundanity of their shared lives, their long time together. Here, she just knew what was going to happen. She had known he wasn't going on holiday anymore, known it from the moment they kissed. She ran her hand over his shoulder, down his arm, and took hold of his fingers.

"Fine with me." She smiled at him in the darkness. He took a deep breath.

"When do you have to go back to New York, Kate?"

It was Tuesday. Tuesday, and she had to be back for work on Thursday.

"I . . . I don't know."

"Tell me." He clutched her hand.

"Tomorrow night," she said quickly.

There was silence. She could hear a siren outside in the street, rushing toward the hospital.

"And what if you were to lie?"

"Lie?" she said, not understanding. She moved closer to him; they were on their sides, facing each other.

"Say . . ." His voice was soft in her ear. "Say there was a problem with your visa and you had to stay here a bit longer."

"I couldn't do that," she said immediately.

"Of course you couldn't," he said, rushing to agree with her. His voice was light. "It's just that I've been in love with you for five years, Kate. I was sort of hoping perhaps now . . . maybe . . . before you screw everything up again and fly back to New York to hang out with your mum and an assortment of embittered writers and crazy old couples in your apartment block . . ." He was whispering in her ear now, so softly in the dead quiet of the hotel room, his lips tickling her skin, "Well. I was hoping we might have some more time together. For this."

"For this?"

"This."

"What is *this*?" she said, desperately wanting him to tell her the answer, but he cut her off as she finished the sentence.

"We'll worry about all that later. Let's just say it's imaginary, it's an interlude. Who cares what happens afterward?"

But she knew he didn't mean that.

"Stay, Kate. I love you. Don't go back. Stay for just one more week."

"OK," she said, ignoring the hammering in her chest. "I will."

"Do you want to?"

Like someone had sucked all the air out of her lungs, Kate felt her chest, her heart, cave in, as if she were swooping down low over something, losing her senses. She blinked, trying to steady herself. She put her hand up to his cheek.

"More than you could possibly imagine."

We'll worry about all that later. I love you.
   More than you could possibly imagine.
   I've been in love with you for five years, Kate.
   Five years, Kate.
   Stay, Kate. I love you.
   Stay.
   OK. I will.
   Stay.

When they weren't in bed, they were walking through the park, and when they weren't in the park, they were sitting in a café somewhere in between the park and her hotel, Bayswater, or Marylebone. In the dog days of July, going into August, no one bothered them. Apart from crowds thronging Westminster Abbey or Madame Tussauds or the Tower of London, the city was empty. They went to the Turbine Hall at the Tate Modern early one morning, but it was crammed with people and they only wanted to be with each other, so they walked along the river instead, ducking behind into the old wharfs around Blackfriars Bridge, by the Oxo Tower. They went to Borough Market and bought pies and cold lemonade and ate on the benches outside Southwark Cathedral. They walked along Marylebone High Street, weaving in between pubs in tiny mews streets, they sat outside eating Lebanese food, hummus with diced lamb and pita, they walked along Clerkenwell Road, stopping to drink cold glasses of rosé in elegant bars normally stuffed with workers. The city was theirs—no one troubled them and they troubled no one.

No one at all. Zoe was away visiting Mac and Steve's parents in Edinburgh, Francesca was on holiday with some friends in Italy—oh, the luck. She'd established via email that her father was in the recording studio, Dani and Lisa were with Lisa's parents in Cornwall. It was her and Mac, that summer, and she didn't know what was going to happen, but for once, cautious, sensible, shy Kate Simply Didn't Care. All she cared about was him.

His laughing, kind eyes—how could she have thought they were cold?

His easy, quietly authoritative manner: the hotel tried to overcharge her when she extended her stay, until Mac stepped in, his negotiation technique far superior to Kate's (which was to be flustered and furious), and she ended up paying almost nothing for the tiny, happy little room that became their whole world.

The way he laughed—properly laughed, with helpless gulps and shouts that consumed his whole frame—when she told him a story that amused him, about Betty's new boyfriend, or about the old days, or something that had happened to her in New York.

How in his sleep he sometimes sighed, so deeply, and seeing him in repose, strangely vulnerable, almost broke her heart. She wanted to look after him, to protect him, to make sure he wasn't ever hurt again, especially by her.

His hands on her body—she watched them moving over her, watched him, his face, and knew she would never be happy again unless he was by her side. And as the days moved into a second week, and they stopped lotus-eating and realized they were going to have to make a plan of some sort, the dreams came back.

She'd had them before, after Steve died, all the time, and only going to New York made them stop.

She would dream she was back somewhere where they'd been that day—in a tiny little Italian restaurant in Soho, eating sage-and-butter ravioli, kissing Mac in between bites and drinking red wine. And Charly would appear at the table next to her, and then Sean. Or they would walk past the window and stare in. They never said anything, just watched her, smiling, demonically. And she never knew when they were going to appear, sometimes the dream would last for ages, and only then, at the end of revisiting the lovely walk she'd had with Mac through Battersea Park, would Charly suddenly walk casually out from behind a tree, her long hair ruffled by the summer's breeze, and Kate would awake, sweating, terrified. And another memory of a beautiful day with Mac would be ruined. She couldn't sleep, and he didn't notice, couldn't help her, and she started to hate him for that.

She ignored it for a few days, the voice in her head that dripped poison into her ear, but she knew it was only a matter of time before she admitted it.

Admitted that if she really loved Mac, the only way not to hurt him now was to go.

It grew hotter and hotter as August drew near, and now they had spent nearly two weeks together, barely a moment apart, other than lavatory breaks. Or when Mac had to go back to his flat to pick up more clothes. Their tiny, bare hotel room and the London of tourists in the summer was their world, and though someone cleaned the room each day, clothes, shoes, possessions were flowing across it like water by nighttime, when they lay asleep, the covers thrown off, Mac's arm draped over Kate.

Yes, Kate would decide, as she lay by his side, watching him during those stuffy, airless, dark nights. He does love me. She knew that.

But Kate also knew that while Mac thought he'd forgiven her, it was only a matter of time before he started to hate her for it, to blame her for the death of his beloved brother, for making her best friend, his sister-in-law, a widow—all these things. It would happen: it was a way off yet, but it would happen, and it would gradually poison everything—that's why she'd left London in the first place. She had tried to separate herself from it all. She had put an ocean between herself and what had happened, and now it was starting to catch up with her.

In the last few days of their time together Kate slept less and less, and Mac's arm across her body, over her shoulders, weighed her down more and more, and the dreams became more and more regular, and the weather grew humid and frayed her nerves even further, and he was crowding in on her, more and more. She could sense him clinging on to her, even as she tried to push away, knew he was reaching out to her for reassurance because he felt her rejecting him. He would kiss her, draw her toward him, open her legs to let him inside her, and she let him, wanting him desperately, trying not to cry with love for him even as she wished he'd just leave her alone, alone. Alone, a unit of one, so she wasn't bothered by him and how he made her feel.

So she had to leave.

The question was how. And when. And one night, her thirteenth night back in London, it came to her, suddenly.

"Ill? Your mother? How— What do you mean?"

"She fainted today. She was in Saks. She banged her head,

she's unconscious." Kate stood on the other side of the bed, trying not to panic. "There's a flight at seven. I've spoken to someone at Virgin. I'm on it."

Mac had gone back to his flat to pick up more clothes, check his post, his messages, run some errands. He had left her there, in their cardboard world of the hotel, promising he'd be back by three, and he was, to find that everything had changed, to find Kate surrounded by clothes, her eyes red, curiously withdrawn from him.

He ran his hands through his hair. "My God, Kate. That's awful." He came around to her side of the bed as she stuffed her meager, much-worn clothes into her bag; every one had a memory now.

"What did Oscar say?"

"He said to come home. He'll meet me at JFK."

The black cotton broderie anglaise sundress—she had worn that when they hired a boat on the Serpentine, Mac rowing, Kate reading him Sherlock Holmes stories, and covertly giving him sips of illegal wine.

She watched him hugging himself, his hands shoved under his armpits, his body language tight, panicked. "But what do they think. . . . Do you want me to speak to him, to someone at the hospital, find out what's going on?"

"God, no. No, Mac, please. I just need to get home. They think she's going to be OK, that it's just a concussion, but . . ."

The polka-dot navy and white shirt—she had worn that the night it had rained, five days ago, when drenched, soaked to the soul, they had given up trying to stay dry and had run back to the hotel, his white T-shirt virtually transparent, her hair like rats' tails, both of them laughing silently, almost hysterically.

He was shaking his head, his eyes full of damned sympathy, concern, emotion for her. She hated it, hated him for feeling like that, herself for making him feel like that. He moved toward her, and put his arm around her.

"Oh, Kate—darling . . ."

That skirt, the one she had worn the first day she saw him; she bit her lip, bowing her head over the bed, as he released her and took her hands in his.

"I wish you weren't going. Shall I come with you?"

For a second, Kate leaned against him, allowing herself to indulge what it would feel like to say yes. To just breathe out and give in. To say, yes, come back with me, actually, stay with me, let me stay with you. I love you, I want to be with you, to stay with you forever. Love me, let me love you.

Kate rolled all these words around in her mouth, unspoken. But she had to go, and when he found out how she had lied he would start to hate her, and by the time she came back to London again, he would properly hate her, think she was a lunatic, and her work would be done.

Two years of Kate's pushing everything down, deep, deep down inside her, guilt and mourning, not just for her friend's death, but for the lives she'd left behind, were finally catching up with her, she knew it. And now it pleased her to be mad. That's how miserable she was.

"I'll come with you to the airport," Mac was saying.

Kate ran her hands through her hair. "No."

"Of course I will."

"No," she said. Her voice surprised her. She turned to him. "Please, Mac. Can you just take me to Paddington, put me on the Heathrow Express. I hate airports so much. I don't want to say good-bye to you there. Please."

It was true, the only true thing she'd said since he'd got back, and he didn't realize it. But he nodded, bewildered.

"Of course."

She waited till she was on the train. He even got on with her, put her bags on, having charmed the guard into letting him through the ticket barriers. She tried not to cry as he kissed her, told her he loved her.

"I'll be over as soon as I can," he said, kissing her hair, the way he had done the first time they'd kissed, outside St. James's. "I'll call you. Call me when you get there, but I'll call you."

"Sorry, sir," said the kindly guard who'd let him climb onto the train with her. "We're about to leave. You'll have to get off."

He stood up.

She didn't stand up. She just said, "I'm sorry."

He looked at her, puzzled.

"Bye," she said. "Mac—" She held out her hand.

"I've written you a letter. It'll explain everything."

"*This train is about to depart. Please stand clear of the closing doors.*"

"In the drawer by the bedside table. At the hotel. I'm sorry."

He looked even more bewildered as the doors closed and Kate sank back into her seat, not looking to see if he was watching, not knowing. She was shaking so hard she thought she was going to be sick, and the train pulled away, gliding seamlessly out of the station, and she didn't look around once.

Dear Mac,

Mum's not ill, I made it up because I had to leave. I'm sorry.

I can't be with you, not in the way you want. It would have been nice, but it just can't happen. After everything that's happened but especially because of Steve. Can't you see that?

I expect you'll hate me now, but don't feel bad about it. After everything I've done to you it would be weird if you didn't.

You'll never know what these last two weeks have meant to me. In another life I love you.

Kate

Part Four

Thirty-five

*K*ate woke after five and lay in the darkness of her flat, staring at nothing.

How long, she didn't know, but after a while, she realized Mac was awake, too. He was breathing heavily, half asleep, but he wasn't asleep. She knew it because she wasn't, either, and she remembered how he used to sleep back then, last summer, while she lay awake, praying for the sunrise. She didn't want to move, though, to move things on; she wanted to stay there in his arms, feel his body next to hers, their legs entangled, caught between being asleep and awake, this state of security and the next state of uncertainty, for as long as possible, until dawn slid through the slatted blinds.

She turned over, so her back pressed into his chest, and his arm slid around to hold her. Kate blinked in the darkness, her eyes aching already with fatigue. Why had she let it happen?

Because it was always going to, a little voice inside her head told her. *Because the two of you have unfinished business.*

She blinked again, staring at the crumpled edge of the duvet.

Because you're lonely.

Because he understands.

But he didn't, that was the trouble. He pushed into her space, he brought back the past, he invaded her, he upset her, every single time. And she even more so with him. It was like an old scab, she had decided. They were bad for each other, yet they couldn't stop picking at it, opening it, because of everything else it covered.

Mac moved against her, drawing her closer into him, so there was nothing between them. She could feel him against her thighs, his muscles against her back. He sighed; she didn't know whether it was conscious or not. He kissed her shoulder, gently, the back of her neck, and stroked her arm, and was still again. They were quiet, in the dark room, and Kate stared out again as a cold, heavy tear streaked onto her pillow. This, this tenderness was what got to her the most. This was why she'd left London. The agony of complication, of entanglement.

And then Mac spoke.

"You're awake, aren't you?"

Kate cleared her throat. "Yes."

She rolled over and rubbed her eyes in an effort to look more half asleep, less with it, than she actually was. In reality her mind was whirring, flipping over possibilities and endings like a pinball machine, but she said, after a moment, "You OK?" She leaned in and kissed him, somewhere on the chin. He didn't react or reply in any way. "Hm," she said, and closed her eyes again, jokingly. "Hey. You OK?"

He put his hand on her neck, and pulled her toward him. "Yeah. Just thinking." He kissed her back.

"About what?" Kate said. He was silent again. "What?" She pushed him. "Hey. Don't go silent on me. About what?"

"Your flat," he said. "I finally get to see your flat."

Of course. "You've never been here, have you."

"No," he said. "You were with Sean—and then, afterward . . ."

Afterward.

"Do you like it so far?" she said softly into his ear as he drew her toward him. "Do you like what you've seen?" She touched him in a way she knew he liked, that only they knew.

"Hm?" He pushed her away but then he sighed, laughing softly. "Oh, Kate."

"I'm looking for a new tenant," she said, moving into him, wrapping his arms around her, feeling calmer as he responded to her.

"That's strange," he said. He nibbled her ear. "I'm looking for somewhere to rent."

"I remember," said Kate. "We should talk. I could do you a discount. Mates' rates."

"Mm. Kate's mates' rates." He kissed her, on the mouth, her neck, her ear. "Only—I don't think we're mates," he said. "Do you?"

"I'm sorry you feel that way," said Kate, rolling on top of him, smoothing her hands over the muscles in his shoulders. "That'd solve all my problems." She kissed him, running her hands through his short, scrubby hair. He froze.

He lay still beneath her, then he pushed her off him, gently. "Nice. Always the same."

"What?"

"You're really going back there again, aren't you?"

Kate had the feeling of being outmaneuvered. She rubbed her face, pushed her hair out of her eyes. "What?"

"New York. You're really going to go back. Again. Aren't you?"

"You know I am." she said. He pushed her hand away.

"Screw you, Kate," Mac said. He sat up. She stared at him, astonished. "God. You never want to face up to it."

"Mac!" Kate said, sitting up too, turning into him, leaning on one hand. "You were the one last night saying it was a one-night thing! What the hell—"

He looked furious. The words wrenched out of him. "Of course it's not a one-night thing!"

"Don't shout at me," she said, furious. "Don't shout. You *said* this was a one-night thing! And I said we shouldn't do it again, it would hurt too much, and you were all 'No, Kate, give in to it, it's only one night,' and here you are blaming me because I'm leaving in a few days. *God,* Mac, you're like the reverse of one of those stupid dating books!"

"What do you mean?" He looked at her coldly.

Kate knelt in front of him, suddenly hating her nakedness. She wrapped the corner of the duvet around her body. "Why are you doing this to me, trying to force me into a corner, when last night you made it clear this was only for one night?"

"Look, this was never about one night. Stop trying to sound like a lawyer, Kate. Stop avoiding the issue. The issue is you. You always run away." He counted off on his fingers. "The first night we spent together."

"I didn't run away then!" Kate was practically shouting. "You ran away! You shagged me and then went to bloody Scotland and never called me!"

"I didn't need to, did I?" He threw the words in her face. "You were sleeping with your flatmate a week later, what did it matter?"

She put her hands over her eyes, wanting to block it out. "That's not true—" she said.

"I even turned up at your engagement party. I told you not to marry him," he said, throwing the words in her face.

"That's what I mean!" Kate shouted. "You're being ridiculous! It's always on your terms, Mac. What was I supposed to do with that? Leave him, in front of everyone, just because you appear out of *nowhere* after two years and start drunkenly hinting at some dim and dark secret? I thought I loved him! I thought this was it!"

"It wasn't, though, was it?" he said grimly.

"Exactly," she said, shaking. *I never loved him the way I loved you. Never.* "So don't you dare make me feel guilty about it. You bastard." She turned away from him, but he carried on, ignoring her.

"Kate, you even ran away after Steve died, and I thought you were the only one who could help me through it." He banged his fist on the mattress. It made a deadening whooshing sound.

"You really thought that?" she whispered. "But I was the last person for that—"

"Last year, when we had everything, you did it again." Mac rubbed his face. "Everything. I told myself you were damaged, you'd had a hard time, that, you know, perhaps it was worth one more try. And now, when we're here in bed together, and I'm actually thinking, Well, despite everything we said last night, isn't it clear now, isn't it obvious we're great together, and you turn around and offer to rent your bloody *flat* out to me."

"Oh," she said. "OK."

"I don't get you, Kate." He was standing by the bed, watching her. "I just don't get you."

"No, you don't," Kate said. "You think you can fix everything, and you don't understand you can't."

"What does that mean?"

She climbed out of bed, naked, her back to him, and pulled on her blue velvet dressing gown. Standing in front of him, she said, "I ran away because I needed to work everything out myself. I know it was crap of me. But that's the way it was."

"But, Kate—it didn't need to be like that," he said, bewildered.

"It did." She rubbed her nose. "Mac, listen to me. I'm the one who should have died that day. Not Steve." She hated, hated saying this to him.

He winced. "It's not like that."

"It is," she said, moving closer to him. "He pushed me out of the way. He saved my life. Did you forget that?"

"It doesn't matter," he said, but she heard the note of hesitation in his voice, and that was enough for her. "Kate, what happened, happened. You have to accept that."

"I have accepted it," she said. She was quite calm. "Now I'm back, I can see I'm getting used to it. But that doesn't mean I don't feel guilty about it every single day. Don't you see that it's impossible for us to be together? There are some things in the past that just can't be overcome. You'll love Steve, and Zoe, for the rest of your life. But if it hadn't been for me, your life would have been completely different. So much better." She put her hand on his chest; he caught it, held it there. "I wish I could change that. More than anything else. But you can't move away from that, no matter how you look at it."

His hand tightened on hers. "You can't look at it like that, Kate."

She whispered, "I do, though. I do. You have a choice. Your brother, or the girl who was responsible for his death." Her throat was dry; she couldn't swallow.

Was it getting lighter in the room or was she imagining it? They stood there, perfectly still, neither wanting to move, to choreograph the next step. His hands were always warm. She could feel his heart beating in his chest. She prayed that he would understand.

"I don't understand," he said finally. He opened his fingers; her hand dropped to her side, heavily. "I've tried so hard with you."

She hated the way he boxed her in, like those nights at the end of the summer when she couldn't sleep, trapped under the weight of him, and the weight of her feelings for him. "What are you looking for, some kind of reward?" she said sharply.

"Why do you always push people away?" he said, pulling on his shirt and buttoning it up swiftly. "Why don't you want someone to look after you? To care about you?"

"Don't patronize me," she said angrily. "You know it's not about that. This is about you trying to sort everything out, your way."

"What's wrong with that?" He pulled on his jacket. "You've got a damned funny way of looking at things, Kate. I'm trying to help you."

"You've got a damned funny way of helping," she said bitterly. He was facing her again; there were only a few inches between them. "Don't be such a hypocrite."

"How am *I* a hypocrite?" he said.

"Because you come back here with me and we have sex and it's great and we *know* it's a one-night thing, and then you start making me feel horrible again," Kate said, her voice thick. "You always do. You always do."

"That's called life, Kate!" Mac said furiously. "That's what life's like! You can't lock yourself away forever. You can't put your heart in a safe somewhere and hope no one touches it, comes near you! You can't sleep with me just for some human contact without having the fallout afterward." He put his hands on his forehead, kneading the skin with his knuckles. "My God. This is crazy."

"I think you'd better go," Kate said.

"I'm going," said Mac. "Don't worry. I've learned my lesson with you, Kate. Finally."

She picked up her house keys, lying on the dresser, and caught sight of the post. She had picked it up when they'd got back the previous night, stumbling around each other in the hall, his hands inside her coat, pulling her toward him, the promise of the night ahead intoxicating them both. She had held the letters, crumpled in her hand, thrown them down as they came in. She snatched up the pile again.

Kate Miller
Flat 4
Howard Mansions
London W9

"No . . ." she whispered, stopping herself.

"What?" Mac said. He looked at her. "What is it?"

"Nothing," Kate said, snatching the letter up. "Bills."

He looked curiously at the envelope in her hand. "I know that writing. Who's the letter from?"

"No one." Her stomach hurt.

Mac sighed softly. "God, Kate, you just won't change, will you."

"It's from Charly," she said. He took the letter out of her hand. "She's been writing to me."

"She— What?" He froze, the paper half opened.

"She's having a baby. Mac, she's—"

He was watching her. "She told you that?"

"Yes," she said. "She's pregnant. That was the first letter."

"What do the others say?"

She was cold in her dressing gown, the night was still black, and there he was, dressed, ready to go. She wanted him out of the flat, now.

"Kate, what do they say?"

"It's my problem," she said. "Let me sort it out."

Washed up, single, living with your mummy. I always said you were a bit of a loser, didn't I?

"Forget it," Mac said again, and the sound of his voice was awful. "You're right. It's too complicated, all of it. This is over. I'm sick of trying to mend you."

"I don't need mending!" Kate shouted, nearly screaming. "I'm not one of your bloody patients! Just leave me alone!"

"Well, I will, then," he said. He picked up his bag and turned toward her. "You were right Kate. I can see it now. This would have been a disaster. Thanks for proving me wrong." He shook his head at her. "It took a while, but I'm glad you were right."

• • •

Kate heard the front door close gently. It wasn't even light, and he had gone. She crawled back into bed, to find she was shaking, juddering from head to foot. She was freezing cold, and now she couldn't stop shaking, even if she'd wanted to. The letter was still in her hand. The light from the blinds in her room fell in stripes over the words, shafts of black and white on the difficult, messy handwriting.

Kate

You didn't call me, Kate. I've written four times now and nothing. And I bet you're wondering how we knew you were back, aren't you? Wouldn't you like to know WHO TOLD ME. Well, if you won't even have the courtesy to ring me I'll have to do something about it. I'll have to come and see you. Don't worry, I've got the address. See you soon.

CHARLY

Thirty-six

When the morning finally arrived, Kate was still freezing. She hadn't bought enough winter clothes and she hopped around the flat, trying to stay warm. At the bottom of the closet, beneath some of her old trainers and a squashed black felt hat, she found an old sweater. She pulled it on, gratefully, and sat down in front of her computer. She was bone-tired, but she reasoned it was no more nor less than she deserved. Kate knew, with a certainty born of experience, that it would be a few days after what had happened last night, early that morning, before it would start to hit. At the moment, she just felt numb.

So she poured herself some coffee and opened her emails. In among messages from Kate Spade about their summer collection, enticing offers from Amazon that promised her 30 percent off a box set they thought she'd want but she found vaguely insulting to be offered (what had she bought recently that made them think she'd like a Jeremy Clarkson DVD?), and entreaties from disenfranchised Nigerian aristocrats were hidden three emails. If she wanted a wake-up call, she got it.

The first email read:

> Dear Kate,
> I trust your father is recovering well; please pay him

my respects. I have left several messages on your cell phone and sent you numerous emails, since I haven't heard from you about when you will be returning to your job here at Perry and Co. Please could you be in touch at your earliest convenience, otherwise I will consider your contract of employment here to be terminated as of the end of this week.

Yours,

Bruce Perry

The second one said,

Darling!? Where are you?!! I haven't spoken to you in days, what have you been up to? How is London? I saw a picture of Hyde Park with the daffodils out in force in the *Times* yesterday, it and made me think of when you were little and we used to walk through Kensington Gardens after your flute lesson, do you remember? I took you to Barkers for lunch in the cafe after your grade 4 exam, wasn't it? It made me miss London terribly, isn't it funny! Oh, darling, I miss you!! Please call, let me know you're OK. Oscar sends lots of love. He is standing behind me as I write this. Darling, one more thing, you will be back in time for Oscar's 60th, won't you? (He's not standing behind me now.) He would be so upset if you weren't there.

Must go, darling xxxxxxxxxxxxxxxxxxxxxxxxxxxx
Mummy xxxxxxxxxxxxxxxxxxx

And the third one had been sent at eight that morning. It was called "Perfect" and it simply said:

Kate. You NAILED it. Loved the article. I knew
you could do it. It's fresh, it's fun, it's really sweet!
Readers are going to love it.
I want to talk to you about a contract. And your
next column for us. Don't book any flights! Call me
as soon as you get this.
Sue

Kate leaned back in her chair and stretched her hands above
her head, high into the air, till her sides ached. She drew her legs
up under her chin, pulling the tattered old sweater over her knees.
Her heart was hammering inside her chest. She'd known that
email from Bruce was going to come; over the last week or so,
she'd deliberately avoided calls from the agency, reasoning to herself that they were getting on fine without her, and the real reason
Bruce was getting in touch was to fire her and replace her with
the bodacious Lorraine. But now—she bit the tip of her finger
thoughtfully. Did she really have the nerve to email Bruce back
and tell him to stick his job? Wasn't that just saying she wasn't
going back to New York?

She knew it wasn't. No, if the last few weeks had taught
her anything, it was that she should not be doing that job anymore. She had to start being brave and get out there, not molder
away at Perry and Co. She had been quiet and diligent, but her
heart wasn't in it, she didn't enjoy any of the books Bruce represented, she didn't believe in the world of Perry and Co., where
one author—Anne Graves—held sway over everything, an author who'd long ago stopped trying to write good books and was
merely content to deliver something half baked year after year,
later and later, because millions of people across the United States
had been convinced by her publishers that hers was a name they
could trust. She didn't like Doris, and Doris hated her. She was
pretty sure Bruce didn't like her much, either. It wasn't a job she

cared about. Why had she let herself do it for so long, then? Kate shook her head.

She had told Mac last night that since she'd come back to London she was finally working things out for herself. Well, time to put that into action. She pressed REPLY and typed Bruce a long, apologetic email, taking full responsibility for her behavior and thanking him for everything, and then wrote out a separate card, which she addressed and stamped, in a fit of organization. Right. Done. And it felt pretty easy. Liberating, in fact.

She was halfway through a reply to her mother, telling her to calm down in as nice a way as possible, when the phone rang. Kate checked her watch. It was ten thirty. She wasn't due at her dad's till about three. She clutched the now cold mug of coffee and picked up the receiver.

"Well?" a brisk voice demanded on the other end of the phone. "What on earth happened last night?"

"Francesca," said Kate, with some relief. "Hello."

"I had a meeting at eight thirty this morning, just got out of it, otherwise I'd have called sooner. So . . . ?"

"Why do we have this relationship where all of a sudden all you're interested in is me and Mac?" Kate complained. "How are you, Francesca? What's happening with Pav, have you seen him lately since you slept with him by accident at the Christmas party? What are your hopes and dreams?"

"Shut up," said Francesca. "Pav's back with his girlfriend, the stupid twat. And as for you and Mac, that's practically the only thing I know about you in the last two years, since you disappeared off the face of the frigging earth. And I still don't even know what happened! Man!"

Kate took a sip of her coffee and pulled unenthusiastically at the untouched toast that sat next to her, cold and slightly wet. "Look, Francesca . . ." she began warily. She wasn't ready to be reminded of it all yet. She paused. "It's pretty horrible, so . . ."

Francesca's voice softened. "Oh, Kate. I'm sorry." She sounded genuinely contrite. "I wasn't calling to force you to tell me, honest. I just wanted to make sure you were OK. It was such a weird vibe last night after he arrived, between the two of you. I can't believe Zoe doesn't know something's going on. Don't you two ever *talk*?"

She sounded like Mac. "Well, we left together," said Kate defensively. "She probably imagines . . ." She didn't say anything else.

"Look," Francesca began. "Whatever happened between you two—"

Kate interrupted, curiosity suddenly, overwhelmingly, getting the better of her. "What time did he get back this morning?"

"Well, some time after six o'clock," said Francesca. "I was in the shower when he came in. He was quiet as a mouse, too. But I didn't see him. I yelled out 'Bye' when he was in the bathroom when I left and he yelled back."

"Mmm," said Kate. "What—what did he yell back?"

"Well, 'Bye,' too." Francesca sounded apologetic. "Sorry."

"Right," said Kate. She knew he wouldn't have said "By the way, I'm in love with Kate, and I left her this morning, but I'm just back here for a shower and change of clothes and then I'm going to buy her a big bunch of flowers and go back to her flat to shag her senseless again and then take her out for lunch somewhere nice, possibly by the river." But a small part of her hoped he would. She stamped her foot. Stupid girl.

Francesca asked curiously, "So he left you at—what, five?"

"Five thirty, yeah."

"Blimey," said Francesca. "That's early."

"Yes," said Kate. "Oh God, Francesca. He was so angry."

"About what?"

"Well—" Kate sighed. "Give me a couple of minutes to fill you in, and if the yen starts to crumble you have my permission to cut me off. OK?"

So she told Francesca everything. About the night together all those years ago. The affair last year. Last night. The letters from Charly. How he'd left.

When she'd finished, Francesca was silent, and then she said, "Wow."

"I know, sorry."

"Yeah. Wow." Francesca exhaled loudly. "You two are hopeless."

"That's the problem," said Kate. She added sadly, "Do you know something? I promised myself I wasn't going to think about it for a little while, but I just can't help wondering if that's the last time I'll see him. And it's probably for the best."

She didn't know what she wanted Francesca to say. She just wanted her to be honest.

Francesca made a strange sound, and then she said, "You know what?"

"What?"

"I think you may be right."

"Oh."

"Oh, babe. It's hard, but really—how would it ever work? You're both too . . . messy from the past. He's got his own stuff, too. His job's really busy—he's looking for somewhere else to live, you know."

"Yes. I know." Kate bit her lip, grimacing. She thought for a second and said, "I was so sure it'd work last year. I kept having these dreams, kept thinking I saw . . . I saw Sean and Charly. You know? Everywhere I went." She'd never said any of this before. "It was like my punishment. Even though I knew they were dreams, they were so real, it was . . . awful."

"Forget about her," said Francesca.

"I can't," said Kate. "Now there's this letter thing." She banged her fist gently against the wooden surface of her desk. "God, I don't want to see her."

Francesca made a huffing sound. "Course you don't! She did you a favor, though."

"How so?"

"Getting you away from Sean, in my opinion," she said. "Imagine if you'd married him."

"Yeah. Maybe," Kate said uncertainly.

"No 'maybe' about it. You were such a little mouse in his presence," Francesca said. "You weren't yourself. You stopped saying interesting geeky facts, you stopped talking about your job—and you had this really important job, too, while he was moving stupid program data around from one computer to another! You'd sit there and gaze up at him like he was . . . Zeus or something!" Her voice was loud; she obviously realized it and said more softly, after a moment, "And as for that cow, Charly, well. I just think it was bad luck, you know? We all have these friends we make who we think are the greatest things since sliced bread. Especially at work. You just got really unlucky, that's all. She was a bitch, you always knew she was a bitch, but you never really knew she was *evil*, did you? Who could have known."

"You're right, you know." Kate nodded, blinking in amazement.

"I think they're probably miserable together," Francesca went on. "You know, Bobbie saw them last year, in some Vietnamese restaurant in Dalston. It was BYOB and Sean hadn't brought the wine and Charly was having this massive go at him."

"Gosh," said Kate, fascinated. "Is that true?"

"Yep, she looked awful, apparently," Francesca said with relish. "But she was always one of those people whose looks were going to go early on. Good riddance to bad rubbish, I say. And, God, you know we all wish we could change what happened that day, but the one thing I don't think any of us would change is you splitting up with Sean. He wasn't right for you. He's weak. A weak, weak man."

This was all news to Kate, and she was astounded. "I had no idea," she said, but as she said it she realized pretty much all of it made sense. "Why didn't you say any of this to me?" she asked Francesca.

"When?" said Francesca, snorting loudly. "Kate, when?"

"Yeah." Kate nodded, startled at the easy honesty of this conversation. "I know."

"Let me ask you something," Francesca said. "Have you talked to Zoe about any of this?"

"No," said Kate. "No way. She's got enough on her plate."

"I think that's your problem," Francesca said elliptically. "You should have told her."

"Maybe." Kate squirmed in her seat. She still felt guilty about Zoe, in a variety of ways. "One thing at a time, eh? Hey. Let's have dinner tonight. My treat. To say thanks. You've been an amazing friend since I got back, don't know what I would have done without you."

"Hm," said Francesca darkly. "Well, I don't know about that. Dinner'd be nice, though. Where?"

"You pick."

"Great." She was silent. "Yes. I've got an idea. I'll—I'll text you when I've booked somewhere." She changed tack suddenly, and Kate forgot the strange tone in her voice. "Oh, God, did you hear about Betty's new boyfriend?"

By lunchtime, Kate felt much better. She'd accomplished more that morning than she'd ever expected to, and it filled her with an intoxicating sense of freedom. She spoke to Sue, who was so kind, so positive, and asked her to do another article for next week, and then to Lisa, checking on her dad and her plans to see them all that afternoon.

Francesca, in her bluntly affectionate way, had made her see things she'd never thought of before. And she was right about

Mac, too, little though Kate wanted to hear it. Perhaps it was best to sweep all of this out, with this new sense of purpose she had. Consign it, once and for all, to the past. She didn't understand him, though she thought she had. But she understood his wanting to preserve his sanity, to not want to get dragged back into all of that again—even though it had been so good. Still.

She was having a shower when she heard the phone ring again, but they didn't leave a message. She got dressed, humming, and popped the "Thank you for everything" card she'd written to Bruce into her bag. The feeling of lightness that was washing over her did not vanish. She ran down the stairs, staring out the windows at the front and back of the building that gave out onto the blue sky. Another beautiful day. When would this gorgeous weather end? Because it had to end sometime.

As she flung open the door, patting her bag to make sure she had her keys, Kate screamed with surprise. There, on the doorstep, grinning maniacally at her, just like she had in those dreams, in Kate's nightmares, was Charly.

Thirty-seven

Kate stared at her. As if she were in a museum staring at a curiosity piece.

"Hello, Kate," said Charly.

Almost calmly Kate noted Charly's hair was thinner; perhaps that was the pregnancy, though; it sometimes made your hair fall out. She knew that, one of those random facts she'd picked up somewhere. It fell lankly about her shoulders; it was a bit too long.

"What are you doing here?" Kate said, steadying herself against the door. Everything felt as if it were in slow motion. She looked down, dreading seeing Charly's pregnancy in evidence, the child she was carrying, hers and Sean's baby. Charly had a neat, nice bump. She was wearing a stripy top, a pretty long gold chain, flat shoes, skinny jeans, a little jacket. The uniform of a thousand girls who cram into TopShop on Saturdays, only that on someone heavily pregnant it looked different.

"Did you get my letters?" said Charly. She'd forgotten her voice, that curiously husky, yet high-pitched, slightly mockney voice. "I wasn't sure."

"Yes," said Kate, nodding politely. "Yes, I did get them. Lovely, they were."

"I didn't mean the stuff I—" Charly began, but Kate interrupted her.

"Look, Charly, I'm late, and I have to—"

When she looked back on this encounter, she found it hilarious that she might have just walked away because otherwise she'd have been ten minutes late for Lisa. Though she should have done—who was Charly to cause her to keep Lisa waiting?

"I need to talk to you," Charly said simply.

"OK," said Kate, crossing her arms. "Fire away."

Charly was waiting for her to expand on this; when she didn't, she said, visibly discomfited, "Well—I want to say sorry."

Kate watched her, breathing slowly. She just didn't know how to react. Why wasn't she feeling more emotional? Why wasn't she trying to kick Charly, why didn't she spit on her, or run away, calling her vile names? Wasn't that what she deserved? Charly was vulnerable now, so much more vulnerable than she'd been when they'd been friends. And Kate just couldn't do it.

"How did you know I was back?" Kate said suddenly.

"That doesn't matter." Charly waved her hand impatiently, and Kate saw a flash of the old Charly—imperious, careless of others, concerned only with herself, not this watered-down, colorless version in front of her now. "Can I—can I come up? I just want to talk to you for a moment."

Kate stared at her, anger finally hitting her. "Are you serious? You want to come up—up to the flat? This flat?"

"Yes," said Charly. She looked obstinate. "Only for a bit."

"No way!" said Kate, almost laughing. "This is a joke." She walked down the steps, shaking her head. "I'm going, Charly, bye." She started walking down the road, as fast as possible.

"Sean's having an affair," Charly said loudly after her.

It was eerily quiet on the street, and the words echoed. Kate stopped and turned around.

"What?" she said.

"He's having an affair." Charly came down the steps, slowly; Kate noticed how she shuffled, her movements were painful. "With someone at work. I don't know her. I know who she is, though."

There were lines around Charly's mouth that hadn't been there before, sharp little lines that made her lips look like a rosette when she spoke. From smoking, Kate knew—from sucking on endless cigarettes, pursing her mouth. She looked again at Charly, and she couldn't even remember why they'd been so close, but she felt a pang of sympathy for her, for this girl in this situation. This girl. Because Charly was this girl, the one who'd taught her how to do tequila slammers, taught her how to chat someone up in a bar, made her grow her hair and ditch the glasses, sat through countless shopping expeditions, patiently saying yes or no to everything Kate tried on. Who'd argued with their landlord when they needed a new sofa, insisted on sending back a bottle that was corked, who'd stayed in on Friday nights with her, watching *Friends* and *Frasier*. She had made her laugh, made her confident, made her feel like a person in her own right in the world. She had shaped her life, been a shot in the arm, been the spark on a fuse.

Kate had forgotten all of that.

She'd had to.

And now—

She faced her. "What do you want me to do about it? Although, I know how you feel."

"Yes, you must," said Charly quietly. "Look—" She grabbed Kate by the arm. "Let's just go there and talk, can we?" She gestured to the pub down the road. "That's why I've been writing to you. When I knew you were coming back— look—" She licked her lips; her eyes were misty with unshed tears. Kate was transfixed. "I have to make my peace with you before this baby comes. I sort of think it'll make everything all right." She swayed a little on her feet.

"You OK?"

"I need to sit down," she said impatiently, with a flash of the old Charly. "Just one coffee or something. Sean's picking me up in an hour." Kate's eyes flew wide open. "It's OK, he's just going to wait around the corner, you can be gone by then. God, I hate being pregnant." Kate was silent. "I do. I wish I was . . ."

Don't say it, Kate thought, *please don't say it.*

"I wish this had never happened. I wish I'd never met him."

Kate wanted to walk away; she was repulsed by her, by what she was saying, by the fact that Steve was dead because of her and Sean. But she couldn't just leave her there. Walk away and not finish this.

"OK," said Kate. "I'll need to call my stepmother. Just one coffee, then."

The pub was twenty yards away—anonymous, brown, neutral, serving burgers and tapas and coffee for young professionals, not old men. It was slightly soulless; Kate had never been in there before, and she was glad of that suddenly. She turned to Charly.

"I've only got fifteen minutes. OK?"

"Fine," said Charly.

They walked into the pub silently and sat down.

"It was the attraction mixed with the dislike, you know," said Charly, sipping her coffee, rubbing her stomach, her feet up on the other side of the banquette. "I was so used to getting anyone. I know it sounds crap, but I was. He was different, you know. He really hated me."

Kate nodded. She had made up her mind to say as little as possible. She was just going to ride out the numbness, the absence of sensation before the pain starts, when the bandage is pulled off.

"He hated me, and then one day when you were out of the flat, at a meeting about your new job, he came over. You were late. I said he was being rude. He just ignored me and sat there waiting for you." She curled a section of hair around her finger; God, thought Kate, she doesn't even know I'm here. "We had a big argument and then suddenly—well . . ." She trailed off. "We were doing it. In the sitting room." She looked away at the memory.

"God, I hated him," she said. "Really despised him, for making out he was such a wannabe family man, all lovey-dovey with you, crawling up to your dad and all your friends, and then screwing me when you were out, or Jem was out, or . . . wherever we could."

After all this time Kate didn't feel angry. She wondered, almost curiously, why, how she could hear Charly talking like this and not feel anger. She just felt sad for her younger self, for how stupid she must have looked.

"The day of your dad's wedding, you know? He was vile to me all day, and then he was furious because he couldn't have me. And what did he do? He proposed to you instead." She shook her head, marveling at herself, at him. "His face the next day, when you came out of your room and told me . . ." Kate swallowed. "Like it was a game, you know? Part of it all. We were so into each other, the things we would do to each other—it was like a drug. It scared me. I think we wanted to get caught by the end. I certainly did." She stirred her coffee and looked directly up at Kate. "I was glad when you walked in on us." Her eyes opened. "Isn't that awful? Really glad. I thought, OK, well, at least it's out in the open now. I was glad."

Kate spoke then, her voice craggy with misuse. "But— Charly, what happened after— How can you look at it like that?"

"Well, of course that was awful," said Charly. "Of course it was." She looked uncomfortable. "Absolutely devastating."

This is unreal, Kate thought. She's a robot. She's not a real person at all. She said, tentatively, "Did you feel like maybe . . . with Steve's death and everything . . . that you had to stay together, after all of that? Prove it was real to everyone?"

"Of course not," said Charly sharply. "We were always going to end up together, me and Sean. We just wouldn't have wanted that to happen. That's all."

Kate didn't know what to say. Because she just didn't believe her.

They made polite conversation after that. Where was she having the baby? Dick Whittington? How nice. What was she going to do, would she go back to work? Three days a week at *Your World!*, she'd see how it went. They were living near Bethnal Green, how was the flat? Good, great, but Sean had to do some more work to the nursery, he was being crap about it, and he still hadn't finished the plastering in the hall, it was really annoying. . . . It was funny how hilariously perfectionist Sean had been about getting their flat right. He'd obviously tired of DIY over the years. Kate told her about seeing Sue Jordan, but she was unwilling to discuss much more. There was something about Charly that deeply unsettled her now. Something desperate, as if a part of her had died and the rest of her knew it but couldn't work out quite what was wrong. She seemed to have shrunk, too—Kate realized that her heels were always so high it gave the impression of natural height. And when they were living together—well, she'd just been a different girl, confident, totally sure of herself. Kate had been pretty much the opposite.

Strange, then, that she had everything Kate had wanted, and Kate didn't want it anymore. She wanted to be on her own, to walk to the tube station and go and see her dad, her sister, and her stepmother. She was so, so glad she didn't have to get in a car and go home with Sean. Strange, she barely thought of him, because she hadn't allowed herself to, so angry she had been with him, and so strange that he should have slipped out of her life so easily. When leaving Zoe, Francesca, her father, Dani, and Lisa, not to mention Mac—leaving all those people behind in London—caused her pain, constant, low-level pain.

I thought I was dead inside, she told herself as Charly described in some detail the new girl at *Your World! I thought I'd shut all of that out . . . and that's the reason it made me so unhappy. Because I love them, I love them all. And shutting out Charly and Sean—it was easy, because they're . . . not the people I thought they were.*

The realization hurt her, but it comforted her, too, because that's what real life is all about. It hurts to love people because you expose yourself to them, and they can hurt you, so much. Here in front of her was the girl in whom Kate had had complete, idolizing faith, and she had broken her heart. She and Sean.

Charly's phone vibrated on the table, jangling loudly into Kate's thoughts. She started.

"Oh . . ." said Charly, picking it up. "He's waiting around the corner."

"In case I go mad at the sight of him and throw something at him?" Kate said, trying not to sound like that was exactly what she wanted to do. Charly smiled vaguely, like she wasn't really taking it in.

"Yeah . . ." She put the phone in her bag. "Listen. We have to talk about it. Did you know?"

Kate didn't understand what she meant. She shook her head.

"Did you know—when he was cheating on you?"

"Oh." Kate felt awkward. Just because it made her feel stupid. "Er . . . you know what? I don't see why I should tell you." She smoothed her fingers across the wooden varnish of the table, leaving a fingerprint smear.

Charly's head drooped a little; she stroked her bump for the first time. "OK. OK, yes. Of course. I can see why."

Glad you can see why, you complete mentalist, Kate wanted to shout, but she didn't; she couldn't. Instead, unbending a little, she said, "Look. If you want to know . . . No. I had no idea. I trusted him, which was my mistake." She paused. "You'll never trust him, will you?"

"What do you mean?" said Charly, blinking violently, as if someone were shining a bright light in her face.

"I mean you can't trust him, because you met him because he was my boyfriend, my fiancé, and you slept with him behind my back for—what, two years? When I was your best friend, you were everything to me, he was everything to me." She smiled, to hide her grimacing, as tears filled her eyes. She blinked them back, as if she were surprised at their appearance. "And you wonder why you can't trust him after that? How could he betray me like that? How could you? So the two of you are locked together in this kind of weird old web of . . ."—she was running out of words now—"web of *something,* I don't know, and you deserve each other, you *deserve each other, Charly,* and I can't feel sorry for you. Because he did it before and it ruined my life, and it did, actually, kill someone. Or had you forgotten that bit?"

Charly flicked her hand languidly, even though she was still blinking strangely. "Of course I hadn't. But this is different, this time. It's some girl at his company. I know who she is—"

"Shut up," said Kate, standing up. "Look, just shut up, I'm going." She grabbed her purse and keys and turned around, and there he was. Sean was in the doorway, twice as large and American-football-player handsome as she remembered, and she just stared at him. Her hands flung out involuntarily and her purse slid to the floor. She bent down to pick it up, and he said, "Kate. Hi. So . . ."

His eyes raked over her. Kate raised her hand to her ponytail, swinging behind her head, and clenched her hair in her hand. She gritted her teeth.

"Hi," she said, and she raised herself up as tall as she could, thanking the Lord and all His seraphim for her height, the gangliness at school that she used to hate and now loved, and the fact that she had put on her high-heeled boots that morning. "I was just going, actually. Bye, Sean."

And with that, she turned on her heel, something she had always wanted to do, and strode out, feet clacking loudly on the wooden floor, and for the first time in her life she felt like Charly must have felt, walking away from all those situations, totally in control, and it meant nothing to her, nothing at all. She carried on walking, oblivious to the sound of Charly calling her name.

Thirty-eight

*K*ate caught the tube to Holborn that evening. She was meeting Francesca in Exmouth Market, and she was early. She walked through Bloomsbury, hands sunk deep into the pockets of her jacket, and she looked around her as she went. The streets were busy, as always in Bloomsbury. Students, tourists, old couples, people sitting outside the Brunswick Centre under heated lamps. She walked around the edge of Coram's Fields, through the sedate, quiet Mecklenburgh Square, and crossed Gray's Inn Road. She loved the fact that in this part of town it seemed as if every other house had a blue plaque on it, marking the presence of some worthy person who had lived there. Often they were incredibly famous and you stopped and said, "Huh! Thomas Hardy lived here? Wow!" surprised that one of the greatest novelists in the English language had chosen to live in an OK but not-that-nice Pooterish villa overlooking the train tracks leading into Paddington. Just as often, however, they were people of whom Kate had never heard, but she liked that, too, liked knowing that at 21 Mecklenburgh Square lived both Sir Sayyid Ahmad Khan, a nineteenth-century Muslim reformer and scholar, *and* Richard Henry Tawney, British historian and writer (but not at the same time). Kate's own favorite, as a late convert to karaoke, was David Edward Hughes, (1831–1900) who had lived at

4 Great Portland Street. He had invented the microphone, and she would always be grateful to him for that.

It had been a long day and a longer night, but now she knew her time in London was coming to an end, and she owed it to herself to keep on going. Things kept falling into place these last couple of days. Not necessarily the way she would have liked, but perhaps the way she might have predicted. Mac had said she kept her heart locked away. Well, if that's what it took to get her through that strange afternoon with Charly, then fine. She thought about Charly, about how she couldn't see past her nose, how she hadn't altered at all, apart from the baby growing inside her. Kate saw now, the way she never had before, that they were totally different in that respect. Charly had seen it; she hadn't. For Kate had changed outwardly—she dressed better and had nicer hair and bought flowers for her flat and could talk to people at parties more than she had when she was twenty-two. But that didn't mean she was different. She was the same, just more grown -up. Same Kate. That, after all, was what was happening to them all, like it or not.

But she knew the next stage, where she felt all of this more deeply, would hurt her when it happened. She hated leaving London with her relationship with Zoe still so formal. She didn't know how to cross the final divide that separated them. Perhaps that had been what forced her to drive Mac away. But she couldn't think about that yet.

So she didn't—she walked instead, and she watched people go by, and when she got to Exmouth Market she was still early, so she walked a little farther, up to Sadler's Wells, where *Rigoletto* was on that night. The audience was just starting to mill into the theater. She stood for a while watching them all, the excitement of the pretheater crowd, the pretty fairy lights that hung in the trees outside. From her position on the opposite side of the road she could see people's expressions, could tell if they were tired or excited or apprehensive or if they'd had a bad day; the deliciousness of observing others unaware of it. She felt totally alone, a unit of one, and it felt good to be on the other side of the road, watching from the sidelines.

When she reached The Ambassador on Exmouth Market, a few doors down from Moro, she decided to go in, even though she was still a little early. It was a sparse, frugal-looking place, with white walls, floorboards, and a collection of junk-shop furniture, but the menu was all fresh, local produce, the wine list was great, and Francesca loved it there. But as Kate opened the door, someone else behind her held it open for her.

She turned around.

"Zoe?" Kate said in surprise. "What are you doing here?" She kissed her in the doorway, and they got tangled up in each other's arms, until Zoe pushed her friend firmly over the threshold.

"I'm here to meet you," said Zoe. "Francesca's not coming."

"What? Why?" Kate said.

Zoe's expression was set. "She rang me. We had a talk. And I'm here instead."

"Right," said Kate, and she felt guilty.

"Francesca told me about Mac," said Zoe, propelling Kate firmly to a rickety table and chair. She pushed her down on the shoulder, and sat down opposite her.

"Oh," said Kate, waving to signal for a waiter. "What—what did she tell you?"

"That you slept with him and he ran out this morning."

Kate felt nervous, Zoe looked furious. "It wasn't like that. Look, Zoe, I didn't tell you because—"

The waiter appeared. "Goodeveningladies." He rubbed his hands together impishly. "Well, well. Can I—"

"Can you give us a moment," said Zoe firmly. "Just a little while. OK?" She nodded at him. "Oh. Tell you what. Bring us a bottle of white wine in about five minutes." She turned back to

Kate. "Where was I. You, Mac . . . um, you . . . yes." She crossed her arms. You didn't tell me. And you didn't tell me that you came back last summer, and you didn't see any of us."

"Well . . . I did, you see, I . . ." Kate faltered.

"Oh, I know about that, too," Zoe said. "You and Mac. Oh, Kate."

"Zoe—"

Zoe looked around the room, which was pretty empty, and she said in a clear voice, "She told me about Charly, about the letters."

Kate's heart was racing. Zoe was being scary. She hadn't seen her like this since—since when . . .

"For God's sake, Kate, why didn't you tell me any of this?" said Zoe. She looked down, and smoothed the gnarled varnish of the table with her fingers.

"About what?" said Kate helplessly.

"Exactly," said Zoe, shaking her black hair. "Exactly. About everything, Katy. Why don't you tell me anything anymore?"

"You've got enough on your plate," Kate said, taking her hand. "I can't bother you with all of that. I don't want to after everything that's happened—"

"That's *exactly* it." Zoe banged her fist on the table. "You're my best friend!" she said. "We tell each other stuff, OK?" She looked down. "Well. We *should* tell each other stuff, anyway," she said quietly.

"I can't ring you up and tell you about Charly and Sean, not after what I did to you," Kate exclaimed. Her throat felt thick. "I can't say, Oh, by the way, I saw my ex-fiancé today, and his pregnant girlfriend, who's been writing me weird letters, and neither of them seems to care, and it's all my fault. . . ."

Her voice grew louder. The waiter watched them, openly curious, and Kate dropped her voice.

"I said to Mac this morning . . ." she said. "I told him, too. . . . I don't think you understand what happened that day."

"I do," said Zoe. "Kate—"

Kate held out her hand. "He saved my life. He pushed me out of the way. I was the one running away. I always run away. And Steve was the one who saved me." She swallowed. *"And it should have been the other way around."*

"No," said Zoe.

"It's true." Kate balled her fingers into her eye sockets. "It was my fault. I should have died. It was my fault."

"It wasn't your fault," Zoe cried, interrupting her. "Kate, it wasn't your fault! There's something I've never told you."

There was silence.

The two friends looked at each other.

"It's not your fault," Zoe said, covering Kate's hands with hers. She spoke softly, leaning in. "Look at me."

Kate kept her hands pressed to her eyes. She found it impossible to look at her friend.

"Oh God." Zoe said something under her breath. "I should have done this a long time ago. Kate, oh, Kate." She pulled her fingers away from her face, staring at Kate, her eyes ablaze. "It's not your fault! Look, you are *not* to blame for this, and I can tell you that till I'm blue in the face but you have to believe it yourself."

"You told me to go," Kate said softly.

"Of course I did!" Zoe cried. "It was the funeral, I'd lost my husband six days before, and I was seven months pregnant! Of course I told you to go, I was crazy! Because you kept coming around and trying to help, and no one could help me, *no one*, and you just didn't get it, and I . . . I . . ." She shook her head. "I'm *not* going to cry. I wanted you out of my hair for a bit. You know? And you were so busy hating yourself I think you thought you were unclean or something, and better out of it, and so you left without even saying good-bye! And I hated you for leaving!" She banged her fist on the table again. "You were my best friend, I'd just lost my husband, and you ran out on me when I was about to have another baby!" Her voice cracked. "I needed you, Kate. More than anyone else then I needed you. And you left."

"You never said." Kate tried to justify herself, but even to her ears it was weak.

"Neither did you," said Zoe. "Neither did you. And it's all so ridiculous, Katy. Because if it's anyone's fault it's mine, you know. I'm the one who should hate myself."

"What?" said Kate, almost laughing. "You? Are you joking?"

"No, no," said Zoe, and she leaned in again. Her eyes bored into Kate's, a clear, unflinching gaze. "This is what I mean." She swallowed. "It was never your fault. It was mine, if anything. You know. You see . . . I knew about Charly and Sean."

It was quiet in the restaurant; Kate stared at Zoe, unblinking, till she could feel her eyeballs dry. She didn't know what to say. "You knew . . . you knew they were having an affair? You . . ." She trailed off.

"Yes." Zoe nodded, her eyes never leaving Kate's. "I knew. Steve told me. We had huge rows about it. I wanted to tell you. But I didn't know what to do. I thought perhaps it would burn itself out. I couldn't destroy your world. You were so happy, you'd been such a shy, unconfident thing, and now there you were—" She smiled at the memory. "You were suddenly all grown up, all happy and glossy and successful, and you had this wonderful life, and you *adored* him. You just adored him." Kate opened her mouth to speak, but Zoe held up her hand to stop her. "I couldn't destroy all that for you. So I kept trying to get Steve to work on her, get her to see what she was doing." She grimaced, biting her lip, and her voice was unsteady. "Or to talk to Sean, make him understand how stupid he was being. I thought it might work out. . . . You'd never need to know. So I never told you.

"We knew what Sean was doing. We knew it was going on. Steve's the one who made the decision to drive around there that day. I had lunch with you to distract you. And you know, I can't help thinking—if Steve or I had told you months earlier, none of this would have happened. You see?

"Steve was responsible for his death. Not you. You're the last person who should be blaming yourself. He . . ."

And then Zoe's face crumpled, and she slid her tiny hands over her face, fingers pressed furiously to her skin, and she cried.

"I was so wrong." She sobbed. "It was all my fault. I was so wrong, and I'll live with that for the rest of my life. Without Steve, for the rest of my life. Oh God. I'm so sorry, Kate."

Kate pushed her chair out and stood up, she crouched on the ground next to her sobbing friend, and threw her arms around her, and they stayed like that, not speaking, just holding each other, for a long time. Out on the street people carried on walking by, and Kate watched them, unseeing, as she hugged Zoe tightly, the view blurred with tears. She couldn't speak.

"She said we needed to talk," Zoe sobbed, dashing tears away from her cheeks.

Kate cleared her throat. "Who said that?"

"Francesca. She said we were both being stupid. . . . We have been, haven't we?"

Kate nodded. She brushed a tear away from Zoe's cheek with her thumb, and sat back down in her chair. "We have," she said. "Not anymore, but we have."

This was their reckoning, the buildup of everything that had needed to be said for two years and more, and strangely there was little else to say. Zoe sat back and breathed out heavily.

"Pff!" she said, smiling rather soggily. She blew her nose loudly on the paper napkin.

The waiter looked up at the noise; these crazy girls who burst in to a nice quiet gastropub, started yelling at each other and then sobbing hysterically—were they going to order something, at last, finally, at last? He clutched his notebook hopefully.

Kate wiped her cheeks with her fingers. They were both silent, staring at each other, as the waiter approached.

"Can I get you something to drink?" he said, a little nervously.

"Ooh, yes," said Zoe. "Yes, please." She flicked the wine list with her finger. "A bottle of that, please." She put the menu down again as he retreated. "Well," she said. "Well, well."

Despite herself, Kate opened her mouth to ask Zoe something, and then she shut it again, and smiled at her friend. It was all retread, and it would always be there for discussion. She was just relieved that it was all out in the open. What a day, what a day, she thought.

"Well," she said. "Gosh."

"Indeed," said Zoe.

Kate grabbed her best friend's wrist. "Look. We're OK now, aren't we?"

"Of course we are," Zoe said crossly. "We were before, if you hadn't been such an ostrich about it. We've always been OK. I love you, Katy. It'll take a lot more than Charly Willis and Sean Lambert to shake us. Argh," she said, her mouth a wavy line of distaste. "I can't believe it. I bet he cheats on her, too. You mark my words."

Something stopped Kate from telling Zoe this was true. She didn't know why, she just knew she didn't want to be involved with them anymore, didn't want to poison Zoe's life with them, either. Best to walk as far away as possible from it all, that was it. As the waiter set the glasses and some bread down on the table, she said instead, "Who's got the children?"

"Mac," Zoe replied briefly.

"Oh, right." Kate poured the wine. "That's nice."

"Very nice of him to come over twice in two days, but that's Mac for you," said Zoe. She exhaled deeply again. "Phew, I feel about ten years younger."

Kate raised her glass. "You look it."

"Well, while I'm on the subject," Zoe said. "You and Mac. Look, I know you two have some weird kind of sex thing going on—"

"It's not a weird sex thing," Kate said hastily. "And it's not—"

"Let me finish." Zoe waved her arms at her peremptorily. "Whatever it is, it's weird, anyway. And don't think I didn't know something was going on, by the way—he used to freeze whenever anyone mentioned your name—"

"Nice," said Kate.

"I just wish you two could sort it out." Zoe flapped her hands at Kate. "I know it's silly, but it's true—I *know* he likes you, you know, and you quite clearly have a thing for him."

Kate pulled at a piece of bread. "We've been there," she said firmly. "Look, Mac and I have always had—we always have—well, we'll always be close, OK? But it's a timing thing. I just think it wasn't meant to be."

"Why do you think that?" Zoe put her elbows on the table.

"It's timing," Kate said eventually. "We had a chance at it. I think there's too much water under the bridge for us to go back and start again."

"I don't buy it," said Zoe.

"It's true," said Kate. Francesca thought it was true, too. And she was right, she knew. She was starting to see everything much more clearly. "Look at my mum and dad. I actually think they're partly still in love with each other, or at least they think they are. But the timing's wrong now. They couldn't get back together even if they were free to. They've got different lives now, they live thousands of miles apart. . . ." She thought of her father's rage, his loathing of Venetia mixed with his open lust and admiration for her, all of which had peppered Kate's teenage years. She had left him, like Kate had left Mac—perhaps for the same reasons, or perhaps for others, Kate still didn't know.

"No, Kate," said Zoe. "It's the opposite. I've known you since you were five. You're not about to repeat the mistakes your parents made. OK? You're nothing like them."

"Well, that's not true," said Kate. "They're my parents."

"Yes, but genetics aren't everything. I think a lot of stuff skips a generation. Especially now that I've got children. I see what they've got that neither of us had. And I'm telling you, you and Mac are not your mum and dad. Seriously."

"He's always trying to fix things," said Kate. "I wasn't ready. I want to sort it out for myself."

"Fair enough," said Zoe. "But you can't blame him for trying, can you? Not if he's in love with you? And I've seen him with you. He is. In love with you."

Kate looked away. "Oh, darling. He's not. He just wants to make everything all right. Sort everything out, wipe the slate clean. Honestly, after last night—well, this morning—it's over. Really." She shook her head. "I'm going back to New York, and that's that."

Zoe looked disappointed. "You really are?"

"Yes," Kate said firmly. "But properly this time. I'm getting a place of my own, moving out of Mum's. And I'll be back lots, if this column for *Venus* comes off. You're going to come out and visit, too. Hey!" She waggled her finger. "You could come with Diggory! Leave the children with your mum for a few days!"

"Steady on there," said Zoe, laughing. "We've had two dates, Kate. We're not about to start hopping over to New York on mini-breaks. But I'll come! Yay!"

"Great," said Kate. "Even Dad's coming in a few months, when he's better, and he's bringing Lisa and Dani." She thought of her mother briefly. "I'll tell Mum if you're in town. She'd love to see you. But I wouldn't dare tell her Dad was staying with me."

"You need to ask your mum what happened between those two," said Zoe, reading her thoughts. "I've never understood it, myself. Don't you want to know?"

"Sort of not," said Kate, holding her wineglass to her cheek; she was hot.

"Why not?"

Kate tried to explain. "I don't know. If the last couple of years has taught me anything, it's that . . . there are some things you're just not meant to understand."

"I'll drink to that," said Zoe. "Cheers."

They clinked glasses and smiled. The waiter reappeared with the menus.

"Will you ladies be staying for food?"

"You bet," said Zoe. "And—can you bring us two glasses of champagne, please?" Kate leaned forward. "We should raise a glass, not to everything that's happened, but to us," Zoe said as the waiter retreated. "Seriously. Never forget I love you, Kate. We all love you, me and Flora and Harry."

In under a minute, two glasses of champagne appeared on the table, and Zoe raised hers. "To Steve, to you, and to me," she said, sticking her chin out. "Steve, we'll always drink to you, darling." She held her glass high in the air and looked up to the ceiling, then back at Kate. "To us, all of us."

"To all of us," Kate agreed, and they drank.

Thirty-nine

"So, what time's your flight tomorrow?" Her father pushed his hair back out of his face.

"It's at two." Kate held up her hand to shield her eyes from the sun. She shook her feet out, stretching on the wide steps. "I've got loads to do and I haven't done it, still. Got to see Mr. Allan now he's back again, got to pack, of course, and I've got to make sure everything's tidied away properly, you know."

"Of course," said her father, who was utterly uninterested in domestic matters unless they specifically pertained to him. "Yep. You know, Kate—"

Kate leaned forward. "Dani, perhaps don't go any farther. OK? It's a busy road." She turned back to her father. "I meant to say, that reminds me. I've got to drop the spare keys off at the estate agent's, too. They're showing people around next week."

Her dad hadn't mentioned finding a new tenant for her flat since she'd first seen him and she wondered if he'd just forgotten or was being tactful. She wasn't sure. He turned to her now, smiling.

"I'm glad," he said. "Good, so you are going to rent it out again?"

"Yes," Kate said. She put her hands out behind her and looked up at the clear blue sky. "I can't have it empty, I need the money, you need the money. You've been so kind, Dad, thanks a lot. I don't think I ever thanked you properly for bailing me out of the flat after Sean went off."

Her father looked embarrassed, and a little flustered. "Don't be ridiculous," he said. "Not at all, who wouldn't?"

"I know you want a tenant in there again," said Kate. "They say it'll be a couple of weeks, honestly—"

Daniel Miller put his hand over his eldest daughter's. Dani sat at their feet, a few steps below. "Kate," he said softly. "You misunderstand. I wanted you out of that flat because I couldn't see how you could ever be happy there . . . after what happened. Not because I wanted the rent. Please." He sat back, shaking his head. Just as Kate felt herself breaking into a grin, he rather spoiled the effect somewhat by adding, "*Please*. That my daughter should go without a home? Never!"

"*Never*," Dani bellowed loudly at their feet. "Oh, *never*!"

Kate laughed, but her father scooped his younger daughter up into his arms. "You monkey," he said, tickling her.

"*Monkey*," said Dani, dramatically. "Oh, monkey, monkey, monkey."

"You used to do that, too," said Daniel, tickling Dani, who was wriggling and screaming.

"Do what?" Kate said.

Dani screamed loudly with pleasure and Daniel released her, a flash of irritation on his face. "Shh, Dani," he said. "You used to mimic me when you were a little girl."

"Like that?" Kate was amazed.

Her father scratched his chin. "Oh yes. You'd appear in the kitchen after we'd put you to bed and repeat these dreadfully pompous things I'd said during the day but had obviously forgotten." He chuckled. "It used to make me so crazy, but your mother said you'd grow out of it."

"That's so funny, I don't remember that at all."

"Well, she was right," Daniel said. "You grew out of it."

High up in the sky, a tiny plane, almost invisible, cut a white trail through the blue expanse above her. Kate shook her head.

"Thanks, Dad," she said.

They were silent for a moment, as Dani watched them.

Daniel sighed. "Isn't this lovely."

They were sitting on the steps in front of the Albert Hall, which was eerily quiet for a Thursday afternoon; Kate had met Daniel and Dani for coffee, and they'd gone to Patisserie Valerie on the Brompton Road, and Dani had demanded a huge strawberry-filled pastry, of which she only managed three bites. Lisa was picking up Daniel's prescription and running some errands in her vast SUV; Daniel therefore was in charge of his daughters for a couple of hours. Afterward they'd walked to the Albert Hall, nostalgia for the old days overcoming Daniel and Kate, and there they sat, looking down toward the Royal College of Music, Daniel's alma mater, quietly chatting and waiting for Lisa to pick them up as Dani ran around the balustraded terrace, singing softly to herself. She had told Kate she was a princess or Maria in *The Sound of Music,* she hadn't decided yet.

"So what will you do back in New York?" her father asked.

"I'm not sure," said Kate. "Sue's going to give me some freelance work, and I'll start contacting people. . . ." She paused. "My column's in next week's edition of *Venus,* so let's see."

"How can the Girl About Town write a column about New York?" her father asked wryly.

"Maybe it'd be good," Kate said. "Girl About New York Town instead." Daniel said nothing. "Maybe interviews, I could be a stringer for them, do their stuff out of New York, contact other people I knew from *Venus,* see what's available. . . . We'll just have to see."

In truth, it had been so long since she was in the magazine world she wasn't sure if anyone would remember her. Kate Miller, one of the youngest features editors in town at twenty-seven, the girl who disappeared off the face of the earth. Writing the column for Sue had been enormous luck, she knew it, and she was still almost speechless with gratitude to her, although, as Sue put it, "You deserve a bit of good luck, Kate. So get over it."

Now she was older, wiser, calmer, saner, and she didn't know what the future held for her in New York—she just knew she was going back there, even though—

"And you don't want to stay here?" her father said, sitting up straight and fiddling with his cuffs, interrupting Kate's thoughts as Dani, who had overheard this, danced over to them.

"Hey, Kate!" she said. "Will you stay?"

"No," said Kate, scooping her little sister into her arms. "But I'll come back lots to see you, and I'll take you to the zoo next time to see the giraffe." Dani was going through a big obsession with giraffes. Kate blew raspberries onto her sister's neck, and she screamed. Daniel looked weary suddenly and a little bored.

"I'm going to get a place of my own there, too," Kate said. "Dad, you should come over when you're better."

"Well, I'll have to, with the Manilow album," her father said with bravado. He looked around at the Albert Hall, glowing red behind him. "And they want me to do another series of *Maestro!* For Christmas, if I'm up to it."

"I'm not sure about that," said Kate, frowning, but Daniel ignored her.

" . . . So yes, it'll be pretty hectic. . . . Anyway," he said casually. "You're moving out of your mother's, then?"

"Well, it's about time," Kate said, releasing Dani, who clambered onto the step below and positioned herself in between Kate's legs. "Poor Mum and Oscar, I should think they're longing to have some time to themselves, now they've had a chance to get used to me not being there this past month."

And then her father said impulsively, "Give her a message, will you?"

The tone of his voice reminded Kate of utter desperation, of the way she had to struggle not to mention Mac's name to people, to ask how he was, just trying to glean some minute, significant detail about him. She stared at Daniel in surprise.

"Mum? Yes—of course, Dad, what is it?"

Her father pursed his lips and gazed ahead, into the distance, his aquiline profile set. He looked like a Roman bust in the Victoria and Albert Museum, Kate thought. He was silent for so long she thought he wasn't going to say anything, and she was about to chip in instead, to tell him about how Mr. Allan had seen him play here all those years ago, when suddenly he said, "Tell her I still think about Sheffield."

Kate was disappointed. She'd been expecting something more romantic. *You are the key to my violin case and my heart.* Well, something like that. "You still think about Sheffield?" She repeated it, uncertainly.

"Yes."

"Well—but Dad. Will she know what that means?"

Daniel clutched his hand to his heart briefly. "Yes," he said simply, and then was silent.

Dani wrapped her hands around Kate's ankles as Kate sat next to her father, thinking how strange it was that he was suddenly so human to her now. And wondering, wondering what it meant.

"Yes, it's much better now," Lisa said, biting her lip as she turned the monster car around a corner. "He sleeps through the night now, and he's in such a good mood now, thank *God*."

"I hear you," said Kate. "He seemed to be today, that's for sure."

"It's up here?" Lisa asked suddenly.

"Yes," said Kate. "Thanks, Lisa, it's really kind of you to drop me off."

"Not at all, not at all." Lisa sounded cross. Kate turned to watch her, but her expression was unreadable behind her huge mirrored wraparound shades. Kate cleared her throat.

"Lisa," she began. "I just wanted to say—thanks, you know."

"You've said thanks," said Lisa.

"No, I mean—for this past month or whatever. It's been—" Kate searched for words, and realized she had them already. "It's been lovely. Just wonderful. I had no idea how—well this would work out," she was going to say, then realized you couldn't really say that about a father's near-death experience. "I've loved seeing Dad, and getting closer to Dani and—and you, Lisa." She sounded about ten years old; she stopped. "Thanks, anyway," she finished. "I don't think it could have been easy sometimes."

"You're right," said Lisa neutrally.

"Oh . . . right," said Kate, slightly taken aback.

"You were pretty nasty to me at first, Kate, you know that, don't you?"

"No I wasn't!" said Kate defensively. "I wasn't!" She knew as she spoke that she wasn't being convincing.

"You were," said Lisa. "It's a fact, let's not dwell. It wasn't so much you, anyway. That boyfriend of yours—yuck. He treated me like I was a Thai prostitute practically, your dad's young mistress."

"Really?" said Kate, fascinated. "God, I'm sorry. I was different then, things were different then . . . I . . . he . . ."

"You weren't that different," said Lisa as they turned onto the Edgware Road. "You were the same, Kate. Same cross, gangly, geeky little girl who was the apple of her daddy's eye. You still are." She held out a hand as Kate opened her mouth. "But then you were living the life you thought you ought to be living. Now—well, I'm sure you wouldn't ask for any of what's happened. But it's been good for you."

"Er . . ." said Kate. "Thanks?"

"You should thank me," said Lisa bluntly. "Your father's a nightmare to live with, you know he is." She grinned. "Imagine if you had to cope with all of that on your own. I can quite see what your mother had to put up with. You should love me, you know."

"I do love you," Kate said, realizing it was true.

"Right, fine," said Lisa, sticking out her bottom lip. Sun bounced off her sunglasses. "Right," she said again, as they drove up Maida Vale toward the flat.

Kate looked out of the window, at the streets she knew so well; this time tomorrow she'd be back in New York, sitting in the dining room with her mother and Oscar. How strange to think it, and yet—

"He still talks about her, you know," said Lisa. Her voice was deathly quiet, almost under her breath.

"Who?"

"Your father. Still talks about your mother. In his sleep, a lot of the time. Just says her name, I don't know why."

"Really?" said Kate, and she could believe it.

"Yeah," said Lisa, turning into Elgin Avenue. "Yeah. She's quite a ghost, your mother. He'll always love her, you know." She pulled over.

"I don't think so," said Kate.

"I know so," Lisa said, turning off the engine. She patted Kate's hand. "You look so like her these days. It's really strange."

Then she leaned over and kissed her on the cheek.

"Don't run away again, like she did," she said. "Come back soon. Not just for your dad. For Dani and me, too. OK?"

"OK," said Kate, trying to see Lisa's eyes through the glasses. She hugged her. "Thank you—for everything."

"Whatever," said Lisa, waving her hand dismissively. "Safe flight, you. Call us, OK? And don't leave it so long this time."

It was six o'clock; her last night in the flat in London for who knew how long. Kate let herself in, wearily, and looked down in surprise. There on the floor, slid under the door, was a hand-written note; her blood ran cold, fear spiraling in her chest. She looked again. It was attached to a magazine.

This is the kind of post I like getting; hope you do, too. Your first piece for <u>Venus</u>, enclosed. Congratulations, Kate. I always knew you were a star.

SUE JORDAN

Forty

*I*t was Saturday, and the day dawned cloudy and rainy, the sort of weather you only get in Great Britain, where one can't imagine there was ever such a thing as a blue sky or a sun shining on those sad daffodils, flattened by the wind of the previous night. It suited Kate's mood. She drank tea in the kitchen, looking around her home in the damp gray light. Her bags were packed, she was ready to go, there was nothing more to be done—other than see Mr. Allan, who was going on the Heathrow Express with her.

There was a sad back-to-school feeling to the day, like the previous few weeks of spring and sunshine had never really existed, but Kate knew they had. She knew she was different, that her time back in her hometown had changed her, for the better. She was stronger, she was back to her old self—no, not her old self, perhaps, but on the way to being her own person, for the first time since she was a young girl, probably.

As she was putting her copy of *Venus* back in her dresser, and wondering when she should go up to Mr. Allan, the doorbell rang.

"It's Geraldine Garley," a voice came loudly over the intercom. "Hi there. From Prince's, the estate agents? I just want to measure the flat, my colleague didn't do it yesterday. Can I come up?"

"Of course," said Kate, pressing the buzzer.

• • •

Geraldine was short, stocky, and very determined to impress. She was also clearly furious that she was having to do this.

"It's a busy time of year for us, Kate," she said, pointing the electronic measuring gun at the opposite wall and zapping it viciously. "And I don't see why I should have to pick up Nigel's pieces just because Nigel is a total and utter w— Oh!" she said, coming to and remembering where she was. "Seventeen, six. Great. Nice place," she said, looking around.

"Thanks," said Kate. She perched on the edge of the sofa, watching her. "Do you want a cup of tea or anything?"

"Tea? No thanks, Kate. I'll just—fifteen. OK, and nine inches. Well, you know what they say about nine inches, eh!" she bellowed loudly.

"I do, indeed," said Kate, trying not to wink like someone out of a seaside postcard.

"So, why are you moving?" Geraldine asked. She got out a clipboard. "Jesus! He hasn't even filled out the— Men. That's men for you! Bloody useless! Damn Nigel! Well, now I've gone and done it, Kate, I've sworn in front of you and we're absolutely not supposed to. Please accept my apologies."

"Don't worry about it," Kate called from the bedroom. "It's fine, honestly."

"So where you off to?" Geraldine said, following her in.

"I'm going back to New York," said Kate. "I live there. I was just over here for a bit, so I'm renting the flat out again after I've gone."

Geraldine was only half listening. "That's great, Kate. That's great. You like New York, do you?"

Kate loved the way people asked questions like this in London. It was basically a polite way of saying, "Are you stupid? Why do you live there?"

"Love it, yeah," she said. "It's great, you ever been?"

"Couple of times." Geraldine finished scribbling down something and looked up. "Tell you what, though. If you're talking about cities, I prefer Paris."

"Really?" Kate said. She was surprised; she didn't know why. She had Geraldine pegged as more of a Las Vegas kind of chick. "Do you?"

"Yeah. Paris is lovely. Really beautiful. Dog shit and stuff, and it stinks of cigarette smoke, but it's great. You can walk anywhere. It's small, too. I liked that. Me and my boyfriend went there just before Christmas last year." Her face lit up. "Walking along the river. All those pretty little streets and stuff. Lovely. You want to think about going there. It's so romantic."

"That's nice," said Kate.

"Yep, it is," Geraldine said, hugging herself. She came to. "Well, it will be again, if I make my bloody bonus. I'm the one who paid for it."

"Well, fingers crossed," Kate said. She added, jokingly, "If you rent this flat first, perhaps you can go to Paris again."

"That's what I'm thinking, and if Nigel thinks he's getting his useless little hands on it—oh my God, I'll kill him, Kate!" Geraldine chuckled. "I'll kill him. Oh, now. Look. I've done it again. Lost my temper. My God. My apologies."

"It's really OK," said Kate, seeing she looked quite alarmed.

Geraldine hit herself gently on the head with her clipboard. "Best be off before I get myself into more trouble," she said. She looked over at Kate's bags. "Nice to meet you, anyway. You going soon?"

A voice behind her in the open door made her jump suddenly.

"She's going in five minutes, and I've come to collect her."

"Mr. Allan!" Kate said, turning around to greet her neighbor. She kissed him on the cheek. "Oh, you're really here. I really have to go. Oh dear. Thanks again, Geraldine."

"Thank you, for choosing Prince's," said Geraldine, almost bowing, and she shut the door behind her.

"Who on earth was that young lady?" said Mr. Allan, coming into the sitting room and looking around him in bemusement.

"Estate agent," said Kate, putting the remote control on top of the TV. "OK."

"I could hear her voice from the flat upstairs. Extraordinary. Well," he continued, "this is a sad day, isn't it?"

"Oh," said Kate. "Don't, Mr. Allan. I'll cry, honestly." She held her hand out to him. "I don't want to go. I'm feeling homesick already."

"Cry? Rubbish," said Mr. Allan. "You are a strange girl, Kate. Here you are, back off to New York, which you were constantly telling me is the best city you've ever laid eyes on, and all of a sudden you don't want to be there anymore? Honestly." He picked up a case. "Make up your mind."

"I'll take that one, it's—" Kate was going to say "heavy." She corrected herself. "It's lighter."

"Rubbish," Mr. Allan said again. "Now, before we go, here we are. Let me give you something." He rummaged around in the capacious pockets of his overcoat. "I have a present for you. Where did I put it? Here."

He produced a paper bag with something wrapped inside it and a plastic case. Kate unwrapped the bag.

"It's chorizo!" she said. "Er. Thanks?"

"Fresh from the lush plains of Mallorca." Mr. Allan smacked his lips. "Now," he said. "You can't take that into the States with you. There'll be six-foot-seven immigration officials all over you if you try to enter the country with that on your person. So, I thought I'd look after it for you."

"You're going to look after a Spanish sausage for me," Kate said.

"There's another present," Mr. Allan said, ignoring this. "Now, where—ah, in the case. There we go."

"*Chappell Quartet: Songs for Lovers,*" Kate read out. "This is you?" she asked.

"Me and the band, yes," said Mr. Allan. "We cut that disc in 1960, you know. On my tenth wedding anniversary. To the day." He nodded. "Yes. Thought it was the last word, and then three years later that kind of music was absolutely dead. We became what we are," he said, lovingly holding the CD and gazing at the playlist. "A band of old fogies. Even back then, when we were relatively young. Ha-ha."

Kate's eyes flicked over the songs. " 'That's All' " she read out. "Well, of course that one. 'There's a Small Hotel,' 'I Get Along Without You Very Well.' 'I Remember You'—that's Oscar's favorite. Oh, Mr. Allan. What a beautiful album cover, too. I love it." She paused. "Thank you. Thank you so much." Her finger rested on the last song. " 'It Never Entered My Mind'—I don't know that one."

"Rodgers and Hart," Mr. Allan said, filling the gap. "Saddest song in the world. So beautiful. Listen to it." And he sang it, quietly. His voice was croaky, a little shaky, but true.

She took the CD and put it in her bag so he wouldn't see her eyes filling with tears for him. There was silence.

"What will you do?" she asked him, breaking the tension. She wanted to know.

"Me? Oh, you know. I'm not sure."

"Will you stay here?" said Kate.

"Well, again, I'm not sure." Mr. Allan blinked, looking around the room as if searching for something, and she realized with fear that he was older than she liked to admit. "Sheila wants me to live with her, and you know, that's fine, I get on with her, but I'm pretty happy here, you know? I lived with Eileen here for over forty years. Of course, it'll be strange that she's not there anymore. Getting into my hair." He smiled. "But I have my friends, I'm going to do some gigs, I think, for old times' sake. I've got to clear out the flat a little bit—not too much, though. And you know, I've got my memories, and as the song goes, 'I've got my love to keep me warm.' "

"But what about if you—" Kate began, and then stopped.

"I'm old enough to be able to look after myself," he said firmly. "I don't need anyone."

Kate wanted him to understand. "Yes, but take it from me, Mr. Allan. No man is an island. You need to rely on people, people who care about you."

"Well, I can, I can," he said rather snappishly. "All except you, of course."

Kate stepped back as if he'd slapped her.

"I'm sorry, my dear," he said gently. "I don't mean it like that, of course. I just mean that . . . you know what?" He took off his glasses and fixed her with a steely but kind stare.

"What?" said Kate, returning his gaze.

"I'll miss you. That's all. I will bloody miss you, Kate. You coming back into my life just when I needed you most—it was a bit like an angel, the vicar said. You are an angel."

"Me?" Kate was astonished. "Are you sure he meant me?"

"I mean you," Mr. Allan said seriously. "You arrived as they were taking Eileen's body away. If that's not someone looking out for me in my darkest hour, I don't know what is. I thank God for it."

"I really don't think—" Kate began, and then she stopped.

Mr. Allan walked into the center of the room. "You can say I'm a silly old fool who doesn't know what he's talking about, his wife's died and he's got a God complex, but there are things we don't understand, and there are things that are awful that happen for a reason, far beyond our ken. And I believe someone sent you to me to look out for me in the days after Eileen . . . went." He picked up the heavier suitcase. "You gave me strength. Strength to carry on. Now, you think about that, dear Kate, next time you're telling yourself everything's your fault and no one loves you."

Mr. Allan wheeled the suitcase to the front door.

"We're going now," he said. "We'll be late otherwise. I don't want you walking around this flat saying good-bye to everything. I want you to walk out of here with your head held high, and we'll go to the airport in style. God bless you, Kate."

Terminal 3 at Heathrow was like Armageddon. Plastic sheeting everywhere, walls open to the elements, the low sound of drilling, bags lying around on trolleys, in a worryingly relaxed way— Whose bags where they and why were they just casually being abandoned?—and queues and queues of people, some of whom didn't even seem to be sure for what purpose they were queuing. When Mr. Allan stopped one old lady and asked her if this was the queue for the check-in to JFK, she said, faintly, "I don't know. I've been here for nearly an hour and nothing's moved. I've lost the will to live."

The screen on the board said the flight was scheduled to depart on time, at 2 p.m., but at nearly 1 p.m., Kate still hadn't checked in. As she and Mr. Allan waited, shivering in the breeze from the open wall nearby, Kate said, "Shall I tell them I'm—"

"I have already, if you're going to New York," a man in front of her said firmly, as if he took pleasure in grimly disabusing her of the notion that her case was special. Again, a very British trait, she thought. He added, irritably, "I told them my flight was at two about an hour ago, and they said it'd be moving in a minute."

"Ooh, the liars," said Kate, trying to sound lighthearted, but feeling increasingly stressed. She wanted to leave; she'd made up her mind to leave; she had to leave. *Please,* she said in her head, *don't let there be some hitch. I'm not mentally equipped for a hitch. I'm mentally equipped to go to New York. Don't mess with me, Lord.*

"Honestly," she said, turning back to Mr. Allan for the third time, after they'd been waiting for half an hour. "You should go. I'll be fine, just go."

"No, no, no!" said Mr. Allan, rocking on his heels, his eyes shining. He liked a bit of drama. "I'll wait to see you through security. Come now, my dear. What else will I have waiting for me at home?"

"I just—" Kate impatiently stamped her feet to keep warm. "This isn't a very good good-bye, that's all. Dribs and drabs. And I don't want you to get cold."

"That's very kind of you," he said. "But I'm not a child. I'm fine."

Fifteen minutes later, just as Kate was starting to accept that she might, very possibly, miss the flight—for what if she and the man in front were the only ones not to have checked in yet and they simply didn't hold the plane?—salvation arrived, a woman with a clipboard and an understanding manner, and Kate and her companions were ushered into the until now empty first-class section to be checked in. Mr. Allan looked around him anxiously.

"You OK?" Kate said. "Nearly there."

"Yes, yes," said Mr. Allan. "About time."

"Wow," said Kate, hauling her bags onto the conveyor belt. "At last," she said, trying not to sound chippy to the woman checking her in. "Is it a full flight?"

"Yes," said the woman behind the desk, her mouth pursed in disapproval. "It's a full flight, madam, and I'm afraid you're very late to be checking in."

"But the—" Kate began, trying not to yell something unforgivable.

"Stay calm," Mr. Allan whispered in her ear. "Close your eyes and count to ten. God bless you, Kate."

Since there were only two possible responses, going mad and shouting at the woman or remaining totally silent and counting to ten, and since she wanted to get on the flight and didn't want to risk violence, Kate bit her lip, closed her eyes, and counted to ten.

And when she opened her eyes, the woman was staring at her strangely, and when Kate turned around, Mr. Allan had gone.

"Where did he go?" she said.

"Who?"

Kate waved vaguely at her side. "The man who was with me. The old—the elderly gentleman. Where did he go?"

The woman shrugged. "I don't know. Sorry. Didn't see him."

"Yes, but he can't have just disappeared," Kate said, trying to stay calm. "He didn't just vanish into thin air. Didn't you see him at all?"

"It's very busy here this afternoon, in case you hadn't noticed," the woman said with a real edge to her voice. "Was he checking in for the same flight as you? Because if so, he's very late as well and needs to come to the desk. Otherwise, madam, I think you'd better go through."

Kate looked wildly around her. "But—he was just with me! I can't just leave him."

"Excuse me," came a voice behind her, and she wheeled around.

"If you're not going to move out of the way," said a hard-faced lady with a bag clamped under her arm and an embarrassed-looking man next to her, "then we'll miss our flight and I will actually be entitled to sue you for compensation."

"Oh my God," Kate said. "Are you serious?" She said this with such force that the woman stepped back, clearly wondering if she was dealing with a psychopath. "My friend—Mr. Allan—he's gone missing. He was here a second ago and now he's gone off, and this lady won't help me at all, and just because that holds you up for ten seconds, you want to sue me?"

"Look, just please excuse me," said the woman, her face a rictus of unpleasant smugness. "Some of us have to catch that flight."

"Stupid cow," Kate muttered. God, she hated this country, and she would be glad to leave. She picked up her passport, casting a disgruntled look at the check-in lady, and slunk away, her heart racing.

Where was he? Mr. Allan wouldn't have just left without telling her—would he? She didn't know what to do. She couldn't leave without saying good-bye to him, but she didn't want to miss her flight. What would he say if she did? Or perhaps he wanted her to stay so much he'd done this on purpose?

Kate shook her head; he wasn't that bad. Or was he?

She hung around outside the men's room for a few minutes, anxiously checking her watch and feeling a bit weird, but there was no sign of him, and five minutes later she was hurrying through departures, worry seeping through her, draining her. She was late, she was worryingly late, and she didn't know what to do. The hall was thronged with knots of people, occasionally stepping aside to make way for a stewardess clacking her way through the crowd, pulling a trolley behind her, or airport staff in attractive fluorescent jackets. She was right about airports, she thought. They were stressful and, in this case, totally, horrifically chaotic—and they were the least romantic places in the world.

It was one twenty-five. She'd have to go through; she couldn't wait. She hoicked her bag over her shoulder, took a deep breath, and got into the queue for security.

She was fishing through her things, making sure she wasn't carrying her little bottle of perfume, when a voice said, "Thank God. There you are."

She looked up in confusion. "Mr.—" But the words died on her lips.

Mac was standing in front of her, behind the security ropes, breathing raggedly, sweating slightly, shaking. Kate jumped, and her hand flew to her mouth.

"You . . ." she said, but the words died on her lips. She stared at him, both hands on her cheeks.

"Where the hell have you been?" he said, almost angrily. "I've been looking for you for twenty minutes!"

"What on earth . . . you . . ." Kate began again. "Where's Mr. Allan?" she said incoherently. "Did you see him?"

"Yes, of course I did," said Mac. "I saw you in the queue. I was waving at him to come away, and when he did, I explained everything and got him to step aside so I could surprise you." He grimaced ruefully. "He said to give you his love, and he told me to get on with it, but by the time we'd finished talking, you'd disappeared. It's so bloody crowded in here," he said wrathfully. "I couldn't see you, and I nearly missed you, and, Kate—" He took her hands away from her cheeks and clasped them in his own. "I wanted to see you."

"Step aside, please, miss," said someone behind her. Kate looked at her watch and stepped aside. People started filing past her toward the security checks.

"I know you've only got about a minute," he said, reading her thoughts. "I know—this is all wrong, it's too rushed, it shouldn't have been like this. I've been waiting for you for God knows how long, but I found out from Zoe when your flight was going, and I knew I had to come down because, Kate—I love you. I'm sorry about the other night."

"It doesn't matter," Kate said. "I'm sorry—you were entitled to it. After the way I treated you, it's the least I could do—" She moved forward a little, and someone pushed past her, knocking her even closer to him.

"Kate," he said. "It's not a game with me, never has been. I didn't just want a one-night stand with you. I'm glad I left last week. I don't want to crowd you, freak you out again."

"You were right, though," she said. "I shut you out. I had to, Mac. That's why I don't deserve you."

Mac's face was without expression; but his eyes held hers. "It was stupid of me. Pathetic. I suppose a part of me wanted to hurt you, you know."

"I hurt you," Kate said. "You—"

"It doesn't matter now," he said.

"It does," Kate said quickly—too quickly. She wanted to talk to him as much as possible in the time they had left. "It does. You and me—we've never been you and me, have we? We've never really been on a date—unless you count two weeks together non-stop as a date." She smiled, and he smiled. "That's what I worry about, I suppose," she said.

"I know what you mean," Mac said. "That it'll never get any better than this for us, that we're not destined to be a couple, just ships that pass in the night?"

"Yes," she said, relieved that he understood.

"But I don't think that's true," he said. He cleared his throat. "All along, I've been trying to make things right, and I was wrong. *You* were right. I just wanted to tell you that. I came here to tell you . . ." He smiled carefully at her. "We've done everything the wrong way around. I was wondering if you wanted to go on a date sometime."

"A date?" she said, shaking her head at him. The crowd behind her swelled, pushed her forward.

"Yes," he said, his fingers holding hers. "How about we go for a coffee one day. Or perhaps a pizza. There's a lovely place in Battersea. Or go to the cinema, see a play."

The noise around them seemed to get louder; someone appeared behind them, trundling a case full of bottled water for the newsagents behind.

"Hey," a voice said next to her. "Hey—you were in front of me, weren't you? Aren't you coming?" The man who'd been behind her in the queue appeared at her side. "You know they're about to close the gate?"

He moved on brusquely, shaking his head, leaving Kate gazing at Mac. She gripped his hands tighter.

"This is—impossible," she said.

"I know. I know, darling. I'm going to say this quickly. OK?"

"OK," Kate said, smiling. He leaned forward and kissed her.

"I've got an idea," he said. "You see, you know and I know what's been wrong with you and me. We've done it the wrong way around. We fell in love with each other the first night, and then we went backward and backward, till we were like passing strangers to each other. Don't you agree?"

She couldn't say anything; she just nodded. He slid his arms around her waist. "I don't know, but perhaps we should start from the beginning again. I'm staying in London, I'm looking for a flat. Stay here, too. Come on a first date with me. Let's do it the right way around."

"This is the final boarding call for flight BS080 to New York. Would all passengers for flight BS080 please go to gate twenty-seven. Gate twenty-seven for flight BS080 to New York."

"How can you be that sure?" she cried. "What if fate's trying to tell us something, that we'll never be together? That we've tried, you know we've tried, and it'll never work?"

He paused, and swallowed. "I don't believe you," he said fiercely. He clutched her wrists.

"You do," she said. "That's why you left last week. You do. And I think I do, too. I think it's too late."

"Kate." Mac's face was white, his nostrils flared. "Don't do this."

"I love you," she said, tears streaming down her face. "I don't want to go."

"But you are, though, aren't you," he said, and he stepped back from the tape barrier that separated them. "And you know what? I don't think I should have come here today. Perhaps you're right."

She watched him, as did her fellow passengers, who were gaping at them curiously. Her hands dropped to her sides; but he caught one, her left hand, and pressing her palm to his face, kissed the ball of her thumb, gently.

"Perhaps you're right."

And then he was gone.

Kate swallowed and turned back to the queue. One thirty. She looked at one of the guards, showed him her ticket. His eyes opened wide.

"You'd better go through now," he said, and pushed her along, down toward the fast-track queue, and she disappeared through the archway, toward departures, away from Mac, farther away from London.

Forty-one

There was a sign on the way into Manhattan from JFK airport. Kate had noticed it before; it had been there for a while. It said:

WELCOME HOME!
FROM YOUR FRIENDS AT
AMERICAN AIRLINES

Kate had slept the sleep of the emotionally exhausted all the way there, unusual for her, and woken up with panda-smudged mascara eyes and what she told herself was a clear head. Before passport control she ducked into the ladies' room, washed her face, put on some tinted moisturizer and lip gloss, put her lenses back in. She wasn't going to walk back out looking like she'd just come back from a night out with Pete Doherty, that's for sure.

She was fine, she told herself. She was back. She wanted to talk to someone, she wanted to say, "Hello, I'm Kate, and do you know what's happened to me? Do you know where I've been?" Because suddenly she wanted to talk. She wanted to explain how she felt, she wanted to clap her taxi driver on the back (gently, so as not to throw off his suspect steering even more) and say, "How do you find your job? Because I've just left my job, and I'm really pleased about it. Except I have to find another one PDQ—pretty damn quick, that is!" She wanted to give him an interesting fact as the beautiful gunmetal skyline of Manhattan loomed up in front of them. She wanted to say, "Have you tried the whispering wall in Grand Central Station? You can hear what someone's saying from thirty yards away? It's amazing."

or

"When they built the Brooklyn Bridge, there were the first cases of the bends, because the men who were doing it were diving so deep and coming up so quickly, isn't that interesting?"

or

"My best friend, Zoe, had a third date with this bloke called Diggory yesterday, and I've had to come back here and I don't know how it went! It's her first date since her husband died, three years ago, isn't that incredible of her?"

or

"I'm going to see my mum again and I feel like it's for the first time in years, which is weird because I only saw her a month ago. It is weird. But I feel like I understand her a bit more, Mr. Taxi Driver, are you listening, do you care?"

and, finally,

"Can you take me back to the airport, please? I think I've made a terrible mistake."

But she didn't say any of that—of course she didn't.

And then she rode into Manhattan, and the sky was blue and the cabs were yellow and the trees were green, and it was its old, glorious self, and they rode through the park, cutting across town to the Upper West Side, and Kate hung out of the window, not wanting to talk now, like a dog on a family trip, her eyes eagerly scanning everything in the city she loved so much. The supermommies, jogging with their strollers, the businesswomen in pencil skirts and thick, massive trainers, striding fiercely back from the office, the families heading home after school, the harried businessmen crouched on the edge, the lines of traffic with cars honking and drivers yelling, the noise, the cheerful, aggressive, straightforward noise and bustle. She had missed it so much, longed to be here so much, it was the balm to her soul that she always needed, and never more so than today.

Strange, then, that it felt so odd to be back. When she'd moved here, she had been wildly, ecstatically in love with the place, with everything about New York, with the Upper West Side, with the fact she could walk to the world's best deli in five minutes, the fact that she could shop at Anthropologie, her favorite clothes store, the fact that she could eat burritos from Chipotle whenever she wanted, that the sidewalks were wide and people were friendly and polite, that things worked, and when someone came to mend something they actually mended it, instead of scratching their arse and saying, "I could do it . . . but it'll cost you, I'm afraid. . . . Best to just buy a new one." But as the cab climbed through the streets up toward Riverside Drive, Kate looked out of the window and smiled. But it felt different; she didn't know why. She had just loved it here, loved everything about it, but it wasn't where she belonged. The thought shot through her, disloyally, before she could dismiss it.

They were crossing Amsterdam Avenue. Was it the same for Venetia, she wondered? Did her mother truly belong here, or would she always long to be back in London? Kate honestly didn't know the answer. They were drawing up outside the apartment now, and the driver popped the back of the cab and hopped out to fetch her suitcases. She paid him and he immediately zoomed off, leaving Kate standing on the curb, staring up at the apartment building, wondering for the second time in a few weeks, though in a different location, why she was here.

• • •

The first time Kate had come to visit her mother in New York was the first time she'd ever been to the city, and she remembered it still with a clarity undimmed by her subsequent residency there. She was fifteen. It was summer, the school holidays, and everyone kept saying it was far too hot, humid, unbearable even. But Kate had loved it. Maurice, the doorman, had just started to work at the building, a month after Venetia and Oscar had moved in there, and he called Kate "Newbie," and said she should call him the same. Her mother took her to Bloomingdale's and bought her clothes—primary colored, Benetton-esque sweatshirts that didn't suit her at all, but that she adored and kept in her drawers for years afterward. They had ice-cream floats and they rented boats in the park. The city was curiously empty, everyone else was away, New York was theirs; Oscar taught her all the lyrics to "Manhattan" on that very same subject. They saw *Les Misérables*, which Kate and Oscar adored, but Venetia thought was awful. And she was with her mother, most important, for three whole weeks. Time to tell her lots of things—about her bedroom at home, about school, about Zoe, about how they were putting on *Macbeth* the following term, about how she had kissed Gavin Roberts *twice* now, once at the party Jude had in her parents' garden while they were away, then the following week outside the cinema on the Finchley Road, where they'd gone to see *The Crying Game*. Did this mean Gavin was her boyfriend? And perhaps they would talk about Dad—about how sad he was without her, about how shocked all their friends were that she'd gone, left Kate behind and gone.

They didn't talk about that, of course. They talked about everything but that, and nothing else, because Venetia didn't ask, and something about her mother told Kate not to ask. They shopped, and chatted, and walked, and lazed on the sofa in the stifling apartment, and sang as Oscar played the piano, and after three weeks Kate went home again, hugely grown up, on the airplane by herself, and when she got back the next morning to the rickety old house in Kentish Town, she found her father asleep on the sofa, sunlight strobing through the gap in the rug that served as a makeshift curtain in the sitting room. Daniel wanted to know all about her mother, but Kate didn't tell lots. She wanted to keep the memory safe, holy almost. And thus was her postdivorce relationship with her mother formed, and it had continued to be the same.

She realized now, as she stood at the bottom of the steps up to the apartment building, that they were neither of them perfect parents, and they suffered from her idolizing them both. They'd tried. They hadn't deliberately wanted to hurt her. They were just a bit hopeless, no better and no worse than any parents, and that didn't mean she loved them any the less. But a lot of water had gone under the bridge since she was last here, though it wasn't that long ago. Where had she heard that phrase? She shivered, and climbed the stairs.

As she banged through the front doors, Maurice leaped up from behind his desk and said, with a huge smile on his face, "Kate! Why didn't your mother let me know today was the day you were coming back? Well, well. Give me those bags, young lady. I'll call the elevator for you. It's great to see you! You have a good trip? How's your father?"

"He's much better, thanks," said Kate, squeezing Maurice's arm. "How are you?"

"I'm good, I'm good," said Maurice, putting her bags by the lift. "It's been pretty crazy around here, you know, though. Mrs. O'Reilly's been sick, but she's getting better. Your mother got a new spring coat, Kate—it's beautiful. You know the board's finally talking about getting quotes in to have the floors redone? Yes, I know." He nodded solemnly at the importance of this as Kate stared at him. "Plus," he finished, "don't get me started on the new coffee machine they put in at Rick's!"

The lift doors clanged open. "Thanks for the info," said Kate.

"No problem," said Maurice. "It's great to have a young face around the building again!"

"Thanks, Maurice. I'll see you later," said Kate, getting inside. "It's great to be back."

"Oh my goodness!" a voice cried loudly as Kate emerged from the lift. *"My baby girl is back!!"*

A pastel rush of cashmere and strawberry blond hair pulled her out of the lift and wrapped itself around her; Venetia had been prowling the corridors, alerted by Maurice to her daughter's arrival. She stepped back, holding her daughter's face between her hands, and her large blue eyes sparkled with pleasure.

"Hi, Mum," said Kate, submitting gratefully to her mother's embrace as Venetia hugged her again. "How are you? Oh, it's good to see you." She sank into her mother's embrace, remembering how she smelled—a mixture of Chanel perfume, shampoo, and some kind of hand cream. Venetia's cashmere sleeve was soft, her cheek was soft, her hair was soft—her cheekbones were sharp, though, and she crushed Kate's face against her own angular bones, hugging her tightly as she did.

"I have missed you *so much!*" Venetia cried, stroking Kate's hair so heavily that it hurt. "I have missed you! Haven't I, Oscar, haven't I?"

"Yes," said Oscar, who had appeared at the doorway and was watching his wife and stepdaughter in fond amusement. "Hello, Kate, darling." He kissed her warmly on the cheek and stepped back, wiping his hands surreptitiously on the tea towel that was over his shirtsleeved shoulder.

"Look at you," Venetia said then, staring at her curiously. "You look different. Did you get a haircut?"

"No," said Kate, clutching a strand of her hair. "I didn't."

"You look—did you lose weight?"

"I wish."

"You look a little angular around the face," Venetia said, looking her over with an appraising stare. "I think you did lose some weight, darling. Which is strange because no one in England eats vegetables."

"Yes, that's totally true," said Kate, taking off her jacket. "I haven't eaten a single vegetable in over three weeks. They don't grow them there, you know."

Venetia ignored this. "Oscar made lunch," she said, smiling her great big smile. She slung Kate's bag over her shoulder. "He made burritos."

Kate was ravenous. "Lovely," she said.

"Let's eat," said Oscar. "We'll eat and then we can talk. We want to know how you are. How was it, being back? Not too horrible, I hope? We were worried about you."

"Bless you," said Kate as they came into the apartment. It looked so small somehow, like a doll's house. She looked around as if she hadn't been there for years and years.

"We need to talk about tomorrow," said Venetia. She held her daughter's hand.

"Tomorrow?" Kate said blankly.

"The party!" said Venetia. "Come on, Kate, you haven't forgotten! A *month* back there and you've forgotten everything, haven't you?"

Why do you think I came back? Kate wanted to say crossly. *For this stupid party. Why else do you think I'm here?* She looked at her mother curiously, trying to imagine her back in England, trying to think of her as an actual mother, or sitting in a room with her father. She couldn't see it. Venetia pushed her hair out of her eyes with her arm and smiled at her daughter, her beautiful, clear skin almost luminous in the sunlit hallway.

"It's OK," she said then, in her low, luscious voice, and Kate remembered then how she could do that, how she sort of always understood. They stared at each other for a moment.

She's the same height as me, Kate thought. *She even looks a bit like me; I'd never noticed before.*

She'd been too busy hero-worshiping both of her parents to notice how she might be like them, the best and the worst, and it was in that moment, there in the hallway, that Kate put the rest of her childhood behind her, and she knew it.

"Come on," Oscar said fondly, watching them both. "If the flatbread wilts now I'm blaming both of you."

"Hah," said Venetia, going into the dining room, clutching Kate's hand. "So, tell me everything. Did you see Zoe? And is Francesca still as hard as nails? How's your father? Is that child still a nightmare?"

"Zoe had a date last week, Francesca's really well, actually, and Dani is surprisingly adorable," said Kate, sitting down. "Sorry, Mum, but she is."

"Why should you be sorry?" Venetia sounded disingenuous. She took a sip of water and hummed.

"No idea," said Kate, pouring her mother some wine. "Dad's much better, too. He's back in the studio next month, doing an album for Christmas."

"Oh, really?" said Oscar. "Already? What is it?"

"It's—it's an album of Barry Manilow songs," said Kate. "Come on. You know, he's a really good songwriter, actually," she added defensively as Oscar and Venetia howled derisively with laughter. "Oscar, you like him!"

Oscar held up both hands in defense. "I'm sure he is," said Venetia, smiling at her daughter, her face alight with some strange emotion Kate could not place. "It's just—come on, darling. When we were married he was with Deutsche Grammophon, doing Paganini's most obscure concerti. It's—er—it's just different, that's all."

Kate suddenly remembered her father's message. *I still think about Sheffield.* She watched her mother, searching for some clue. *Parents,* she thought, smiling back at her. They are strange. And she thought of how Lisa was yesterday, and Oscar, and how they were practically parents to her—better, in lots of ways. Mum and Dad are mad, she realized, though she knew it, of course, and she merely nodded at Venetia and carried on, deliberately changing the subject.

"But, yeah, they're all really well."

"Good," called out Oscar, placatingly, as Venetia sipped some water thoughtfully. "So, what else is new?"

"Oh. Well, I saw Charly and Sean," Kate said casually.

"You *what*?" said her mother, holding her water glass in mid-air, as if she'd been frozen. "You—what? How come? What?"

"I saw Charly. And Sean." Kate was smiling.

"Oh, my . . . grrr," said Venetia, tossing her hair and making a strange animal sound in her throat. "My goodness, if I saw that little—that little *madam*—what wouldn't I do to her. . . . What happened?"

Kate sketched in, very briefly, the story of the letters and the meeting itself. When she'd finished, Kate looked at her mother curiously—she was almost red with anger.

"My God, the nerve," Venetia muttered. "So what happened?"

Kate swallowed the rest of her drink. She was silent for a while. "You know what? I got over it, that's what happened. It was the most satisfying cup of coffee I've had in a long time."

Her mother looked unconvinced, but Oscar, who missed nothing, emerged from the kitchen at that moment carrying the burritos and the little bowls of guacamole, sour cream, cheese, and chili, and he said simply, "So, sounds like it worked out for the best. Back to normal."

Now was not the time to say, "I'm moving out, by the way." Now was not the time to tell them about Sue's offer. She was home again, back in New York—she had decided to come back and she was going to make it work now, strange as it felt. "Yeah," said Kate, quelling the feeling inside that she had. "I think it did." Her fingers dug into her thumb as she remembered Mac's face, his lips on her palm, what he had said—she felt pain, sharp, shooting pain, and then she looked up and smiled. She had made her decision—for better, for worse—and she was back.

Forty-two

*A*nd gosh it was lovely being back, waking up in New York at the beginning of summer. The weather wasn't too hot, she didn't have to go back to Perry and Co., and so Kate realized the next morning that she was free to simply get on with her lovely life now in New York, starting with Oscar's much-anticipated birthday party that evening. She got up early, rang Betty and left a message, wanting to fill her in on everything, unsure of how best to explain it all to her. The last time she'd seen Betty had been her last night in New York. She had nearly kissed that guy Andrew; how weird it was, how far away it seemed, like another life.

During the day Kate helped her mother; they went to the grocery store, dropped by the caterers to deliver the sign for the cake that Venetia wanted on top: a little plastic man playing the piano, naturally, with HAPPY BIRTHDAY written above. In New York even the cake decorations were better.

She picked up Oscar's present, the complete Beethoven piano sonatas that she'd had bound, with Oscar's initials stamped in gold on the front, at a store off Columbus Avenue, and she and Venetia had their hair blow-dried, Venetia reading the *Times* and laughing gaily with the hairdresser, Kate flicking avidly through *People,* desperate for a fix of the U.S. celebrity gossip that she'd been sadly missing since she'd been in London.

The salon was a few blocks away from the apartment building. Kate and her mother walked back together, arm in arm, toward Amsterdam Avenue. The streets were unusually quiet, but the blossoms were out everywhere, frothing, frivolous. When she'd left, the leaves had barely been out; now the best of the spring was here, and she always thought this was when she loved New York the most. Kate felt as if she were in a film. They walked under the white and green trees like characters in a Madeline story, in a Fred Astaire movie.

"I missed you, darling," said Venetia. She looked from left to right as they crossed the road. "It's funny I always still do that, isn't it!" she said, patting her head. She had wrapped a printed silk scarf over her hair, to protect it from the Manhattan winds.

"What?" said Kate, watching her.

"Look left and right, when I only need to look right, you know, streets in London and all that." Venetia was babbling; she took Kate's hand and pulled her across the wide road, almost running. "I did miss you, darling," she said as they reached the other side.

"Oh, Mùm, I'm sorry," said Kate. "I missed you, too—I've been so lucky, having you let me stay here—" She clutched her mother's arm. "Honestly—what would I have done if I couldn't have come to you three years ago?"

"Don't be silly," Venetia said. "Gosh, though," she said, in her artless, dramatic way. "I sometimes think you would have been better off."

"What do you mean?" Kate asked, bewildered.

Venetia released her arm from her daughter's clutches. "Well," she said, considering carefully. "Are you your mother's daughter?"

"Well, obviously I am," Kate said.

"I mean, perhaps running away isn't the answer. It was for me. I don't think it was for you."

Kate saw what she meant. They were on a street corner; she could hear someone playing the piano; she stopped, listening out for the music, straining to hear notes.

"What is it?" she asked.

"Don't know," said Venetia briefly. "I can't hear it."

But Kate could hear it. It was "Rhapsody in Blue"; how delicious, how clichéd, someone in their apartment on 77th and Broadway playing Gershwin, framed by the cherry blossoms. It was almost too New York—that had been what she loved about the city: it was a cliché, a wonderland, all for her. She remembered something then, as she watched her mother, who was fixing her scarf in place.

"Mum," she said, and added carefully. "Dad asked me to tell you something."

Venetia stopped.

"What?" she said. "He . . . did he have a message for me?"

"Yes," said Kate, wondering how she knew. Venetia's hand fluttered on her cheek, then her breastbone.

"Let's walk," she said softly. "Tell me."

She set off at a long, fast pace, which Kate matched; they were physically very similar, she'd realized, and she wondered where she'd got her height from then, from her mother or, like Dani, from their father? The music faded away, the languorous, slicing phrases disappearing as they walked. She fell into stride with her mother, and they were silent for a few seconds, and then Kate said, "Well, he said to tell you he still thinks of Sheffield."

It sounded so prosaic when she said it. "Sheffield." Like "Terminal 3."

"Sheffield," said her mother. She was looking at the ground. "Wow."

"Yep," said Kate, hating this, wishing they were back at the apartment. This was it, though.

"Are you sure?" said Venetia "Nothing else?"

"No," said Kate, feeling guilty. "Sorry."

"Sheffield . . ." said Venetia. She glanced at her daughter, her expression unreadable. "Thank you, Katy. Thanks."

"But, Mum—what does it mean?" Kate said, unable to quell her curiosity.

Venetia walked on a little farther, past another apartment block, past a slew of pink blossoms. Her mother sighed, and threw her head back a little.

"Kate—Kate," she said. "Can I ask you something?"

"Yes," said Kate, nodding furiously.

"Do you know why I left your father?"

"Um," said Kate, not wanting to sound too eager. "No, actually, Mum, I don't know why."

"Well, I should have left it another year," her mother said, almost conversationally. "I should have waited till you were fifteen or so. You were too young and it was wrong of me. I will have to live with that for the rest of my life. You know?"

"Mum, I don't—"

Venetia was babbling, her voice quite without its usual girlish inflections. "It doesn't matter, because I pay for it every day, in one way or another; when I think about how I let you down it breaks my heart every day, but I just couldn't take it anymore." She took a deep breath. "And, God. I must say, your father saying that just goes to prove it."

"What?" Kate said. "About Sheffield? What, Mum? What does it mean?"

Venetia turned to face her, and Kate saw her mother as a woman, the woman she must have been.

"It's the reason I left your father," she said, with a tiny laugh.

"And it was selfish of him to ask you to give me the message, wicked and selfish."

"It wasn't like that . . ." Kate felt uncomfortable. "We were talking about you and I always wondered . . ."

"There's no big secret," Venetia said. "You think there's some big secret. There isn't." She wrinkled her freckled nose and exhaled loudly. "God, Kate, I left him because he was a nightmare to live with. He made me miserable. I used to find any excuse to go to the shops, pop out for milk, and I'd cry all the way there, all the way back." She began counting off on her fingers. "He criticized me constantly. I never knew where he was. And if I asked him— pfff! Oh, he'd go mad. He belittled me in front of everyone. He slept with countless other women, he had these terrible rages, he never did the shopping"—listening to this, as it filtered through to her head, Kate loved the fact that sleeping with countless other women was almost on a par with not doing the shopping—"and it got to the point where I couldn't take it anymore."

Her eyes were sparkling with tears, and Kate stroked her arm. "Oh, Mum. I had no idea," she said, trying to work out what to say. She knew her father had been a nightmare to live with, he still was, but she had been protected from it—by her mother, by him—because until she grew up and had a mind of her own, she was still his little girl.

"He's a monster, Kate." Venetia was laughing, almost hysterically. "And I can say that because I still love him. I'll always love him. I just can't live with him. We weren't good for each other. We made each other miserable. That's why I ran away."

"That's all?" Kate said, and hurriedly corrected herself. "I don't mean 'that's all'—it's a lot, Mum, it's just I always thought there was some terrible secret. . . ."

"On our thirteenth wedding anniversary he was playing with the Hallé in Sheffield. The Mendelssohn. I surprised him in the dressing room beforehand. He was with the first trombonist," said

Venetia. "She was sitting on his lap." She shook her head. "God, it sounds like a French farce. So ridiculous." Drawing herself up a little, she said with touching dignity, "And I am not ridiculous. But she was just one of many, and, God, she was so young! About twenty! I couldn't take it anymore."

"That was 'I still think about Sheffield'?" Kate asked with incredulity. "I thought it'd be some wonderful romantic story."

"In Sheffield? In a dressing room with peeling wallpaper and a cheap little brass player with big tits?" said Venetia bitterly. "God, no." She put her arm around Kate. "Is he cheating on Lisa?"

"I have no idea," Kate said, feeling a stab of loyalty to Lisa, understanding even more so now that her life must sometimes be difficult. "But, you know, I don't think so," she said. Venetia looked at her.

"You and me—we were both in the same boat, that's why when you turned up here, so strange. You wouldn't talk about Sean and Charly, or Steve, or Zoe, or anything—that's why I just let you stay, didn't put any pressure on you. I wanted you to feel you had a home here, that you didn't have to worry about anything."

It was sunny on the wide street, but Kate felt a cold wind blow over her heart, suddenly, as she saw how prescient her mother had been. Venetia took her arm and they carried on walking.

"And when you came back last year after those mysterious two weeks away—I know you were away that long darling, Maurice told me, really, I'm not stupid—well, I didn't say anything, because I knew you just had to work it out for yourself."

"Yes," said Kate, nodding violently. "I did. I think I have now, Mum—but I think I've screwed it all up even more."

"How so?" said her mother.

"Every how so," said Kate. "There was this man. I should have been with him from the start." She turned her head toward the sun, blinking. "He's the one I was with in London. Zoe's brother-in-law. Mac."

Venetia nodded. "I know Mac. I remember Mac. That good-looking doctor who spent all night of your engagement party pretending not to look at you. Nice man."

Of course she knew, Kate thought. Venetia missed nothing. "I left him, I wasn't ready. . . . And now I think it's too late."

"Why do you think he's the one for you?" Venetia asked almost conversationally. She waved an elegant hand at someone walking along the sidewalk, on the other side. "Hello, Karina!"

"Um—" Kate tried to sound articulate. "You know Sean?"

"Yes."

"Well, he was wrong for me and I couldn't see it. Because everything was disguised with him. He was good-looking, but he was bad inside. He was tall and comforting, but actually he let me down." Kate carried on talking, though her throat was tight, sore. "I thought I needed someone to look after me, and actually I was better off on my own."

Venetia was nodding violently. "Go on," she said. She patted her daughter's arm, comfortingly. Kate could hear the birds singing, loudly now, in the trees.

"Mac—he's right for me, and he wanted to look after me, too, but I didn't want that. I couldn't see it. It's exactly the opposite. Sounds mad, I know."

"It's not mad." Her mother looked sad. "I wish it had been the same with your father."

They were opposite the apartment building now. She kissed Kate on the cheek.

"Let's go inside. My darling baby'll be wondering where we've got to."

Venetia tripped up the stairs, almost skipping. "Hello, hello," she cried, as Maurice came out from behind the desk.

"I'll see you girls later," he said. "Mr. Feinstein must be very excited."

"He certainly is," said Venetia.

Maurice said, "He really is a very lucky man, Mrs. Feinstein."

"Oh, he knows it," Venetia sang, looking up at Maurice from underneath her lashes as the lift doors sprung open. "Baby, he knows it."

Kate sighed. "Come on, Mum," she said, trying not to laugh. "It's nearly party time."

Back at the apartment, the Robertsons had rung to say they were definitely coming, but Joel Robertson was worried about what to wear, and Mrs. Cohen was now coming solo, because Mr. Cohen wasn't well, and Mrs. Da Costa had popped by to offer to help. Oscar had (a) drawn up a list of songs that he might, if asked, possibly consent to play for the (hopefully enthusiastic) gathering and (b) crossed it out and started again, several times.

"I don't know what to do for an encore," he said fretfully as Venetia and Kate arrived back. "What if they want something . . . you know, really jazzy."

"Darling, give 'em the old razzle-dazzle," said Venetia, depositing the bags on the sofa and taking off her wrap. "You'll be wonderful. Won't he, Kate?"

"Of course he will," said Kate loyally, extracting the coffee beans they'd bought from the bags and putting them in the little galley kitchen, as Venetia flung her arms around Oscar and kissed him.

"Oh, Oscar darling," she said, repeatedly kissing his cheek. "Birthday boy tomorrow, party tonight, ooh-la-la! Look!"

Oscar grabbed her hands, and brought them in front of him. Kate watched them, torn between slight embarrassment and real affection.

"I have a present for you, Venetia, darling," he said solemnly. "Kate, you too. Wait there."

And he vanished down the long parquet-floored corridor toward their bedroom. Kate stood next to her mother, rather excited—what was it?

He reappeared a minute later, carrying two little bags.

"Tiffany?" said Venetia. "Oh, Oscar, no . . ."

Kate looked at the pale blue confection being held out to her. "Oscar. Wow," she said, taking it and opening it up to find a little box, wrapped in white ribbon. She opened it, feeling almost nervous.

Nestling in the white silk padding was a chain and a pendant. A platinum chain, with a heart-shaped pendant, covered in diamonds, a tiny thing that bulged and glittered in the light from the lamp.

"Oscar!" Kate cried. "Oh my God. You shouldn't have!" She looked up to find her stepfather watching her, a curious expression of sadness mixed with—what was it? Love? Kindness, emotion? All those things, probably, were written on his face. She hugged him.

"I love you Kate," he said, his voice choking with emotion. "Dear girl, thank you for coming back for the party."

"Of course I would—"

He gripped her arm. "I know what it cost you," he said. He shook his head, forbidding her from further speech. "You were right to come back, but I know what it cost you. I love you," he added, as Venetia, who had been having considerable trouble with her box, managed to get it open to reveal a diamond tennis bracelet, dotted with hearts, and the screams of joy that greeted the unveiling of this present could, as Mrs. Cohen said to Mr. Cohen, on the floor below, be heard all the way in Hackensack, and what could they ever do about it? Sweet girl, Venetia, but, boy, was she loud.

So from midafternoon onward a stream of caterers, waiters, and servers flowed in and out of the apartment, setting up the buffet, building ice sculptures, arranging flowers, and moving furniture, so that the vast living room was split into two, with the piano and room for a little dancing at one end, and chairs at the other end for people to sit and eat.

Kate's mother, though she loved to pretend to be a drama queen, was, in fact, intensely practical in many ways; it amused Kate, the codependency she and Oscar imposed on each other, each behaving to type around the other but actually more than capable of finding the salad dressing and booking a doctor's appointment (Oscar) and booking a car and filing tax returns (Venetia).

So, actually, at seven o'clock Venetia and Oscar were ready for their guests, who were due to arrive from seven thirty. The caterers had left but the waiters had remained, the sun was starting to set over the park, fiercely red, flooding the last light of the day into the big airy room, and only Kate wasn't ready.

Because Kate was in her room, staring at her phone. One side of her hair was pinned back, the other side hung like a curtain across her face. She was in her dress, but her feet were bare, and her room was littered with makeup, shoes, clothes, half unpacked, half still in bags and boxes. She pressed 1-2-1 again and listened to the message, barely able to understand what she was hearing.

"Hello, Kate. It's Geraldine Garley, from Prince's? The estate agents? We met on Friday? I just wanted to let you know we showed the flat today, to a gentleman, and I think we may have a tenant, Kate. He can move in on Monday!"

Kate had listened to the message four times already. She liked this next part.

"I must say, I've never dealt with such a speedy let, in all my years here. Well . . ."—there was some hilarity in the background of the message: the sound of her colleagues laughing—*"I've only been here eighteen months, you know. But . . . still, it's incredibly fast."*

Then there was some rustling of paper; Kate held her breath again, even though she knew the ending.

"*A doctor, actually. He says he knows you. Kate, isn't it a small world? Dr. Mac Hamilton his name is. Anyway, he said he'd already seen it the previous week? I didn't know you were showing it before then, Ms. Miller. He wants it from Monday, and that's why I had to let you know. . . . Um . . .*"—she cleared her throat, a degree of perplexity in her voice—"*And . . . he specifically asked that I ring you and tell you something—he said he knew you? OK. He said he had to see it again to realize he didn't want to let it slip through his fingers. He said it doesn't need fixing, that it's perfect as it is. Well, so I should hope so. There's one more thing, what else did he say? Hold on*"—more rustling of paper—"*Hold on a second. I wrote it down. Right, he said . . . 'Tell her I'd be happy to take her out for dinner to discuss it.'*" There was a pause. "*Oh. I don't get that part! I hope he still wants the flat. Nigel, where have you put the—*"

The doorbell buzzed, and Kate jumped and the phone fell out of her hand. The first guests had arrived.

"Kate, dear?" Oscar called. "Are you coming? What are you doing in there?"

And Kate stared around the room. "I don't know," she said, in blind panic. "I'm an idiot. I don't know."

Forty-three

*A*utumn came, after a terrible, wet summer, and surprised everyone by bringing a beautiful, gentle September. Kate was always annoyed by people who claimed, with the air of one who is a little bit original, to "love" autumn. Everyone always said it was their favorite season. What rubbish, she always thought. It wasn't just that it started getting darker at night—what's good about that? It was that it rained. It was slippery. Leaves fell everywhere and made everything more slippery. It was impossible to dress, because one spent the whole time longing to don one's new autumnal clothing, usually involving brown or gray knitwear of some description, and when one did, one stepped outside for the day to realize that it was actually 23 degrees.

Kate wrote as much in her column that last week of September, and as she gazed out of the window, toward the just-setting sun, she chewed her pen (which she hated herself for, it was a disgusting habit, and she'd once got a splinter of biro caught in her throat and nearly choked) and pressed SAVE. The weather was changing today, definitely, she thought. Summer was definitely, finally over. It was nearly October.

She didn't want to be late. She looked at her watch: six o'clock. Pushing herself up and away from her desk, she stood up and stretched, yawning loudly. She went into her bathroom, which still had the smell of fresh wallpaper. At Zoe's insistence, she'd had the bathroom wallpapered, in this gorgeous black-and-white Swedish cartoony design she'd seen in a hotel in New York. It was waterproof, and she loved it. She'd had Hollywood star lights put up around the mirror in the bathroom, and she switched them on, slapping her face and looking critically in the mirror. She looked back at herself and smiled, though part of her still thought that growing out her bangs was a mistake. At least it was getting to the stage where she could get away with an insouciant, swept-up jeweled-clip effect.

With surprising speed Kate put on some powder, some mascara, and some lip gloss, and then pulled on her little black cropped linen jacket, which was her summer/autumn jacket/coat dilemma salvation (she'd written about that the week before in her column, and was still going through the emails from readers about where they could buy it and what to do when it got colder). She wound her scarf around her neck and, shutting the door lightly, paused at the top of the stairs.

"Night, Mr. Allan!" she called up.

The door opened, after a few seconds.

"Have a lovely evening, Kate," came a faint, warm voice. "I heard the yawn, thought you must be about to go out. Do enjoy it. Let me know, won't you?"

"Of course," she said. "I'll be up tomorrow morning for coffee. OK?"

"OK," he said.

"What are you listening to?"

"Miles Davis. Miles Davis, you ignorant girl. Good-bye."

"Bye!"

The door closed, and she ran down the stairs.

The air was rich with rain and wet leaves as Kate came outside. She smelled woodsmoke, drifting on the evening air from the gardens down the road. People were hurrying out of Maida Vale tube station as she crossed the road and ran inside, glad of the warmth of the usually stuffy Underground. Well, she thought to herself, autumn really is here if I'm glad that the tube's warm. It's the sign.

She sat down on the train and pulled open her book. Her mother had just sent her *The Talented Mr. Ripley,* which she'd never read before, and she was enjoying it with the sort of addictiveness you usually get with chocolates or, in Kate's case, Marmite. The train was quiet, going the wrong way back into town. When they got to Marylebone, someone skidded on a free evening newspaper lying on the ground; he paused in midair, waving his arms, and then reached out to grab the pole next to Kate; she reared back in alarm, holding out a hand to stop him from falling. He steadied himself and smiled at her, embarrassed, and she smiled back at him, embarrassed that they had almost had contact, that he had almost looked foolish. But other than that it was quiet, almost soporific, and Kate's eyes closed just a little.

She was tired. She had babysat Harry and Flora the night before while Zoe and Diggory went out to dinner for his birthday. She was still recovering. Last week she'd babysat while they went to the final Prince concert at the O2 arena. The children had been exhausted from a big afternoon at the park and they'd fallen asleep right away. Last night, however, had been a nightmare of getting up, going back to bed, bad dreams, arguments, bargaining, and recriminations (on Kate's part, in her head). She thought, resentfully, that the sooner Diggory moved in with Zoe and they stopped having to go out on dates the better. Francesca always got out of babysitting because of her long hours. Mac seemed to want to, the crazy man, but then he was their uncle, and his working hours meant often he couldn't. Kate got stuck with it more than she wanted and she moaned vociferously about it to Zoe. But really, she couldn't have loved it more.

She was remembering the rhyme Flora had been chanting the night before, the pat-a-cake, pat-a-cake one, and it chimed exactly with the rhythm of the quiet car, and she might easily have missed her stop had her book not fallen into her lap and roused her with a start. She hopped off the train, her heart beating fast.

Tickets to *Much Ado About Nothing* had been sold out ever since they'd announced who'd be in it: a famous Hollywood star who'd never acted on the West End before, but the reviews were amazing, and people genuinely said she was pulling off the part of Beatrice, that the chemistry between her and the grizzled, experienced Royal Shakespeare Company actor doing Benedick was so amazing it had to be seen to be believed. Kate couldn't wait. It was her favorite play. She got off the tube a stop early, at Oxford Circus, and walked through town, past Liberty's, through Soho Square, stopping to look in the windows of shops, smiling at the hardy drinkers still out on the sidewalks. She walked fast, weaving in and out of the throngs, avoiding eye contact, hugging herself against the now chilly evening, enjoying being out, being bumped by people, living here, walking toward the theater, toward him. . . .

Down the side alley, before Great Windmill Street, was the theater, and there, waiting for her, like she knew he would be, was Mac. He was holding two programs.

"Hello," she said, her heart beating even faster. She kissed him.

"I got two programs, you see," he said. "After the program debacle of the Open Air Theatre date, I thought I'd better not risk it."

"You're learning all the time," she said. "I missed you."

He wrapped his arms around her. "I missed you, too," he said, and kissed her again. "How was your day? Did you get the column done?"

"Nearly," she said. She took his hand. "I've got tomorrow as well. How was yours. Did you do that craniotomy?"

"Tracheotomy. Stop watching *Grey's Anatomy*," Mac said, grinning. He scratched the side of his face and touched his knuckles lightly against her cheek. "Where are we going afterward?"

"Back to mine?" she said.

"I meant for food, but back to yours is fine," he said, fishing in his pocket. "Although Francesca says to tell you she's away all weekend. Oh, and my room needs serious vacuuming."

"Why does she think I'd want to know about that?" Kate said sternly. "Isn't the vacuuming your problem?"

"Two separate points," said Mac hurriedly. "Very separate. She's away all weekend. First point. Second point, I need to hoover."

"Great," said Kate. "So I'll come over on Friday evening and you'll have hoovered."

"I can guarantee it." He smiled at her she smiled at him, they looked at each other for a long, long time.

"Let's go in," he said eventually. "Are you ready?"

"Oh yes," Kate said. "I'm ready."

Acknowledgments

I would never have finished this book without the support and encouragement of Clare Foss, my favorite Headliner in an extremely crowded field. Thank you so much, Clare. Thanks, too, to everyone else at Headline but especially, as always, to Jane Morpeth. And Marion, for telescope advice!

First of all, thanks to my wonderful mum and dad. Huge thanks to Pippa and Rebecca as ever for everything, and Brendan and Caroline O'Reilly, Thomas Wilson, Jo Roberts-Miller, Sophie Hopkin, Nikki Barrow, and Clare Betteridge. Thanks to the following people for the conversations we've had about why we live where we live: Vicky Watkins, Pamela Casey, Nicole Vanderbilt, Lance Fitzgerald, PJ Mark and Simon, Megan and Jasper Mulligan. (Special thanks to Bea, Felix, and Harriet for the flowers.)

Thanks, as always, to Mark Lucas, and everyone at LAW, Kim Witherspoon and David Forrer (and to Mr. Forrer for the Chrysler Building fact). And to Louise Burke and Maggie Crawford at Pocket Books, who make me love NYC that little bit more.

Huge thanks to everyone at HarperCollins, especially Victoria Hughes-Williams, Helen Johnstone, Sarah Radford, Lee Motley, Clive Kintoff, Wendy Neale, and Amanda Ridout. I am eternally grateful to the super-talented Claire Bord for every little thing, thanks so much, CB. Finally, to Lynne Drew, who is amazing. Thanks for understanding that the brand diamond is in my sitting room.

INTRODUCTION

The Love of Her Life
Harriet Evans

Meet Kate Miller, a young twentysomething professional who whiles away her days as an assistant at a literary agency in New York City. Kate has grown content with her quiet, almost solitary lifestyle when she learns that her father has fallen ill and she must return home to London—and the memories of her past, which she had tried to leave behind her.

Kate had been on top of the world in London: employed in her dream job, engaged to a wonderful man, and surrounded by friends. Then, one day, it all came crashing down. In response, Kate did the only thing she knew how to do, and ran away.

Returning to London makes Kate realize that she must confront the ghosts of her past. She starts on a journey that tests her resolve, opens old wounds, rekindles old friendships, and, most important, brings her face-to-face with the love of her life.

QUESTIONS AND TOPICS FOR DISCUSSION

1. When preparing to return to London, Kate remarks, "It will be hard. . . . I had to go back sometime . . . Just wish it wasn't for this, that's all" (p. 12). If not for her father's illness, do you think Kate would have gone back? Would she ever have returned to her old self in New York, or did she need to go back to London to rediscover herself? Do you agree with her that she is "too good at running away" (p. 21)?

2. Discuss Kate's "new self" vs. her "old self" (p. 14). Which Kate do you like better? Which one do you think Kate likes better? Would "old" Kate have shrugged off Andrew the way "new" Kate had at the beginning of the novel?

3. The scene where Kate reenters her old apartment is full of tumultuous emotion. What does Kate see that rips her feelings of comfort away and reminds her "why she was here" (p. 31)? Why do you think what she saw had that effect?

4. How does the author's use of foreshadowing intensify the moment when the reader finds out what really happened in Kate's past? How do the flashbacks add to this element? How would the book have been different if it started right after Kate graduated from college?

5. Kate and Mac's first encounter results in nothing more than a one-night stand, or so it seems. Why do you think Kate remarked that that night she had a "strange sense of certainty, one that she never got back again" (p. 108)? Does she ever get that certainty back? Why doesn't she make the effort to contact Mac once he leaves?

6. Sue Jordan, Kate's old boss, criticizes Kate for her current career choice. What is Kate's response? Why do you think she initially resisted Sue's offer to write the column? What does Sue mean when she says, "we're all the same, you know, it's just different versions of being the same" (p. 180)? Do you agree?

7. As the events of the novel unfold, it appears that Kate is becoming deeply entrenched in the city she tried to forget. How do her struggles with staying or leaving affect her interactions with Mac, Zoe, Francesca, and her family? Do you agree that "if the last few weeks had taught her anything, it was that she . . . had to start being brave and get out there" (p. 354)?

8. When Charly and Kate finally see each other after so many years, were you surprised to learn about Charly's boyfriend's ongoing infidelities? Why do all the good memories of their friendship come flooding back? Discuss how their conversation at the pub leads to Kate saying ". . . you [and your boyfriend] deserve each other, Charly, and I can't feel sorry for you" (p. 368).

9. Kate goes through a tremendous transformation throughout the novel. What makes Kate become comfortable with the person she is? Or does she never reach that milestone?

10. Before Kate returns to New York, Lisa remarks ". . . you were living the life you thought you ought to be living . . . I'm sure you wouldn't ask for any of what's happened. But it's been good for you" (p. 385). Do you agree with Lisa? Which experience do you think helped shape Kate the most? When is she at her weakest? Her strongest?

11. Did the ending of *The Love of Her Life* surprise you? Is this where Kate is meant to be? Is this the man whom she is meant to be with? Do you think she might run again, or is she here to stay? And why?

A CONVERSATION WITH HARRIET EVANS

Q. What comment do you hear most often from your readers? How do you respond?

A. I guess it would be that they liked the characters, and my response is "Thanks very much!"

Q. What do you want your readers to take away from *The Love of Her Life*? And is there a "love of her life" out there for every woman?

A. *The Love of Her Life* is my favorite of my books, because I wanted to write a book about someone who wasn't the blond, blue-eyed, homecoming-queen type, who was a bit of a geek but who grew up, had some pretty awful things happen to her, and found out something really important, which is a love of her own life. Be proud of being the geek and it'll work out okay. I totally think there's a "love of her life" out there for everyone. I don't know that you always end up with them, and sometimes you don't recognize them as that for a while, but they're definitely there.

Q. You worked in publishing as an editor. Did you ever work in a place as boring as Perry and Co.? What is the worst job you have ever had? Have you ever had a boss like Sue Jordan?

A. Never as boring as Perry and Co., but my first job was at a very old-fashioned magazine in London, and it was completely awful. It was like *Dynasty* set in an old people's home—full of very embittered women who'd been there for years and couldn't understand why they weren't working at *Vogue*. Lots of articles about interesting road signs and amusing things cats do, but such a toxic atmosphere. I lasted five months and it nearly finished me off. Luckily, most of my bosses since then have been fantastic, and my last boss was a fantastic woman. I learned loads from her.

Q. You currently reside in London, where you grew up. Did New York ever present itself as a potential home? Or, do you prefer someplace else?

A. I love New York so much! I would absolutely love to live there, and part of *The Love of Her Life* is totally about me imagining what that would be like! Oh my goodness, it's my favorite place. I've always lived in London, but who knows. . . .

Q. Where did the inspiration for Kate Miller come from? Without getting too personal, are any of the characters in *The Love of Her Life* based on anyone you know?

A. Kate is the most like me of my heroines—or me when I was younger, although I always see myself as a super-mysterious romantic figure, and the reality is so not true. I think there are bits of people I know in all my characters though, and what's interesting is how I can have written someone and then, only a few months' afterward, I realize that subconsciously they're based on X, or they say something the way Y would in my own real life. It's like you put lots of information into your brain and you don't know what's going to come out.

Q. Can you talk a little about why you decided to get into writing fiction? What is your writing process like? How do you create such strong tension and drama in your work? Your characters' emotions are so authentic; how do you manage that?

A. I've always known I was going to write one day. I worked in publishing and was reading lots of women's fiction there. Some of it was fantastic, some of it was terrible, and we'd all sit around and say, "I could do better than that!" One day, I realized I was going to have to do something about it. So I did!

I don't really have a writing process. One day I'll suddenly think of a "thing" that's the motif of the book, but then often it won't end up being in the book at all. For *The Love of Her Life* it was Berkeley Square in London and the song "A Nightingale Sang in Berkeley Square." I realized I wanted to write a big, romantic novel set in London, because New York always has romantic comedies set there, whether it's *Sex and the City* or *Annie Hall* or any number of books, and London doesn't. So I'll swirl around thinking about that for a while and then start writing, and then I'll delete most of what I've written, and then write some more. And so it goes. . . . It's my editor saying, "This isn't tense or dramatic enough!" and me rewriting it!

Q. You make mention that you are a fan of old films. Which one is your favorite, and why?

A. I have loads. My ideal job if the writing goes up the Swanee would be a film doctor, one of those people who prescribes films depending on your mood. But just to pick a few:

(a) *Brief Encounter* is just the most romantic, sad, lovely, fantastic film. The more I watch it, the more I love it.

(b) *Roman Holiday*—Rome AND Gregory Peck; what's not to love?

(c) *Some Like It Hot*—the best songs. Curtis and Lemmon, hilarious and sweet.

(d) *Singin' in the Rain*—possibly my favorite film of all time. I defy you not to love it. Songs! Dancing! Totally subversive! So brilliant.

Q. Tell us about your latest cocktail invention: "The Harrie"—how did you discover it (and how good does it actually taste)?

A. I am telling you, if you make "The Harrie" and your party doesn't go with a bang, I will be astonished. The combination of gin (heavy hitter) and bubbles (bit of sparkle) is the perfect one. I actually first had it when I was meeting publishers with a view to having my first book, *Going Home,* published, and one of them, who is a very brilliant woman, made this cocktail, because there's sloe gin in the book. I since owe her many happy evenings. . . .

Q. What is next for you?

A. Writing the next book, which is set in Rome (hurrah! for Gregory Peck again), and booking a holiday somewhere sunny. And right now, packing for my weekend by the seaside.

Enhance Your Book Club

1. Harriet Evans recommends a cocktail she calls "The Harrie": mix one part sloe gin to three parts champagne. Make some for your book club and give it a try.

2. People make connections between Evans's writing style and director Richard Curtis's style. Rent Curtis's *Love Actually* and see if you like it.

3. Ever had an Andrew, Mac, or Sean in your life? Care to tell the story? Spend a night with your book club talking about old flames!